THE
PAINTED
LADY

THE PAINTED LADY

Lucia Grahame

LOVESWEPT®

DOUBLEDAY

NEW YORK LONDON TORONTO SYDNEY AUCKLAND

LOVESWEPT®

PUBLISHED BY DOUBLEDAY

a division of Bantam Doubleday Dell Publishing Group, Inc.
1540 Broadway, New York, New York 10036

DOUBLEDAY, LOVESWEPT, and the portrayal of the wave
device are trademarks of Doubleday, a division of
Bantam Doubleday Dell Publishing Group, Inc.

Book design by Tasha Hall

Library of Congress Cataloging-in-Publication Data

Grahame, Lucia, 1946–
The painted lady / Lucia Grahame. — 1st ed.
p.   cm.
I. Title.
PS3557.R225P34   1993   92-39009
813'.54—dc20   CIP

ISBN 0-385-46830-X

Printed in the United States of America
June 1993

1   3   5   7   9   10   8   6   4   2

FIRST EDITION

THE
PAINTED
LADY

Prologue: Paris,
September 1888

"Who is that woman?" murmured Anthony Camwell, just as his dining companion, Philip Harborough, broke off a monologue in midsentence to take another swallow of wine.

The two young men were sitting at a corner table in the low-ceilinged dining room of the Coq d'Or in the Rue Montmartre. Both were English, but Philip, who had come to Paris a few years earlier to study at the School of Decorative Arts, now made his home there. Anthony was merely a visitor.

"Woman! What woman? You haven't heard a word I've said!" exclaimed Philip. He had shaggy brown hair and a drooping moustache, and his sack coat, though obviously well made, looked as if he had slept in it.

Anthony leaned back in his chair with a cool, amused smile. He was fair-haired and clean-shaven, and the flawless tailoring of his impeccable evening clothes whispered of Savile Row.

"You are unjust, Philip," he said, subtly mimicking Philip's aggrieved tone. "I have been hanging upon your every syllable as if my life depended on it."

Yet even as he spoke, his gray eyes traveled back across the room to a table where an exuberant party of six were clinking their goblets—five of champagne and one which appeared to hold nothing stronger than *eau minérale*. It was the abstemious member of the group who had captivated Anthony's attention. She seemed, in a way, so familiar; he might have known her for years. But he had never seen her previously; he was certain of it, for had he glimpsed her only once before, she would not be a stranger to him now. He would not have allowed her to be.

"You liar! Your eyes have been wandering for the better part of an hour! I'll stake a bottle of Château-Lafitte that you have no idea what I've just told you!"

"Very well, but I won't hold you to it," was Anthony's unruffled reply. "You've been boasting that the man to whom you have rented half of your studio—I assume it was the divanless half—is the greatest unsung genius in all of Paris. I congratulate you. At least now one may hope that *something* of value will emerge from your atelier."

Philip sputtered for a second. Now and then he produced exquisite pen-and-ink sketches of Parisian life, but having an independent income, he worked only when he felt like it, which was not often.

"So you think my white nights produce nothing of value!" he cried.

"They might, Philip, they might," Anthony told him. "But only if you would put down your glass, send the ladies home, and take up your pen once in a while. However, tonight I will not lecture you. For once, I want to discuss a far more serious matter than your poor, wasted talents—who *is* that woman at the far end of the room sitting across from Marguerite Sorrel?"

Philip twisted in his chair to follow his companion's gaze.

"You don't know Frederick Brooks!" he cried. "Now *there's* a man who can paint! And the woman with him? His wife, of course! And favorite model, as *you*—"

He was halted midstream by the expression on Anthony's face.

"*That's* Fleur Brooks?" exclaimed Anthony with mingled wonder, disbelief, and ill-concealed dismay.

"As *you* ought to know!" concluded Philip. Then, immensely gratified at having gained his companion's full attention, he added, "I'm shot, Tony, if I've ever seen *you* thrown! What's done it to you?"

He *had* been thrown.

So that black-haired angel who'd fired his imagination in ways no other woman had ever done was Fleur Brooks.

Anthony had recognized the famous Madame Sorrel from evenings at the theater, but how had he failed to place her lovely companion? His own cousin, Neville Marsden, had helped to lift Frederick Brooks from rags to riches by buying up one canvas after another. And Fleur Brooks must have modeled for at least half of them. How often had those haunting green eyes gazed down upon him from the walls of his cousin's home in London! But even Frederick Brooks's consummate skill had not done justice to the roses in her cheeks, much less conveyed her air of gentle, effervescent joy, as enveloping and seductive as the scent of Spanish jasmine on a summer night's breeze.

For the last hour he had watched her showering subtle, affectionate attentions upon the high-spirited fellow at her side, and he had felt the unfamiliar sting of envy. He had sensed, rather than heard, the soft ripple of her easy, generous laughter at her companions' unintelligible jokes. He had been a silent witness to every tender favor she bestowed. Even now he felt his pulse race as she reached up, almost as if she could not help herself, to smooth her husband's thick, reddish gold hair with graceful, delicate fingers. Then she leaned forward to whisper something into Brooks's ear, and Anthony saw her lips brush his cheek.

He pulled his eyes away.

For not only were the Brookses one of the handsomest couples in Paris, they were uncontestably the most happily mated.

But in the end, he could not keep his gaze from straying back to her. The enchantment was too strong. Across the room, she glowed quietly, like an unwavering beacon.

"Frederick Brooks is a lucky fellow," observed Philip, following his friend's eyes once again.

"A lucky fellow, indeed," murmured Anthony.

"Would you care to visit their table?"

"What! Do you know the Brookses?"

"No, but I do know Théo Valory—La Sorrel's husband. He is ignoring me tonight because we have quarreled. But it's been three weeks already, and if I were to pretend that I had been in the wrong, I could probably patch things up with him this very instant!"

"Oh, don't think of swallowing your pride on my account!" protested Anthony hastily. "Besides," he added with a wry smile, "you *are* my friend, I hope, and it could hardly be counted as an act of friendship to urge the moth closer to the flame."

He spoke lightly, but in fact he was feeling so helplessly corroded with envy, an emotion he had always regarded as far, far beneath him, that he was ashamed. He would have gladly forfeited his birthright, his name, and his bachelor freedom for the privilege of walking home in Frederick Brooks's shoes. To think of leaving the tavern with that woman on his arm, of leading her to a moonlit bed beneath a skylight in a breathless, silent room, and of losing himself in her warmth and sweetness until the sun rose upon them both. . . . Oh, if he were the man at her side, *he* would never have lingered so long at the Coq d'Or! He would not be calling now for yet another bottle!

But it seemed that the ebullient group was at last starting to break up. The two young men who'd completed the table of six were rising to their feet and had begun to make their farewells.

"That's Guy Hazelton," observed Philip, tipping his head toward the dark-eyed one with the mane of chestnut hair. "He was at school with Brooks back in England, but lately he's become even better friends with Madame than with her husband."

Anthony shot his friend a quelling glance. Surely Philip, who knew everything about everybody, could not be insinuating some illicit liaison between Fleur Brooks and Hazelton? The woman was obviously head over heels in love with her husband. It was impossible to mistake that look upon her face.

"And *that's* Lord Harry Boulmer," Philip went on, warming to his subject. He dropped his voice. "It's not widely known, of course, beyond their intimate friends, but he and Hazelton are lovers."

Anthony felt the muscles in his face relax. His enormous faith in his own astuteness would have been rudely shaken had Philip persuaded him that a woman could smile at her husband the way Fleur Brooks did while carrying on an affair with another man.

But what difference could it make to him whether Fleur Brooks was a faithful wife or an unfaithful one, whether her circle of friends was wide and generous or narrow and exclusionary? If it were ever wide enough to include him, he was certain his life would become a hell as well as a heaven.

Although the number at his table had shrunk, Brooks still seemed intent upon making the party last. Now he was trying to fill his wife's glass with champagne, but she'd covered the goblet with her hand and was shaking her head and laughing up at her husband with a look that Anthony would have sold his soul to have aimed at him.

After a short while, he managed to persuade Philip to move on to the Café Nouvelle-Athènes, which was already filled with some of the city's most spectacular women.

But tonight Anthony Camwell barely noticed them.

At the Coq d'Or, Fleur Brooks, who had abstained from the champagne, was intoxicated with happiness.

They had come to the tavern, one of the oldest in the quarter, ostensibly to celebrate a commission that Frederick had just won, but for Fleur every such occasion—and lately there had been many—was also a celebration of her own impending joy.

More than five years had passed since a benevolent twist of fate had brought Frederick Brooks into her life, and so much that was equally amazing and wonderful had happened since. . . .

How insistently had she been warned that to marry the artist would be to condemn herself to a life of stark poverty and terrible disillusionment! Yet here she sat amidst gaiety and plenty, still wildly in love with her dashing husband and at last, after five years of marriage, about to realize her most cherished dream. In three months, she would be a mother.

Now, as she smiled at the sly way Théo Valory had just capped one of her husband's jokes, her thoughts were already drifting away from the Coq d'Or and back to the house off the Rue du Mont-Cenis, where the nursery walls were painted with scenes from fairy tales, where piles of warm flannel blankets and soft little wrappers, all of them hemmed and embroidered by her own hands, waited to receive the baby she carried.

Now at last she understood completely her husband's extravagances, which had once worried her—his compulsion to shower her with luxuries that far exceeded her wants. She felt similarly driven; nothing could be too good for this passionately longed-for child who would never be shabbily dressed, who would never feel cold or want or rejection, who would be shielded by love from the smallest discomfort, the tiniest disappointment, who must never, never know pain.

As for herself, she was dressed tonight with aesthetic English simplicity in the virtually waistless style immortalized by Rossetti and Burne-Jones only because of her condition. Her closets, in contrast, were full of elaborate, expensive gowns, many of them from the House of Worth, selected and paid for by her doting, spendthrift husband. But he could easily afford it now; during the last three years his paintings had begun to command higher prices than she, in even her most soaring fantasies, had imagined possible.

.   .   .

The hours wore on, and fatigue began to steal through Fleur's veins. But Frederick, who inevitably grew ever more lively and gregarious as night progressed, did not wish to leave. It was close to midnight; the crowd was swelling, friends and acquaintances were still stopping at their table, and Frederick was basking in admiration and trading bon mots. It was his night, his celebration; he looked so disappointed when Fleur at last whispered to him how very tired she was becoming that she immediately wished she had cut her tongue out instead.

"Only another half hour," he cajoled. "After all, you've had nothing to drink—you can hold up for a bit longer, can't you?"

The half hour grew into an hour. In the end it was Marguerite who saw how pale Fleur had grown and insisted that they leave the tavern immediately.

"But why didn't you *say* something, darling?" cried Frederick to his swaying, exhausted wife. Overcome with remorse, he sped her home and helped her into bed.

Once she was lying down, he remarked that he thought he might as well be off again—perhaps he could still catch up with Marguerite and Théo, who had gone on to the Nouvelle-Athènes.

"I wish you'd stay," Fleur whispered.

"Now what would be the use of that?" he chided her gently. "I'm wide awake and you're already half asleep! You need to rest— I'd only torment you by talking all night!"

"I wouldn't mind," murmured Fleur, who loved to fall asleep to the sound of her husband's voice. But she instantly regretted her selfishness. "Well, kiss me good night, then," she said, and lifted her arms to wrap them around his neck.

In the Nouvelle-Athènes, Philip Harborough, too deep in his cups now to resent Anthony's inattentiveness, was recounting a violent argument which had erupted between two friends of his over the worthiness of Edouard Manet's *Olympe* to hang in the Luxembourg Museum.

Anthony's eyes no longer wandered; but they had a distant, abstracted look which might have betrayed to a more alert Philip how far his thoughts had drifted.

He had left the Coq d'Or because the vision of Fleur Brooks, glowing with love and joy, had awakened in him a desire that still seared him with its intensity. He wanted her, and even now, after he had removed himself from temptation, the hunger was as strong as ever.

And he had, only a few days earlier, made plans to visit Brooks's studio with his cousin Neville later that very week.

To go . . . or not to go.

To become her husband's patron, to mount images of her upon his walls, to gain the privilege of bowing to her in the street and of visiting her home . . .

Or to walk away from that tantalizing beauty and cleanse the acrid taste of covetousness from his palate?

It would have to be the latter. He knew himself too well to suppose that he could easily tolerate the continual sting of thwarted desire. He prided himself upon his sense of honor.

With a sigh of resignation, Anthony lifted his glass and began halfheartedly to inspect the roomful of glittering women.

But soon the image of Fleur Brooks's incomparable warmth sliced through his heart again like a tender knife, and after that the brilliant glare of the Nouvelle-Athènes illuminated nothing but her absence.

A short while later, the sight of Frederick Brooks strolling alone into the café shattered Anthony's regard for him completely. Despite the man's undeniable gifts and his obvious charm, Brooks was a fool. Why the devil wasn't he at home with his wife? There was no one else in Paris—or anywhere—to compare with her.

No, certainly he would not go to Brooks's studio with Neville. In fact, it was pointless to remain in Paris; none of the city's sparkling temptations could satisfy him now. He might as well return to his less alluring life in England the next day. It was his best hope of breaking the spell Fleur Brooks had cast.

. . .

In the bedroom of the lavishly appointed house off the Rue du Mont-Cenis, Fleur was jolted from the threshold of sleep by a sudden, agonizing pain.

Sometime around three o'clock, her husband ambled home. By then it was over; she had lost the baby. In the two and a half years that followed, she lost everything else as well, and the next time Anthony Camwell saw Fleur Brooks, she was a penniless widow.

PART ONE

1891 – 1892

I

Frederick, my careless, brilliant, laughing husband, was dead.

He had squandered his talents, wasted his wealth, and exhausted his store of goodwill. And finally, one February night, he never came home.

Sometime around dawn, a body, bobbing in the chilly waters of the Seine, came to the attention of the gendarmes. A would-be wit among the party which retrieved the corpse reported that it had been practically pickled in absinthe.

A drunken misstep had cost him his life.

Of course I knew it was my fault. For a period of nearly two years, I'd sunk into a private sorrow from which I had been unable to rouse myself until the summer before Frederick's death. Meanwhile, our marriage had come apart at the seams.

I'd failed my child and I'd failed my husband as well. Now both were lost to me.

But fate, which had stolen everything that really mattered, was generous at least in one respect: Although Frederick's incessant borrowing had cost us nearly all our friends long before he met his sorry end, the three who'd most stoutly refused to be exploited remained true and were now my greatest consolation and support.

They were the actress, Marguerite Sorrel, my closest woman friend; her artist husband, Théo Valory, who'd been Frederick's ally through thick and thin; and Lord Neville Marsden.

At the time of Frederick's death, of course, I did not consider Lord Marsden an intimate friend. He had been Frederick's patron—his first. But even after he'd stopped commissioning paintings, even after we'd had to move from the charming house off the Rue du Mont-Cenis into our last home together, a miserable fifth-floor garret on the Boulevard de Clichy, Lord Marsden, amazingly, still called upon us and would sometimes wander sadly through the north-lit room that held Frederick's easel. At first it pained me that he no longer exclaimed with pleasure over what he found there; I thought he was being unkind. But false enthusiasm would have been worse.

Once or twice I overheard his mild attempts to make Frederick face up to his decline and the reasons for it, but as usual Frederick laughed and refused to admit to any failings or limitations—he was as good as ever; if he drank, it was only for inspiration. It seemed he had moved forward too quickly for his patron, whose exquisite tastes were perhaps a little too *arrière-garde* to permit him to readily appreciate the direction Frederick's art had taken; one day, however—or so went Frederick's litany—the world would trace the unbroken trajectory of Frederick's genius and marvel at the ignorance of those who had stared so uncomprehendingly at the highest evidence of it.

I ought to have defended Lord Marsden's position, of course, for I knew he was right; I knew, as any reasonably sensitive and observant person must have known, that the great artist who still lurked within Frederick had not been untrammeled by his excesses, it had been dulled and drugged by them. But I never reproached him—not once during those first two bleak years after my tiny daughter had broken loose from her fragile mooring three months before her time and had died, before my eyes. All too conscious of my own failures, I lacked the confidence with which I might once have tenderly urged Frederick to try to change his ways—until, of course, it was too late.

By the time I finally summoned up the will to shake off that incapacitating grief, Frederick's slow but fatal dissolution was well under way. For months thereafter I had labored to break its grip on him; I'd gone on my knees and pleaded with him to struggle against it; I'd showered him with the tender little attentions that I had so selfishly withheld during my own long and lonely travail. I'd begged his forgiveness for having surrendered so weakly to the blow that had struck us both and for having failed to fill his life with the smiles he craved. He'd said there was nothing to forgive now that I would try to be happy again.

If only he had understood that it wasn't a matter of trying. I had always *tried* to be happy for him. It was just that for that one terrible period in my life I had not been able to manage it. Sometimes I even entertained the subversive thought that if only Frederick hadn't so refused to acknowledge the reality of our loss and the legitimacy of my grief, if only he hadn't been so determined to treat the painful matter as something of which it was best not to speak, something to forget as quickly as possible or to pretend had never happened, if only he hadn't been so repelled by my long face and the unshed tears that hovered behind it, I might have recovered my spirits more quickly.

But he hadn't and I hadn't, and all we could do in the end was to try to reverse the disastrous course our lives had taken. And then—just when I dared to believe that we'd come to the turning point, just as my smiles came more easily and he began to take more comfort from them than from a bottle, just when his canvasses had begun to burn again with that hot brilliance, just when he had seemed on the verge of reaching out to me again in the night, as he had not done for so long, and just when my blood had at last begun to sing softly again at the thought of what might happen if he did—it had all been snatched away.

But I was no longer the same woman I'd been when I lost my

daughter, and once the first tide of despair and disbelief had sub-
sided enough to permit me to think clearly, I vowed that I would
never again succumb to the paralysis of despair.

I had come to this wisdom too late to save Frederick.

But I could still save myself.

No one was more generous, in the days immediately following
Frederick's death, than my warmhearted friend, Marguerite Sorrel.

Childless herself, and with a superficially brittle and worldly
air, she had never comprehended the depth of the wound that the
loss of my daughter had inflicted, nor had she been able to do
anything to ease it.

But Frederick's death was another matter; not only had she
adored him as a friend, she was also far too much in love with her
own mercurial husband not to feel my new grief profoundly.

She understood my need to surround myself with memories, to
fall asleep at night on the bed linens which still carried Frederick's
scent. Toward the end of his life, we'd slept on opposite sides of
the bed, carefully observing, although never overtly acknowledging, the invisible boundaries of our respective territories. Now—
too late—I crossed the lines.

Of course Marguerite, with her busybody nature, insisted upon
attacking the dusty disorder which always likes to steal in upon
the heels of a domestic tragedy, but she was sensitive enough to
avoid the room which had served as Frederick's studio. Here I
could still take some comfort from the paint rags and crumpled
pages ripped from Frederick's sketchbook that littered the floor. I
smoothed the wrinkled sheets out one by one.

I did not linger too long over the memories, however. After
two weeks I washed the bed linens, threw out the rags, swept the
floor, and, not without one searing flash of pain, wiped away the
charcoal smudge that Frederick's thumb had left upon a window-
sill.

Then I was ready to face the future.

I knew, of course, that I would never love again. No man would ever know me as Frederick had . . . no man who did could have gone on loving me with Frederick's accepting, uncritical, unflagging, and wholehearted devotion.

It never ceased to amaze me that Frederick, knowing of my origins, had actually made me his wife—and *after* I'd given myself to him! But Frederick had loved me back in England when I was seventeen—even when I'd blurted out the humiliating truth about my grandmother, he'd loved me—and he had never stopped loving me, nor I him. When things were at their worst, when any other couple would have been at each other's throats, savaging each other's souls with bitter accusations, it was not so with Frederick and me. Instead, as I'd retreated gracefully into the quiet, undemanding depression that had been like death in life and Frederick had consoled himself with alcohol, it really seemed that these stratagems were what allowed us to keep love, if not its splendid early passion, alive.

A fortnight after Frederick's death—it was the same day I finally began to clean up the little studio—Lord Marsden left a card inquiring after me with Marguerite, who had been acting as my doorkeeper. But by then I saw no reason to hide myself from anyone.

So I quickly sent my thanks for his kind inquiries to his temporary address in Paris, the Hotel Bristol.

Lord Marsden would always have a special place in my heart. He had done so much to help establish Frederick's reputation only a few years earlier. It was the elusive dealer Julien, of course, who had actually engineered Frederick's dizzying rise to fame and fortune. He had insisted on showing Frederick's *Othello* series to Lord Marsden, and not only had the enthusiastic viscount purchased all six of the *Othello* paintings, he'd also commissioned one of a favorite scene from *The Winter's Tale*. It was of the moment when the supposed statue of Hermione reveals herself to be a real woman of flesh and blood. I posed for it.

When the viscount arrived to deliver his condolences in person, I was genuinely delighted to see him.

"It is customary," said Lord Marsden, "for friends—and I hope you will consider me a friend—to ask whether there is anything one can do to lessen the hardship of such a bereavement. In my case, these are not idle words. If there is anything, anything at all I can do that may ease your difficulties at this sad time, you have only to say the word."

I swallowed my pride, for I knew that I could not afford to let the opportunity pass. My situation did not allow it.

"Then I will take you at yours," I told him, and was relieved to see that he really did look pleased, rather than becoming stiff and uneasy, as I'd half feared. "But I must assure you that my circumstances are not nearly so desperate as you may have imagined."

This was true. At first I had supposed that the sudden cessation of visits from Frederick's creditors was due to some nice reluctance on their part to harass me too soon upon the heels of his death. I ought to have known better—they had never exhibited much chivalry before. The truth was, as I had by now begun to discover, that they had all been paid off.

Frederick, it seemed, had spent the last day of his life making good his debts.

And how he had done it was a complete mystery.

He'd still had money in his pockets when his body was found, and it felt like a small fortune to me, once I realized there were no other claimants to it. But I couldn't stretch it out forever.

"It seems," I now observed to Lord Marsden, "that Paris is daily becoming more popular with our countrymen. But perhaps you have noticed the difficulties some of our visiting compatriots encounter when they try to make themselves understood on this side of the Channel?"

"I have," said Lord Marsden with a little smile.

"Well, for most of the past year I have been offering French lessons to our English visitors, and I know that you have a great many connections. . . ." Here I stammered a bit with embarrassment but forced myself to go on. "So if you should hear of anyone who wishes to achieve greater fluency, and would not mind paying a very modest fee for lessons, I hope you will think of me. I can't ask you to testify to my abilities, of course, but if you would at least mention my name—"

"I should be very glad to," interjected Lord Marsden quickly. "And I think I *can* testify to your abilities—Julien swears that you speak like a native, and your late husband once confessed to me that he'd have had the very devil of a time, after you first came to Paris, had you not worked so patiently to help him master the finer points of the language."

I felt a belated but sincere little twinge of gratitude for my grandmother, who, even after she had washed up for the last time, figuratively speaking, on an English shore, pregnant, unmarried, and cast aside by her protector because the child she carried was not his, had clung to the language of her native land. She'd been fluent in both English and Italian, but she had always spoken only French to me. It was the language of love, she used to say.

Of course, love had not meant quite the same thing to her as it did to me.

Lord Marsden was as good as his word. Within a few weeks, I had acquired several new students and was gaining confidence that I would somehow be able to make my own way in the world. Of course, I'd have to exercise my hardworking grandmother's lessons in frugality for the rest of my life. But instead of bemoaning my fate, I was glad to have had that stringent education, which she had prayed I would never have to use.

By late April, the Concours Hippique horse show had for over a month been drawing English visitors, along with *Tout Paris*, to the Palais de l'Industrie, and the demand for lessons was growing. I suppose there was a sort of cachet in learning French from the widow of a well-known artist who was now on his way to becoming a legend, having died so tragically and with a certain morbid glamour so long before his time.

By this time, although I still missed Frederick keenly, I was not indifferent to the benefits of my new independence. It was a condition I had never known before, having been so dominated by my grandmother and then having had to assume so many mundane responsibilities during my marriage to Frederick, whose artistic temperament had held him to a more elevated plane.

Yes, I hungered for my incomparable husband more than I can say—but not so much for his body, to which I had been virtually unable to respond for two years, as for the sheer warmth and vitality of his presence.

However, I found it easier to adjust to my new life than I had supposed; and the very notion of ever marrying again remained wholly inconceivable.

Then, one June morning, more than four months after Frederick had been laid to rest in the Bagneaux, where the paupers sleep, Lord Marsden, who had continued to call upon me during his extended visit in Paris, asked whether he might introduce to me his cousin, Sir Anthony Camwell, who had just arrived in Paris for the Chantilly Derby. Lord Marsden would be returning to England soon, but his cousin, he said, intended to remain longer, for he was an art collector and had become fascinated with French and Belgian Symbolist painting. Lord Marsden was aware that, although Frederick had largely scorned the Symbolists for being too ethereal, I had not shared his opinions on that subject. It was true that the pale, rather attenuated saints of Puvis de Chavannes lacked the robust and vigorous splendor of Frederick's best works, but I did not think any the less of them for it.

I had heard Sir Anthony Camwell's name before. At the very height of Frederick's success, the baronet, who'd apparently been remarkably struck by the beauty of some of the paintings that decked his cousin's walls—particularly the one of Hermione—had arranged to visit Frederick's studio with Lord Marsden. It might have been another great coup for Frederick, for Sir Anthony was said to be very rich. But the visit had not materialized: At the last minute Sir Anthony had sent his regrets and, with what could only be regarded as cavalier incivility, had not even proposed another date! Not even the courtly Lord Marsden had offered any explanation for the baronet's precipitous withdrawal.

I'd hardly cared; I'd just lost my child and was almost beside myself with regrets that seemed too deep for tears. But even Frederick had been crushed by Sir Anthony's sudden loss of interest in his work, and although the severity of his disappointment was not at all the kind of thing that Frederick could have found the words to express, it must have shaken his self-confidence, for, in spite of his success, Frederick suffered from a growing anxiety that his work might suddenly become unfashionable. It was most unfortunate that Sir Anthony's thoughtless little blow had fallen on Frederick at a time when I was too demolished myself to perform the complex job at which I had become so skilled, that of bolstering Frederick's spirits whenever they flagged without actually acknowledging that they *were* flagging—a condition he would have indignantly denied.

But now at last I would meet the arrogant and ill-mannered Sir Anthony Camwell, whom chance had linked so closely in my mind with my own greatest failure and with Frederick's subsequent decline. Out of regard for Lord Marsden, however, I voiced no objection to the proposed introduction. Perhaps since Sir Anthony was planning to spend some time in Paris, Lord Marsden had a view toward helping me acquire yet another pupil. Or perhaps Sir Anthony had come to regret the earlier lost opportunity —now that Frederick's death had permanently secured his reputation and had sent the value of his works soaring. Perhaps he wished to snatch up anything still in my possession. But I had nothing to sell.

I had nothing left at all of Frederick's mature works, except five gorgeous but blazingly indiscreet canvasses that had been rolled

and bound almost as soon as the paint had dried and had been
relegated, in our final home, to the back of a deep closet behind a
barricade of ordinary domestic clutter. Frederick had promised me
long ago that no eyes but ours would ever see those brilliant,
damning masterpieces.

This time, Sir Anthony did not excuse himself from keeping
the engagement. On the appointed day he arrived at my door in
Lord Marsden's tow.

Although I had been predisposed to dislike him, on account of
the subtle injury I felt he had done Frederick, he was Lord Marsden's cousin, and I was determined to be cordial on that account.

But, alas, he appeared to be everything I had feared he would
be—and worse.

He was young—much younger than his cousin—and as tall as
Frederick, although with not so massive a frame.

No one, in fact, could have been more unlike Frederick. He
was as handsome, it is true, but in an entirely different way.

Frederick's vitality had given an irresistible charm and magne-
tism to a face that might have otherwise been merely pleasant. Sir
Anthony's features had been chiseled with such flawless precision
that he seemed to feel no need to exert his personality at all in
order to enliven them.

No, there was not one ounce of Frederick's endearing spontaneity in Sir Anthony Camwell. More than anyone I had ever seen,
he exuded a cool, quiet, almost lazy self-possession, the kind
which proclaims itself to feel under no obligation to ingratiate or
please.

From his silk hat to his fine leather shoes, he was attired with
studiously understated elegance. Indeed, all that prevented him
from being the perfect gentleman's fashion plate, in swallowtail
coat, gray-striped trousers, dove gray waistcoat, and snowy ascot,
was the fact that his hair, which was pale blond in color and rather
long, hung loosely around his well-cut features, undisciplined by
any pomade. That single suggestion of insouciance gave the

perfection of his appearance some slight interest that, in my opinion, would have otherwise been entirely wanting.

And as soon as he spoke, he dispelled my misperception that
he might be a candidate for French lessons. For although Sir Anthony had not been born to the tongue, he used it, in a low voice
which I found disarmingly pleasant, with as much appreciation
and sensitivity as if it had been a woman and he her lover.

But he did nothing to suggest that he wished to impress anyone with his fluency. Indeed, he spoke very little, and although
unerringly polite, he was so unforthcoming that I began to imagine he had been dragged along against his will.

Lord Marsden was warm and voluble, attentive and amusing;
his cousin was remote and virtually mute. At first I thought he was
unspeakably bored; soon I began to sense that behind his indifferent facade, he was alert to everything, although he contributed
nothing. Perhaps, as he was undoubtedly accustomed to luxury, he
was dismayed by the shabbiness of his present surroundings.

When I made a polite effort to bring him into the conversation, which had been bubbling along quite easily without his help,
his response was not encouraging.

"How long are you in Paris, Sir Anthony?" I asked him at one
point.

"Several months possibly, Madame Brooks," was his not very
illuminating reply. Then he fell utterly silent as if he could think
of nothing further to add.

With an inward shrug, I turned all my attention back to Lord
Marsden. One thing I particularly liked about Lord Marsden was
that I could speak to him of Frederick without pain. Lord Marsden
had known Frederick at his best and at his worst, and it was
Frederick at his best that he remembered. Now, instead of dredg-
ing up our mutual sorrow over Frederick's death, he and I began to
discuss a commission that Lord Marsden had proposed to Frederick before the final tragedy. By that time even Marsden had come
to see that Frederick was regaining his powers, and he had tenta-

tively indicated to Frederick his interest in commissioning further scenes from his beloved Shakespeare. In consequence of that, Frederick and I, during the last weeks before his death, had been reading the history plays aloud to each other at night. That was when I'd at last dared to believe that we had truly reached the turning point and that the closeness and the passion between us, which had been so damaged, might one day be fully restored.

Now as I recounted to Lord Marsden one of Frederick's wicked puns about *Henry V* and the Hundred Years War between England and France, out of the corner of my eye I caught Sir Anthony gazing at me with an unfathomable expression. It nettled me. I was proud that instead of collapsing with grief I had managed to accept my loss so well and could smile and laugh when I spoke of Frederick to those who had loved him, too. But I interpreted Sir Anthony's unrevealing stare as evidence that he was appalled by such levity in a woman who was only four months a widow.

For this, I decided to tweak his nose a little.

"And what is the object of *your* invasion of France?" I asked Sir Anthony. "Is it conquest?"

He did not answer immediately. The expression which I had taken for disapproval turned very slowly into a faint, rather private smile.

"Yes, Madame Brooks," he said at last. "As a matter of fact, it is."

By this time I was really annoyed by his laconic replies to my questions. I decided that I would no longer allow him the luxury of withdrawing into himself and leaving the entire burden of conversation to his cousin and me.

I was about to make a pointed comment when his eyes began to sparkle a little. It seemed that he was about to amplify his statement, after all.

"But France has nothing to fear from me," he said. "The territory I hope to win is really very small."

"I would hardly call it insignificant," I replied. "I understand that you are an art collector, so you may as well admit that you have come here to plunder."

Sir Anthony looked entirely unchastened.

"That is a strong accusation," he said, still with that half smile. "But if it *is* plunder to admire something of extraordinary beauty and to dream of possessing and cherishing it, then I am guilty."

It was at this point that I began to find Sir Anthony more intriguing than I had at first suspected. It seemed that he had the French gift of conversation; in speaking of a most ordinary matter, he had given his words a subtly flirtatious twist. It's a courtier's trick—the sort of thing which gives a woman pleasure without making her feel compromised.

"If you intended only to dream," I replied, "I would not be concerned. But I fear you are about to besiege poor France with a far more powerful weapon than the longbow and will march off with all her treasures."

At this he actually laughed. It was a delightful laugh, low and soft like a caress.

"I suppose you are referring to my pocketbook," he said with unembarrassed candor. "But mine will be a very hollow victory, Madame Brooks, if I take back to England only what I am able to *buy.*"

Before I could puzzle out the meaning of that remark, he assumed a far less playful tone and began to quiz me very earnestly about my own admiration for the Symbolists.

Pleased at having managed to pry him out of his shell of reserve, I responded in the same vein, and a lively discussion ensued among the three of us.

At the end of the visit, however, when I expressed the polite hope that Sir Anthony would call again, I never imagined that he would pursue the acquaintance.

II

But Sir Anthony made a second call. Again he seemed to have come as a sort of reluctant equerry to Lord Marsden. Again his manner was distant, and this time I did not put myself to the trouble of trying to draw him out. Toward the end of the visit, however, he surprised me by making a languid remark to the effect that the dealer, Julien, with whom he was slightly acquainted, had once mentioned that I had an extraordinarily fine eye.

"Monsieur Julien is more than kind," I said, coloring a little, for the point that Julien had made to Sir Anthony was a rather sore one with me. Julien was forever praising my discernment, but when I'd dragged myself out of the slough of despond to face the fact that Frederick had drunk and gambled all our money away, and that he had buried his splendid gifts in a haze of alcohol and false bravado, Julien had done something I found it painful to recall.

I'd been desperate to find a means of supporting Frederick, since he could no longer support me.

So I had gone to Julien, bashful and anxious, to remind him of all that extravagant praise, and to remind him, too, of the explanations he had long ago made for his initial refusals to examine

Frederick's work—he was old, he was tired, he was already over-stretched, he hadn't the energy or the inclination to take on a new talent—all of which suggested that he might welcome an opportunity to entrust some of his burdens to another person. I'd asked him timidly whether he would consider making me his assistant and teaching me what he knew. I offered to work for nothing at first, until I had proven my abilities. I told him there was no task so lowly that I would refuse it. I would have washed his floors, swept his grates, dusted his marble busts, and trudged all over Paris on menial errands, if only he would take me on and educate me in the secrets of his trade.

And he'd said no.

What his objection came down to was that I was a woman, and not only a woman, but a lady, a delicate flower from an English hothouse.

I might have laughed in his face had I not been so angry and disappointed. *Me*—a lady!

But it was my own fault. It was the illusion I'd intended to create from the moment I'd first arrived in Paris and had strolled its fashionable boulevards on Frederick's arm, wearing the polonaise-style silk dress he'd bought for me from what was left of the little nest egg he'd inherited and scarcely knew how to manage. The dress had been a wild extravagance—one of the very few to which I'd surrendered before I was able to persuade him that until he had established his reputation we would have to make every centime do the work of two.

Eventually, even when not so exquisitely attired, I managed to pass myself off to all of Paris, with the exception of my husband, as a mysterious, splendid, and refined creature. Not a soul could have guessed the truth about my origins, the humiliations of my youth, or that my gloss had come, not from a privileged upbring-ing, but from my grandmother's ruthless determination to make me an even more successful courtesan than she had once been—a fate I'd eluded by the skin of my teeth. I'd loved Frederick from the moment I set eyes on him, but it was to escape my grandmother and the repellent destiny toward which she was so intent upon driving me, that I'd fled with him to France.

After that she always told me I'd pay for it, that one bitter day I'd learn that I could have taken far better care of myself than Frederick would.

Of course, when it came to that point and I'd tried to take care of us both, I'd failed miserably. When I'd pressed Julien to elaborate upon his polite refusal, he'd confessed that it wasn't merely my gender and presumed refinement which so unsuited me for his trade, it was my nature as well.

"You're too . . . transparent, Madame Brooks," he'd told me. "You're not subtle enough, you show your hand on your face, you can't conceal your enthusiasms, you can't dissemble. You have the eye, yes, but not the instincts for this business. I'm sorry."

Now I lifted my eyes, those liabilities which hid too little, to Sir Anthony's face.

He had just finished asking whether I would object to joining him on his next visit to the Louvre; it would give him pleasure to savor its fabulous collections in the company of a real connoisseur.

Although the words themselves flattered, I expected, from the tone of his request, to find an expression of bored indifference upon his face, and certainly it seemed as if he were making an effort to wear precisely such a look. But for a second his eyes gave something else away; it was impossible to define the significance of the mute appeal in them. I only knew that some feeling had flickered across his face which seemed entirely out of keeping with our brief and casual acquaintance.

In an instant it was gone. As I tried to absorb its meaning, I did not realize that two little furrows must have appeared on my brow, until Sir Anthony broke the silence again.

"I beg your pardon, Madame Brooks," he said hastily. "It was a most unsuitable suggestion under the circumstances. I do hope you will forgive me. . . ."

By now he was stumbling over his words—this polished, impeccably bred English gentleman! But I understood exactly what he meant. In issuing his invitation, he had not demonstrated the proper consideration for my bereavement.

Perhaps I ought to have felt embarrassed for him. Lord Marsden did, I think, for he was determinedly studying the cracks in the wall, and although his face was impassive, his eyes suggested that he was trying not to smile at his cousin's discomfiture.

But I wasn't embarrassed. Not at all. I felt a warm rush of delight. As haughty and impenetrable as Sir Anthony's manner appeared to be, it seemed that neither the inherent arrogance of his class nor the rigid discipline of English schooling had entirely eradicated his humanity. In that moment he seemed very young indeed and endearingly vulnerable.

"Oh no! It was not an unsuitable suggestion at all!" I exclaimed. "Quite the opposite! My late husband was the very *last* person to have begrudged me such an innocent pleasure as you have proposed. He never had any regard for hollow social forms, you know, and still less for weeping and gnashing of teeth!"

Sir Anthony laughed.

"I must confess," I went on, to assuage any awkwardness he might still feel, "that I take issue with the ladies of the Faubourg St.-Germain where the etiquette of mourning is concerned, for I believe it is unhealthy to wallow in one's sorrows. I would be delighted to accompany you to the Louvre, Sir Anthony. I used to visit it so often, and I have missed it."

Had I gone to the Louvre alone, everyone might have felt sorry for me, a frail figure in black. Certainly I would have looked gratifyingly woebegone, for I would have felt Frederick's absence so keenly as to make pleasure impossible. But Sir Anthony might well distract me very pleasantly from any unmanageable onslaughts of loneliness and self-pity, and I found I welcomed the possibility. I was so tired of dwelling on the sorrows and failures of my irreparable past. I was twenty-five years old. I wanted to enjoy myself.

"It is most kind of you, Madame Brooks," Sir Anthony was saying in his low voice.

We smiled at each other until, by shifting slightly in his chair, Lord Marsden called us back to an awareness of his presence in the room.

As a fiacre carried us toward the Louvre, Sir Anthony asked me which of its collections I most wished to see.

"But *you* are the visitor!" I protested. "The choice is yours."

"But *you* are my guide," was his lazy rebuttal. "How can I learn from your enthusiasms if you won't reveal them?"

He spoke in the calm and measured way that I had at first misinterpreted as a symptom of chronic ennui. But today I observed a hint of restrained gaiety in his manner that told me he was as intent upon enjoying himself as I was.

By the time we arrived at the Louvre's Pavillon Denon, we had agreed that the antique sculpture collection must be our first port of call. I was a step or two ahead of Sir Anthony, who had paused to leave my parasol and his umbrella in the custody of an attendant, and the crush of visitors was so great that, rather than diving forward, I hesitated momentarily from a vague and rather irrational fear of becoming separated from my companion.

Then I felt his warm hand at my waist guiding me subtly toward the left.

I was very glad that Sir Anthony was behind me and could not see my face: His touch, brief and light but supremely assured, had unleashed a tidal wave of pure physical feeling in me, and during the moment or two that it took me to reestablish the connection between my tingling body and my practical brain, I could feel that my cheeks had gone scarlet. Sir Anthony, had he seen this, might well have once again imagined that he had offended me. He could not possibly have guessed how infrequently, in recent years, I had known a man's touch. And not once during that time had my body responded as eagerly as it had to this stranger.

By an effort of will, I managed to slow my racing pulse and

turn my eyes calmly upon my companion, knowing that they betrayed nothing.

In the Rotonde, we contemplated Melpomene, the muse of tragedy, moved on to admire the first Lycian *Apollo*, and presently came to the wonderful Silenus tending the infant Bacchus.

"Have you ever been to Florence, Madame Brooks?" Sir Anthony inquired as we stood before the affecting pair.

"Oh no," I said, with a pang. That unknown city was laden with private significance for me. My grandmother had once lived there, for what I suspected was one of the few truly happy intervals in her life; Frederick had studied there; and in the early days of our marriage we had often promised each other that one day we would visit it together.

Frederick.

I seized upon his name as a defense against the amazing flood of sheer animal hunger that had swept through me only minutes earlier.

"My husband studied in Florence," I told Sir Anthony, "and we often planned to visit it together. He wanted so much to show me Michelangelo's *David*."

"Oh yes, the *David* is perfection itself," agreed Sir Anthony. "But if you ever go to Florence, be sure not to overlook his *Bacchus*, which is in the Bargello. I like it better than the *David*, even if it is not so impressive a work."

"And why are you so fond of it?" I asked with a little smile, for it amused me to think that while my drunken husband had favored the alert and utterly sober David, the sober Sir Anthony would harbor a preference for the god of intoxication.

"The *Bacchus* himself is exquisite, but the little satyr at the god's feet is utterly enchanting," explained Sir Anthony. "When you come upon those eyes from a certain angle, it seems like a living thing. The first time I saw it, it brought me up short. I felt as if I'd stumbled upon something from another world."

As he went on to describe, in his low voice, the effect of that seductive, pagan gaze, I wondered what wayward string in his reserved English soul had vibrated to it so strongly.

"How you surprise me!" I told him artlessly, as we moved on. Regrettably, I had never mastered the art of proper English conversation, which dictates that, unless one is with intimate friends, one must rigidly confine oneself to the most impersonal subjects. However, I had already gone too far to turn back, so I plunged on. "I would have taken you for a worshiper of Apollo, not of Bacchus!"

"And you'd have been right, I suppose," said Sir Anthony with a rueful laugh. "Certainly Apollo is far more admirable. He never spoke a false word, you know. But Bacchus was always gentle, even in anger, while Apollo, as you must recall, could be very cruel."

"Cruel?" I said. "Apollo, the healer?"

"He slew Niobe's children," Sir Anthony reminded me.

I felt my face close up.

"Yes," I murmured. "He was very cruel."

Thereafter, for a time, every image I saw evoked thoughts of destruction and loss and drew my mind relentlessly back to the sorrows I had come here to forget. They seemed to chastise me for the frivolous spirit in which I had undertaken the day's adventure.

But once we had moved into the Salle de Psyche, the frivolity of my nature began to reassert itself—with some help from Sir Anthony.

We spent a long time admiring the *Venus de Milo*.

"The perfect woman," I remarked as I studied the serene loveliness of her features.

"Not quite perfect," said Sir Anthony dryly.

I glanced up at him.

"You don't regard her as the ne plus ultra of feminine beauty?"

His eyes lingered on me with the same unrevealing expression I had seen in them at our first meeting.

"No," was all he said.

But later, just before we left, we agreed that we must pay our respects to the *Nikè of Samothrace,* and Sir Anthony admired her so extravagantly that at last I felt compelled to observe, "So *that* is your *belle idéale!* A woman with wings!"

He gave this comment a moment or two of earnest consideration before he rejected it cautiously.

"Nooo," he said. "Not quite."

But then his mouth began to twitch.

"I prefer women with hands," he announced, and then added, after a tiny pause, "and lips."

There was nothing insinuating in the matter-of-fact way he said this. His tone was not at all suggestive. It was simply mischievous, and I laughed.

"I suppose you favor the works that have been restored, then," I said.

"What, the ones all patched together like Frankenstein's monster with heads that don't belong to them!" He sounded highly insulted. "Certainly not! I detest sham! Battered and broken she may be, but this lady has at least kept her integrity."

For the remainder of our visit, I enjoyed myself wholeheartedly. It wasn't until I was alone again that I reviewed my behavior and berated myself for having drawn our conversation toward a level of such ease and intimacy. Sir Anthony had only followed my lead. I knew very well that had I been more reserved, had I behaved in a manner more appropriate to an inconsolable widow, he would have respected my distance entirely. . . .

But to think of all the little pleasures I would have missed!

III

The rules of polite conduct require a widow to mourn no less than two years for her departed husband. During the first year, she must not go into society.

For a woman whose child has died in infancy, three months is considered the proper length of time to grieve.

It seemed that I had turned the etiquette of bereavement topsy-turvy.

As I lay in bed the night after my jaunt to the Louvre, I recalled vividly the feeling of Sir Anthony's light, confident but unassuming hand upon my waist; it was as if some neglected and half-forgotten inner bowstring, pulled tauter and tauter over the years, had been lightly plucked.

Better for me had it remained in oblivion.

Already it was beginning to tighten again—but this time I could feel every teasing, agonizing increment of tension.

It had nothing to do with Sir Anthony Camwell, of course. What was he? A rich and idle dilettante who'd sought some brief amusement in my company. A grave and reserved young man who seemed to consider his words too carefully before he spoke: Even that small witticism about the *Nikè of Samothrace* had sparkled in his eyes well before he'd shared the joke with me.

I felt myself blush in the darkness. The remark of his, which had seemed so innocent amidst the austere classicism of our surroundings, now struck a hot little flame in my drowsy mind, and I let myself wonder for a moment or two just how Sir Anthony Camwell would use a woman's hands and lips. . . .

What was I thinking! I had never thought of any man but Frederick in so bold a way. And Sir Anthony, of all people!

I turned over, pressed my face into the pillow, and inhaled with faint hopefulness, but Frederick's familiar scent was long gone.

The bed was too warm, that was why I couldn't sleep.

I sat up and flung off my blankets.

I couldn't keep my thoughts from straying back to my childhood as I lay down again.

My grandmother had always worried I was too hot-blooded. "I live in fear," she used to say, "that you'll throw yourself away on the first man who strikes a match to your loins."

And so I had.

My mother had, too. Against my grandmother's wishes and to her fury, she'd married a poor, but ambitious, man for love, and had paid the ultimate price for that piece of folly by dying as I entered the world. My father begged my grandmother to raise me and promised that he would send money to support us to the extent that he was able. Soon afterward, he'd sailed for America. He never returned. He sent money faithfully, but he never communicated with us otherwise.

I had written to him, upon my marriage to Frederick, telling him that I could manage without his further assistance but begging him to continue sending money to my grandmother until Frederick and I were able to assume that responsibility. How I'd hated having to ask even this of a man I had never known.

The only other letter I wrote him was to tell him, two years later, that Frederick and I were at last in a position to assume responsibility for my grandmother's financial support and to thank him again for all he had done in the past.

After that, his checks to my grandmother stopped coming.

Now, as I tossed between the sheets I could hear my grandmother's voice again, cautioning me to resist dangerous impulses, warning me never to do anything in the heat of passion that might later bring me to grief.

She'd been true to her own counsel. With what businesslike determination she had gone about her career! She had raised me, and no doubt my mother, as well, with the same ruthless single-mindedness.

She'd distrusted joyfulness and encouraged me to do likewise. But her advice had the opposite effect. Her tales of her youthful exploits were so unromantic that they'd made me swear I would never follow in her footsteps. She spoke of her lovers in terms of their wealth and station, and their gifts to her, but never did she display any hint of tender feeling . . . except when she touched upon the few months she had spent in Florence with an overly emotional Italian count who had allegedly attempted suicide after my grandmother had coolly deserted him for a much wealthier but considerably less noble protector.

When I'd lived with her, it seemed that her sole remaining pleasure in life was to open the strongbox in which she kept the odds and ends of jewelry that were to be my only legacy. She loved to display these cherished possessions. Each had a story, the full details of which emerged only as I grew older. The rose pearl had studded the collar of a marquis before the besotted nobleman had it set in a gold ring for her; it was only the first of many such rewards for her favors. The silvery mask, which had a little tearlike diamond at the corner of each eye, had come from an aging crony of George IV; she had worn it, but not much else, at a splendid masquerade. Dear God, what would Sir Anthony Camwell think of me were he to know that *this* was my inheritance!

Years later, when my grandmother was dying, she'd made me swear that I would never bail Frederick out of debt by selling any of the pieces she was leaving to me.

The day came, of course, long after my grandmother was gone, when those jewels might have saved us. It was after Frederick had finally begun his erratic recovery; he had produced and sold two paintings that were at last worthy of his talents.

But as soon as his creditors got wind of this, they came banging at our door more insistently than ever, and the money couldn't be stretched far enough to satisfy them all.

That was when I told Frederick that we had to sell the jewels and clear our debts up altogether.

"No, darling," he had said, with a weary sadness that made my heart ache. "Your grandmother was right, you know. Those jewels are the only insurance you'll have, if anything should happen to me. I won't let you break your word to her. It was I who plunged us into this morass of debt and it's my job, not yours, to pull us out of it."

So the promise wrung from me by my poor dead grandmother remained inviolate.

In some ways I still felt as if she had never died; she'd impressed herself so forcefully upon me, that whenever I was hesitant or indecisive, she would charge in upon my thoughts with her worldly, unwelcome advice.

"A baronet!" she'd have cried out, had she known of today's adventure. "But *what* on earth were you thinking of! That dress— why, it makes you look like a lump of charcoal! Good heavens, girl, black *can* be very effective, you know—*if* it's worn correctly."

And she'd have been taking in seams, stripping away every inch of excess fabric, until the black clung to my figure like a blazing invitation.

"There," she'd have announced with shameless satisfaction. "Now you look deliciously vulnerable, very much in need of . . . protection. Not even your well-behaved chevalier can remain immune to *this* for long."

Of course, *I* would never stoop to such ploys. The last thing I wanted to do was to draw to myself the kind of pointed attentions that my grandmother had regarded as the only kind worth having. Nor was I interested in a pointless flirtation.

A pleasant friendship, yes, but that was no reason to take in my dresses!

I tried to steer my mind away from the channels the thoughts of my grandmother had suggested. But it wandered among them longer than it should have and nudged me with a truth I had been trying to dismiss.

Sir Anthony's mere physical presence had had a subtle but undeniable impact upon me. Being in the same room with him made me feel as if I'd drunk a little too much from a bottle of rare old wine.

I tried to pretend it wasn't so. I tried to ignore the disturbing feeling or to push it away, but now, alone in the darkness, I felt a warm, slow thrill as I let the guilty awareness fill my mind.

What was it exactly that made his company so pleasant in ways that had nothing to do with the words he spoke or the things we did?

Was it that calm air of expectant stillness, which made me feel almost as if he were lying in wait for something, like a lion lounging indolent yet alert in a sea of tall golden grass? Or the quiet grace with which he moved—which compelled not only my eyes but my senses?

The truth was—and even in the darkness I could feel my cheeks burn as I acknowledged it—that I liked to watch the way he used his body: I liked the way he got up from a chair, the way he walked across a room, even the slow, lazy way he smiled.

I liked his low voice, too, and his understated way of speaking —soothing, but with enough bite to keep you on your toes.

He was very different from Frederick, who'd moved with an expansive, exuberant energy; who'd filled up a room as soon as he entered it, with his body, with his voice, and with his robust laugh that could lift you up like a great warm gust of wind. Frederick, who'd never waited for anything. Frederick, whose language was the language of superlatives; it was how he'd talked, how he'd painted, how he'd moved. It was how he'd lived.

No, Sir Anthony Camwell was nothing at all like Frederick. And therefore, I assured myself, if our pleasant acquaintance were to continue to develop, it would certainly be as innocent as it was enjoyable.

IV

To fully appreciate the treasures of the Louvre would take far longer than a lifetime. Sir Anthony and I had given ourselves less than a day. But when he'd returned me to my door, he'd said nothing about repeating the adventure. Perhaps I had disappointed him. I had not revealed the discerning and critical eye he had looked for in me. I had not explained, in disengaged and pedantic tones, why this piece of work, although charming, is indisputably inferior to that one. I had not detailed with dispassionate condescension the small failings of great talents, nor had I pointed out, with perverse smugness, the little flashes of genius in obscure works that are commonly overlooked.

No. I had artlessly exposed to him the very worst evidence of an undisciplined mind and an uncultivated eye: I had expressed my enthusiasms!

True, he had encouraged me to do so, but a man whose tastes had surely been shaped by a Cambridge or Oxford education must have been quickly bored by my lack of erudition.

On the following day I received a rather formal but extremely gracious note from the baronet thanking me for the time I had spent with him. It concluded with a hope that we might visit one of the Louvre's other galleries at some unspecified future date.

I responded with what I hoped was a reserved and dignified yet encouraging reply.

Before a week had passed, another note in Sir Anthony's severely unembellished hand informed me that an engagement which he had not been anticipating with much pleasure had mercifully been called off. This freed him for the afternoon of the following day. If I cared to revisit the Louvre with him, I had only to send word. Of course, he hardly dared to hope that I would likewise be free on such regrettably short notice. . . .

My inexplicable but growing fascination with Sir Anthony prompted me to try to read between the lines of his economical pen.

He was rich, unattached, and sojourning in a foreign city—surely his time was his own. He might have easily pinned me down days ago had he issued his invitation in person at the end of our last excursion, when it would have been rather awkward to refuse. On the other hand, perhaps there really were a great many unpleasant demands upon his time; there was a suggestion of earnestness in his nature which might have made it difficult for him to turn his back on the needs of others.

In any case, had I not wished to pursue our acquaintance, he had given me, by issuing his invitation only one day in advance, a fine opportunity to make a refusal that would not seem contrived. But surely he knew by now that I had no pupils on Friday afternoon—the time of the week he and Lord Marsden had called upon me, the time of our first visit to the Louvre.

Of course I was pleased to accept.

Sir Anthony and I fell rather quickly into a pattern of spending our Friday afternoons together, and for the most part, we sustained the pleasant, easy tone we had established early on.

I was now convinced it was at Lord Marsden's instigation that Sir Anthony had begun to squire me. The Paris Season was over and the viscount had returned to England, but I supposed that, out of his long-standing regard for Frederick, Lord Marsden had been reluctant to leave me bereft of the courtly and unimpeachably correct companionship he himself had so kindly provided during the early months of my bereavement. Certainly this seemed to be the role that Sir Anthony had now assumed, and if Lord Marsden's attitude toward me had been that of a benevolent uncle, Sir Anthony's could best be described as cousinly.

In September, Sir Anthony returned to England. We spent our last afternoon together at the Luxembourg Museum but barely commented upon the paintings. Indeed, I was all but oblivious to them. A real sadness that our lazy summer afternoons were coming to an end had me in its grip.

My regrets were made more difficult to bear by my consciousness that it would not do at all to express them; such a confession seemed very out of keeping with the lighthearted tenor of our relationship.

But when at last Sir Anthony handed me down from the fiacre onto the Boulevard de Clichy, his hand clung to mine for perhaps a moment longer than necessary, and when I met his gaze, I saw a much softer glow in his eyes than I was accustomed to find there.

He escorted me up the narrow stairway to my door, where we made our farewells on the dim landing.

"You have been very generous with your time this summer, Madame Brooks," he said, taking my hand again. "I don't know how to express my gratitude."

"Oh no," I said quickly. "All the gratitude is mine. You have helped me through what might otherwise have been a very difficult and lonely time. I can't thank you enough."

He smiled. But still my hand remained in his. It seemed that neither one of us wished to be the first to sever that innocent connection.

"I fear I shall miss you," I confessed at last.

Sir Anthony looked oddly gratified by this admission.

"I am flattered," he replied softly, "for I *know* I shall miss you."
I felt my cheeks flush faintly. And still my hand rested in his.
"I hope to return often and soon," he went on, his own face coloring slightly. "Paris has come to feel like a second home to me."

"I hope it will always seem so," was all I could manage, as I gently disengaged my hand.

It wasn't until after the fiacre had carried him away, however, that I began to fully comprehend how much his companionship had meant to me. Those afternoons had been the high point of my week.

They must have been all that had kept at bay the terrible reality of my losses, for without Sir Anthony's tactful and undemanding company, my grief and loneliness returned with a vengeance. Even more disturbing, however, my thoughts did not entirely confine themselves to my dead husband.

It was Frederick's name I whispered when I clung to my pillow in the dark, but, to my shame, the lips that came to me in waking dreams were not Frederick's lips . . . and this unsettling development had begun long before the end of summer.

If I'd been wiser or more experienced, no doubt I would have more carefully examined my tangled and obscure feelings where Sir Anthony was concerned. But I could not see the need: I regarded him as a very minor player in the drama of my life. The kisses that my drowsy imagination allowed him were not chaste ones, but I never allowed my mind to race beyond them to visions of greater intimacy.

In any case, my black gowns were my protection. The rules of correct behavior required me to continue my mourning for nearly eighteen months more, and it was my prerogative to stretch it out even longer—for decades, if I chose to. From behind my barricade of black, a fortification that demands both sympathy and respect, I could keep life's complexities and ambiguities at bay for as long as it suited me.

And if my interest in Sir Anthony was not entirely innocent, that was nobody's business but my own. Certainly Sir Anthony himself would never know.

By summer's end, of course, I supposed that he might have been fleetingly attracted to me. Harmless flirtations between men and women who are entirely unsuited to one another are very common, as everyone knows, but sensible people can be trusted not to act on them. And Sir Anthony Camwell was eminently sensible. He impressed me as the least impulsive, most judicious person I had ever met in my life, and if a dishonorable or foolish thought had ever wandered across his mind, I was certain that he would have routed it instantly.

Even if his attraction to me had been stronger and more enduring, he could not possibly have acted upon it. He would never insult me by trying to claim a husband's privileges outside the bonds of matrimony, and he could not possibly think of marrying me. He was of ancient English stock and the whole weight of English tradition would require him to take a wife from a family with a bloodline as unsullied as his own. In a year or two, he would be thirty; it was time for him to begin looking seriously for a bride. Perhaps it was this very recognition of the demands and responsibilities of his station that had called him back to England and ended his pleasant dalliance in France.

The more that I tried to consider his situation from this practical point of view, however, the sadder I felt. He would make a proper marriage to some thin-lipped, cold-blooded English girl with a puritanical streak even broader than the one I had glimpsed in him. She would embody everything that I most detested in the English upper classes. Her blue eyes would bulge with confused incomprehension should her husband ever attempt to infuse her with the enchantment he'd once felt under the gaze of a marble faun. But what did these things matter? She would bring him the kind of pedigree that could never be mine, and equally important, she could give him children. Who was I? A creature of murky lineage who had not even been able to carry my beloved's child to term.

For a while I lashed myself with these painful thoughts as if I imagined that by intensifying my loneliness I could surmount it faster, but it was the note I shortly thereafter received from Sir Anthony that lifted my spirits. He intended to make another, very brief visit to Paris in October and hoped that I might be able to spare him an afternoon.

We spent a good part of it idling over a bunch of autumn grapes outside a café in the Boulevard des Italiens, while the October sunlight fell upon us. I felt oddly happy and oddly shy.

"And how did you find England?" I asked.

"As lovely as ever," was his reply, "and as imperfect."

"Imperfect?" I repeated. "In what way?"

I have always regarded insular England as very imperfect when compared to cosmopolitan, democratic Paris, but I was curious to know in precisely what way Sir Anthony Camwell found his native land wanting.

His lips curved into a hint of a smile.

"It hasn't quite the charm for me that Paris has," he said, flashing me a sidewise look that I found difficult to interpret. "Of course," he added after a pause, "*you* must feel this even more strongly, for you are English by birth and yet have chosen to make your home here."

"Oh yes," I told him cheerfully. "On the great railway line of life I regard Paris as one stop short of heaven."

Sir Anthony's smile broadened.

"And where on the line do you put England?" he inquired.

I wrinkled my nose as I considered this for a minute or two.

"I don't know," I replied at last. "It is so very smoky, you know, I fear it must be rather close to hell."

Sir Anthony burst into laughter, but when he spoke again he sounded more piqued than amused.

"So that is your opinion of England," he said. "Don't you think you are being unjust? There is a good deal more to England than smoke."

I popped a grape between my lips and considered this with an air of skepticism.

"I have no warmth in my heart for England," I said at last.

"But you *were* born there, were you not?" he asked.

I had the feeling he was trying to draw me out.

"Yes," I said in a tone that was meant to slam the door on that subject.

"I hope that one day you will find a reason to think better of your country—and mine," he said.

"*This* is my country now," was my only reply.

He was watching me thoughtfully but did not press me to explain my antipathy for England.

"Have *you* ever thought of making your home here?" I asked in the hope of injecting a lighter tone back into the conversation.

"Me? Oh, I've toyed with the thought, but it's really out of the question."

"Why is that?"

"I have . . . responsibilities," was his rather vague response.

It occurred to me then that Sir Anthony had never, in his conversations with me, made any reference to his blue-blooded family or to his great wealth.

Well, there was no use pretending they didn't exist and that they would not shape the course of his life and every choice he would ever make.

"Oh, I suppose you mean the vast Camwell estates," I retorted lightly. "Don't you pay someone to manage them for you? What's the point of being rich if you still insist upon wearing the harness of dreary responsibilities?"

To my surprise, the usually even-tempered Sir Anthony did not seem amused by my offhand remark.

"I see," he said. "Perhaps you're right, Madame Brooks. What's the point of life at all if it's not to throw off all responsibility and do whatever you feel like doing at any given moment?" He paused for a minute and then added in a tone that managed to be both mild and scathing, "That's quite an ideal, isn't it?"

I thought it sounded very appealing, indeed, but, even so, his cool words hit me like a little slap. I shot him a quick, rather startled glance.

What a Roman standard he espoused!

I wondered what he would think of me were he to discover that I was someone who had weakly collapsed under grief for nearly two years rather than honoring my sacred responsibilities to my husband.

"I beg your pardon," I managed after a few more seconds. "I spoke too carelessly."

But at the same time, he was saying, "Forgive me, Madame Brooks. I spoke too harshly."

"Not at all," I said. "You were quite right to say what you did."

"No. Actually, I was being thoroughly disingenuous. You see . . ." He hesitated with something like embarrassment and then plunged on rather awkwardly. "I like being rich. I love being able to do pretty much as I please. I'm afraid I deny myself very little, if you want to know the truth. It's not something of which I'm proud. And the fact is that I love my home in England. I can't imagine choosing to live elsewhere for any length of time. I only wish . . ."

"You only wish what?" I prodded him.

He lifted his head and gave me one of his slow, charming smiles.

"I only wish there were a little more of Paris in it," he said enigmatically.

I resisted the fleeting temptation to take this cryptic remark as a personal compliment.

"Perhaps you ought to hire a French chef," I proposed.

He broke into that soft laughter again.

"But I already have one," he confessed. "You see, I *do* indulge every whim! But something is still wanting. And a French *chef* is not quite what I have in mind, at this point."

At *that* point, as luck would have it, I caught the eye of Monsieur Julien, who was strolling silkily down the boulevard. As he was known to both of us, we invited him to join us and our conversation quickly assumed a more urbane and inconsequential tone.

It seemed that Sir Anthony had once again dropped one of those seemingly innocent but hauntingly provocative remarks that kept me awake at night when I ought to have been deep in slumber.

So a French *chef* was not what he had in mind to enliven his English home.

It was difficult to avoid the conclusion that what Sir Anthony wanted was a woman.

So he had come to France to find a wife.

No doubt, then, he had spent the vast bulk of his Parisian hours, above and beyond the few he devoted to me, in the salons of the Faubourg St.-Germain, politely conversing with young, convent-educated virgins whose blood was as rarified as his own.

I must be a very dog in the manger, I thought, for I did not like the vision my thoughts had conjured up any better than I had liked my earlier vision of him wed to that prim-mouthed, pop-eyed hypothetical English miss.

V

I did not see Sir Anthony again before his return to his beloved England, where he remained for more than two months.

On All Saints' Day I visited Frederick's grave in the Bagneaux with a wreath of immortelles. He would have laughed at such a trite act of devotion.

December came. I celebrated Christmas Eve and most of the following day with Marguerite and Théo. They were so lively that it was impossible to feel much loneliness when in their company. Théo, perhaps out of deference to the season, did not indulge his famously contentious nature as much as usual. Marguerite, who relished every aspect of holiday-making, was in her element. And I had had a card from Sir Anthony, who was spending the holidays in Devon at the home of Lord Marsden's sister-in-law and her large family. He told me that he would be back in Paris in January.

I had never spoken of Sir Anthony to Marguerite or Théo. I wanted to keep him separate from the rest of my life, somewhere where he could not bump up against people who had known and loved Frederick. And I did not wish to invite speculation about the nature of his interest in me, especially on the part of Marguerite, who had the soul of a matchmaker and could be wickedly suggestive when the mood took her. I had seen her victims writhe under her pointed tongue.

Yes, I knew her. She would insist that Sir Anthony's interest was not as innocent as I knew it to be. She would declare that with a mere coup d'oeil I could subjugate any man I chose. She would never give me a moment's peace regarding the outcome of this friendship that could lead nowhere. Besides, it was Frederick I missed, Frederick into whose life I had fitted like a hand to a glove.

Still, I counted the days until Sir Anthony would be in Paris again.

We had planned to visit the Musée de Cluny on the Friday following his return. But the spectacular winter afternoon—intensely cold, intensely bright—made me repent of my promise to spend it indoors, among tarnished-looking Flemish tapestries and medieval woodcarvings depicting the gruesome martyrdoms of ecstatic saints.

I suggested an alteration in our plans to Sir Anthony.

"I've been a prisoner to my pupils all week long," I told him. "How I long for exercise and fresh air! Can I persuade you to forgo Cluny and settle for nothing more than a long walk?"

What I had in mind was a climb to the still unfinished basilica of Sacre-Coeur, which is at the very top of the Butte Montmartre. I thought *that* would be grueling enough to settle my restless spirits.

But although Sir Anthony proved cheerfully amenable to a change of plans in general, he seemed somewhat torn with respect to Sacre-Coeur.

"Or perhaps . . . ," he said, "if you wouldn't find it too . . ."

And here he paused as if inwardly debating the propriety of the sentence that hovered on his lips.

I waited, half annoyed, half flattered. Frederick would never have hesitated—he'd have burst out with his suggestion, no matter how bold. On the other hand, Frederick had never treated me with quite the same tact and delicacy that Sir Anthony invariably displayed.

"Madame Brooks," said Sir Anthony, at last, to my astonished delight, "have you, by any chance, a pair of ice skates?"

I quickly unearthed the skates I had not worn for . . . how long? Four years? Then a pell-mell carriage ride to Sir Anthony's hotel in the Rue de Castiglione to fetch a gleaming pair of skates that looked as if they had never been worn at all.

And at last on to a frozen lake in the Bois de Boulogne. It was ringed with the glowing braziers of chestnut sellers. Over the ice flew dashing men in tight black breeches and gaiters and graceful women in accordion-pleated skirts.

Sir Anthony led me onto the lake. Our feet left the lumpy, frozen shore, no longer earthbound, and we began to sail over the ice. It felt as smooth and hard as marble and as slick as butter beneath our blades.

Sir Anthony skated with the same languid grace that I admired in everything else he did, and now, as he held me, his rhythms became mine as well. His long, slow strokes were more fluid and assured than mine would have been, had I skated alone. For a moment I resisted the impulse to let my feet follow the fearless sweep of his own. It seemed too thrilling—almost dangerous. Then I surrendered.

We soared lazily over the lake like a pair of hawks hanging in the sky, barely moving their wings at all as they let the air currents carry them.

The enchantment went on until I lost all sense of time. No giddy pyrotechnics, no calligraphic swirls and loops, only those strong yet indolent glides, each one lasting almost too long before the next one came to keep us aloft.

Bundled as I was in heavy winter underwear, a heavy black dress, and a heavier black coat, I could barely feel my partner's left hand on the small of my back. The suede-gloved fingers of his other hand, however, were firmly interlaced with mine. In spite of my black wool gloves, I was intensely aware of his gentle grip, and I gleaned all the private pleasure I could from knowing that we could sustain this innocent, delicious connection indefinitely.

The distance between us was small, almost insignificant, and filled with our heat. I felt my cheeks glowing; was it from that warmth or from the frosty air?

My eyes fell shut. I felt Sir Anthony's arm bring me a tiny bit closer, and I knew that here on the gleaming lake we had at last lighted upon the purest expression and finest culmination of our unlikely friendship.

Anything more would have alarmed me; anything less would have left my vague, restless hungers unslaked.

But this was everything I could ever want.

For one perfect afternoon I felt complete.

Afterward, he whisked me off to a modest little restaurant near the Opéra. At this early hour, the dining room was nearly deserted, so it was with a sense of luxurious privacy that we took our seats.

Our conversation was desultory and marked with long silences. Once or twice when I caught his eyes, I saw that curious tenderness flickering there. I thought again of the impossibly deep and prolonged pleasure I had known in his arms. My skin blazed; I quickly dropped my attention to the *canard à l'orange* on my plate.

A few minutes later, Sir Anthony cleared his throat softly.

"Madame Brooks," he began. The assurance with which he usually spoke was gone. He seemed as diffident as he'd been when he suggested skating on the lake. "I wonder if I might ask . . . do you ever have any time to yourself during the week—other than Friday afternoons, I mean?"

"Oh yes," I said. "I never have pupils on Sunday."

"Oh, but that's perfect!" he exclaimed. Then his voice faltered again. "I mean, if it would be agreeable to you . . . I have a sort of call I must make before I return to England, and I wonder if I might ask you to accompany me."

He wanted to introduce me to his friends?

I thought it was a terrible idea!

We had just achieved perfection; what could possibly be gained by attempting to push the acquaintance beyond its obvious limits?

"Oh, I don't know," I demurred. I speculated on how my shabby black dresses—they made me look like a milliner's assistant —would appear when set against the brocaded satin upholstery of a drawing room in the Faubourg St.-Germain, and on how they would contrast with the silk gowns of the ladies there. "I'm sure that any friends of yours would find me shockingly bohemian," I added.

"Not this family," he said. "They will like you just as much as I think you will like them. But I can't pretend that it is merely a social call. Among other things, Monsieur Salomon makes doll-houses."

I started to laugh. What on earth could the staid Sir Anthony Camwell want with a dollhouse?

"Aha!" said I, laying down my fork triumphantly. "So you *have* decided to buy a house in Paris!"

"I have," acknowledged Sir Anthony gravely. "And I hope I may depend upon you to help me select just the right one."

"I would be delighted," I said. "But really—what is the occasion? Have you a little niece?"

"Not I!" I thought I heard a slight edge in his voice. "I was an only child." Then he continued more lightly. "No, this is for a great-niece of Neville's. She has a birthday coming up, and Neville has no knack at all, you know, for picking out gifts for small children. His tastes are overly sophisticated."

"And you have the talent he lacks?"

"I like to think so. What Neville has forgotten is that children can entertain themselves for hours with not much more than a couple of stones or an end of chalk."

I thought that a rather odd remark to come from this scion of wealth. Surely *he* had never been obliged to entertain himself with nothing but rocks and a piece of chalk! What an absurd notion! His childhood birthdays must have been princely celebrations.

Of course there was a slim possibility that he had been raised in the horrible tradition which makes *all* pleasure suspect. I knew of a vicarage where a pet cat had once been drowned in the well simply to teach the children not to become too attached to earthly things.

But I doubted that Sir Anthony had known such harsh treatment. Someone had grounded him in the virtues of kindness and consideration, had honed off the edges of what could easily have been an overbearing arrogance. I could hardly condemn the stranger's handiwork.

On Sunday, therefore, we found ourselves in an ancient gray house in the Rue Vieille-du-Temple, where we mounted a stairway as steep and narrow as my own to find ourselves before a door which bore a plate proclaiming this to be the establishment of Abraham Salomon, *"Fabrique de patins à roulettes et jouets."* A little factory of roller skates and toys.

Monsieur Salomon, who must have been at least seventy years of age, welcomed Sir Anthony warmly and expressed his pleasure at making my acquaintance. Then, after leading us through a dining room in which virtually every surface seemed to be covered with miniature houses, he lifted a curtain and ushered us into a low garret whose function I was at first hard-pressed to identify.

It contained a bed and a washstand, so perhaps it was a bedroom.

No, there was an iron stove; it was a kitchen.

But it was the only kitchen I had ever seen, other than the one I had once shared with Frederick, where the fragrance of paint and varnish competed triumphantly with that of onions and garlic.

Here Monsieur Salomon introduced me to his wife, Anais,

who sat at a worktable varnishing yet another dollhouse, and to his daughter, Rachel, a danseuse of perhaps thirty or so who, I soon discovered, produced ballets for the provincial theaters. Today, however, she sat beside her mother making artificial flowers.

I was too fascinated by the jumble of ribbons and roller skates, pedal-lathes and bandboxes—one of which was occupied by a skinny cat—to contribute much to the conversation that began to swirl about me almost as soon as Sir Anthony and I had taken our seats.

Mademoiselle Rachel almost immediately proceeded to dredge up from the depths of Sir Anthony's mind every image it still contained of any ballet he had seen in London since he had last called upon the family, and Sir Anthony obliged her gallantly, as if he had taken special pains to make note of the sort of technical details in which he knew she was likely to take a particular interest.

He then encouraged Monsieur Salomon to reminisce about his youthful days as a circus tumbler, while Madame tried to feed me, scolded me for being too slender, and, in the end, would not allow me to depart without copies of recipes which she guaranteed would put meat upon my bones.

I could not help but be amused by the terms of affection which punctuated nearly every sentence the Salomons addressed to one another. To her parents, Mademoiselle Rachel was *"ma cocotte."* The others were inevitably "my dear husband or wife" or "my darling mama or papa." Even the cat was *"mon cher moumoutte."*

This surfeit of endearments might have been almost stultifying had they not been flung about with a guileless warmth and sincerity that both touched and charmed me.

But at last it was time to leave, and after we had made our selection of a little toy house for Lord Marsden's great-niece, we departed. Outside, the winter sky was growing dark. Without saying much, we began to walk rather aimlessly through the cold streets until we found ourselves at the river. We were close to the spot where draymen and cavalry officers bathe their horses in the late summer afternoons, when the sunsets last forever. But the gentle days of summer were long past.

We lingered by the floating apple market near the Hôtel de Ville; here boats from Normandy moor every autumn and remain through the winter until all their fruit has been carried off in great baskets.

The sweet-tart scent of apples hung on the icy air, like a ghostly reminder of autumn's abundance. Sir Anthony was to return to England on the following day, and tonight, after the last cold red glow had vanished from the western sky, I would fall asleep alone in that empty garret in the Boulevard de Clichy.

I thought of the Salomons' cluttered, overflowing kitchen, where sunlight must pour through the huge windows even at this time of year to coax such luxuriant greenery from Madame's little red herb pots. Had my daughter lived, perhaps even now I might have been in a kitchen not so very different from theirs. Frederick, at the table with our daughter on his knee, would be cleaning his brushes, and I'd be across from them, slicing potatoes and carrots for our dinner. . . .

Never, never had I so dreaded going back to my . . . dwelling place—it hardly deserved to be called a home.

I felt a surge of anger. How I wished Sir Anthony had not taken me to the Rue Vieille-du-Temple. Of course he had not done it to be cruel. He could not have guessed the effect it would have upon me. He had never known what it was to live in a garret with love and turpentine and a view of the rooftops.

Nearly all the light had gone from the sky. For once, perhaps because he could not see my face, Sir Anthony's customary sensitivity to my moods failed him.

"Did you enjoy yourself this afternoon?" he was asking.

"Oh, very much so," I roused myself to answer politely. "The Salomons are delightful."

"An extraordinary family," Sir Anthony was saying.

Something in the way he said this irritated me, no doubt because my nerves already felt raw.

"Extraordinary?" I said. "Very charming people, to be sure. But extraordinary? I don't think so. Why there must be at least a thousand families in Paris just like them."

If only I were still part of one of them.

"What do you mean—just like them?" he asked with a laugh.

"Oh, close-knit, hardworking, talented. You know."

"And as warm toward one another?"

"But of course!" I said impatiently, as if he were being obtuse. "Good heavens, what can be more natural than parents who love their children, and husbands and wives who love one another!"

With his usual equanimity, Sir Anthony merely laughed that low laugh of his.

"I suppose you're right," was all he said.

VI

In March, with my usual disregard for polite behavior, I went into half mourning. The proper thing would have been to wait at least three months longer—preferably six—before shedding my black garments in favor of the old gray dresses I'd begun to favor when I'd stopped caring about making myself attractive to Frederick. Later he'd said they were fit for nothing but paint rags.

No, the change from black to gray did not signify any improvement in my spirits. My loneliness had sharpened with a vengeance during the dark days of winter. *That* was why I wore gray.

I knew that black was infinitely more becoming; I had even succumbed at last, during the past summer, to my grandmother's ghostly advice on how to increase its allure. Now I felt ashamed of that impulse; now I *wanted* to look as drab as I felt.

During Sir Anthony's prolonged absence, he wrote often, mostly about a reception and show that he was organizing on behalf of Henri Caylat, a painter whose works Sir Anthony felt deserved wider attention than they had yet received. He had begun making the arrangements with Caylat during his visit in January. The event was to take place here in Paris at the end of April.

I was surprised that Sir Anthony should have undertaken such a venture. Although I had heard of Caylat, I had never seen any of his works. He'd been brutalized by the critics years earlier and had scarcely been heard of since.

But Sir Anthony seemed quite set up as he planned the event. When I worried that the critics and gallery owners would never come, Sir Anthony replied that no matter how much they despised Caylat, they would make it a point to be there. Sir Anthony had a reputation for providing superb food and drink whenever he entertained.

When I pointed out that neither Pommery and Greno nor magnums of Bollinger had ever softened a critic's heart, Sir Anthony parried with the statement that he had no hope of altering anyone's opinion of Caylat's painting; but once the critics had seen the studies from Caylat's sketchbooks that he'd persuaded the artist to mount and display, never again would they be able to dismiss him with the charge that he could only daub because he'd never learned to draw.

My hopes were not high for the success of the event, but it was difficult not to respond to Sir Anthony's enthusiasm, dry and understated though it was.

With the same vague determination to keep the various strands of my life rigidly separate that had prevented me from introducing Sir Anthony to Marguerite and Théo, I did not invite the Sorrel-Valory ménage to Caylat's show. If Caylat was as dreadful as he was reputed to be, and if Théo was in one of his uncharitable moods, no sneers would be crueler than his.

There were several reasons, I suppose, why I failed to recognize the singular position in which I found myself on the day of Caylat's show. At first I thought Sir Anthony must have felt uncertain of his own judgment and hoped that the presence of Frederick Brooks's young widow would add prestige to the event—for lately it seemed that Frederick had enhanced his reputation tremendously by dying.

I'll admit that this attitude of mine was rather cynical, but it lasted only until I entered the rooms Sir Anthony had hired for the occasion.

I was so enraptured by the astonishing display that I could think of nothing else. I had heard Julien disparage Caylat once or twice; he'd even mocked Sir Anthony for being his patron. He thought Caylat was a savage and Sir Anthony a fool.

But he was wrong.

And I knew that I had been wrong, as well, in ever having accepted Sir Anthony's presentation of himself as someone whose eye needed training.

So captivated was I by the brilliance and boldness around me that I scarcely considered much else. Certainly I did not think as much as I ought to have about the fact that Sir Anthony was as attentive to me as he was to the artist himself, that he seldom left my side for very long, that he introduced me with something like pride to everyone he knew.

Lord Marsden was present. Although I was familiar enough with his tastes to feel certain that he could not fully share Sir Anthony's enthusiasm for Caylat, I was very happy to see him once again. Soon, however, I had the uncomfortable sense that he was watching me rather too closely. Before long, I became convinced that he was studying me with the intensity he ought to have devoted to the paintings around him! I wondered uneasily if it was on account of my dress. Because this was a special occasion, I'd worn one of the black ones, with touches of white, but now I worried that I had followed my grandmother's advice too assiduously and that the altered dress detailed my curves too boldly.

I concluded, with acute embarrassment, that it would be wiser to stick with the gray ones from now on.

Although I was enjoying myself, I had to leave Caylat's show earlier than I would have liked. During the latter part of winter, I'd acquired a new pupil, an American girl who had come to Paris to study music. Due to her other commitments and my own, I now had to devote part of my Friday afternoons to her.

Sir Anthony, of course, was obliged to stay. He wanted to hire a carriage for me, but the weather was so fine that I refused his offer.

I had walked only a block or two homeward and was still dreaming of the visions I had left behind while paying little attention to the ones in front of me, when a well-dressed gentleman, pale-eyed and with graying yellow hair, approached me.

"Madame Brooks," he said.

I was not in the habit of speaking to strange men in the street, but that day I was so preoccupied that when he spoke my name I assumed he must be an acquaintance. I stopped and roused myself belatedly from my private reverie to realize that I had never seen him before in my life.

I averted my eyes and started to walk on.

"Surely Madame Brooks would not snub an old friend of her late husband—although she now enjoys such elevated companionship," said the stranger.

To be accused of snobbery was more than I could bear.

"I am afraid that I do not know you," I said in the most neutral tone I could manage. "Why do you say my husband was your friend?"

"Because he was kind enough to show me an aspect of his talents that his other admirers have not yet seen," replied the stranger, and I knew from the way he said it that he did not, in fact, number himself among Frederick's admirers.

To hear Frederick referred to in slighting tones was unpleasant but, alas, not outside the realm of my experience. During the last years of his life, Frederick's lax attitude toward his financial obligations had given a number of people good reason to speak unkindly of him. But those days were over; he had paid every one of his debts before he'd drowned.

I started to move past the stranger.

"But soon all Paris will be talking of it," he said.

There was something ominous in his tone. I knew it was a threat. I supposed it was an idle one. Nevertheless I could not let it pass.

I turned on him.

"I don't know who you are," I told him, almost in a whisper. "Nor do I wish to. But I will tell you this: If you ever lift so much as your little finger to smear the memory of my husband, I will find you, under whatever rock you have crawled out from today, and I will cut out your heart."

"I'll be waiting for you," said the stranger with a calm smile, and moved on.

I was trembling. But really, there was nothing anyone could do now to harm my beloved Frederick. He had taken himself far beyond the reach of vengeance or malice.

In May, toward the end of another brief visit to Paris, Sir Anthony suddenly announced that he wished to visit the forest which had provided so great an inspiration to the *en plein air* landscape painters of the sixties and seventies. Would I care to accompany him to Fontainebleau?

I remember the start of our journey so well. He brought a picnic lunch of cold chicken, a salad, and pears, and since we were rather late setting out—the whole adventure having been undertaken on the spur of the moment—we ate it on the train.

Our conversation was light and careless; we laughed at everything and nothing. I had never seen Sir Anthony in so expansive and mellow a vein. Perhaps he might have said the same of me.

When we arrived at Fontainebleau, we quickly agreed that we must forgo the convenience of a hired carriage and explore the huge forest on foot. I'd always loved long walks, and in Sir Anthony that day I noticed a new, restless energy, which I supposed he wished to burn off. I imagined that it was due to the effects of springtime on the masculine psyche; perhaps he had fallen in love at last. Perhaps that explained why he had spent more time in England lately.

But I was no longer inclined to speculate about the kind of woman to whom Sir Anthony Camwell would be likely to give his heart; I did not like the feelings those thoughts invariably engendered. Now I merely told myself that I hoped she would be worthy of him.

It was so warm a day that I left my coat at the railway station, along with our picnic basket, and set out into the forest dressed in only an unseasonably light summer dress. It was almost threadbare in places, but really very modest, for I had patched and mended it carefully.

It was one of the dullest of my gray ones—not alluring at all. The costly gowns which had once filled my closets were gone now; I had sold them long before Frederick's death to staunch the unending flow of bills. All my vanities seemed to have died with my daughter; today I did not even carry a parasol.

Sir Anthony, too, was dressed in summer clothing, although his attire, despite its simplicity, was of a quality far more impressive than my own. Perhaps it was these outward manifestations of the vast social gulf between us, a gulf I took completely for granted, that made me so ill prepared for what happened that afternoon.

We had been enjoying ourselves immensely, having ventured rather deep into the fairy-tale forest with its magnificent old trees and fantastic rock formations, when the weather changed.

The first sign was only a cloud passing over the sun, but a little later the sky darkened alarmingly and large, slow raindrops began to splash upon the leaves above us and spill down from them onto our heads. Then the clouds burst open.

"Oh, Madame Brooks, you'll be soaked," said Sir Anthony. He sounded chagrined, as if he blamed himself for having carelessly exposed me to some dreadful peril. He stripped off his jacket and quickly placed it over my head and shoulders.

"And now *you'll* be soaked!" I exclaimed and lifted the jacket in a vain effort to shield him from the rain as well, as if the garment could be miraculously transformed, like loaves and fishes, to meet the present need.

In the next instant, as neither of us was willing to leave the other unprotected, we found ourselves standing with our arms around each other, his jacket only half covering us both.

I heard a muffled sound, as if a sigh, torn from his throat, had been reined in before it could escape.

I could feel the beating of his heart, and through my thin garment, I felt something else as well. Not being a maiden, I understood its meaning and knew that I ought to pull away. But a flame had leapt up the full length of my body and held me to him. My breasts were straining against the light fabric of my gown so urgently that I feared the seams would not hold them. I longed for his mouth; the hunger made me shiver.

All of my rigid notions about what was possible, about what was permissible, about what I sought from him, about the potential of his heart and that of my own—all these came tumbling down like rocks in a landslide. I was too weak even to think of trying to reassemble them.

In that moment he might have done anything he liked with me.

Past and future, consequences and responsibilities, the rules of conduct, all had been blasted into insignificance. I would have laid myself open to him fully so that he might find and take from me anything and everything he had ever desired in a woman. I would have withheld nothing. I would have given myself to him for an hour—or for a lifetime.

Yet, to his credit, my companion, if he felt my heat, did not take advantage of it. In the suspended seconds before I found the strength at last to draw gently back, he did not move his lips to mine; he did not alter the position of his hands to encompass my willing flesh more intimately; he did not even tighten his embrace.

I disengaged myself and turned away.

"It's useless to fight nature," I said shakily, trying to conceal my own embarrassment and to save him from feeling any. "We might as well give in to it."

Of course I had said the wrong thing!

"The rain, I mean!" I added with one quick glance back at him to make sure he had not misunderstood me.

But a veil had fallen away from his gray eyes. For one blinding moment they were the windows to his heart: They told me that he loved me, that he had always loved me, and that he always would.

It was too much. I felt as undone as the mythical Semele, who'd bound her lover Zeus to a promise to appear before her in all his Olympian splendor. She could not endure the blaze, and died.

But I still lived and breathed and heard Sir Anthony say, "I suppose you're right," in the most ordinary of tones, and when I dared to look at him again, it was as if nothing at all had happened.

After that, however, things were not quite so easy between us.

The storm was brief, the sun returned, our light clothing did not take long to dry, but we were bedraggled in appearance and chastened in manner as we climbed aboard the train back to Paris. Whenever I tried to speak during the two-hour ride, my voice sounded strained and artificial. I was glad that Sir Anthony seemed disinclined to conversation.

The next day he returned to England.

VII

My belated recognition of the true nature of Sir Anthony's feelings struck me with the force of a blow.

How well he had hidden them. Never could I have guessed, during all the hours he had devoted to me, that he had borne the weight of an unspoken desire as strong—no, stronger—than that which had flared up so suddenly in me.

Or could I have?

Yes. As I reviewed the entire course of our friendship from this new point of view, I was forced to acknowledge, with wonder and humility, that almost from the beginning every action of his had bespoken a generous and loving heart.

His plans to spend the previous summer in Paris, of course, had been made before he knew me, but he must have been taken with me immediately. *That* was why he had pried me out of seclusion—at least as much seclusion as a woman who has to earn her living may allow herself—and drawn me back into the very heart of life. And not into the hectic and superficial life of pleasure-loving society, where so many people hide their private disappointments. No, those leisurely afternoons in the Louvre had drawn me out of the isolation of my purely personal regrets back into the whole tender and terrible drama of human existence to which art bears witness.

What a context in which to be gently guided toward an acceptance of my own losses!

My imaginary rivals—at last I could admit that this *was* how I regarded them—the shrill, horsey English girls, the satin-gowned, high-bred, ivory-skinned little angels of the Faubourg St.-Germain —they had never existed.

The hours Sir Anthony had spent with me were not those he could spare from his pursuit of a suitable bride, but those he knew I could spare, given the demands of my work.

I had become his reason for loving Paris. I was the piece of Paris that he longed to possess.

I thought of the showing he had arranged for Caylat and of my obstinate blindness to the full significance of the event. I was the woman he'd worn upon his arm; he had made a public demonstration that day not only of his regard for the painter but of his regard for me.

Yet his deep, innate courtesy which had endowed him with so much tact and sensitivity, not to mention that severe, Roman sense of honor, had kept him silent, and still did.

Humbled as I was, I was very far from elated to discover that I was loved by the man who had so captured my imagination.

I knew what his silence meant.

We had both been playing with fire. He knew it as well as I did, and he knew that nothing could come of it.

His respect for me was almost palpable. Even now I was still convinced that he would never insult me by making me his mistress; it would have cost me my livelihood and my independence. I might have lived in less grim surroundings and worn prettier clothes, but after his desire had been satiated, what would become of me? I could never return to my life of modest respectability. I would have to find another protector or be dependent upon him for the rest of my life, like an aging nanny whose services were no longer needed but who was kept on a pension out of consideration for all she had done in the past.

No. He would never put me in that position.

And marriage was out of the question.

I could not forget his vague allusions to his "responsibilities" in England.

Surely he had some kind of family there, although I knew none of its members, beyond Lord Marsden. But inevitably there would be the usual ancient traditions to carry on.

When he married, he would be obligated to select his bride from the same proud caste: a lady who could be presented at Court, who would do him credit in the ballrooms of Mayfair, in the drawing rooms of Belgravia, and on the hunting field, a lady who could never attract malicious gossip about her dubious lineage or her raffish friends, a lady who could give him the requisite son—the most compelling reason for an English landowner to take a wife.

Anything less would be a slap in the face not only to the society from which he had sprung but to his family.

And Sir Anthony, I was sure, placed a very high value on ties of blood and familial affection—his comments about the Salomons were proof of that.

Under the weight of all this knowledge, I felt my heart would break. Not for myself, of course. I had come to terms long ago with the impossibility of it all.

No, I assured myself, it was for Sir Anthony, bound as he was by his own strict code, that my heart ached.

I knew that it was far more difficult for a man, with passions so much wilder and harder to bridle than anything a woman could feel, to refrain from acting on his hungers. This imbalance of nature was something my grandmother had impressed upon me; she'd said it was woman's only real source of power.

And yet he had refrained.

What was I to do with all this new and daunting knowledge?

If I had subscribed to the same principles that Sir Anthony seemed to embody, perhaps I would have found a way to end our friendship. I might have claimed that I had taken on more students and that they left me no hours of leisure at all. I might have pretended, improbably, that I had been censured by my friends and Frederick's for having flouted the etiquette of mourning and had been brought to realize the error of my ways. It would be awkward but not impossible to break the connection completely. Even if Sir Anthony suspected that the reasons I gave were specious, he would understand and respect the impulse behind them.

But I could not give up his friendship. How could I exile from my life the man who had reintroduced me to all the little pleasures I had thought were lost or blighted forever?

He had given me happiness—a quiet, undemanding happiness, very different from that which I had known with Frederick, but a true happiness, nevertheless.

How could I turn my back on it now and sink into a gray and tedious life of duty and self-denial?

I could not do it.

If Sir Anthony were truly suffering, surely he was free to extricate himself. All he had to do was to claim that his vague responsibilities were calling him home to his odious, beloved England. Permanently. One day he surely would.

Thus ran my thoughts, as I tried to unravel the snarl of my emotions.

What they amounted to was this: I did not want a life in which Sir Anthony played no part. I could not give him up altogether, whether or not it would have been wiser and kinder to both of us to have done so.

But I could not put this to myself quite so baldly. That might have obliged me to examine my heart more honestly and to recognize not only that I was already half in love with Anthony Camwell but also that I was very far from loving him enough to sacrifice my own small portion of happiness for his sake.

Instead I gave a great deal of thought to what was in Sir
Anthony's heart and as little as possible to what was in my own.

He was back in England now and had told me that he would
be unable to return to France for some time. Perhaps the lengthen-
ing intervals between his visits were his way of trying to loosen
the unacknowledged bonds between us.

Rather than applauding the judicious intent I attributed to him,
I seethed with impatience. Now that I had at last penetrated his
careful facade, how I yearned to see him again! The awareness that
both his desire and his restraint were stronger than my own, made
the prospect both terrifying and thrilling. We were walking a
tightrope, from which we must never allow ourselves to fall. Yet
what could ever satisfy us short of the final reckless plunge?

VIII

It was during Sir Anthony's absence from Paris that I received a note from one Marcel Poncet. He was an art dealer, he said—although I had never heard of him—and had acquired some paintings of Frederick's which he believed might interest me, although he understood that my purse was very thin.

I thought it kind of him to acknowledge my circumstances. This was not the first time a few of Frederick's minor works had found their way back onto the market, and even they were always far beyond my means. Monsieur Poncet's thoughtful note, however, implied that if I had a particular interest in those he possessed, perhaps an arrangement of periodic payments could be worked out. I knew my financial situation would not allow such an extravagance, but I replied with a note in which I agreed to meet with him anyway, for I was curious to discover which of Frederick's patrons had either tired of his works or fallen upon hard times.

The door to the little shop was locked when I arrived. I rang the bell.

When the pale-eyed man with graying yellow hair opened the door to me, I choked back a startled gasp.

He smiled.

"So we meet again, Madame Brooks. I hope you have not brought your knife."

I did not take the hand he offered.

"I can have no business with you," I said coldly, and stepped back onto the pavement.

He moved into the doorway.

"Au contraire, madame. I think you will find you have some very urgent business to attend to here," he said, fixing me with a keen gaze. I hesitated, unable to step forward or retreat further as I struggled to assess what threat he could pose to Frederick's memory.

No, it was impossible. I turned and started to walk away.

"What shabby dresses you have taken to wearing of late, Madame Brooks," he went on smoothly. "Golden fetters are far more becoming—and conceal your beauty less."

Then I began to understand him.

I turned back.

"You have seen that painting?" I whispered through frozen lips.

"I own it. And four others."

Around me I could still hear the slow clopping of the hooves of carriage horses, a ripple of birdsong, the soft chatter of a pair of lovers who strolled down the pavement arm in arm, yet my world had darkened and narrowed down to this man, this doorway.

"You look ill, Madame Brooks. Perhaps you will step inside."

There were several little armchairs in the front room of the shop. I sank down upon the edge of one.

"Well, you had better let me see them," I said expressionlessly at last. I was reluctant to follow him toward the back of his shop, but if I were about to be blackmailed, I supposed I ought to assure myself that he really had the goods. No doubt I would be paying for them for a long, long time.

He led me to a dusty back room.

Yes, there they were—all five of them.

I took in the display with only the briefest of glances, then turned away.

Sitting opposite him once again in the front room, I strove to remain coolheaded.

"Have you a receipt for what you paid for those?" I asked after a while.

Poncet took a sheet of paper from his pocket, unfolded it, and handed it to me. There was Frederick's bold signature and the date. It was the day before his body had been found in the river.

"Do not think too badly of your husband, Madame Brooks," said Poncet gently. "He wished only to protect you from the continual harassment of your creditors. He assured me that he would buy these paintings back from me within the year. You were in no real danger. But it has been more than a year. And of course his death has increased the value of these works immeasurably."

I absorbed this silently. Then I asked, "Has anyone else seen them?"

"No one but my daughter. And that was merely because she was thoughtless and unlocked a door which she had been told to leave shut. She is at an age when the young tend to be self-righteous and cannot smile at the ways their jaded elders sometimes choose to amuse themselves. She was, to put it mildly, appalled to stumble upon this other aspect of the refined Madame Brooks. But she will not speak of it to anyone."

"What do you want from me?" I asked wearily.

"It is not my wishes, Madame Brooks, but *yours* that we are here to discuss." The dealer smiled. "I know the market for paintings of this sort. It is my speciality. A number of wealthy gentlemen keep private collections like this for their own entertainment. I can think of *one* Englishman in particular who will be astounded by what I have to offer and who is able to afford it."

I swallowed the last remnants of my pride.

"If you are referring to . . . the baronet," I said haltingly, having found myself unable even to speak Sir Anthony's name under such distasteful circumstances, "I beg you, Monsieur Poncet, do not offer them to him."

My voice trembled somewhat. I could not bear to think of the chivalrous baronet's regard for me crumbling as violently as it must, were he to ever see these paintings.

"How could I refuse the appeal of such a lovely woman?" said Poncet. "No, I do not think it will be necessary for *me* to approach the baronet in order to realize the full value of what I have to sell."

I was so relieved to hear this that, although his tone was not as reassuring as his words, I barely noticed the peculiar emphasis he had given the latter. Still, I could not bring myself to thank him for his willingness to spare me the ultimate humiliation.

"Very well," I said, and rose to my feet to leave. He still held all the cards, but he had agreed not to use them as I most feared. Now I wanted only to escape from the shop and to have nothing more to do with him.

"One moment, Madame Brooks," he said. "Perhaps you are not acquainted with my methods of doing business. When I have works like this in my possession and am preparing to dispose of them, I make sure that it is widely known. There is always a great demand for well-executed paintings of this sort, but I must confess that the quality of these is far beyond anything that has ever before passed through my hands. And I have never encountered a case where the artist was so famous and so immensely talented or where his subject was a woman so well known and so well re-spected. You cannot imagine how many gentlemen will spring at the opportunity to come to a showing such as the one I arranged for you today. It will be well publicized and well attended, I can assure you, and the setting, of course, will be far more accommo-dating than this poor little shop. Most of the gentlemen who will attend the sale will do so, no doubt, purely to amuse themselves. But there *will* be a number of serious buyers and they will bid against one another for each of these splendid portraits."

He paused to let me savor the hideous prospect, and then continued.

"That was my original plan for disposing of these paintings, but it occurred to me that you, as the widow, might also have an interest in them, and, if so, that you might be grateful for this opportunity to avoid having to confront the . . . enthusiasm of the gentlemen you will otherwise be bidding against. . . . You do not seem appreciative, Madame Brooks."

I did not respond. So the sale of the paintings would be a circus—not a discreet, private transaction between himself and some harmless, hoary old seigneur doddering about in a moldering chateau and trying to rekindle the sensations of his rakish youth.

"I know your situation is difficult at present," Poncet went on. "That is why I am prepared—at no little sacrifice, I must say—to make you a special offer. A modest but regular monthly payment from you will keep these paintings a secret between you and me—at least until you are in a position to pay for them in full."

"And how do you imagine that I could ever pay for them outright!" I inquired with a sharp, bitter laugh.

"Oh, I think you'll find a way," said Poncet suavely. "And, in the meantime, the slightest monthly token will prevent matters from coming to a head."

But the amount he named, when I pressed him to be specific, was staggering, far more than I could earn from the lessons I gave. And if I failed to meet his terms, the resulting scandal would surely deprive me of even that precarious livelihood. I could imagine the kind of "pupils" who would come to me once the paintings had been unveiled, and what they would expect from their "French lessons." I wanted time to think.

"There is absolutely no way I could meet your demands in my present circumstances," I said at last. "Would you consider accepting one payment immediately, as proof of my good faith, and giving me . . . perhaps six months to work out something else?"

How I hated to have to bargain with him! And I had no idea what the "something else" might be. But I was desperate for time.

"I might consider that," he said, like a cat playing with a mouse. "Tell me what you think you can do."

I made some rapid calculations in my head and finally named a figure which I felt confident I could manage to come up with if I were to part with two or three of my grandmother's treasures.

"I could have a draft for you by the end of the week," I told him.

"That will buy you three months," he said. "No more."

"Four," I said, feigning a firmness that was a complete sham. I had nothing with which to influence him; I held no cards at all.

"Ask me more sweetly, Madame Brooks," he said. "Soft words and tender smiles can work wonders on a man. That is a lesson I think you will need to learn rather quickly."

I struggled to swallow my revulsion.

"Could you give me four months, please, monsieur," I whispered at last with a tremulous attempt at a smile. But tears of furious impotence stung my eyes.

"Three and a half," he conceded. "And only because you have asked so nicely. I regret that I cannot afford to be more lenient, but that ought to give you adequate time to arrange your affairs . . . *if* you take to heart the lesson I have given you. I will expect the next payment—the first of those you will make to me each month—at the beginning of October."

It was already the middle of June.

I stumbled homeward in a daze. The young American lady, who presented herself promptly at four for her lesson, at last ventured to remark that I did not look well at all.

"I am so sorry," I said, forcing my horrible preoccupation to the back of my mind and rousing myself to greater efforts. I spent more time with her than usual that day, to compensate for my inattentiveness at the outset of the lesson.

But at last I was alone and able to reflect upon my grotesque predicament.

How had I failed to realize that the paintings were gone? That was simple. I had not gone into the depths of that jumbled closet where they ought to have been for months. Since Frederick's death I had scarcely opened the door. Now the mystery of how he had flung off the last of that terrible burden of debt was solved. And I had told myself that he must have finally enjoyed a long overdue streak of luck at the gaming tables!

But how could I blame him? If he were looking down upon me now from some other world, he must be sharing all my anguish. How could he have dreamed that his final gamble would lead to this? It could never have crossed his mind that he would not make it home that last night, that he would never be able to ransom those scorching canvasses from Poncet before the year was out.

But there was only one avenue which might ever allow me to meet Poncet's demands, at least for a time, and thinking of my dead husband would not make it any easier for me to embark upon it.

I would have to take up, with quiet discretion, my grand-mother's profession. No doubt that was what Poncet had meant to imply when he'd told me that I would need to learn the subtle ways that a woman can work her will upon the stronger, the richer, the more powerful sex. But even this did not offer a sure solution; in a business which puts a premium on youth, I was already too old, at twenty-six, to achieve more than a modest success. I was sure I could never rival the *grandes horizontales* of Paris. Could I even earn enough to keep him from acting on his threats? And what would become of me as the years advanced and my earning power declined?

The day would surely come when those paintings could no longer be hidden.

I could see myself, rough and coarsened, living hand-to-mouth as my grandmother had, being frigidly cut by the self-same re-spectable ladies and gentlemen whose soiled linen I would wash and iron, whose dirty floors I would scour on my hands and knees.

She had been right about everything, everything. She had looked straight at the world as it was, not as one might wish it to be.

"Oh, Frederick," I whispered into my pillow that night. "Where are you now? I need you!"

But my lost Frederick could not answer my desperate prayer. It took a living man to do that. It took Sir Anthony Camwell.

He had told me, before his departure in May, that he did not expect to return to France again until July. Yet three days after my meeting with Poncet, Sir Anthony made a sudden, flying visit to Paris and called upon me the very morning after his arrival.

I had spent many sleepless hours since Poncet's revelation and was already steeled to make the speech I knew I must. I intended to tell Sir Anthony that I would see him no more. Perhaps he would attribute this to the revealing incident at Fontainebleau, for I was at a loss to invent a better explanation. But sooner or later, some part of the truth must become apparent to him—the paintings themselves might remain a secret, but I could hardly hope to conceal, equally well, the means I would have to take to keep them one. I remembered how proudly Sir Anthony had introduced me to friends and acquaintances on the day of Caylat's triumphant show. I felt ill as I thought of the shame that would redound to him when Paris began to whisper that the lady he had honored so greatly had set out along the primrose path.

"You are unwell, Madame Brooks!" exclaimed Sir Anthony before I had a chance to do more than welcome him.

"Oh no, I am merely a little tired," I demurred.

"Then you have been working too hard! While I—" Here he broke off. I sensed that he was profoundly agitated behind his polished veneer.

"Can I do *any*thing for you? I really ought to let you rest and come back another time," he then proposed with anxious solicitude.

"Oh no, not at all," I said, uncertain as to which of his contradictory offers I was addressing. I could think of nothing further to add. The moment had come to bring our brief but precious friendship to an end.

My mind was spinning. My prepared speech had slipped from

my memory, and I sought helplessly for a gentle way—yet one which would leave no opening for questions or objections—to tell him that I would not see him again.

"Madame Brooks," he broke out rather breathlessly before I could say more, "let me tell you what has brought me back to Paris. I have been thinking of you constantly since I was last in France, and I find myself unable to hide my feelings any longer, although I know it is premature to express them. I have struggled to keep my distance until the passage of time would make my declaration less unseemly. But I cannot continue to be silent. I *must* tell you that everything you have done since the day I first saw you, and every word you have spoken, have convinced me that you are the only woman on earth whom I could ever love."

I lifted my eyes to stare at him with blank astonishment. I might have read his heart at Fontainebleau, but he had always been so reserved! And it seemed inconceivable he could have chosen *this* wretched moment to make his passionate avowal. I barely comprehended the full significance of his words.

"I never dreamed," he continued, "that I could love anyone as I have come to love you. Madame Brooks . . . Fleur . . . you have already won my heart. Will you take my hand as well?"

Really, I must have been particularly dim that day: It was a full minute or two before I grasped that he was asking me to marry him.

"But you hardly know me," I stammered at last, still thinking of the paintings but not yet perceiving that he had offered me a way out of my impossible dilemma. It was incredible that he should wish to take me—me, Fleur Deslignères, the granddaughter of Holwich, Kent's most notorious and least upstanding citizen—back to England, to be introduced to his well-bred friends and to be installed in the very heart of his family circle.

"I know the woman you are," he was saying. "And I know that nothing on earth could ever alter my regard . . . my love . . . for you."

The irony of this was almost more than I could bear. He knew nothing of the woman I was, nothing. He knew only the woman I had been with him.

"Will you have me?" he whispered.

He wanted to marry me! Who would have dreamed that his nobly restrained passion could at last have driven him to propose such a mésalliance!

But he was rich and generous, and if I were very careful with what he gave me, perhaps I could keep Poncet permanently at bay. Sir Anthony himself need never know.

My whole soul cried out against what I was about to do, but I am afraid that those cries were not quite as strong as the horror I had struggled to repress at my every thought of the only other route out of my difficulties. After all, to give myself legitimately to a man I liked so deeply and sincerely was a far less hideous prospect than that of selling myself to a series of men I neither liked nor loved.

I struggled with my conscience, I fought to maintain some semblance of calm, and finally I managed to answer, "Yes, Anthony, I will."

I can't say that he looked as elated as one might have expected. He seemed to be waiting hopefully for something more. I knew what was wanted, but I could not quite manage it. So instead I did what I imagined was the next best thing and said, "It will be an honor—and a joy—to be your wife."

He dropped to his knees by the arm of the sofa, took my clenched hands in his own, and very gently began to loosen my fingers.

"Are you quite sure?" he whispered. "Perhaps it is too soon for you to give your heart to anyone. Tell me, Fleur, do you love me at all?"

My recurrent vision of the only alternative that remained to me, should I deny him what he hungered for, was so alarming that it filled my voice with real feeling as, wild with relief and despair, I cried out, "Oh, yes, yes, yes! I do!"

I remember only fragments of the rest of that feverish conversation. He took me in his arms once or twice, but now that the moment had come, when I was at last free to yield to the warm pressure of his body against mine, when I might have given him my lips boldly with no need for self-recrimination on either his part or mine, my blood did not surge with fire. I felt utterly numb and exhausted; he must have noticed this, for every so often he anxiously renewed his inquiries as to my health.

I kept assuring him that I was well, that my pallor was simply the result of having slept badly the night before.

"Then you must sleep now!" he declared. "Let me warm a cup of milk for you. It may help to relax your nerves," he continued, and added with a regretful smile, "which I fear I have only jangled further."

"Oh no!" I said, trying to smile as well. "I am rather tired, it is true, but I have a pupil coming within the hour. I can't risk being half sedated when she arrives."

"But you must send her away," he decreed. "You have obviously been pushing yourself beyond the limits of your endurance."

I took a deep breath and swallowed my annoyance. I was still my own woman, although I would not be for long.

"No," I said firmly. "I will *not* drink hot milk. I will *not* send my pupil away. And I will not marry you if you persist in ordering me about like this!"

Instead of looking chastened, he laughed.

"How right you are," he said tenderly. "Forgive me, Fleur. I swear to you that I will *never* give you any reason to regret the new life you have chosen with me."

IX

No regrets! What a vain promise!

Regrets had become the treacherous prevailing undercurrent of my life; every time I imagined that I had risen free of them at last, they dragged me down again.

I was drowning in regret.

My whole life was about to become one huge and irreparable lie.

But I was too drained and demoralized to fight it any longer.

Sir Anthony remained in Paris only long enough to put into motion the machinery of matrimony—we were to be married in August here at St. George's English Church. Before he returned to England, he expressed some concern about how I would adapt to my new surroundings. Did I wish to visit Charingworth, his ancestral home, and arrange alterations to its decor that might suit my taste better than its present furnishings?

I did not. I waved a hand toward my threadbare carpet and faded curtains and asked him, with a laugh, if he really imagined I might find his splendid country house wanting in any way.

Privately I knew that my new surroundings, however ornate, could never begin to console me for the loss of my freedom or for marriage to a man for whom I must never permit myself to care too deeply.

For I already knew that if I allowed myself to feel too much for him, if I were to trust him too completely, I might be tempted to pour my heart out. And if I were ever foolish enough to confess the truth, I was sure to lose everything.

He held me in his arms and gave me a tender kiss before he left me. With any encouragement, his kiss might have been less restrained, but although I felt almost comforted by the warmth of his arms, the physical desire which had ravished me in Fontainebleau did not flare up again.

Everything inside me seemed frozen. Perhaps the chill had taken hold when Poncet had presented me at last with the invoice for all the passion which had been unleashed within my first marriage. Perhaps it had come over me the first time I'd found myself obliged to lie to Sir Anthony, telling him I loved him when I could barely comprehend the true nature of my feelings. A week ago I had been anxious to see him again; I'd been restless with thoughts of those forbidden embraces I knew he yearned for yet denied himself, and when I'd dreamed of being close to him once again, of knowing that the lightest touch of his hand would carry the weight of a wild, inadmissible passion, I felt as if my skin had been touched by a hot wind.

But no more.

Now I could hardly wait for him to depart for England and relieve me, at least for a time, of the obligation to invent cheerful answers to his affectionate questions.

Once he was gone, I could at last begin to think more cool-headedly about all that this marriage would require of me and could try to devise some way of rising to the challenge.

But when I was finally free to devote my attention to these pressing matters, I found that the mere prospect of becoming Lady Camwell filled me with stark terror.

I recalled a joking remark Lord Marsden had once made to the effect that his cousin sometimes seemed to hold himself to an almost inhumanly high standard of conduct. Lord Marsden had punctuated this observation with an indulgent laugh, but now the memory alarmed me. No doubt it was true; and no doubt Sir Anthony would hold his bride to the same relentless standards. He might be kindly and diffident in France, where he came for pleasure, but who knew how he might behave in his own domain? Would that inflexible morality I had sensed in him from time to time be the law by which he ruled his household?

Oh, there were a thousand reasons why this marriage could never work! But somehow I would have to keep it limping along for as long as I could.

If Sir Anthony had proposed to me a week earlier than he actually had, how would I have responded? I would have had to ask him to give me time to think—it was all so unexpected. Then I would have had to examine myself as to whether I honestly loved him or believed that I might be coming to love him. I would have had to explore every obstacle to closeness of which I was now becoming painfully aware. I would have been obliged to confront him with all the things in my past that were sure to scandalize his friends, his family, and very likely my high-minded suitor himself.

Now I no longer had any of these luxuries—of time, of fearless soul-searching, or of candor.

I would have to marry him whether I loved him or not. I would have to conceal from him anything and everything that might suggest how unwisely he had chosen his wife.

I would have to mimic love without ever allowing myself to feel it. I would have to suppress any impulse to speak too freely: I might expose my loneliness, an incessant nostalgia for my old life, or my continual longing for Frederick; I might make some thoughtless and revealing allusion to my grandmother, or voice an opinion that someone in my privileged position could scarcely be expected to hold. One careless word might shatter the illusion of love, not to mention the identity I had acquired not only by marriage to Frederick but by my own efforts as well—that of the mysterious, refined, reserved, and elegant Madame Brooks, who had won Anthony Camwell's heart without even trying.

Oh, there would be countless areas where a misstep could cost me dearly.

I would have to adapt myself quickly to a very unforgiving harness or risk exposing myself to constant criticism and scandal-mongering, for surely the freedoms that generous-spirited Paris had allowed Madame Brooks would never be tolerated in the upper echelons of English society.

If only there were someone I could talk to!

I thought, with a sharp pang of loss and longing, of my dear friend, Guy Hazelton. I had not seen him for years, not since he'd given up his life in Paris to return to England with his beloved Harry.

Of course, like me, he was the sort of person who would be shunned by English society if he were ever to stand in the light of truth. In Paris, his inclinations were not looked upon with nearly the same horror that is felt for such things in England. In Paris, his passion for Harry had not been entirely clandestine; within the small, tightly knit circle of our closest friends, it had been as casually accepted as his friendship with me.

How I missed him!

To him alone I might even have been able to confide every agonizing nuance of the tangle in which I now found myself ensnared.

What a relief it would have been to pour all my troubles into his discreet and sympathetic ear. I had always been able to tell Guy things I could barely discuss with anyone else—not with Marguerite, not even with Frederick. Frederick, although he had known virtually every salient fact about my life, had never cared to know how I *felt* about anything that made me less than joyful.

He had been the same with Guy. Although Guy and I had become the closest of confidantes, Frederick had held back; he'd made it his business to avoid knowing anything about the anguish

Guy had suffered for months before he'd found the courage to reveal the dangerous secret in his heart, only to find that his love for Harry was returned.

To Guy alone had I ever admitted that I still bore the scars of having been virtually an outcast in the town where I had been raised, and that it was this that had made me so determined to present one face to Paris even as I showed another one altogether to my husband. To Frederick, I was his *fleur du mal.* To Paris, I was only his devoted and angelic wife.

I'd had few secrets from Guy. But Guy had faded out of my life, through no fault of his own. I had not seen him since the night of my miscarriage, when we'd dined at the Coq d'Or.

Afterward Guy had written to me several times from London, but I had never been able to answer his cheerful letters. How easily I might have talked to him about the devastation of losing my child. But the painful task of trying to put it on paper proved far beyond my power. Eventually his own letters had stopped. When at last I broke my silence to write to him of Frederick's death, it turned out that he had moved long ago from the West End flat which was the only address I had for him.

It was entirely possible, however, that I would run into him again in England. I hoped I would. At least it was *one* thing I could still anticipate with real pleasure.

But suppose that some day the scandalous secret about his own private life came to light?

I knew that *I* would never turn my back on him; never could I close my door against a beloved friend.

But the doors behind which I must live in England would not be mine to open or to close. Certainly I could never assume that my future husband would unlock his gates to every pariah I might choose to claim as a friend.

And I knew that if he proved to be as rigid and intolerant as I feared he might, I would turn away from him with a heart of stone. What *were* those "responsibilities" of his, after all, if not some feeling of obligation to uphold the standards and morals of the narrow and ungenerous society which had spawned him?

As I considered all the difficulties, real and imaginary, that lay in wait for me, my sense of hopelessness became almost unendurable. I began to feel as if I were under a lifetime sentence of transportation and bondage.

I loved Paris and hated England. I didn't want to live there, and certainly not in the antiquated luxury of some baronial manor, where my every breath would be drawn under the frigid eyes of a huge staff of disapproving servants whose lineage would almost certainly compare favorably with my own and who would probably discern this pretty quickly.

As for my future husband, I hardly knew Sir Anthony—and he knew me not at all. But shallow as my knowledge of him might be, one thing I *did* know: I knew exactly the expression that would appear on his face were he ever to glimpse the paintings which had delivered me into his hands. I had already seen that look once.

Now my whole life would become one unremitting effort to keep the dangerous truth hidden from him even as we shared the greatest intimacies that can exist between two people.

In such stony soil how could love take root? Already every impulse of mine to be open and yielding and generous had been crushed. I could never afford to drop my guard again.

It was just as well. For what if I had fallen in love with Sir Anthony *before* Poncet had sprung his trap? What if my heart *already* belonged to a man who would surely turn from me with disgust and condemnation were he to plumb my secrets?

I would do everything in my power to keep that knowledge from him forever. But I was hardly confident that I could really manage this, and to think of having surrendered myself to him completely and *then* to fail in covering up my sins! The agony of his rejection would be insupportable.

No, he must never have my heart; this was my best protection. This way no matter what happened, he could never really hurt me.

Even if a day came when all his esteem for me turned to ashes, at least I would not have to suffer the anguish of being coldly cast aside by a man I worshiped, a man who would meet Poncet's price to protect his own name from scandal, but who would never forgive his wife's deception. I thought with a shudder of the unbending Marquess of Londonderry, who, years ago, upon discovering love letters from his wife to another man, had informed her, in a note, "Henceforth we do not speak," and had not violated that edict since.

Yes, it was a good thing that I had never allowed myself to fall blindly in love with Anthony Camwell.

In the midst of all my turmoil, this was my surest consolation.

The days passed, and I grew calmer. I assured myself that a mere portion of the generous allowance my husband had already promised me, so that the new Lady Camwell might be suitably gowned and able to indulge every whim, would easily keep Poncet satisfied. As long as I was careful to give nothing away, my secret would be safe.

X

Still I could not always keep the panic down.

Sir Anthony returned to Paris in July. When I opened my door to him, I watched his eager smile fade. He said nothing as his searching gray eyes inspected me. I submitted to his gaze, half fearful that my guilty secret was emblazoned on my face.

"You've become very thin," was all he said.

His voice was noncommittal. Was it an accusation of some kind? Had he already begun to discern my myriad imperfections?

"It's all the excitement," I stammered with a false laugh. "I've hardly had time to eat!"

Still he did not smile.

I shivered, as if awaiting a verdict.

"Aren't you going to invite me in?" he asked at last, still in that level, unsmiling voice.

With another little gasp of chagrined laughter at having kept him upon the landing, I opened the door wider. He stepped inside.

I followed him into the drawing room. It still had a few touches of the bold color with which Frederick's taste had invested

it: on the vermillion blanket which was draped over the chaise
longue to hide its worn upholstery sat the plump yellow silk pillow which had lain behind my head when I'd posed as Frederick's
wanton and inviting *Odalisque.*

Now she belonged to Marcel Poncet.

I shivered again and tried to shepherd my thoughts into less
perilous channels.

Sir Anthony arranged himself elegantly at one end of the sofa.
I placed myself at the other, keeping a distance between us. I was
intensely aware of him. Soon I would be all too well acquainted
with that lean, graceful body.

Still he said nothing.

I knew I ought to be overflowing with a lover's chatter, offering him tea or coffee and madeleines, and babbling about my
trousseau. Again I had the feeling that he was waiting for something. But I could not speak.

The tense silence pricked at me like a thousand needles. I
began to understand how guilty prisoners could be driven to make
desperate confessions—without even a finger having been laid
upon them.

Had Poncet gone back on his word? Was it possible that Sir
Anthony *already* knew?

I met his eyes more fully and saw, to my relief, that the expression in them was not accusatory. It was thoughtful, grave, expectant.

The prolonged silence was becoming as unendurable as a
tickle. I could feel myself weakening.

But I lacked the courage to lay myself open and to ask for his
help. Instead I equivocated.

"I'm a little . . . ," I began tremulously.

He waited.

"Yes?" he prodded me at last.

"A little . . . frightened," I said in a whisper.

"Frightened?" He didn't laugh or make light of my admission,
as Frederick surely would have. "Of me?"

"Oh no! Never of you! It's just that . . ."

Here I broke off again. He waited patiently but offered a small, encouraging nod to help me onward.

"It's just that I fear I may not be up to the demands of such a different kind of life," I said finally.

"What demands would those be?" he asked in his calm, unruffled way.

"Oh, you know . . ."

"But I don't. At any rate, I don't know what *you* have in mind. Tell me what you mean, Fleur."

It was so strange to hear him call me Fleur, after having been Madame Brooks to him for so long. Fleur. He said it as if he loved it on his tongue.

I felt myself floundering.

"Ah, well . . . living up to your family's expectations, for example. I'm sure I'm not at all the sort of woman they would like to see you married to!"

"My family!" he exclaimed with a short, rather harsh burst of laughter. "You already know Neville, and he adores you. There's no one else, really, except for my mother, but she lives at a safe distance; I really don't think she'll give *you* any trouble."

The edge in his voice when he said this did not soothe my vague uneasiness.

Then he added, "Are you quite sure that it is only *my* family you're worried about? What about yours? You *are* English, aren't you? And you've never said a word about them. Why *is* that?"

He issued this challenge in a gentle, encouraging tone, as if to assure me that I had nothing to fear by revealing all.

I licked my lips nervously.

"I really have no family to speak of," I said at last.

His continued silence drove me on.

"I . . . ah . . . I was raised by my grandmother. She was French, but she lived in England. Her name was Emilie Deslignères."

I don't know why I felt compelled to tell him her name. Perhaps it allowed me to imagine that I was being heroically straight-forward about my ignoble origins. But of course the name could mean nothing to him. She'd been notorious in our own little vil-lage, of course, mainly because she had never attempted to hide her scarlet past, but she was hardly one of the great scandals of her era.

"Deslignères," repeated Sir Anthony in that almost flawless ac-cent which I loved because it made him seem less . . . English. "What a beautiful name. And your parents?" he then pressed softly.

"There's nothing to tell, really. My mother died when I was born. My father . . . went away." I swallowed painfully. "His name was Hastings. That was my name, too. Caroline Hastings. But my grandmother didn't like it. So she called me Fleur and gave me her last name."

Sir Anthony looked amused. "That was good of her," he said, as if he were trying to keep fond laughter from spilling into his voice. "I like it better."

I smiled back edgily.

With a sudden air of restless impatience, Sir Anthony stood up and began to pace the carpet in his slow, measured way.

Finally he stopped and stood before me.

"Fleur," he said, "if you think your family connections—or any-thing else—could possibly affect the way I feel about you, then you still have no idea how much I love you."

"I just . . . don't want to embarrass you," I murmured awk-wardly.

He dropped to his knees and took one of my half-clenched hands in his.

"How could you embarrass me?" he whispered. "I know there are differences between us. I know that our opinions and attitudes and the ways we are accustomed to thinking about things will sometimes clash. I know your life has been very, very different from mine. But what do these things matter? If we love each other, how can anything drive us apart?"

I stared back at him hopelessly. Never had I felt so cut off from him by my secret; yet never had I felt such a rush of warm emotion for him. If he had taken me in his arms at that moment, I might have told him everything.

But instead he released my hand, stood up again, and wandered to the window. He lingered there for a moment or two, staring down at the busy street.

When at last he turned around, his face still wore that grave and thoughtful expression. But now he seemed more serious than ever.

"Forgive me, Fleur," he said. "I never meant to ride roughshod over your reservations. If you have doubts about the step we are about to take, if you are uncertain about your love for me, or whether you truly want this marriage, you have only to say so. There is no need for us to rush into anything."

I stared back at him, mute.

"But if you love me as I love you, what is there to fear? All that matters is what we feel for each other. Surely you know, better than anyone, that love will always adapt and evolve and recreate itself to meet every problem. With *that* star to guide us, how can we go wrong?"

A thin streak of bitterness shot through me. What did he know about love? He had never been married. He had never been assailed by the demons in whose face love is as helpless and impotent as a newborn child. Love hadn't saved my daughter. Love hadn't saved Frederick.

But at the same time I knew he was promising me something extraordinary. He was telling me that he was prepared to be flexible and forgiving, that he knew there were ways in which we were certain to disappoint each other and fall sadly short of each other's expectations, and that he believed we could still go on loving despite them, that we could reinvent love over and over to meet every new challenge, that it would grow and flourish, not wither and die in the first winter frost.

He was assuring me that all my unspoken fears were groundless.

It was a beautiful illusion. How I longed to believe in it; if only experience hadn't taught me that it was dangerous and false.

He was still standing against the window. The light behind him made a halo of his fair hair.

"Are you ready to love me, Fleur?" he asked.

Perhaps all my sleepless nights and anxiety had made me slightly delirious. All I knew was that for a moment he seemed to exude both calm assurance and an almost hypnotic power.

He was waiting for my answer.

I knew that if I said no, that I was not ready for love, he would not abandon me; he would, to use his own words, adapt.

But the force that seemed to radiate from him, almost against his will, was irresistible.

How could I, impoverished, exhausted, and desperate, resist everything that had combined to drive me into his arms?

"Yes," I said.

PART TWO

1892 – 1893

XI

The wedding was carried off with a minimum of pomp and circumstance. Not even Sir Anthony's mother or her second husband, Lord Whitstone, came to Paris for the occasion. They excused themselves on the grounds that Lady Whitstone was in poor health. When I remarked to Sir Anthony that I hoped his mother's illness was not a serious one, his rather dry laugh and terse reply suggested that he regarded neither her absence nor her illness as cause for concern.

Marguerite Sorrel was my matron of honor; Lord Marsden, the best man. Although Neville Marsden was a generation older than Sir Anthony, who was barely two years my senior, it was plain to see how close was the bond between them. Always kindly and urbane in his manner, and blessed with a wit that generated an atmosphere of smiling conviviality among all the members of the wedding party, Lord Marsden had that sublime talent of eliciting one's best self.

But I noticed even his humor take on a slight edge when he made a few casual asides to Sir Anthony about the absent Lady Whitstone. These gave me an alarming picture of my new mother-in-law. I gathered from the one or two oblique remarks not meant for my ears that she was cold, ruthlessly willful, and outspoken to the point of rudeness. I was very glad that she had remarried and that we would not be required to share Sir Anthony's home with her.

Théo Valory's tongue was not as suave as Lord Marsden's. The hotheaded painter was susceptible to fits of surliness and had recently exhibited an unfortunate tendency to envy and disparage his actress wife's popular successes, which far outshone his own. Unfortunately, his defects of character were never more pronounced than when he had the opportunity to rub shoulders with the beau monde he detested and to imbibe unlimited quantities of good wine.

I sympathized with Théo, whose abilities deserved more recognition than he had yet received. He had all of Frederick's technical skill and more, but he refused to abandon certain idiosyncrasies of style which would have shocked Frederick's wealthy patrons had Théo allowed Frederick to show his works to them. He used color in deliberately jolting ways; he violently and intentionally distorted perspective; and he painted only scenes of common life, completely lacking in grandeur. He prided himself in his refusal to pander to anyone's taste and yet could not bear to risk rejection and ridicule by exposing his work outside his own poverty-stricken but aesthetically impeccable coterie.

How he and Frederick used to fight! The case of Paul Gauguin —who had virtually abandoned his wife and children to answer his muse—was a case in point, Frederick declaring that any man who'd do such a thing was a soulless, unfeeling cad and could never create great art. *Only* a man who could make such a choice, retorted Théo, was capable of greatness!

I was enormously fond of Théo. Yet I so hated to see his understandable dissatisfactions express themselves in hurtful ways that I had half dreaded his presence at the wedding reception. My fears were realized when one of the guests commented upon the enormous popularity of the play in which Marguerite was currently appearing, a frivolous and delightful farce. Marguerite's performance was its chief attraction, but far from enjoying her triumph, Théo had lately begun to imply that the roles she took were proof of her limitations. If she was serious about her art, he said, she would choose to hone her mediocre abilities by performing in the more demanding realm of the experimental, avantgarde, and generally insolvent little theaters he loved.

"Ah yes," said Théo in response to the guest's remark, "La Sorrel has such a knack for playing to the indiscriminate taste of the masses."

Marguerite was far too polite to counter this in public, but I saw her lovely mouth tighten. Out of the corner of my eye, I saw, too, that Sir Anthony had stiffened slightly. But when he spoke, his tone was mild.

"She is greatly admired, isn't she," he said, and then continued with consummate politeness, "however, I am not quite so ready to condemn the popular taste as 'indiscriminate' as you are, Monsieur Valory. Surely you must agree that the ability to appeal to theatergoers of every station is a sign of the greatest artistry. It requires enormous talent to touch such a wide audience, to illuminate not only our differences but our common hopes, desires, and fears. Your wife, Monsieur Valory, is brilliant."

Marguerite, although hardly unfamiliar with adulation, looked as if she might burst into tears of gratitude. But Théo gave Sir Anthony an insolent, disbelieving stare and then shifted his glance to me. I knew him well enough to read the silent message in his eyes: *How could you have married such an insufferable prig? You—who were wed to my dearest friend?* I could imagine only too vividly how he would pillory the baronet later on at his local brasserie, among his own circle, which until today had been mine as well.

Although I detested Théo's gratuitous jab at his wife and although the views which Sir Anthony had expressed were precisely the ones I myself held, I found, to my acute discomfort, now that Théo had been challenged, my sympathies were entirely with the artist.

Lord Marsden had turned toward Théo.

"I am not acquainted with your work," he said, "but Madame Br
—my cousin Fleur, whose taste and judgment I respect unreservedly, tells me that it is astonishing, that it startles the eye into new
ways of seeing. I have been hoping I might prevail upon you to let
me see it for myself. When may I visit your studio?"

Théo flushed. Frederick and I had often begged him to let us
bring Lord Marsden to his studio, and Théo had always refused,
claiming that he was loath to take advantage of his friend's success. But never had he been approached so directly. I held my
breath.

"Any time you like," responded Théo in a sullen tone. "But I
warn you, I'm nothing like Brooks."

Sir Anthony and I spent the night in his suite at the opulent Hôtel
Continental. I dared to hope that the web of expansive goodwill
which Lord Marsden had so artfully spun around the wedding
party would cling for at least a short while afterward, long enough
to cocoon me through my wedding night. But among the congrat-
ulatory cards that filled our room was a note to me from Marcel
Poncet telling me that he now found himself obliged to double the
price of his silence.

There went my hope of being able to manage my allowance
cleverly enough to avoid raising suspicion.

My spirits shriveled like leaves in November.

Until now Sir Anthony had refrained from ever seeking more than
a chaste kiss or an innocent embrace. I had been grateful for this,
although at the same time it had exacerbated my sense of guilt.
Even passion could not drive *him* to throw his principles to the
winds. He had always treated me like a lady.

Some day—perhaps only a month or two from now, it all
depended upon how rapidly Poncet's greed swelled and upon how

skillfully I was able to placate him—my husband would learn how wrong he had been. I could hardly bear to think of it.

That miserable awareness kept me as lifeless and cold, when he finally took me in his arms, as I had been when I'd received his kiss at the end of the ceremony that locked us in matrimony. The fires which had blazed for Frederick and had flickered dangerously for a moment in the forest of Fontainebleau had gone out forever.

But I could tell from the way the gentle stranger who was now my husband had begun to handle me that he was seeking to engage me fully in the ancient dance of love.

I didn't want that. I didn't want to be drawn into anything I might be unable to control. I was prepared only to submit passively to the restrained power that I had sensed—or imagined— lay within him as he had stood at my window and asked whether I was ready to give myself to him.

Still I knew that I must make an effort to demonstrate the love I had professed to feel.

But I was at a complete loss as to how to do this. How *would* a newly married, utterly respectable woman display her ardor? My experiences with Frederick could hardly serve as a blueprint. He'd been a free spirit, and we had not even been married the first time we'd let passion carry us away.

I thought the business might be easier if the room were dark, so I asked my husband to put out the light. He assented without protest to this request, although I sensed he was somewhat taken aback by it.

In the sheltering darkness, he was as tender and considerate as he had always been.

He sat down upon the edge of the bed and drew me toward him. He was touching me as carefully as if I had been the most fragile of blossoms.

I felt his hands, slowly stripping away my clothing piece by piece, and then his lips on my skin. I shivered, neither with cold nor with passion but with a wracking, fathomless sadness. I could not speak.

It was so odd to experience his gentle, exploring touch, never unpleasant or clumsy, but always somehow distant and muted, as if my nerves had been deadened and muffled, as if my body had been laid away in thick rolls of cotton wool.

I tried to be as pliant and obliging as possible, but I was unable to rise above a lassitude born of guilt and despair, self-loathing and anxiety, as I allowed him to use me.

Nothing short of love and its attendant passion could have eased the ordeal. I knew now why I had once been able to give myself to Frederick so fearlessly and that it had, after all, had nothing to do with hot blood! But I could not call upon love now. Darkness was my sole, flimsy protection, the one barrier I could raise against the intimacies I dreaded.

Oh, why was I so frightened? Whatever private longings he might harbor, surely my decent, well-bred, chivalrous husband would not dream of shattering my psychic boundaries with the kind of behavior to which my grandmother had assured me that no true gentleman would dream of subjecting his wife.

He did not.

But even at the climax of his lovemaking, I felt a thousand miles away.

I lay beneath him, understanding at last the magnitude of the impossible role I had been driven to take on: I had sold myself to him. I was nothing more than a mistress—as emotionally distant as my grandmother had said one must be—but one who had committed herself to the lifetime job of pretending to be warmhearted, open, and affectionate. But of how this fictitious creature might behave in bed I had not the faintest idea.

Certainly not as I had: I was barely able to open my lips to my husband's kiss. He had not pressed me; instead he'd simply moved his mouth downward to the hollow of my throat.

As for the rest . . . there had been no escaping it, but it had awakened nothing.

When he was finished with me, he shifted his body to the

empty space at my side. I almost imagined I could taste his disappointment.

I was disappointed, too, although I could never have told him so. I was sure I would have been far less painfully aware of my shortcomings had he merely shown the same indifference to my lack of excitement that Frederick had latterly displayed before he had tired of me altogether.

I felt like a tight, locked casket, with all my guilty knowledge sealed inside. I half believed that, if he had only the will to do so, my husband might have used his own lithe body to drive it open, releasing every secret and reawakening every desire. Perhaps with a little more insistence and a little less restraint, he would have wrested from me both truth and passion. But that would have put me entirely at his mercy.

Still I felt it was incumbent upon me now to do *something*. I turned toward him and brought my lips to his cheek. I heard his soft sigh.

He was staring up at the ceiling and did not speak. I moved closer and hesitantly rested my head against his smooth chest. He put his arm gently around me, and I lay there, like the survivor of a shipwreck, stranded beside a stranger, and counted my losses. I mourned, rigidly and with dry eyes, for Frederick, who was dead, and for my little dead daughter, and for the man beside me, whose joyous expectations were perhaps already dying in the face of what I knew to have been so grave a failure on my part, and for the innocent, idyllic happiness I had tasted in the Bois de Boulogne and once again on the morning we'd set out for Fontainebleau. Now that was as dead as everything else.

Perhaps if I had yielded then to the almost overwhelming urge to weep for everything that had slipped through my fingers, it might have released me to feel something beyond guilt and fear and the terrifying hollowness which seemed to be all that remained of me. But as usual, I held back the tears, which could never have been more inappropriate than on my wedding night.

XII

For once in my life, I longed for my grandmother's practical, earthy advice. With what zest she would have risen to the challenge of instructing me in how to hold a man's love, even if I could not return it, and in how to fan the flames of passion even when I lacked any heat of my own.

But her voice, which had once railed at me so insistently, had fallen silent. Perhaps it was because I was now in a realm where her heartless manipulations had no currency. Could any of her clever stratagems withstand the blinding light of my husband's love?

I soon discovered how weak they really were.

I knew that our wedding night had been a disappointment to him, and I was determined to find some way to make up for it. I did not act on that wish immediately, however, for I still had no idea how to go about this.

The morning after the wedding we set out by train for Lyon. From there we would go to Nice, and then on to Greece by water. During the ride to Lyon our conversation was amiable; but once we were in our hotel room, all my anxieties returned. That night was not very different from our first night in Paris; in Nice, it was the same. My husband always took me with tenderness and restraint. I would lie passively beneath him until he had spent himself, and then when I was free of his weight, I would move, almost apologetically, into the shelter of his arms. He never turned away from me. He never suggested that our relations were any other than what he wished them to be.

But I knew he was troubled.

While we were at sea, I had a little respite, for we slept in separate beds. It was a mixed blessing; although I had not enjoyed my conjugal duties, I'd almost welcomed what followed them.

I did not take this as a hopeful sign, however; it only made me feel worse. What a hypocrite I was! I couldn't respond to my husband's lovemaking, and yet, as faithless as a lost dog that had stumbled into a new home, I liked to fall asleep cradled against that long, cool body.

In the daytime, when my husband seemed relaxed and almost cheerful, I tried to convince myself that my coolness at night was pleasing to him, that it was really what any well-bred Englishman would naturally wish to find in his bride. My grandmother had always insisted that although English gentlemen craved passion and abandon in their mistresses, they would be horrified to find the same qualities in their wives.

But where my husband was concerned, I was increasingly aware that my inert passivity was too pronounced even for his gentlemanly tastes. I would have to change.

In Athens, I recalled a fragment of my grandmother's counsel. It told me what I must do.

"A clever mistress," she'd once said, "will study her lover as carefully as any general studies his enemy's position. If she watches and listens closely, she will quickly learn his strengths and weaknesses; she will discern what pleases him and what does not.

Every time he betrays a certain desire or inclination, however subtly, she gains power and he loses it. All she has to do is take that power and use it."

Of course I'd never had to employ such tricks with Frederick. I'd practiced some of the other techniques she'd described to me—the kind it would be unwise to reveal any knowledge of to my new husband—but I'd done it only because it had excited me to give back to him the kind of pleasure he gave me. It had never been a matter of trying to gain ascendancy; we'd been co-conspirators, spurring one another on to bolder demonstrations of passion. Our natures harmonized.

But now, where nature had failed, perhaps artifice could triumph.

That night I took greater pains than I had done before to please my husband's eyes. I clothed myself in the one truly alluring nightdress from my small trousseau. It was made of the softest lace imaginable, and had a deeply scooped neck. I had bought it for my wedding night, but that night I had worn no nightdress at all.

I unpinned my hair and let it tumble loosely over my shoulders; I already knew that my husband loved to see it unbound. It made a glossy black nimbus around my pale face and bare throat.

Then I walked slowly into the sitting room.

My husband was on the sofa, still absorbed in the newspaper he had taken up while he waited for me to prepare for bed. At first he didn't look up. I felt subtly rejected.

"Anthony," I said.

I saw him press his lips together and fold the newspaper carefully, as if he were bracing himself for something. With a flash of genuine remorse, I understood, far more fully than I ever had before, how troubled he was by our unacknowledged difficulties—by the incompatibility of our bodies that was rooted, although only I knew how deeply, in an incompatibility of spirit. It would be even worse for him, I realized, because *he* had no way of knowing what was at the bottom of it.

He lifted his head at last, almost reluctantly. I saw the resolute set of his mouth soften. A slight flush came to his cheeks; a hopefulness that I had not seen since our wedding day sprang to his eyes.

"Fleur," he said.

He sounded surprised, almost dazed.

I was somewhat stunned myself to think that my deliberate maneuver could have such an instant and obvious effect. It made me feel both elated and ashamed.

I forced myself to stand motionless and let him look at me. The white lace might have been molded to my body. It was loosely woven but held me tightly.

After my husband's eyes had taken their fill, he stood up and came to me, still with that air of wonderment.

"Fleur," he murmured again huskily, putting his hands upon my shoulders.

I tipped my head up and nearly parted my lips to his mouth, which was moving down to mine. It wasn't a calculation; it was an impulse. To at last be able to give my mouth over to one that didn't reek of alcohol! Toward the end the fumes Frederick gave off had made me feel nauseated. But a cleansing, healing kiss might—

I moved my head just in time. If I gave in to that one fleeting but genuine hunger, who could say where it might end? It might start with a kiss and end with my needing my husband—in every way.

But sooner or later my blackmailer would surely raise the ante beyond anything I could possibly scrape together.

Then he would go to my husband.

And after that, my husband would never look at me again the way he had tonight, would never bend his head tenderly to bring those firm and gentle lips to mine.

Once he had absorbed those images of me splayed out upon the canvas, he would be lost to me as irretrievably as everything else I'd ever loved.

I couldn't risk letting myself come to love him, too.

Having evaded the perilous kiss, I rested my head upon my husband's chest and swayed against him, weak with the knowledge that I had narrowly escaped a sensation that might easily have swung out of control. In this precarious marriage, control was everything.

"What is it, Fleur?" my husband was asking softly. His mouth was buried in my hair.

I reminded myself of the part I must play.

"We don't have to . . . sleep apart any longer, do we?" I murmured.

"Oh, Fleur, sweetheart, did you mind?" He sounded astonished and remorseful. "I'm sorry. I thought it might be . . . more comfortable for you."

"No," I whispered. It was as much the truth as it was a lie. I never felt my loneliness and isolation more than when he was making love to me; I never felt it less than when I was falling asleep in his embrace.

"What's gotten into you tonight?" He was stroking my body gently through the fine lace.

"I don't like it when we're apart."

"You've missed me already?" The gratification in his voice was faint but unmistakable. At least *one* of my grandmother's lessons had begun to prove sound.

"Yes," I whispered.

I could feel his relief at being able, at last, to believe that I wanted him the way he had let me know, with so many subtle signals, that he longed to be wanted. He lifted me in his arms and carried me into the bedroom.

Again I asked him to put the lights out. I knew my part would be easier in the dark. But the faint, watery light of a quarter moon trickled through the two long casement windows. One of them was wide open. The other seemed to have been painted shut. We had tried to pry it open earlier and had failed.

Now we sat on the wide bed facing each other.

My husband's fingers were unfastening the tiny mother-of-pearl buttons at my wrists. Then they moved to my breasts. His palms cupped me lightly. The sensation was not one that I was able to enjoy; my breasts had not given me any real pleasure since —well, for years.

But I let out a little sigh and arched my back slightly as if I craved this touch, as if I were straining to give him greater possession. My left nipple had broken its way through the loose network of lacy threads that held my breasts and was wholly exposed to him. He brushed it tenderly with the pad of his right thumb and began to stroke and flick my right nipple until that one, too, sprang free. I raised my hands to his shoulders, gripped them, and moaned softly.

The sound of his breathing told me how much this pleased him.

His hands lingered at my nipples for a while longer and then moved on to the row of flat little shimmering buttons that ran from the top of my breasts to the bottom of my hips and held the soft lace tightly against my skin.

My husband began to release those buttons slowly, one at a time. My breasts spilled out of the lace. He bent his head toward them. I wrapped my arms more closely around his neck and gasped and writhed like a woman in ecstasy as his mouth nuzzled one nipple and his fingertips pulled gently on the other.

In reality, I wanted to wrench myself away. It wasn't his fault. Even Frederick's fingers, which had rarely touched me quite as tenderly and skillfully as these, had become clumsy irritants after my miscarriage. My breasts had been so sore then that the lightest touch was torture. The raw sensitivity had faded, finally, but they had never been filled with the old, sweet yearning again . . . except for one moment at Fontainebleau.

My husband brought his head up and gazed at me in rapt silence. Then he began to unfasten the remaining buttons. He slipped the nightgown down over my shoulders, over my waist and hips and legs, and let it fall from his hand to the floor at the bedside.

"Lie down," he said thickly, as if he'd had to force the words out of his throat. His hands guided me backward. The weak, cold moonlight puddled over the bed like watered-down milk. I lay there in the thin, ungenerous pool.

"You're so beautiful," whispered my husband, looking down at me. "You don't know how much I've wanted you."

By means of another soft sigh, I tried to convey in a ladylike fashion that I, too, was at last plagued by the same fevers.

He slipped off his shoes and then his jacket. It fell to the floor and covered my gown. He removed his tie; the strip of silk glided out of his hand like a serpent and disappeared over the side of the bed.

He lay down beside me, with his body turned toward me and his head propped up on his left hand. With his right hand, he lifted a loose strand of my hair and twined it idly around his fingers.

"I wanted you the first time I saw you," he whispered. I heard him swallow. This openness, this self-revelation on the part of my reserved husband, who had for so long carefully hidden his desires, was painful to me. Nothing burns a liar's eyes as cruelly as the clean light of truth.

I could feel my skin glowing with embarrassment; but I was sure it could pass for the wanton heat he longed to ignite in me.

"I wanted to break every rule," he was saying. "I couldn't believe that a stranger—that anyone—could make me feel that way. I wanted to snatch you up and carry you off like a prize." He let the strand of hair fall back to the pillow and began to trace my jawline with light fingertips. "I couldn't think of anything but you, of what it would feel like to have you . . . like this."

I reminded myself of what I must do.

"I wanted you, too," I whispered hesitantly, turning toward my husband. It was truer than anything I had said to him for weeks, months. I *had* wanted him, for that one brief moment in the forest. Now I could not even remember how it had felt.

"Did you?" he said with something between a soft little laugh and a sigh. But then he grew silent and abstracted.

At last he said gently, "Fleur, don't ever be afraid or ashamed to show me that you want me. There are no rules here, no boundaries. Do you understand me?"

"Yes," I whispered bravely, but I couldn't keep my voice from shaking a little.

He moved closer and seemed about to cover my lips with his mouth. Quickly I moved my head. I lifted my hands and unfastened first the pearl stud that held his collar shut and then the topmost button of his shirt, baring his throat. I twined my arms around his neck and began to shower little kisses upon that long, slender throat and upon his cheeks, his eyelids, his jaw, and his earlobes. He closed his eyes and stretched his neck luxuriously the way a cat will when it is being groomed by another's tongue.

His right knee, still clothed in fine black summer wool, moved up slowly to insert itself between my thighs and drive them gently apart. I yielded with a little sob of feigned urgency.

Instead of insisting upon taking my mouth, he now began to return the little butterfly kisses I had given him. His right hand moved back to my breast. Again his fingers began to stroke and press and pull. I twisted sinuously and made the whimpering sounds of a creature in delicious torment. His breath quickened; his touch grew rougher, more insistent.

I let out long shuddering groans and began to move my hips in sharp, inviting spasms.

"Ah," came his low whisper of triumph, as if he had hunted me down at last.

His left hand was tangled almost cruelly in my hair, like a conqueror's.

His right hand slid downward from my breast, over my stomach, and further still. His fingers knotted themselves in the soft mat of curls that covered my groin and pulled at them gently.

I gave a little sob and increased the rhythm of my hips.

Now his fingertips found the tiny bud of flesh whose long-ago and now unimaginable hungers had brought me finally to this, to the necessity of simulating a forgotten ecstasy.

I could sense his excitement, how he was straining to keep it in check.

He moved his finger still further, down to the gates he'd longed to break since he first saw me. He began to slide his finger inside, as if he reveled in taking possession of this most private part of myself.

It should have slipped in easily, but it didn't.

It hurt.

In my stupendous ignorance, I had supposed that masculine lust and vanity would prevent my husband from comprehending the undisguisable message my unreceptive flesh conveyed. It had taken Frederick months to acknowledge the significance of that desert dryness.

But I'd been wrong.

With a sharp, almost angry intake of breath, my husband released me and pulled away.

He got up from the bed.

Trying to suppress my anxiety and shame, I sat up and leaned over to reach for my nightgown. My fingers found, not lace, but light wool. I came up with his jacket in my hand and held it against me protectively.

I heard my husband give one hard little gasp of disbelieving laughter as he pressed his forehead against the cool glass of the closed window. I saw him bring his right hand up in a fist.

I knew the game was up.

An electric violence, just barely kept in leash, radiated from him. I trembled, certain that he was about to smash the window-pane and would then turn upon me clutching a long shard of glass in his bloodied hand.

I couldn't speak or cry out. I could only wait.

But he merely let his fist fall slowly against the glass and then stood there for a long, long time with his back to me.

He seemed to be fighting for control.

At last he turned around. His face was in shadow.

"Well," I heard him say in a voice that he managed to keep entirely level, "it seems we have some things to talk about."

I clutched his jacket against me with one arm and pressed the fingers of my other hand against my mouth. I really couldn't believe that he would insist upon *discussing* a matter so delicate and so humiliating. I had expected only an outburst of anger followed by hours or even days of silence.

He walked slowly toward me, but no longer with the effortless grace that had once fascinated me. There was something tight and withholding in the set of his shoulders and his back.

I felt sick with a vague dread.

He sat down on the edge of the bed and let out a long, tremulous breath. His shoulders relaxed a little. I released my own breath slowly, almost silently.

He lifted the fingertips of his right hand—it was open, palm up, and harmless—to my chin and tipped my head up slightly so that I was forced to meet his eyes.

I thought I saw something glistening on his cheek. The night was warm; perhaps the effort of keeping such a harness on his anger had caused him to perspire.

"Fleur," he said. And then again, "Fleur."

He made it sound beautiful and tragic.

"Was it always like this for you?" he whispered haltingly. "I mean . . . with . . . Frederick, too?"

I hesitated for only an instant. I really didn't want to sink any further into the quagmire of lies, but I had to answer quickly. Otherwise my reply would seem calculated. If I told him the truth, that it *had* been that way at the end of our marriage but not at the beginning, I feared that he might keep probing until he found out about the baby. . . . I couldn't have withstood that, to reopen that wound which had never really healed, to expose all my pain to him.

So instead I laid the capstone on my prison of lies.

"Yes," I said, and bowed my head.

"Well," he said again, this time with a rather strained little laugh, as if he were trying to leaven all the wretchedness that filled the room like a miasma, "we have quite a problem here, haven't we?"

"It doesn't have to be a problem," I whispered desperately. "It wasn't a problem for Frederick. He never let it interfere. We . . . managed."

"But I'm not Frederick," he said.

I swallowed painfully. If only he were. Frederick would never have subjected me to this gentle, merciless inquisition.

"Is that all you want, Fleur?" he asked after another long silence. "To . . . manage, as you put it?"

"What else is there to do?"

He laughed that low, exhausted little laugh again.

"I don't know," he said. "This is . . . ah . . . outside the realm of my experience." He made it sound almost like a joke, as if he were trying to nudge my spirits up a little. "No wonder you seemed a bit . . . skittish," he remarked. "Why didn't you say anything? I knew something was wrong back there in Paris. But I thought you needed time to get accustomed to me. I never dreamed it was more than that."

"I ought to have told you," I said after another excruciatingly long silence.

"Yes," he said. "You should have. If I had known how you felt about . . . these things, I would have . . . approached you differently."

"Or not at all," I said with a rather hard laugh as I slid my eyes away.

In an instant his hands were on my shoulders. He held me tightly.

"Look at me, Fleur," he said. So I did.

"Don't ever think that," he said. "Do you think knowing this would have made me care for you less?"

Then, with a sudden air of self-consciousness, as if he feared his touch was unpleasant to me, he released me.

"I love you," he said. "And I love you for trying to please me tonight. It was a mistake, and I wish you hadn't done it, but I love you for it anyway. . . . *I* don't know what to do, Fleur. I wish I could *make* you want me the way that I want you. But I'll take your love in whatever ways you *can* give it. All I insist upon is that *whatever* happens between us be real. Do you understand what I'm asking of you?"

"Yes, I think so," I whispered. My eyes stung.

For a second I thought he was going to put his arms around me, but he seemed to think better of it.

"Will you do that for me?" he pressed softly.

"Oh yes!" I said, only because I knew I had no choice. I could hardly turn to him now and tell him that everything was a lie.

"I don't think it will be easy, Fleur," he said. He sounded exhausted now. "We'll have to feel our way. It won't be painless."

"I know."

I was used to pain; it was beginning to feel like an old friend. I could hardly imagine life without it now.

But even so, his next words ripped away one of my few remaining consolations, that little sense of comfort I had gained from falling asleep in his arms.

"I don't want to sleep here with you tonight," he said reluctantly, as if he hated the possibility that his words might wound me. "It's not that I don't love and want you. I do. But I don't want to lie here beside you tonight, wanting you as I do, and knowing that it's not the same for you. I'd rather go on sleeping apart, at least for a time. . . . You can always come to me, you know, if you feel like . . ." He let the sentence trail off.

"Like what?" I whispered numbly.

"If you ever feel like . . . making love. I'll never turn you away. No matter what happens, I'll wait for you. We can go as slowly as you need to."

He was so generous, so patient. I felt overwhelmed and so unworthy that I was almost in tears. I guess he could tell, because he tried to cheer me up again.

"After all," he said with a forced little laugh, "we have the rest of our lives."

But that night he slept on the sofa in the sitting room.

As for me, I did not sleep at all.

XIII

After that the beauties of Greece and Italy made barely any impression on me. I knew I had made a terrible mistake; if it hadn't been for my clumsy and foolish effort to feign passion, the severity of my limitations as a wife might have become apparent more gradually, and my husband's disappointment would have been less sudden and shattering.

Now his subdued air only fed my despondency. His manner had never been particularly effervescent, but where it had once had the delicious tang and crackle of very dry champagne, it now became mild and flat. He tried, of course, to spare me any sense of failure and to hide his own unhappiness.

And I tried to hide mine. During the day, I made sincere attempts to fight my deepening lassitude, and to exhibit the same delight in the glories of the ancient world that I had once in Paris. But it was all false. There was no heart in anything I said or did.

I longed to be able to treat my husband with the fondness that I honestly felt for him, but I was unable to. My sense of guilt, the constant awareness of all that I was hiding, made spontaneity and warmth impossible.

Equally painful to me was my husband's withdrawal of the

simple gestures of affection, unworthy though they made me feel, that had come to mean too much to me.

For a moment or two, when the mystical loveliness of Delphi infused him with wonder and awe and penetrated even my gray indifference, he laid his arm across my shoulders and I leaned against him with a feeling of relief and joy.

The light embrace grew warmer, more reassuring. He started to draw me around toward him. But then he stopped, withdrew his arm, and moved a step or two away.

The abrupt change in his manner left me raw. But I knew he hadn't deliberately intended to hurt me, that in fact he would have gone to almost any length to spare me pain, so as soon as he lifted his arm from my shoulders, I fanned myself with my hat and said, with a gay little laugh, "*Thank* you—it *is* awfully warm here."

He would never know what that brittle remark had cost me, and I couldn't resent the distance he kept thereafter, although I hated it. I respected him for having too much self-regard to subject himself to the frustration of holding a woman he could never wholly possess.

The awkwardness between us did not diminish with time. I knew my husband had expected that it must. Although he had found the path he'd so hopefully set out upon with me a far rockier one than he had supposed, he still believed that the light of love would guide our feet to a smoother road. But I knew *I* would never reach the golden highway—not with those paintings and Poncet's greed hanging over my head like the Sword of Damocles.

The best I could hope for was that things would remain as they were; my husband, in his innocence, still dreamed that love and patience would transform them.

Meanwhile, the exigencies of travel thrust us together in ways that were painful to us both. Every time he took my hand to help me down from a carriage, every time we brushed too closely against each other by accident, I could feel the spark of tension between his body and mine. It kept me continually on edge.

We did not stop at Florence, which was to have been the grand culmination of our honeymoon tour.

We had intended to stay there for a fortnight.

Instead, we passed through it on a train, for in Rome my husband had abruptly proposed that we cut our travels short and return immediately to England.

I did not object. I knew that he was right. In England, everything would be easier. We would not be so constantly in each other's company, so relentlessly pushed up against the invisible obstacles that divided us. In England there would be a thousand other demands upon his time, which would surely give us long hours of respite from each other.

So I never saw Giotto's tower, the *Gates of Paradise*, or Brunelleschi's dome. I never saw Donatello's *David* or Michelangelo's. I never saw the pagan god with the little faun who had stolen my husband's heart. All I saw of Florence was a railway station, a sluggish river, and a few red-tiled roofs.

In England, we took up residence on my husband's large estate, Charingworth. Here I had my own bedroom, and in it I slept alone. My husband had told me his door would always be open to me, but how could I go to his bed when I knew not only that nothing *had* changed but that nothing *could* change?

I had thought that anything would be better than that strained honeymoon which was not a honeymoon. But England was worse. During our travels, my husband's inevitable presence had sometimes caused me pain, but in England his frequent absences from home only deepened my loneliness. He spent a great deal of time in London; he had a house in Grosvenor Square where he sometimes stayed for days on end. The first two or three times he went there, he asked me to join him, but at that period I hoped that a little time apart might make things easier for us, so I declined. After that, he stopped asking.

Sometimes I did travel to London, just to escape for a few hours from the role I had so unwillingly assumed and which was proving to be so uncongenial. But I always went alone, and spent my time wandering restlessly through the galleries of one museum or another. I never slept in Grosvenor Square since, by train, Charingworth was less than two hours from London.

My husband never failed to treat me with the same kindness and consideration he had always shown. But I still could find no way to ameliorate his unspoken dissatisfactions. Every effort I made to appear lively and gay, every small but awkward gesture of affection, felt ghastly to me—always contrived, always calculated no matter how true the feeling behind it.

Most of the time my husband gave the appearance of having accepted the uncomfortable state of affairs with the same imperturbable calm that he exhibited in every other aspect of our life together.

Nevertheless, some question seemed to hover on his lips. And there was one on mine, as well. I often longed to ask him if he really imagined that our ailing marriage was somehow miraculously going to fix itself. What was he waiting for? Surely he would not be content to live like this forever. Yet he took no action. Was he waiting for me?

And what could I do? Go to him with the truth and bring the whole sorry house of cards tumbling to the ground? I knew what would happen then—the shutters behind those clear gray eyes would come down and close me out forever.

Or I could go to him as I had in Athens, willing to try to give pleasure but incapable of receiving it, and expose myself to the same frustration and humiliation.

No. The only other justification for going to his bed would be to give him a child. But that seemed as far beyond my abilities as everything else, and if by some miracle it were not, how could I love the child of this man who seemed every day to be growing more remote? It could never be the one I had lost. And if I *was* foolish enough to love it, what would become of it once the tissue of lies was finally ripped open? Perhaps my husband's strict sense of honor would lead him to declare that I was unfit to raise his child and he would take it from me.

In the meantime, his generosity was unstinting. But while the allowance he provided had so far enabled me to meet Poncet's relentless demands, those same demands forced me to exercise extreme frugality in everything else.

Once my husband, having discovered a new patch on one of my well-worn gowns, asked how I managed to dispose of all the money he gave me.

"Must I account to you for how I spend it?" I asked archly, but never had I felt so threatened.

He flushed. "Certainly not. But I have sometimes wondered. . . ." He hesitated.

"Yes?"

"I know so little about you, Fleur."

"You know everything about me. There is really very little to know."

"Your early life . . . and your life in France." He could not conceal his extreme discomfort; his rising color told me how much he hated to pry, yet it now seemed that he felt driven to override his scruples.

"I have told you everything."

"It is apparent that you have already gone through a great deal of money, and it is equally apparent that you spend nothing on yourself. It has crossed my mind that perhaps you have needy dependents, whom you have been unwilling to impose as a burden upon me, and for whose well-being you have felt compelled to assume complete responsibility."

Now I was the one who flushed.

"If that is the case, or anything like it, there is no reason to hide it from me," he continued. "Certainly there is no necessity for *you* to do without in order to fulfill your obligations, whatever they may be. *Everything* that is mine is yours, surely you know that?"

I thought then, for one terrifying instant, that my poise would crack. I tried to speak, to protest those suspicions which cast me in so much better a light than I merited, but the words caught in my throat. My eyes burned alarmingly. I clung to the image of my grandmother. She would have been ashamed of me; she had always taught me that the last defense in an impossible situation is to present to your enemy an unyielding stone wall. At the time I had thought it was an embittered woman's drivel; now the memory gave me the strength I needed.

"You are completely mistaken," I said. "The truth, if you must know it, is that I have never been able to manage money." How could he know that I'd been the very soul of husbandry during the lean years with Frederick? "I am afraid I am forever coming up short—and with nothing to show for it!"

"Well," he said, "if there *is* anything I can do, you have only to ask."

I was silent.

"Besides," he went on, "you are a very lovely woman, and I wouldn't mind seeing you looking a bit more *soignée.*"

I chose to ignore this oblique request, one of the very few he ever made of me, and continued to wear the same gray dresses I had during my last months in France. Virtually every cent that passed from my husband's hands into mine continued to go straight to Paris, but there was no way that I could appeal to my straitlaced husband to break Poncet's hold over me once and for all.

My husband did not care much for society and made only the minimal gestures toward it that were required of a man in his position.

At Charingworth, we paid occasional polite visits to some of our neighbors, but except for these small acts of neighborly civility, we shunned the endless rounds of fox hunts, shooting expeditions, country house weekends, empty but rigidly orchestrated social calls, and elaborate dinner parties that provided so many people of our station with their sole raison d'être.

That suited me very well, for I had no raison d'être at all, nor had I any love for the upper classes or for their ostentations, prejudices, and frivolities.

The one unmitigated benefit of my new life was my limitless freedom out of doors. Instead of walking, however, as I had done in my youth, I rode the filly with which my husband had presented me upon our return from the Continent. When I was with Andromeda, I was almost happy. She was a glossy little black horse with a white blaze on her face and an endearingly delicate manner. But her fastidious airs disappeared when I brought her to a gallop and her passion for speed was unleashed.

I had not learned to ride at the school in Montreux where my grandmother had sent me for two years, so it was my husband who taught me. He was a superb horseman and under his tutelage I took to the saddle quickly, with a buoyant confidence, expecting that my fearlessness would win me his lavish approval. Instead, even in his restrained way, my husband proved to be a surprisingly demanding and critical instructor. I sensed that it drove him wild, for example, if I either pulled too hard on the reins or grew too lax in my control, but the only indication he gave of this was in the ironic tone of his mild rebukes. Nevertheless, he let no error slide.

After I had licked the first few wounds to my pride, I found that I did not object to my husband's manner of instruction. In fact, our rides together, when he accompanied me on his chestnut stallion, Perseus, were among the few pleasant intervals in our marriage. But they could not compensate for its other disappointments.

XIV

Hardly ever, during this period of our lives, did my husband express the frustrations that must have been gnawing at him. Even when his temper frayed, he kept it as tightly controlled as the fist he had raised against the windowpane in Athens.

One or two such incidents occurred in conjunction with his mother's first visit to us, which she finally condescended to pay in early November, after we had been settled for weeks in England.

Earlier, in a fit of boredom so great that even the idea of seeking out the fabled dragon in her lair offered itself as an appealing diversion from the stately passage of the long, slow days at Charingworth, I had suggested that perhaps we ought to call upon her at her Yorkshire manor.

"I think that is a most unsuitable idea," said my husband, in a chilly voice that brooked no compromise. "You tire so easily, Fleur, I'm sure you would find the trip fearfully exhausting."

It was clear that he was dead set against the notion. I was surprised. Never had he rejected any proposal of mine so unequivocally.

He seemed equally displeased when Lady Whitstone sent us

the letter announcing her intention to favor us with a visit. After showing it to me he proposed, with a flash of that old, acerbic sparkle, that perhaps it was time for a holiday in France. I demurred, saying that I felt very remiss at not having made the acquaintance of my mother-in-law long ago. My husband shrugged and yielded.

Lady Whitstone's stay with us was not a pleasant event. Lord Whitstone did not accompany her—I had once been given to understand by a remark of Lord Marsden's that Whitstone had a poor opinion of my husband, who did not share that worthy nobleman's enthusiasm for slaughtering foxes.

When I finally laid eyes on Lady Whitstone, I was astounded by the resemblance between parent and child. My husband was a perfect, albeit masculinized, replication of his mother: the pale complexion, hers; the white-gold hair, hers; the haughty bearing, the cool gray eyes, the excruciatingly high-bred nose, and the clean line of the narrow jaw, all hers. Only his dark lashes—hers were as light as her hair—and equally firm, but more generously formed mouth suggested that his sire might have contributed anything at all to his makeup.

My husband had been tender enough of my feelings to warn me in advance that Lady Whitstone was obsessive about rank and ancestry. In fact, he added almost nonchalantly, he was certain that she would never have married his father were the Camwells not one of the richest families in England, while her own family, the Cercys, equally ancient but far more distinguished, had fallen upon hard times. His voice was casual, but with an undertone that suggested he judged her harshly on that score.

It was no surprise, then, that one of Lady Whitstone's earliest conversations with me, almost entirely one-sided, was a general dissertation on the importance of maintaining the purity of good blood. Sometime during the conversation, she asked me what my father's name had been. When I told her, she gave me a quizzical look and then went on to decry the unfortunate modern trend, among so many people of impeccable genealogy, to take a mate from the inferior classes, thus polluting England's finest stock with every sort of undesirable characteristic.

It was a theme to which she invariably returned on the rare and brief occasions that my husband left us alone together. Then one afternoon, my husband was called into the village on an urgent matter which seemed likely to occupy him for several hours. Almost as soon as he had gone, Lady Whitstone began to bombard me from across the tea table with more details about the Camwell family's origins, wealth, and noble connections than I had ever wished to know.

When she had finally exhausted the tiresome subject of the Camwells, I scarcely had time to offer her another cup of tea before she began tracing her own immaculate Cercy lineage back to the Battle of Hastings.

"You mentioned that Hastings was your father's name. But *you* went by a different one," she suddenly interjected into her monologue. "Deslignères, was it not?"

I froze. I had mentioned my father's name to her, but I had never told her my grandmother's. This was the first indication she had given of the extent of her interest in my origins, and although I was not warmed by it, I was mightily impressed. I had been very vague about my early life in our conversations. My husband, of course, knew the name I had used before I married Frederick, but I was pretty certain, from Lady Whitstone's atrocious accent, that she had not heard that name from him; she must have somehow found it out for herself. It could only be from the records of my marriage, in Paris, to Frederick. To think the woman would have gone to such lengths!

"Yes," I said, wishing that she might revert to the less volatile subject of William the Conqueror.

"And this grandmother of yours, who raised you, her name was also Deslignères?" persisted the intrepid researcher, leaning toward me and looking somewhat like a well-kept vulture.

"Yes," I repeated, astounded by the depth of her genealogical excavations. "Deslignères," I then added, giving it the correct pronunciation.

"And your mother's maiden name?"

"Deslignères, again," I replied with the utmost politeness.

"What a curious coincidence," she observed. "Or did all the women in your family marry relatives?"

It was at this moment that my husband slipped like a pale shadow into the room.

"So it *was* nothing so very important, after all," said Lady Whitstone of the matter which had taken her son from her side. "Really, Anthony, you are far too quick to respond to every bumpkin's imaginary troubles. It breeds disrespect."

By now I had acquired the distinct impression that behind her elegant and richly clothed exterior beat a heart that harbored very little affection for her son.

"Do you think so, Mother?" said my husband, indifferently settling into a chair.

"You have always known my views on your relations with those people, Anthony. You encourage them to forget your station."

"As if they could!" he murmured. Then, inclining his head toward me, "She thinks I do not take sufficient advantage of 'those people,' Fleur, and instead encourage them to think poorly of me. What is your opinion on the subject?"

"I have never heard you spoken of with anything but respect and affection, Anthony," I told him truthfully. *So there!* was the message I flashed simultaneously at Lady Whitstone from behind my lashes.

"Well, that is only to be expected—I'm the king of the castle and *you* are, after all, my wife," said my husband, in a tone of such cynicism that I was momentarily shaken.

"And every day I see the lengths to which you go to be worthy of such regard," I added with a warmth that astonished me.

He sent me a look that all but pierced my heart, but his face closed up when his mother spoke again.

"Oh, let's not argue about such paltry things, darling. Fleur and I have been having such a lovely tea. You must try some of this lemon cake."

My husband ignored that proposition and instead lounged in his chair, as *fainéant* as a squire at the end of a long day's hunt.

"And what have you and Fleur been talking about?" he asked carelessly.

"Oh, this and that," said Lady Whitstone with a little laugh. "Indeed, I can hardly recall now *what* we were speaking of when you burst in upon us."

"Indeed?" remarked my husband, stretching out his legs. "Perhaps I can assist your memory."

His mother blanched.

"I can remember," I interjected, for I had no confidence in my languid husband's ability to defend me. "You had concluded that I was a bastard and were taking the opportunity to remind me that my mother was one, as well. That *was* your point, was it not, Lady Whitstone?"

Without his having moved a muscle, I imagined for a moment that my husband's demeanor had become alert and watchful. I shot a glance his way, but he was only examining his fingernails.

"Is that so, Mother?" he asked idly, with his gaze on his hands.

"Certainly not!" protested Lady Whitstone, with what seemed to me unnecessary vigor in the light of his apparent unconcern. "I was merely curious about what seemed to be an odd coincidence."

"Then let me enlighten you on that subject," I said. "Like you, my grandmother did not approve of intermarriage between people of different stations in life. In fact, she did not approve of marriage at all. She never married. But I think you already know that. You appear to have taken great interest in the matter and to have done a fair amount of digging on your own."

I expected Lady Whitstone to protest angrily, but she did not. Instead she continued to cast furtive looks in the direction of her impassive son.

"Yes, indeed," I went on. I was beginning to enjoy myself. "Bad blood is a terrible curse. And do you know the worst of it, Lady Whitstone? I will tell you—it's this. I do not even know *who* my grandfather was! Why, he might have been anybody—the butcher, the baker, or the candlestick maker. Just think, perhaps he was even your own father—or your husband's—if either of them were inclined to flout their domestic obligations!"

This was an outright lie. I knew exactly who my grandfather had been. My grandmother had impressed his name upon me, for very much like my mother-in-law, she had adored titles almost as much as she had adored wealth.

Lady Whitstone had gone whiter than ever.

I could not imagine what might be my well-bred husband's response to my outrageousness. There was no excuse for it, other than that she had driven me to the wall with her questions and insinuations. Surely he would be horrified—not only by the appalling freedom of my speech but also at the discovery that I really had no claim to respectability at all.

But when I finally dared to steal a glance in his direction, I saw that he wore an expression of pure delight. He had eased back even further into his chair and was beaming at me affectionately.

"Well, how do you like that?" he said, turning to his mother. "Tell me, have you now managed to accomplish everything that you set out to do here?"

"I don't know what you mean, Anthony."

"You've insulted me, you've insulted Fleur, and you've insulted the whole village. Short of inviting you to whip the stableboy or to beat the dogs, I cannot imagine how we can possibly provide any further amusement for you." He came lazily to his feet and strolled over to pull the bell-handle. Within seconds a housemaid appeared and was sent to fetch Mrs. Phillips, the housekeeper.

"Mrs. Phillips," said my husband when that lady arrived, "it seems that my mother has been called back to Yorkshire rather suddenly. Please arrange to have all her things packed as quickly as possible. She will depart for the station within the hour."

"Yes, sir," said Mrs. Phillips tonelessly, but she moved with an alacrity that suggested real enthusiasm.

"This is ridiculous, Anthony," said his mother through her teeth when the housekeeper had gone. "Whitstone is not expecting me to return for another fortnight."

"Well, do whatever you like, Mother," returned my husband amicably. Then he added, in a voice of steel, "But if you choose to remain here you'll have to be content to wear nothing but the clothes you have on your back, for I guarantee you this, everything else you own will be on the next train to York."

"I have always said you had a vicious streak, Anthony," said his mother. "It was that foul-tempered wet nurse of yours, I'm sure of it. There was venom in that girl's milk."

"That must be it," he retorted with a laugh, and then added in that low and dangerous tone, "But you should thank your stars that where you are concerned, I have had the patience of Job."

They glared at each other like snakes.

In spite of the intense hostility between mother and son that this incident exposed, not to mention the equally violent antipathy that had arisen between Lady Whitstone and me, all three of us fell back upon our good manners pretty quickly and papered over the rift with one final pretense at mutual civility.

We drove together to the railway station.

There we exchanged chilly but polite farewells. We had just put Lady Whitstone on the train, which was about to pull away, when a young man raced up in a dogcart. Tossing the reins to his groom, he gave a joyous whoop, leaped from his seat and dashed to catch the train. The groom lowered himself slowly to the pavement and came around to the head of the shuddering, exhausted horse, which was completely blown from its exertions and all but bleeding from the nose.

My husband's face darkened alarmingly. He watched the train disappear and then strolled over to the groom, whose face was strained with worry.

"Why was this horse driven so hard?" inquired my husband. His tone was casual.

"Young Lord Percy had a bet with his father, sir, that he could leave ten minutes later than Lord Sparling insisted he must if he were to have any hope of catching this train," replied the groom in an expressionless voice.

"I see," said my husband still in the same neutral tone. He continued to observe the trembling animal. Finally he said, "I suppose you'll leave the creature at the livery stable here until he's thoroughly rested."

The groom bit his lip; it was plain to see that, behind his unexpressive manner, he was angry and upset. How could he not feel humiliated by my husband's self-righteous interference in a matter over which the groom himself, it seemed, had very little control?

"I can't do that, sir," he said at last in a very low voice. "My orders are to return with the horse as quickly as possible."

"The horse may die," my husband said.

"So may my wife and baby, if I lose my position," retorted the other with a flash of anger.

My husband flushed more deeply.

"Of course," he said at last. "I beg your pardon."

I supposed there was nothing for it, then, and that the groom would turn away to carry out his inhumane obligation.

But neither of the men moved. I felt they were taking each other's measure.

"The Sparlings can go to the devil," said my husband suddenly. "Let the horse rest. I'll give you a place at Charingworth. You won't be any poorer for it."

For an instant the groom looked as if he might leap at the offer, but still he hesitated.

My husband laid his hand lightly upon the horse, which was shuddering somewhat less violently. The groom appeared to be thinking hard. His face was as unrevealing as my husband's.

"And which one of us do you think will be brought up as a horse thief?" he asked suddenly.

"I'll take up the matter of the horse with Lord Sparling myself," replied my husband. "If you would have no objection to that."

Another long silence.

"Well, I suppose I had better tend to the horse then," said the other man finally, still in the same expressionless voice.

I heard my husband let out his breath.

When the horse had been taken to the livery stable and my husband had assured himself that it was likely to recover, we returned to our carriage. Inside, he turned to me, and I realized, with something like shock, that he must have been exercising enormous self-control for the past twenty minutes or so. He had given so little indication of this that I had not fathomed the depth of his rage.

"Have you any idea how hard that miserable Sparling wretch must have forced that animal to run?" he demanded. "To win a bet with his father! My God!"

His eyes were blazing.

I understood his anger and had almost been wishing that something would occur to ruffle his tiresome, imperturbable equanimity. But not this. The reemergence of that disturbing aspect of my husband—for the second time that day—frightened me, and involuntarily I shrank from him.

He turned away, leaned back in the seat, and closed his eyes. After a while he said quietly, with a rueful sigh, "That's all we need, another groom."

I did not attempt a response.

"Oh well," said my husband wearily. "It will lighten the work of the others, and I suppose that's never a bad thing."

He seemed to shake off the last remnants of strong emotion and turned again to me.

"You don't mind driving back alone, do you?"

"Alone?" I said. "Why? Where are *you* going?"

"I think I had better remain here until the whole business is settled," replied my husband. "Who knows what may happen should Lord Sparling decide to come looking for his lost property." He smiled without warmth. "It seems that I have just become a horse thief!"

That night, to my astonishment, he came to my bedroom. Only moments after I had put out the light, I heard his soft rap at my door.

My heart pounded violently as he crossed the room to me. Was something wrong? Or had he simply tired at last of waiting?

He sat down upon the edge of the bed.

"Did I wake you?" he said.

"No, I wasn't asleep yet. What is it, Anthony? Has something happened?"

"No," he said. He reached across the counterpane to take my hand.

"May I lie here with you for a while tonight?" he asked.

"Oh, of course," I said. My throat was so full I could hardly speak; I didn't know whether it was alarm or a fragile joy that was nearly choking me. Perhaps it was both.

He took off his shoes and stretched out beside me. He was on top of the bedclothes and fully dressed; I lay beneath them in a heavy winter nightgown.

"You were wonderful today, you know," he said.

"I was afraid you'd be . . ."

I hesitated.

"Be what? Shocked by the things you said?"

"Shocked . . . or embarrassed. I ought to have told you about my infamous grandmother long ago instead of springing it on you like that."

"Oh, I don't know," he said with a laugh. "I rather enjoyed it."

Already he was starting to make me feel too good, just lying there next to me, talking in the dark, giving me the simplest and most precious lover's gift, the feeling of closeness, of being a part of something—not alone.

I turned over on my side to face him.

"I'm glad you're here," I whispered hesitantly.

He laid his hand over mine, interlacing our fingers lightly. That felt good, too. We lay that way for a long time, not saying anything, until his hand seemed as much a part of me as my own, as if the borders between our separate skins had dissolved away.

I knew this shouldn't be happening. Innocent as it was, I knew I would have to stop it before I started to need it too much. I'd had a letter from Poncet two days earlier. Again he wanted to raise the monthly payments. God only knew how I would manage to satisfy him. It couldn't last much longer.

"I've been wanting to kiss you all day," said my husband. That was all. He didn't move toward me. He just said it—a simple statement of truth, not a demand, not a rebuke.

My heart ached. Surely there was no danger in it. It was such a small thing; he'd been so patient with me and understanding, how could I withhold something as trivial as a kiss? What harm could it do to bestow that one tender favor?

I moved a little closer and slipped my left arm under his neck. With my right hand I began to stroke his hair. A frantic inner voice screamed at me to stop. I ignored it.

"Fleur?" said my husband, as if he didn't quite believe what was happening.

I opened my lips and brought them to his.

I never wanted it to end.

He kissed with the same languorous grace that characterized everything he did. He kissed as if that one kiss were everything he had ever wanted or could ever want. Even when he moved, so that he was above me, his body half covering me, he never tried to claim more of me than my mouth. All of his energy and concentration were invested in that kiss.

His mouth was so warm; his tongue's lazy exploration of the world behind my lips, so sweet; he tasted so good, so fresh.

I felt my own mouth grow more urgent.

All my careful resolutions to remain in control began to disintegrate. I wanted this to go on forever.

No, I wanted it to go further. . . .

I had forgotten that a kiss could be so seductive.

That was when he took his lips away. I stared up at him, silent with wonder.

He stood up.

"I'd better let you sleep," he said gently. "Good night, Fleur."

I was too dazed to answer him right away.

By the time I could have, he was gone.

I sat up dizzily and tried to comprehend what had happened.

That kiss . . . it had sent little waves of flame skittering through my veins. I could still feel them.

It was too much.

It wasn't enough.

He had said his door would always be open to me.

I opened the door into the gallery and started to walk toward the wing where he slept.

Already my courage was failing. What would happen if I arrived at his bed only to find that the fragile heat he'd sparked in me had dissipated. Or I came to him only to disappoint him once again, and this time in spite of the desire that brought me to his bed? Could I bear another night like the one in Athens, especially now, after the pure magic of his kiss?

My steps began to flag.

There was an open door on my left.

Beyond the threshold was the room where his mother had stayed during her visit with us.

I came slowly to a halt. Suddenly I was cold again.

By the dim light from the gallery, I could see into the vacant room. No trace of Lady Whitstone remained. It was as if she had never been there.

I shivered as I remembered the ruthless speed with which my husband had dispatched her. As unpleasant as she was, what had she done to be thrown out of his house with such chilly indifference? She'd asked a few rude questions and made a few disparaging remarks, that was all. Her crime was nothing compared to mine. And *she* was his own mother.

If he could do that to *her*, how would he treat *me* when the day of reckoning came, as it surely must?

I leaned weakly against the door frame.

I would have gone to him with that kiss still burning on my lips, holding nothing back. If he could wreck my first line of defense with a mere kiss, I could be sure that by the time I got up from his bed, he would have taken my heart. It wouldn't have fallen to him easily, but once it was his, it would be his forever.

Then I'd be lost beyond all hope.

There was no possibility of salvaging this marriage—it was built on sand and was sure to come crashing down.

When it did, I had to be able to walk away intact. I couldn't go, leaving part of myself irrevocably in the possession of a man in whose eyes, from that moment on, I would be only a traitor and a liar. A shameless adventuress whom he'd once been foolish enough to love. A woman without an ounce of integrity. A sham.

I knew that would be all he'd be able to see.

Even if the sham had been transformed into the real thing.

I turned around and went back to my room. The ache of loneliness, after that brief, illusory closeness, was almost more than I could bear. But at least it was familiar and manageable, unlike the imagined fate that had made me feel so weak and ill as I'd stood in the doorway of that empty, stripped-down bedroom.

I wondered how long it would be before the room where I now lay had that same stark, denuded look.

The following night my husband came to me again.

I hadn't yet gotten into bed. I'd been sitting by the window in an old nightdress, with a silver hairbrush in my hand. I wasn't using it. I was staring out into the blackness of the night trying to see where I'd taken the first wrong turn. Was it in sitting for those paintings? Should I have denied Frederick the pleasure it had given him? The pleasure it had given me?

Or had it been in paying Poncet for his silence? I still shuddered to think what would have become of me if I had not. Where would I be now? Certainly not here in this warm, luxurious room. . . .

My husband's knock interrupted my reverie.

My heart leaped and then faltered.

I knew what I had to do. I had to retrieve the ground that I'd lost the night before. I had been thinking about this all day, but I hadn't expected to have to act quite so soon.

I got up and opened the door to my husband.

He saw the hairbrush in my hand.

"Let me do that," he said, and led me back to the armchair in which I'd been sitting.

Reluctantly, knowing that it was a mistake, I handed him the brush.

He brought it to my temples. I closed my eyes for a moment and gave myself over to the sensuous pull of the soft bristles through my hair.

At last I forced myself to turn around. I reached out my hand to take the brush from him.

"Do you want me to stop?" said my husband. He looked surprised.

"Yes," I said. "I don't like that . . . what you were doing."

"You don't like it?" His voice was disbelieving.

"No. I don't like being touched. I'm sorry. I just don't."

My husband did not lay the brush upon my outstretched palm. "So you don't like being touched," he said.

There was no warmth in his voice at all. He struck the back of the brush against his left palm at the end of his sentence as if to give it a harsher emphasis.

"No, I'm sorry, but I don't."

"And I suppose you don't like being kissed either."

"That's right. I'm sorry."

"And last night you were just . . . being a dutiful wife."

"It was such a small thing . . . I thought it would make you happy."

"I see."

He began to stalk slowly up and down the room, still with the brush in his hand. At last he stopped, a few feet from me.

"Tell me something, Fleur," he said. His voice was so much colder than usual that I thought he must be angry, that his patience had worn out at last. When I met his eyes, they had an opaque, closed look. What were they hiding? Anger? Hurt? Or simply disbelief?

"I want to know more about this . . . aversion of yours," he said. "Is it that you dislike being touched? Or that you don't want *me* to touch you?"

What could he be thinking? That I was betraying him with somebody else? It was so absurd that I gasped with shocked laughter.

"I've told you," I exclaimed. "It's not you. It's me."

"Yes, so you've said," he conceded. "And it was the same with Frederick, too?"

"I've already told you so."

"So you have. You must forgive me for not quite understanding how you managed to have the happiest marriage in Paris although you couldn't stand your husband's touch. How did you make it work so well?"

"How can you ask me something like that?"

Now it was his turn to laugh.

"How can *I* ask you *that?*" he cried. Then he dropped his voice slightly. "Because I want to know, Fleur. I want you to tell me *how* you and Frederick were able to make each other so happy."

I felt a flash of rage. How dare he bring Frederick into this! But I knew it would be unwise to reveal my anger.

"Maybe I didn't make him happy," I said sulkily.

"Oh," he said. "Then I wonder who did."

I didn't answer.

"Well? Is *that* how you . . . managed, Fleur? By sharing him?" His voice dripped with something—whether it was disdain or sarcasm I couldn't tell.

I flung up my head.

"I don't know what Frederick did when he wasn't with me. I never asked."

I knew what he did. He drank. I'd shared him with wine, absinthe, champagne, and various aperitifs. His other loves were no mystery to me. They usually announced themselves fragrantly as soon as he got into bed. But it was no one's business but my own.

"And *I* thought you loved him," my husband was saying.

"You *know* I did!" That time I couldn't quite keep the anger out of my voice.

"I don't know anything, Fleur. If I did, I wouldn't be asking."

The house of cards was already beginning to fall.

I moved round to the back of the chair, so that it was between him and me.

"I don't believe what you've been telling me," he was saying. His voice had softened a little; it wasn't quite so icy, but it was still much harder than usual. "I don't believe that you couldn't bear his touch. I don't believe that you loved him but didn't care what he did or with whom he did it when he was apart from you. I don't believe that you could love any man the way you loved him and not give a damn whether or not he went to other women. Maybe it's true. But I don't believe it."

"Well, I can't help that," I said. "That side of marriage that you're so concerned about . . . for some people it's not all that important."

To my amazement, my husband began to laugh again.

"I'm sure you're right," he said. Somehow I felt he was mocking me. "But *I'm* not one of those people. And I don't believe that you are either. Or that you always were."

He waited.

I looked down at my hands. They were clutching the back of the chair. My knuckles were white.

"What happened, Fleur?" he asked softly. "What happened to you between the day we went to Fontainebleau and the day you married me?"

I felt myself go pale.

"I don't know what you're talking about," I whispered.

He gave me a long stare and then shook his head, as if I were some kind of equation he couldn't solve.

"That won't do, Fleur," he said. "It's time we got to the bottom of this." He sounded tired now, and he looked tired as he lowered himself onto the edge of my bed. "It may take a while; why don't you sit down."

I didn't move.

"What is this, an inquisition?" I asked.

I hadn't intended for it to come out the way it did. I suppose it was fear that put the cutting words in my mouth and gave my voice its defensive edge.

I saw my husband's face darken with anger. Then it became impassive.

"Well, if that's how you feel, I'll end it," he said with a shrug. He stood up. "But not until you've answered one question. I want to know what you were feeling when you kissed me last night."

That was easy.

"I wanted to make you happy," I repeated.

He met this with another short laugh.

"No, Fleur," he said. "That's not what I asked you. I asked you what you were *feeling*."

I thought of the intoxicating river of happiness, warmth, pleasure, and desire that had carried me along as I'd given myself over to his confident lips, his warm, wandering tongue. There were a thousand words I might have used—seduced, subverted, lost, longing, scared, captivated, hungry. But one word kept racing ahead of the others. Happy. I had felt dangerously happy.

"Nothing," I whispered.

"Nothing," he repeated. "You mean it gave you no pleasure, no pleasure at all. You simply did it to please me. But it didn't please you."

"That's right," I said. "I've told you, that whole aspect of marriage is disagreeable to me. I know you were hoping that if you waited long enough, I might change. But I *can't* change. I can see how much you want to give me pleasure. But you can't. I wanted last night to be different, too. But I can't help what I don't feel."

He turned away from me then and seemed lost in his own thoughts as he crossed the room to the doorway. Then he lifted his head.

"It's clear that you don't want to talk about this," he said. I stood in guilty, frozen silence, not looking at him.

At last he spoke again.

"I expected more from you, Fleur," he told me.

I was so nervous about facing him the following day that I did not come down to breakfast until very late. I hoped I would have the dining room to myself, but he was still there. I could tell from the way he greeted me, and from the note of his voice as we avoided the subject that weighed upon both our minds and instead spoke of insignificant things, that he regretted the harsh note he had struck with me the previous night.

I felt inordinately relieved. Now that the uncomfortable subject had been thrust back into the shadows again, I hoped he would leave it there for a long time.

Late that same morning my husband left for London and stayed there for a day or two. His manner to me, when he returned to Charingworth, was as kind and patient as ever. But no longer did he come to my bedroom—not to brush my hair, not to lie beside me and talk idly about the events of the day, not to take my hand or to taste my lips.

Although I hoped that this alteration in our relationship would make our life easier, by eliminating the greatest source of tension between us, it did not improve matters. I knew that he had a profound sense of honor, and his manner told me that he still loved me. That alone would keep him faithful, although I had given him nothing to be faithful to.

I could not shake off my bitter awareness of how greatly I had failed him. I brooded upon this constantly; it did not improve my spirits. The self-accusations did not remedy the trouble; they merely affixed the blame.

And although I knew that I was being unreasonable and unjust, I began to grow more critical of my husband, as well. My impression of latent power, which had once made his slow, lazy grace so attractive to me, had been false. He was merely phlegmatic. How else could he have come to accept the grave imperfections of our marriage with such calm imperturbability, leaving any responsibility for trying to overcome them entirely to me?

What could *I* do? I had already tried everything—and everything had failed.

Sometimes I tried to imagine the kind of woman who might have pleased my husband better, but this was a futile exercise. I was never able to envision some wonderful lady whom I might take as a model. All I could see were wispy images of myself—not as I was now, but as I had been in the early years with Frederick.

I knew now I could never produce a convincing imitation of *that* glowing creature—she had been dead for years and was now as unfathomable a stranger as I sometimes felt my own husband to be. And although he might yearn for some modest signs of passion, *that* could not be the woman he looked for in me. He had never laid eyes upon her, she had vanished long before he met me.

And she was surely the last woman who could have pleased him. She was the reckless, shameless creature who had posed for the paintings that were the source of all the trouble.

XV

Of all the staff at Charingworth, it was Watkins, my husband's exacting head groom, by whom I felt most overawed and yet with whom I was most comfortable. Upon my arrival, I had expected the entire household to treat me with thinly veiled scorn due to my plebian background and my inexperience with the role of chatelaine. But this was not the case.

Nearly all the staff, however, had a somewhat independent air. They had welcomed me cordially and behaved respectfully. But while there appeared to be no underlying disdain, it was clear that they were observing me carefully, reserving judgment, always watchful.

Watkins was the most forthcoming. He seemed to approve of my passion for riding and the readiness with which I welcomed any advice he could offer that might improve my skill and knowledge. He also provided me with a circumspect family history by means of anecdotes from the stables. From these I gathered that my husband's father had not been particularly fond of horses and was, in fact, somewhat intimidated by all but the most docile mounts. In contrast, Watkins confided to me, the former Lady Camwell, now Lady Whitstone, had a heavy, rather cruel hand with the bit and used the crop too freely. But my husband was a real horseman, he told me.

"He's not like his father, you know," the old groom said. He gave me a keen look. "Sir Anthony holds the reins very lightly. But don't let that deceive you. He always knows exactly what he's doing."

Since I was well acquainted with my husband's skill in the saddle, I wondered what had impelled Watkins to make this point so portentously. I supposed it was pride in his employer.

But if it was, there was nothing servile in it. And, conversely, it seemed that my husband was able to dispense with his stiff admixture of hauteur and diffidence when he was around the shrewd old man—at least when I was not present. I knew this because I came upon them once, unexpectedly.

I remember the day, because I had quarreled with my husband that morning—well, perhaps it was not exactly a quarrel, for we never quarreled, but we had had another slight disagreement.

I thought I had glimpsed a small but unmistakable flicker of distaste in my husband's eye when I had appeared at the breakfast table in one of my very oldest and plainest gowns, and somewhat later he interrupted the silence of our meal by saying, "I shall be going to London at the end of the week. Would you care to join me?"

I thought this an odd request. It had been some time since he had sought my company in town.

"I really have no reason to go to London," I said thoughtlessly, and then wished that I had chosen more tactful words of refusal.

My husband looked down at his empty plate as if he were committing the design on it to memory. Finally he raised his eyes again and said, "I would like to have you fitted for some new clothes. You seem badly in need of them."

I would have dearly loved some new gowns, but it had become a peculiar point of pride for me to wear my old ones. By this means, I was able to assure myself that I had not married him basely, to indulge my appetite for luxuries, but only to save myself from ruin.

"No, thank you," I said. "Perhaps my gowns do not meet *your* exacting standards, but they suit me very well. My tastes are simple. Besides, I am sure I would find the fittings very tiresome."

My husband pushed back his chair and stood up abruptly, bestowing upon me a look of sheer exasperation. I thought he was about to speak, but he seemed to swallow the words that trembled on his tongue.

"You are angry," I said, surprised.

He bit his lip and then either his expression changed or I was able to read it better. He almost looked as if the insignificant rebuff had wounded him.

"No," he said. "I don't wish to impose my tastes upon you."

For a moment I wished that he would. It does me no credit, I know, but that is what passed through my mind in the brief interval before he turned and left me: I thought what a great relief it would be to be swept forward under the power of a personality stronger than my own, to be carried away despite my own leaden inertia, and with little or no regard for my will.

The feeling passed, or perhaps I pushed it away. I merely shrugged as he departed without another word. It was a fine day, and after lingering over my breakfast, I decided to change into one of my riding habits—for in this department, I was not too proud to accept my husband's generosity—and to take Andromeda out.

As I walked toward the stables, I saw my husband and Watkins so deep in conversation that at first neither of them was aware of my approach. My husband was leaning against the door frame, his hands in his pockets. Everything in his demeanor was relaxed, except for the intensity of his expression as he listened to the words of his ancient groom. His head was bent, his eyes narrowed, and a little smile that gave his face a look of mingled regret and amusement played across his handsome features. There seemed something so intimate about the conversation that, had the groom not been so very old and had his rough clothes not contrasted so greatly with those of my polished husband, they might almost have been father and son.

But now Watkins had observed my presence, and as I came within earshot, I heard him say, as if to seal the discussion, "Well, you know what I think. She's a sound little filly all right, but she needs a touch of the crop to soften her."

My husband looked startled, then lifted his head and broke into laughter. The late autumn sunlight gleamed on his hair and his teeth flashed. I felt a sharp, poignant thrust, as I realized suddenly that he was still a very young man. Ordinarily his youthfulness was concealed by his air of cool dignity.

My husband saw me, and his easy laughter and the charm of his expression faded. I felt a momentary envy of the humble Watkins, who seemed able to evoke that vanished aspect of the man I had married.

"I hardly think that's called for," said my husband in response to Watkins's remark. Then he glanced again in my direction and the now unfamiliar sparkle returned to his eyes. "Although, I must say, the idea *has* got a certain appeal."

My nerves tingled. I ignored the curious sensation.

"How dare you speak of my horse that way!" I exclaimed. Andromeda was the only filly in our stable. Their presumptuous discussion of her outraged me.

I saw Watkins give my husband a piercing, knowing look.

"I assure you, my dear," said my husband, now with his customary grave politeness, "we were not speaking of Andromeda. Are you taking her out?"

"Yes, it's too lovely a day to waste indoors," I said, slightly embarrassed by my furious outburst. I supposed my husband must be thinking of buying another horse. Apparently the two men had been discussing the strengths and weaknesses of the animal which had caught his eye.

"Well, enjoy your ride."

With that, my husband turned his attention back to the groom.

I wished perversely that he had offered me his company, but our rides together were already a thing of the past.

Upon joining such a respectable English family, I had supposed that I must become a dutiful churchgoer. Frederick had held fashionably agnostic views, and I—having witnessed a little religious hypocrisy during my youth in England and having learned a great deal more about it from my grandmother—was an even greater skeptic. But sometimes, when I was out in the countryside astride Andromeda, I would be swept with a restrained but powerful pantheistic fervor.

Nor was my husband particularly devout; it seemed that he attended our village church primarily to maintain his connections to the community, and with what I considered ostentatious humility, he did not even take his seat in the Camwell family's special pew.

I regarded my husband's attendance at the services he did not find particularly instructive or uplifting as silly and hypocritical. I implied this in a comment I made the first time I accompanied him to the little stone church. I had gone chiefly because I was bored. Once or twice the sermon nearly made me giggle, but more often than not the platitudes had me gritting my teeth.

"I can't imagine why you bother to attend," I said afterward. "You don't take it any more seriously than I do. You really go only to polish that upright image of yours, don't you?"

"Not entirely," replied my husband calmly. He could never be provoked to rise to the bait on the rare occasions when I yielded to an unkind urge to needle him. "It's true that I put little faith in conventional dogma, but I do find much to admire in Christianity. The sermons, I'll grant you, tend to be dull and disappointingly shallow—I'm always astonished that a gentleman of such limited imagination would choose what surely ought to be the most challenging and demanding of professions. But it's a living, of course." He smiled wryly at his own slight joke. "And I do believe that, in certain ways at least, the Christian faith has had both a radical and a civilizing influence."

"Civilizing!" I exclaimed. "What *can* you be thinking of? The bloody Inquisition? The Crusades? The persecutions of the Jews? The slave trade? Or was it the burning of witches that you had in mind?"

"Not at all," he replied in his unruffled way. "But surely you'll admit that, whatever the failings of its practitioners may be, Christianity's original precepts are quite remarkable. If you doubt that, try to imagine a time when retribution was the only law. Then think how utterly revolutionary it must have been to suggest that only someone without sin ought to cast the first stone. Isn't that the very essence of a compassionate morality?"

I laughed. "Do you know anyone in England who lives by that code?"

"Don't *you?*" he asked, and I fell into silence.

In spite of such exchanges, I was not often unkind to my husband. Generally, I lashed out only when I felt he was pushing me to display some emotion I could not feel or to make some response when I wished only to be left alone.

But most of the time I felt saddened when I thought of his empty, joyless life, so earnestly and responsibly conducted—and I tried very hard to behave well. Before our marriage I had supposed that once we were in England the ties of family and society would compensate my husband at least in part for my own limitations. But he had no close family ties other than to Neville Marsden, whom we rarely saw anymore, for, to my enormous regret, some slight coldness seemed to have arisen between the cousins.

Moreover, my husband cared as little for country society as I did. He had taken the unrest in Ireland and the agricultural depression in England seriously enough to slash his tenants' rents, which was a major cause of the bad blood between him and the rack-rent Sparlings.

His interest in agriculture I thought very dull. Although we both shared a passion for the outdoors, it did not provide much common ground. Mine was a romantic love of Nature; his, a practical concern with science and natural history.

But still he was always kind to me, and except for my little flare-ups, which were very few and far between, I managed to curb the tongue which guilt and depression had begun to hone to a razor edge.

There was the matter of the camera, for example.

If there was one invention that I detested, it was the camera. In my hierarchy, the medium of paint and canvas soared far above that of the soulless, treated plates that merely absorb whatever image the lens admits.

This had become one of my small, private objections to my husband. I would have preferred that he have no artistic impulses at all, but he had the very worst—he was an amateur photographer.

I did not discover this, however, until I came to Charingworth, at which point I concluded that it was by far the silliest of all his interests and thanked heaven that he never insisted, after my earliest refusals, on attempting to capture *my* image.

He once showed me two or three examples of what he regarded as his best efforts: one was a portrait of Watkins that bespoke the man's character better than any words I could write here; another was a stunningly natural picture of one of the village boys proudly holding a catapult. And how had he coaxed his restless subject into remaining so patient and cheerful during the long exposure? By promising the child the portrait as a present for his mother, and by answering all his questions about the camera's workings.

I told him they were very good, and never admitted my aversion to his hobby. Of course, I did not tell him quite how *fine* I thought them. He was, after all, a dilettante. The superb quality of these particular portraits could only be a happy fluke, and I did not wish to encourage his love of the camera.

We had been married for nearly seven months, our amiable estrangement deepening daily, when, one evening in March, I arrived at the dinner table to find a small package, beautifully wrapped and tied, at my place. I opened the card.

"To Fleur. With my love, which is as constant and enduring as these. Anthony," I read.

Oh, was there really no end to it! He had stopped proclaiming his love for me months ago, and I no longer needed it—I had cured myself of *that* by keeping my distance and by focusing on the inevitable final separation. We did not share a bed and often did not even sleep under the same roof.

Why had he chosen this moment to shame me with such a reminder, however subtle and well meant, of an emotion which I'd dared to hope had faded to mere affection?

"Won't you open it?" he said.

Uneasily, I removed the wrappings and lifted the cover of the green velvet jeweler's case within. There lay a spectacular diamond necklace, made in the dog-collar style, like the ones Princess Alexandra wore to cover a scar on her throat, a style that had been instantly adopted by virtually every lady of fashion.

I appraised it with my grandmother's eye and reeled at the thought of what it must have cost him.

"It's very lovely," I said, closing the box and trying to force some warmth into my voice. "Thank you, Anthony."

My husband arose from his chair and came to where I sat. He opened the velvet case once again, lifted out the jewels, and fastened them around my neck. They lay there heavily, like ice against my skin, a blatant symbol of possession.

As soon as I was able to retire to my room, I did so, on the grounds that my head ached. An hour or so later there was a tap at my door, so soft that it would not have awakened me had I been sleeping. It was my husband, who had not come to my room for months. Leaving the door open to admit the light from the passage, he entered.

"How do you feel?" he asked me softly. "Is there anything I can do for you?"

"No, thank you. My head is no better. When it aches like this, sleep is the only help for it."

"And how are you otherwise?"

"I beg your pardon?"

I saw his slender black silhouette merge with that of an armchair which stood near the foot of my bed.

"You are not well, Fleur. You grow thinner every day. If this goes on, soon you will not even cast a shadow."

"Don't be ridiculous, Anthony. I have always been thin."

"And have you always been so wretchedly unhappy?" he asked.

I was so astounded by the forthrightness I thought I had long ago discouraged forever that I did not know how to answer. Fortunately, he spared me.

"I have tried to respect your delicacy, Fleur," he said, "your disinclination to unburden your heart to me. But I cannot remain silent any longer. It will not do. My hesitation to insist upon confronting your difficulties—whatever they may be—has already driven us apart. Perhaps *that* can never be mended. But something continues to eat away at you before my very eyes. I cannot simply watch and do nothing."

I remained speechless.

"I know that I have wronged you," he continued preposterously. "I have no right to ask for your forgiveness and your trust. But I do. I would do anything to restore your happiness; I would make any sacrifice."

"*You* have wronged *me?*" I finally managed to articulate in a whisper.

"Most assuredly I have wronged you. I know it. You must know it, too. I was too hasty, too eager to make you mine. You were not an unhappy woman when I knew you in Paris, Fleur. But I pressed my suit too quickly and carried you away—perhaps before you were ready to close that chapter of your life. I think . . ." Here he stumbled, but then went on. "I think that you confused an affection which might have developed into love, under more favorable conditions, with love itself."

I felt as if he had knocked the wind out of me.

"You are mistaken, Anthony," I choked out.

"Tell me how."

I tried to say more, but my breath was too ragged.

"My head hurts far too much to have such a conversation now," I whispered at last, hoping the evil moment might be postponed forever.

"But you must have it soon. If not with me, then with *someone* in whom you have faith and confidence. I fear for you, Fleur. Few things can destroy you so long as you face them bravely. Bring your dragons out into the light and stare them down in the open —with someone at your side. It's the only hope. If you go slinking after them into their murky caves, they'll eat you alive. I ought to have said this months ago, but I've been reluctant to impose my own convictions on you. As a result, I've let you suffer far too long —I am ashamed of my cowardice. Now I am begging you to open your heart. Surely you know you have nothing to fear from me."

My heart! That Pandora's box of grief and despair, bitterness, and lies.

"You have nothing to be ashamed of, Anthony," I whispered at last. But there I halted, unable to exonerate him further without incriminating myself. Finally, I said sadly, "I could not ask for a better husband. My low spirits have nothing to do with you. I have suffered from them for years. Perhaps *I* was too hasty in agreeing to become your wife; I ought to have given you time to know me better. Then you might have discovered that I have no dragons—only moods."

My husband considered this sorry blend of fact and fiction in silence for a moment or two.

"And that is all you will say on the subject?" he said.

If only I could say more! If only I could trust him! If only he were not quite so *good,* so upright and virtuous! If only he had had one or two little weaknesses that might have enabled him to comprehend my own!

"It is all I *can* say!" I whispered brokenly.

I could not see his face as his dark shape disengaged itself from that of the chair. He moved toward the light-filled doorway. For a moment he stood there, looking back at me. At last he turned away. The door closed behind him and the light was gone.

XVI

As soon as I awoke on the following morning, fragments of my husband's latest appeal for honesty drifted back to haunt me. I sat up among the bed pillows to sip my coffee from an eggshell porcelain cup, and heard again his calm and level voice begging me to open my heart to him—or to someone—and promising me his support.

But was it possible? Could anyone be so selfless as to forgive entirely? He had said he would make any sacrifice for me; was he prepared even to let me go? Could he really be willing to end the sad charade?

No one, of course, could dissolve a marriage merely for the lack of love. Lovelessness might drag a couple down as surely as a millstone tied about their necks, but it carried no weight in the courts. Nevertheless, there was no reason for us to remain together. Life would be so much easier for both of us if we were to live apart. And my husband *could* set me free in body and spirit if not in name, if he chose. At least there was no child on the way to complicate a separation! Then I could return to Paris, where at least I had friends.

But if he did release me—oh, here was the rub—would he yet

provide for me sufficiently so that I might continue to toss bones to that insatiable monster Poncet, who was forever snapping at my heels? And for how much longer would the monster remain satisfied with bones?

Not long at all, it seemed: That morning's post brought a letter from Paris. The brownish envelope, with its French stamp and no return address, had a familiar look. It would be yet another notice from my persecutor. Amidst profuse apologies, he would announce that once again he must raise the stakes. I could hardly bear to contemplate what this would mean for me.

Well, there was still my grandmother's jewelry.

I opened the envelope, expecting the usual request. But this one was different.

"You must come to Paris immediately," Poncet had scrawled. "It has become necessary to renegotiate our arrangement."

I had no idea what this cryptic and alarming message implied, but I was far too frightened of what he might do to ignore the imperious summons. I sent him a note to advise him that I would leave for Paris immediately.

Then I told my husband I had received word that my dear friend Marguerite was ill.

"Madame Sorrel ill?" he exclaimed. Two fine little creases appeared between his eyebrows. "Why, I had no idea!"

I couldn't imagine why he might; she was, after all, my friend, not his.

"Is it serious?" he asked. His whole demeanor suggested the gravest concern.

"I think not. She says it is merely fatigue—that she has been working too hard. But still I would like to see her to assure myself that it is nothing more."

The clouds left my husband's face; his expression became almost hopeful.

"Oh, but of course," he said eagerly. "You must go to her at once."

He urged me to let him know if there was anything he might do on Marguerite's behalf or to make my journey easier. He even gave me money for the trip.

I realized then that he suspected Marguerite's illness of being a mere invention to conceal my true reason for traveling to Paris; he had come to the happy conclusion that I had decided to follow his advice. To think of it! This man, knowing I could not bring myself to confide in him, was yet so generous as to feel relief in supposing that I was going off to pour my secrets into the ear of my closest friend!

When I bade him farewell, it was with uncharacteristic warmth and deep sadness.

Since my last visit to him, Poncet had moved his place of business to larger quarters and had outfitted these even more ostentatiously than his previous ones. A rather plain-faced, bespectacled young woman, who projected an air of enormous self-possession, presided over a rococo little writing table in the front salon. She rose as I entered and started to inquire how she might help me. But then her face turned crimson. I knew instantly that she had recognized me, and that she fully understood the reason for my visit.

We stared at each other in silence.

She too much resembled the stolid-featured Poncet to be anyone but his daughter. The spectacles magnified her eyes tremendously. But to my amazement what I saw in those two great, limpid pools was not scorn or condemnation. It was distress.

"Please excuse me, Lady Camwell," she stammered at last.

Without another word, she turned and disappeared into a little passage at the back of the salon. Soon I heard, from the rear of the shop into which she had vanished, a murmur of voices and then a man's voice raised in anger. I could not discern his words. Then the woman's voice—higher and clearer—cried, "And *you* led me to believe that you had thought better of it!"

A door slammed.

A few minutes later, Poncet himself appeared, alone.

He was more extravagantly well dressed than before, and although he wore an unhappily preoccupied expression as he stepped into the room where I awaited him, he routed the shadows from his face at the sight of me and greeted me as unctuously as if he had not a care in the world.

"Oh, just tell me the purpose of this meeting," I snapped, cutting off his effusions.

We sat down facing each other across the recently vacated writing table.

"I have been waiting for you to purchase the paintings outright," said he, "now that your circumstances are so improved. But during all these months, you have not done so, although I know that you have the means. I've been patient for as long as I can, but my expenses are increasing. There is simply no way I can continue our arrangement on the present terms."

"Yes, yes," I said impatiently. "You need something more than what I have been paying. Tell me how much. You might have done it by letter. There was no need to waste my time with this journey."

As if I had anything better to do with my time!

"You misunderstand me," he said. "I cannot continue our arrangement on *any* terms. I have virtually no choice but to auction the paintings, as we discussed so long ago."

I froze.

"However," he said, "as a courtesy to that *most* upstanding and respectable gentleman, your husband—who, I am certain, would prefer to have their existence remain a secret—I am prepared to offer him the paintings outright for the price that I quoted to you some time ago. Of course, if *you* can come up with the money yourself, there will be no need for me to approach the baronet."

I stared at him across the table, nearly blind with despair. I could always sell a few more of my grandmother's jewels and buy a few more months, but in the end it would inevitably come to this.

My husband had begged me for the truth. Now he would learn it, but not from me.

"Do as you must," I said wearily and left.

Then I did call upon Marguerite. Théo was not at home, but the sunny rooms of my friend's splendidly furnished house and her equally sunny manner proclaimed the couple were living well.

Marguerite, who had not known I was in Paris, welcomed me with her usual effervescence.

"Fleur," she said, "how wonderful to see you. It has been far too long. Théo will be wretched that he missed you. Sit down. Will you have something to eat or drink? You look a little *faible.* Is everything well with you? What has finally brought you to Paris? Does the *distingué* baronet accompany you?"

"I am here because you have been so ill," I said. "The distinguished baronet remains in England but sends his best wishes for your speedy recovery."

"Ah," said Marguerite with a frown. "Am I the pretext for an amorous tryst? That seems very unlike you, Fleur. Are you sure it is wise? Oh well, how long must I languish?"

"The tryst is over," I answered. "And it was hardly amorous."

For one of the few times in my life, I actually did attempt to pour out my troubles. But once I had begun, I found myself relating the sorry tale in the same brittle manner with which I had parried her initial questions.

Even so, my friend listened quietly and with sympathy.

"Oh, but you must tell your husband *everything,*" she declared the very instant I had finished.

"Are you mad! I can't possibly do that!"

"He will find it out anyway," she pointed out sensibly. "Isn't it better for him to hear it from you than from a scoundrel, who may twist the truth in ways that you cannot imagine. Besides, Anthony seems to be such a good man. Surely he deserves to hear the story from *your* lips."

"He *is* a good man, Marguerite. That's the trouble. He is *so* good, I cannot bear it! Even when I lose my temper and am unkind to him, he never changes."

"Then what is there to fear? Perhaps the truth will even provoke him enough to show more spirit. And did he not say that he would do anything for you? You ought to have told him then. He must love you, Fleur—God knows why, for I don't believe he is one of those men who *likes* to be treated badly," she added wickedly.

"It is impossible," I said. "I could *never* tell Anthony myself. I think I would rather have him believe the worst inventions about me than to subject the truth to his judgment."

I recalled once again, this time with a sharp, unexpected pang that burned for only an instant, how he had defended me against his mother. She had goaded him numerous times in the course of her visit; the insults had seemed to roll off his back. I had never spoken up for him except on that single occasion when he had asked me, so casually, for my opinion of the subtle abuse she was showering upon him. Yet the very instant that lady had unsheathed her claws to me, he had sent her packing. As he would, no doubt, soon have occasion to do with me.

"Don't be a fool, Fleur. Tell him the whole truth. Not only about the paintings—I'm sure they can be nothing to be ashamed of—but about everything. Of course, it will wound him—after all, he is in love with you. But if it shakes him out of that equanimity you seem to find so aggravating, would that be entirely a bad thing? Think what a great relief it will be to have everything out in the open! If anything can breathe life into your marriage, it will be honesty."

"Nothing could breathe life into that marriage!" I cried. "It's too late."

"I don't see why. You have not said one thing that reflects badly upon your husband. Really, he sounds quite wonderful. Why do you assume that he could never understand and forgive?"

"There are some weaknesses a man like that could not possibly understand, much less forgive. You can't imagine what it's like to be married to Sir Galahad!"

My friend fell into a reverie, her expression very sad. At last she roused herself and said, more briskly, "I have told you what I think is right. But you know your situation better than anyone, and you must do as you think best. I believe that you will be making a terrible mistake if you do not go to Anthony with the truth—and quickly, before someone else does. He deserves that from you. But whatever you decide, Fleur, I wish you well. Never, never forget that you will *always* have a friend in me."

I returned to Charingworth and told my husband that Marguerite had been suffering merely from exhaustion. I offered no further account of my visit. For a day or two my husband seemed to watch me with a hopeful, expectant air, but fortunately he never pressed me to reveal what had actually taken place across the Channel.

On the third day, he left for London and remained away for more than a fortnight.

As usual, my husband's absence only made me feel my loneliness and isolation more keenly than ever.

From time to time, I forced myself to reflect upon Marguerite's advice. In my heart, I knew that she was right. Yet, when I tried mentally to rehearse the words I might use to present my husband with the awful truth, I could not imagine finding the courage to speak them.

On the day he was to return to Charingworth, I took Andromeda out for a long ride. It had rained during the night, but now the late March air was clear and fresh. As I rode between the wooded hillsides and the rolling meadows, with their hedgerows about to come into leaf, I began to feel stronger and more hopeful. The world had a clean and polished look. I had the swift urge to do some spiritual housecleaning myself, whatever the consequence might be. Perhaps I *could* face my husband with the truth.

For a long time I wrestled with my pride, but there was no avoiding the fact that there was only one high road open to me. My husband had been right. Marguerite had been right. Nothing would do but honesty.

So, at last, I began to frame the words by which I would confess to my husband simply and fully all that had driven me to marry him and by which I would admit that my claims to love him had been no more than desperate lies.

I could only imagine the pain this would cause him, but certainly my inept deceptions had not spared him much pain. I remembered the unspoken sadness I had felt the first night that I had lain in his arms. My confession would deal the death blow to any illusions he might still cherish about me, but the fatal illness had taken hold the day he gave me his name.

There was no longer any way to sustain the fraud. The one honorable thing I could do now was to let him hear the truth from my lips—not Poncet's.

I knew that I still had time to act. No dreaded envelope from France had yet arrived by post for him: I had been keeping a careful watch.

But when I turned Andromeda's head back toward the house, my resolve began to waver. The whole business made me feel small and unworthy. Was *that* perhaps the real source of my antipathy toward my husband—that his incorruptible goodness made me feel so shabby? It took all my will to maintain my sense of purpose. Could I cling to it until his return?

"Oh, my lady," said Mrs. Phillips, rushing up to me as soon as I came through the doorway. "Sir Anthony has come home and wishes to speak with you in the library."

I thought this very odd. We had grown so far apart that it was remarkable now for my husband to request my presence anywhere.

I felt a clutch of apprehension. It gripped me even tighter as, after having changed from my riding clothes into a dreary little gown, I descended the stairway to welcome my husband home.

XVII

My husband was standing, staring out of the library windows. He turned slowly as I entered the room. He looked amused. I shut the doors behind me.

He held up a brown envelope bearing a French stamp. "I suppose you know what this is," he said.

How had it arrived without my seeing it! I wavered in confusion for a moment, then steadied my resolve.

"I will explain it to you, Anthony," I said in a low voice.

"Why trouble yourself now?" he responded carelessly. "This invitation to a private viewing arrived at Grosvenor Square over a fortnight ago. As you may imagine, it took me immediately to France."

I closed my eyes.

"And as a result," continued my husband in the same pleasant tone, "I have acquired a remarkable collection of paintings. Come and have a look—I'd like to know what you think of them."

"I am sure you know what I think of them," I said. My back was against the doors; they were all that kept me upright.

"Well, yes," said he agreeably, "I suppose I do. After all, you've advanced a considerable amount of money for them. Not that it's spared me from paying the extortionist's price."

I brought my eyes to his and nearly reeled under the disdain I saw expressed there. The kindly concern I had taken for granted for so long had vanished, but not his customary dispassionate, exasperating calm.

"I thought you were a woman of . . . delicate sensibilities," he went on with a little laugh. "I've been deceived."

The coldness of his laugh hit me like a slap.

Was this my patient, tender husband?

I had not forgotten his remarks about casting the first stone. I had consoled myself with them all that morning; they had given me courage. But now those high-minded sentiments were proving to be so lightly anchored that they had gone adrift in the first hard breeze. Perhaps, being virtually without sin himself, he did not feel enjoined by the Biblical precept. But to think that he would have the sanctimonious arrogance to condemn me for those paintings, for having loved Frederick enough to sit for them! I had always behaved as if I thought this must be true, but nevertheless it was a shock to look at his face now and to see there the contempt, the stern, puritanical, ungenerous judgment.

I leaned my head back against the doors and felt something pass out of me like a pain or a fever. When it was gone, it left me harder—and emptier—than before. I straightened my spine and looked directly into my husband's eyes.

"I have often wondered why you married me," he was saying quietly. "You wasted no time in revealing your lack of desire. For a long while, I supposed that your passions had been somehow repressed. I thought that perhaps your late husband was not as gentle with you as he might have been. Or that it was a reaction to your . . . unfortunate antecedents. Now the mystery has been explained."

The scathing reference to my "antecedents" rankled. So, after all, he was his mother's son.

"If it's passion you want," I said in a scornful, brittle tone, of which even an hour ago I would never have dreamed myself capable, "or at least a fair imitation of it, perhaps you ought to take a mistress."

Something flickered in his eyes. He might have been furious. He might as easily have been enjoying himself. It was impossible to tell.

"Why should I continue to squander a fortune upon my mistresses," he asked, "when I have such a wanton under my own roof, and one who's cost me more than all of them together?"

Nothing in his steady voice revealed what emotions lay beneath his cool self-possession.

I managed to keep my face expressionless, but my throat tightened at the implication. I had expected the paintings to scandalize him, but never that they might spur him to resume those forays beneath my bedclothes. He must have sensed my revulsion.

"Oh, you need not fear that I will hold you in a loveless marriage," he said. "But I *will* put a small price on your freedom."

"Oh? And what is the ransom you have set?"

"These paintings of which you are so fond," he said, "suggest that you have far greater talent and enthusiasm for the . . . business of love . . . than you have ever given me reason to suspect. I'd like to see more evidence of it."

"Love isn't a business," I said.

"So I once thought, but it seems that it is. And in that spirit, let me state the terms on which I'll set you free. There are five paintings. You may buy each one of them back from me—in kind. If you are cooperative and really exert yourself to please me, you will leave here with enough money to live very comfortably for the rest of your life."

I know my composure must have failed me then. I could scarcely imagine anything more odious than being forced to perform for this man—who had astonishingly begun to inspire real fear and real hatred in me.

"You seem less than avid," he observed. "Perhaps my offer doesn't entice you. That's all right. If you prefer, we can go along as we are. Of course," he added, his voice hardening, "I ought to warn you straight out that I will assert my rights far more . . . vigorously than I have done in the past."

For an instant, then, as he was speaking, I glimpsed the fury that underlay his calm demeanor. The cobra had lifted his hood.

"And if I should agree to your proposal," I asked, "how long will this farce go on?"

"Not long. No more than a few months, I should think. I haven't found a mistress yet who can hold my interest longer. Of course, I would expect you to provide me with more amusement than most. You were a great disappointment the first time out, but I see now that all you lacked was the proper motivation."

I felt as helpless as a fish twisting in a net. My gaze skipped around the room. On the small table to my right a pensive little nymph fashioned in bronze sat cradled between the horns of a crescent moon. My fingers twitched. I longed to hurl that graceful *objet* through the mullioned window behind my husband. I longed to shatter his restraint and, with it, the civilized, deadly peacefulness of my splendid prison.

Perhaps my husband's fair head offered an even better target. That he could be capable of such casual cruelty, and worse, that he could actually take pleasure in it, made me long more than ever to break free of him at almost any price. But not at the price of hanging for his murder.

Therefore I was obliged to weigh his proposal.

Well, what would it cost me really? A month or two of deadening my sensibilities. This was a skill I had perfected; surely I could withstand a few more of my husband's uninspiring assaults.

So I replied in an easier tone, "You give me little choice. No one would dispute that a few months of bondage is preferable to a lifetime of it."

"Surely not." He smiled. "So we're agreed."

My silence was my assent. He understood.

"Well," said he, sounding very pleased with the outcome. "I think such a bargain demands evidence of good faith. Why don't you come here and demonstrate your readiness to gratify my every wish."

A sickly wave, first cold, then hot, surged through me. I inched toward him guardedly. When I was perhaps a foot or two away, he stepped toward me and took my hot face between his cool palms. There was no affection in the kiss which followed. It was the purest assertion of power. I understood what he wanted of me. Only once had I ever opened my lips to him when we kissed. But the danger it had formerly posed was gone.

Now, as an emblem of defeat, I parted my lips enough to permit the unwelcome invasion. But the heat of his mouth and the careless assurance with which he took possession of mine still stirred me faintly and perversely. Already his new indifference to my own hungers—or, more accurately, to my lack of them—had begun to release me from my burden of guilt; the effect was curious and not entirely unpleasant.

Nevertheless, I pushed him away.

"That was delicious," he said, "although somewhat more grudging than I will expect from you in the future."

His eyes were full of an even greater scorn than I had seen in them previously, as if he despised me for having yielded. Feeling slightly ashamed, I wondered what he might have done if I had not.

"I don't know why you are looking so wretched," he said, as if mistaking hatred for misery. "After all, five nights of obedience and unstinting generosity is a very small price to pay. If you satisfy me in that respect, I'll consider your debt paid. And I think you'll find the next few months tolerable, since we shall see so little of each other. I may visit you here on occasion, but I will not live in this house again until you are gone from it forever. And meanwhile, *you* are not to leave it unless I send for you. Beyond that, all I require is that when we are apart you do nothing to disgrace yourself, and that when we are together you will accommodate my wishes in *every* respect. If you can manage that, you have my word that you will be well provided for when you leave, so long as you never show me your face again. Do you understand?"

"Well enough," I said.

He laughed. "Won't this make an interesting change," he remarked, and then added, "Come into the study."

I remained where I stood.

Coming around behind me, he gripped me by the shoulders and pushed me toward the study door. He was stronger than he had ever given me reason to suppose, and his fingers, pressing into my flesh, made me feel weaker than even I had ever imagined myself to be. He drew a key from his pocket and unlocked the door with one hand while still holding me tightly with the other.

"You had better start learning to do as you are told," he whispered in my ear as he forced me across the threshold, "if you're set on earning your freedom."

My indiscretions were lined up on the floor against one wall. I could not bring myself to look at them—not here. Yet I knew each one. *Odalisque. Artist and Model. Knave and Harlot. Nymph and Satyr. Dancer and Drinkers.*

"Look at them well," said my husband, "so that you'll remember what is expected of you."

From a drawer within his writing table, he produced a slim silver paper knife and used it as a pointer.

"Note, for example, the expression of desire on the female's face," he directed me, indicating the closed eyes and parted lips of the transported nymph. My face. "I'll want you to replicate that precisely."

"That can't be feigned," I whispered.

"Oh, I don't expect an imitation," he replied. "From the trappings in these paintings"—now the paper knife lightly tapped the golden fetters on the wrists and ankles of the odalisque—"it looks to me as if you can be stimulated to . . . the real thing. So *that* was the secret of your blissful marriage."

I leaned against the writing table and crushed a sob back into my chest. My husband stroked the blade of the paper knife absently with his fingers as he gazed with hard, unflinching eyes at my painted selves.

"I could *never* feel passion without love," I told him when I was sure my voice was steady.

He turned.

"I'll teach you otherwise," he said in a voice like a velvet glove. "I'll give you such a taste for loveless passion that, when I'm through with you, you won't be able to survive without it. And then what will become of the cast-off Lady Camwell? Believe me, when this marriage is over, your punishment will have just begun."

This absurd prediction struck me as so ludicrous that, as miserable as I was, I had to leave the room to prevent myself from laughing hysterically in his face.

He did not stop me.

Once I had attained the relative safety of my bedroom, an even stranger thought flickered through my mind: If only he *could* make me feel again.

But there was no danger of that.

I did not leave my bedroom again that day. Nor could I eat the meal that was brought to me that evening. All night long I lay awake, listening for the sound of footsteps at my door, dreading his first assault. Only as the sky outside my windows began to lighten did I fall into an uneasy sleep.

I remained sequestered for all of the following day as well and sent my untouched breakfast tray back to the kitchen. A housemaid, Ellen, brought lunch to me, as she had been directed to do, she said, by Sir Anthony. When she returned to collect this second untouched meal, I told her that she might as well bring dinner to my room that evening. Perhaps by that time I would be hungry enough to choke something down.

As the clock struck the dinner hour, there was a tap upon my door. "You may enter," I called, expecting to see Ellen and a tray.

But this time it was my husband. I drew my dressing gown more closely around me as he approached the bed.

"You are ill," he said with a searching look. There was no kindness in it.

"I did not sleep well," I replied.

"I hope you sleep better tonight," he said. "We shall go to London a few days from now, and I'll be displeased if you are not well rested and in the best of health."

I shuddered, Ellen arrived with my dinner, and my husband left the room.

For the next several days, I kept to my room and my husband continued to leave me blessedly alone. I supposed he was occupying himself with the arrangements necessary to complete his change of residence. I even hoped that by venting some of his rage in making his threats he had dissipated the will to carry them out. Perhaps he had come to his senses and was even now planning to release me into a comfortable separation without exacting his merciless price.

But this was not at all what my husband had in mind. And when he departed for London, I was at his side.

We barely spoke during the railway journey or after our arrival. But my husband did not come to my room that night, although again I lay awake for most of it, fearful that he would. Every creak of the great old house as it settled into its own slumber destroyed any hope of mine.

In consequence of that unrestful night, I rose very late the following morning. I was glad of it, too. It happened that my husband had an early caller, and I would not have been up to the exigencies of playing hostess. But the faint, occasional gusts of masculine laughter that drifted upward from below filled me with resentment, not because they had broken my sleep but because it galled me to be reminded that my husband could be so content with his own lot while I submitted so unhappily to mine. This new

merriment on his part, under the present circumstances, struck me
as unfeeling and shockingly inappropriate.

That he could now be carelessly trading jokes with some light-
minded acquaintance told me, beyond any doubt—in spite of
what I'd imagined had been in his eyes at Fontainebleau and in
spite of all his old gentleness and patience—that he had never
really loved me at all.

I was glad to know this—it made the guilt I could no longer
feel seem superfluous anyway. But it wounded my pride.

His visitor had gone by the time I dressed and descended. Luncheon was about to be served. Having eaten no breakfast and
scarcely any dinner the night before, I was rather hungry. But my
appetite flew out the window when my husband announced that
we would be going out as soon as the meal was over.

"Where are we going?" I asked.

"We are going to have a look at your new wardrobe," he replied.

I fell silent, uncomfortably aware of how worn my dress was. I
did not want to subject it to the ill-concealed contempt of a fashionable modiste.

"Then I must change my gown," I announced, rising from the
table.

"There isn't time for that," said my husband. "Your first toilette
took you half the day, although the results are"—he surveyed my
attire with distaste—"not impressive. However, if you considered
that good enough for *my* eyes, surely it is good enough for the rest
of the world's."

Although I now preferred to avoid his gaze, the untempered
arrogance of this declaration wrung a quick, sidelong glance from
me. I saw a glimmer of amusement in his eyes. Yes, there could be
no doubt; my husband was thoroughly enjoying himself.

I therefore resolved immediately to adopt an attitude of pas-

sive acquiescence, which I trusted would afford him less entertainment than any resistance or protest might.

I expected his carriage to deposit us among the fashionable shops
of Regent Street. Instead, it came to a stop in Maida Vale, on a
quiet little street, well shaded by trees and lined with pretty
houses. My husband escorted me across the pavement toward one
of these.

"What is this place?" I asked uneasily.

"This is where I dress my mistresses," he said. "I took the liberty of ordering some garments for you when I returned from
Paris. Now we will see how they fit."

I stopped dead.

"Please," I said, hating myself for using the word almost as
much as I hated him for bringing me to the point where I must.
"You know that I have been unwell. I am far too weak to subject
myself to hours of standing to be fitted." Or to anything else, I
thought, that may be in store for me in *that* low establishment.

"Oh, I think you'll manage," he said. His hand grasped my arm.
"It can't be any more taxing than holding a pose," he added, "and
you can always lean on me if you are . . . overcome."

I wrenched my arm out of his grip and turned to face him. My
face had reddened. His, too, had colored. But before I could give
voice to any of the bitterness his words had provoked, I realized
that a rosy-cheeked elderly lady proceeding along the pavement
toward us from one direction was well within earshot, as were the
two gentlemen who were approaching from the other.

Already I felt hideously conspicuous, standing outside this undoubtedly infamous house; I would not make a public scene for
anything. My only recourse was to rely on my practiced skill of
suppressing every feeling.

I walked up to the door like a convict to the scaffold. My
husband sounded the brass knocker, and we were admitted.

XVIII

The door was opened by a young woman with blue eyes, yellow hair, and an ingratiating smile.

"Good afternoon, Hélène," said my husband.

"Good afternoon, Sir Anthony," she replied, smirking up at him. "Madame is expecting you."

She led us to an inner sanctum, where a buxom, auburn-haired Frenchwoman, just approaching middle age, gave my husband a very cordial welcome. Her greeting to me was a warm one as well, although considerably more formal. How delighted she was that Lady Camwell would deign to honor her establishment, etc., etc., etc.

I gave this woman, whom my husband introduced as Madame Rullier, a chilling look, but she chattered on.

"Sir Anthony's tastes are most particular," she concluded, lifting a silver-thimbled finger to my husband's face and tapping him playfully upon the cheek. As she was short and he was tall, it was a stretch. "Your whims will cost you dearly, my friend," she said with evident satisfaction. "But *you* have never objected to that."

"I am fortunate," replied my husband pleasantly, "that I can afford them."

Madame met this with a gay little laugh, and then proceeded to wax even more garrulous, this time on the subject of my husband's attire. She admired the intricate stitching of his gloves and the pattern of his tie, and interrogated him boldly as to where he had obtained these articles and what they had cost him. He answered all her questions good-naturedly, while I grew ever more irritated by their peculiar camaraderie.

At last my husband drew Madame back to the matter at hand by asking her how many hours she expected my fitting to consume. She replied that, at the very least, it would take the entire afternoon—perhaps longer, if many alterations were required. Ought she send a message to his club when all was ready?

"Oh no," replied my husband. "I intend to oversee this business personally."

Madame appeared to be as pleased at this news as I was displeased.

"I can see why you would take such an interest," she murmured to him, as she conducted us to a large room hung all around with long mirrors. A fire burned in the corner grate, which was flanked by an armchair on one side and a large sofa on the other. My husband settled himself upon the latter, an audience of one. "How delightful it will be," continued Madame, "to watch the transformation of this little—"

She stopped abruptly, as if she had suddenly remembered who I was. In the meantime, I had grown more stiff-backed than ever, if possible. How dared she speak of me so slightingly? Had I not once been considered one of the great beauties of the most fashionable city in Europe!

"Yes, I believe it will," agreed my husband blandly.

Madame Rullier plucked at my skirt, rolling the fabric between her thumb and fingers and making clucking, disparaging noises with her tongue. She then lapsed into silence for a few seconds and finally burst out, "Oh, I *will* say it—how can you bear to dress like such a grubby little sparrow?"

I swallowed a sharp retort. I saw my husband repress a smile as he leaned back into the sofa and thrust out his legs with the aplomb of an eighteenth-century rake preparing to make his selection of bedmates for the night. That he should appear so at ease and amused routed all my resolutions to endure passively whatever indignities were in store for me.

"My husband takes a great interest in natural history," I told Madame Rullier sweetly. "And, out of deference to him, I dress in accordance with nature's ways. As you know, the male of the species is generally the more flamboyant—the peacock of any pair."

My husband laughed.

"Hmmmph," said Madame Rullier. "Your husband is hardly a peacock. And he is certainly not flamboyant. However, I will not deny that he has exacting tastes and excellent judgment."

"Perhaps in such trivial matters as dress," agreed my husband modestly. "But in matters of greater consequence, I fear I am too easily swayed by what is alluringly packaged."

"Well, anyone can see that is not how you chose your wife!" said the irrepressible Madame, mistaking his meaning entirely. "And *you*," she went on, turning to me, "since you have chosen nature for your teacher, I would advise you to take your lessons from the flower garden. There the sexes strive equally to charm each other with their beauty. They make a far more commendable model than the one you have chosen."

My husband now appeared to grow somewhat impatient. He shifted his position and began softly to tap one handsomely shod foot against the carpet.

"Oh, roses and daffodils may charm the world," I demurred. "They do have a wonderful effect upon bees and butterflies—and poets, of course—but I am sure they are quite indifferent to each other."

"Ah," said Madame with a dismissive flick of her hand. "Bees or poets—it's all to the same end, you know. And now," she declared dramatically, "I shall dress you to charm your husband."

She flung open the door of a spacious closet, revealing a rainbow of jewellike colors. After rummaging therein, she emerged with a malachite green skirt and jacket and a blouse of aubergine silk striped in gold. She draped these over one arm, turned to me, and clapped her hands briskly.

"Whatever are you waiting for?" she asked.

I stared at her.

"Hurry and get out of that ugly dress," she commanded.

My husband had fallen back into his lounging attitude upon the sofa and was gazing moodily at the carpet with his chin on his hand. Now he lifted his head.

"Lady Camwell is accustomed to dressing and undressing with the help of a maid," he said. "Perhaps you could send for Hélène."

"Oh no!" I cried instantly.

"Well then?" he said, and extended his hand toward me in a small, imperious gesture that told me to do as Madame had ordered. And so I did.

Madame Rullier embarked upon her mission to transform me into a charming blossom by energetically tightening the laces of my white corset. Vanity prevented me from protesting—it piqued me to think my waist was not small enough to suit the fashionable Madame Rullier. In the end, feeling extremely weak and ill used, for I had had no breakfast and very little lunch and was now to be deprived even of the sustenance of air, I could not quite repress a pathetic little sob as she gave the strings one final vigorous jerk before preparing to knot them.

"For God's sake, Aurore, don't hurt her!" exclaimed my husband sharply, starting to rise.

Madame Rullier bridled, dropped the laces, and turned to him with an exasperated sigh.

"You *told* me the effect you wanted," she reproved him.

I took a huge, thirsty breath as the whalebone released my rib cage.

"Yes, but that is hardly any reason to bind her so cruelly," said my husband, leaning back. His voice was placid now, and yet I sensed that he was still highly displeased. "Her waist is already smaller than I like them, and her back is very straight. You might as well dispense with the corset altogether."

"Shall I, then?" said Madame, as if she regarded this as a most interesting commission.

"Certainly not," I interposed quickly. "Only do be good enough to leave me a little room to breathe."

Madame Rullier, however, was not about to take her instructions from me. She looked to my husband; he nodded.

She tied the laces then, without yanking on them any further. Next she produced a tape from the sewing box at her feet and began to measure me.

"Your estimates were nearly perfect," she told my husband approvingly when at last she had finished. "I shall have to make only the smallest alterations."

He must have had my measurements from the maker of my riding habits, but nevertheless his expression suggested that he was rather pleased with himself.

"That's a man of science for you," I said. "He has an eye like a caliper."

My husband fixed that cold eye on me.

"I fear I waited rather too long to take *your* measure," he said.

Madame looked with disapproval from one of us to the other. I had an uneasy premonition that she was about to take us both to task for our charmlessness.

"Let me see her in that coat and skirt," said my husband hastily, and thereby deflected the incipient scolding.

As Madame Rullier was completing her alterations to my new wardrobe, my husband inquired about some other items he had ordered and which he hoped were now ready.

"Hélène will show them to you," said Madame Rullier out of one side of her mouth—the other was full of pins.

My husband rose and left us. As soon as he was away, Madame Rullier's manner toward me grew curt.

"Voilà," she said with no enthusiasm as she cut the last thread and turned me toward one of the mirrors I had been studiously avoiding.

"Well, have you nothing to say?" she demanded, after taking the pins from her mouth. If I had been expecting her to tell me how magnificent I looked, I would have been sorely disappointed. If she had been waiting for me to express my gratitude for the miracle she had wrought, she must have been equally so.

"You do not like me," I heard myself say, although I had never intended to voice this conviction.

"And what of it? I am only a poor dressmaker." I thought her humility extremely specious. "And"—she gestured toward the looking glass—"as you can see, I do not allow my prejudices to interfere with my work. Had I loved you with all my heart," she concluded with another burst of the appalling candor she seemed to find so difficult to curb, "I could not have dressed you more beautifully."

"But you like my husband," I persisted, to my own astonishment.

She tilted her head and our eyes met in the glass. Hers were narrowed. She pressed her lips together.

Finally she said in a most unrevealing tone, "What kind of woman would not?"

I shifted my gaze.

Madame bent and began returning her needle packet, her pincushion, and her spools of thread to her meticulously arranged sewing basket.

At this moment my husband returned. The trace of a sparkle lingered in his eye, as if he had witnessed something delightful.

"Were you pleased with what Hélène showed you?" inquired Madame Rullier eagerly, lavishing upon him all the warmth she had withheld from me.

"Oh very," he assured her.

But then he cast a critical gaze in my direction, and his expression grew frosty.

"Do you not like it?" asked Madame.

"I like it very well," said my husband. "It is most becoming. Perhaps not quite as dazzling as some of the others, but I think that may make the transition from drabness a little less trying for her."

I was wearing a mustard-colored jacket and skirt, made of blended silk and mohair; they were trimmed with black braid and cut with almost brutal simplicity. It was, in fact, precisely the severity of the cut which made this costume, as well as all the others, so striking. They were perfectly unobjectionable and the very height of fashion, and yet I felt almost queasy with self-consciousness at the thought of going anywhere in them.

The garments I now wore could certainly be numbered among the more subdued of my new habiliments. Most of the others were even more spectacular: suits and dresses of indigo, magenta, myrtle, cerise, and marigold; blouses of goldenrod, quince, mignonette, peach, and rose. Even the most brilliant tones could not be faulted; they could have been achieved only by means of the very richest vegetable dyes, for they had none of the gaudiness of aniline.

I started to remove the jacket.

"Leave it on," said my husband.

I eased it back over my shoulders obediently as he continued with a laugh, "Surely you were not about to insult Madame Rullier by exchanging her splendid creation for *this!*"

With his back to me, he picked up my ancient dress from the chair where it had been lying. For a second I thought I saw his reflected image press it to his lips, but in the next instant he had turned and was holding it out at arm's length.

"Shall I have that wrapped with the others?" asked Madame Rullier in a mocking tone.

"You may burn it, for all I care," said my husband, letting it fall.

I felt a pang. It was, after all, my dress. It had shaped itself to my very flesh and—as I had not used perfume for years—was faintly imbued with my natural scent. No one could defend it as pretty, but it was sturdy and had served me well.

"No," I said. I bent to retrieve the forsaken gown from the floor. "It is mine and I am fond of it, even if you are not."

My husband shrugged.

"Have it wrapped with the others then," he told Madame Rullier.

She wrinkled her nose at the feel of the fabric as she took it from my hands.

"What *is* the thing made of—haircloth?" she muttered to herself.

"If it were," remarked my husband in barely audible tones when we were alone, "I'd *make* you wear it. Day—and night."

Rather than dwelling on the curious little frisson triggered by this unpleasant suggestion, I merely let my face express how disagreeable I found it. Then I looked unhappily at my image in the looking glass. I might have been wearing haircloth already: I could hardly bear to think how conspicuous I would feel the instant I left the fitting room.

I had never disliked attracting attention and admiration as Frederick's wife. Despite my air of reserve, I had enjoyed it. But now I shrank from the interest of strangers. Surely any eyes I might draw would easily discern both from my mien and from the obvious constraint between me and my husband that not for love had I become Lady Camwell. To dress boldly and expensively, I considered, would be to flaunt my price tag like a banner.

Oh, how my grandmother would have loved my new costumes, I reflected suddenly with bitterness. Yes, that was what I hated about them: they were so relentlessly à la mode. They made me look like a prized and haughty *courtisane*, so well kept and so well appointed as to outshine respectable ladies in tastefulness as well as splendor.

"Shall we go," said my husband, making a statement of it, not a question.

But I did not obey. Overcome by exhaustion, I sank into the armchair where my old, scorned gown had lately lain. Even as I rested my burning forehead on my palm, a glimpse into one of the mirrors told me that my handsome apparel had given my attitude more panache than pathos. I could expect little sympathy from my husband.

"Well?" he prodded me.

I lifted my head.

"You *do* look rather faint," he said. "Perhaps you need air. No— don't try to stand."

He opened a window; it gave out upon a pretty walled garden that lay under an overcast sky. The damp, cool breeze that drifted in carried on it that rich odor so redolent of spring, the scent of moist and fecund earth that proclaims the thaw, the end of winter, the promise of new life. A greenfinch caroled joyfully among the bud-tipped branches of a fruit tree.

"I am better now," I said, getting to my feet after a moment or two. "It's only that—" I stopped. I was famished now, but I disliked expressing to my husband even the simplest physical need.

"Well?" he demanded.

As I hesitated, my stomach decided that it could wait no longer for my reluctant lips to voice its desires. It issued its own unmistakable complaint.

My husband began to laugh.

"It *does* seem that it is now your fate to have your appetites declare themselves however much you try to deny them," he said. "Let us hope this state of affairs will continue."

I glared at him hatefully.

"Come," he said, offering me his arm. "There is a very pleasant tearoom not far from here."

I left the fitting room with mingled feelings. I was grateful for his arm and for the prospect of nourishment, furious at the implication of his remark about my appetites, and both puzzled and faintly alarmed at how well the new tenor of our relationship seemed to agree with him.

XIX

As we were about to depart from Madame Rullier's establishment, Hélène scampered up with a large parcel and breathlessly inquired of my husband what he wished her to do with it. She was unnervingly pretty.

"Why, have it sent along with the others, of course," my husband told her, shaking his head with a smile. "Just as I told you earlier."

Hélène blushed and twinkled.

In the tearoom, when I was certain that no one could overhear us and once the edge of my hunger had been dulled, I asked, "So. Was that one of your mistresses?"

"Who?" my husband responded in a disbelieving tone, "Madame Rullier?" And then, more softly and with a smile, "Or her lovely niece? And why on earth do you want to know?"

"It was an idle question," I said. "It's nothing to me where you go crawling."

He gave me a hard stare, then leaned toward me and said very softly, "I hope that I would never be so unkind to a lover as to require her to attend upon my high-minded wife. I will tell you, however, that I cannot promise the opposite."

I considered the scenario that these words suggested and pushed my plate, with its remnants of cucumber and watercress sandwiches, away. The afternoon had not been entirely unpleasant, but my husband's last remark served to replenish all my ill will.

I spent another uneasy night in my impersonal London bedroom. Again my husband did not leave his bed to come to mine. I almost wished he would. The slight, alarming tang of his words in the tearoom, the suggestion that he might be tempted to try to humble me by asserting his desires in perverse and curious ways—a persistent image of the glowing Hélène reclining smugly among lace-trimmed, perfume-scented pillows in my own bed while, at my husband's direction and under his critical eye, I poured chocolate for the obnoxious minx and arranged her golden curls to his satisfaction—all made the joyless but conventional conjugal act seem blissfully innocuous.

The following day was devoted to the acquisition of gloves and parasols, hats and shoes.

None of this, of course, was undertaken in a spirit of affection or generosity; my husband, however, clearly seemed to enjoy turning me out in a style that at last satisfied his exacting standards.

That evening he took me to hear Alexander Mackenzie conduct the London Philharmonic. I wore one of Madame Rullier's more restrained creations, a superbly simple white dress trimmed with tiny pearls, and over it, a cloak of rose-colored velvet. I barely knew what was played—only that I must sit sedately beside my icy, unbending husband, under a sweeping deluge of music that nearly drove me mad with an objectless longing.

When we returned to Grosvenor Square, Marie, the French

lady's maid my husband had engaged for me upon our marriage, was waiting for me. But to my embarrassment, my husband, who had followed me into my bedroom, dismissed her.

"Take off your dress," he said softly when she had left us.

My heart began to hammer violently. I longed to be back under what I now regarded as the protective eye of Madame Rullier, disrobing in those far less dangerous surroundings.

"If you cannot bring yourself to do as I ask, I will do it for you," said my husband, now in a harder voice, "but that would not be how we agreed to conduct our relations, would it?"

This prompted me to act. My chest felt hot and tight, my fingers huge and graceless, but finally the gown was off. I laid it carefully upon my bed in the hope that its occupation of that terrain might deter other activities from taking place there.

"Now go into the other room," my husband directed, pointing toward a door I had hoped would never be opened.

"There is nothing that proclaims a woman's virtue quite so depressingly as white underclothing," he observed once we had passed into his bedroom and he had closed the door behind us. "It doesn't suit you at all. I hope I never see it on you again."

"Well, you must, I think, if you insist upon holding me to this wretched bargain, for I have nothing else," I told him angrily.

"Then *nothing* is what will have to take its place. So you may as well remove all your prim little rags."

"Oh, what is your object!" I cried, almost beside myself.

He stepped toward me and placed his forefinger lightly under my chin, lifting it.

"You," he said, "are on the verge of obtaining everything your cold heart desires. But before that day comes, I intend to have some pleasure from you, for I have never had any yet."

I was not quite so heavily defended as usual: I wore only a white corset, a long gored petticoat with a narrow ribbon of yellowing lace at the hem, plain white stockings, and sturdy, clinging lisle drawers. I could hardly fault my husband for regarding this get-up as uninspiring—that was precisely the effect it was intended to achieve.

As I began unwillingly to dismantle the flimsy barricades, my husband disappeared within his dressing room. In his absence, I examined my new prison. How I wished my inspection would reveal some ancient priest's hole through which I might escape. But, of course, the house was too new for that—less than two centuries old—and nothing in the room was conducive to flight.

Every element had quite the opposite effect. Velvet curtains of midnight blue hid the windows and shut out the world. More night-sky velvet framed the great bed; these hangings had been drawn back to reveal a billowing coverlet, also deep blue and filled no doubt with the finest eiderdown. There were great soft pillows everywhere—massed at the head of the bed, clustered at each end of the long sofa, propped against the striped-silk ottomans that flanked the fire. Indeed, every object that met my eye issued a wordless invitation to sink into idleness and sensuality.

Now my husband returned with what I recognized as the parcel Hélène had shown him on the previous day. He placed it upon the bed, opened it in a leisurely way, and, laying back the tissue paper, drew out its contents one by one. These he arranged upon the blue ocean of the counterpane. The resplendent, frothy masses of color, brilliant heaps of silk and satin and lace, made a dazzling regatta.

He then removed his dress coat and took up his station in a gold velvet armchair which stood hard by the bed. Beside his chair, a table with a black marble top held a decanter of Madeira and a pair of wineglasses. My husband leaned forward to pour some of the pale wine into one of them, but he did not lift it to his mouth. Instead, he settled back into the chair, crossed one leg over the other, and glanced at the palette of color spread across his bed.

"Now we will see how some other things fit," he said.

I wondered whether the ingratiating Hélène had tried them on for him the previous day, to persuade him of their charms—and hers. But no, it was impossible. She had twice as much flesh on her lovely bones as I did.

Still I hesitated.

Surely my husband could see now how cruelly all this opulent sensuousness must set off my dessicated self.

But he only gave a little lift of his chin, which instructed me, as clearly as if he had spoken the order, to approach him. His face was implacable.

As I stepped forward, I concentrated on obliterating every sensation of shame and hatred. By the time I reached him, I felt nothing: I had willed myself back into that state of somnolent detachment that had possessed me in our marriage bed and upon which I knew I could depend to get me through even this night.

My husband lifted his hand and idly ran the back of a fingernail along the inside of my right wrist. I felt a soft, not unpleasant shiver.

"Try that first," he said, indicating a fragile, low-cut nightdress of sheer black lace. With the composure of an automaton, I drew it over my head. But as I did so the faint scent of fresh, crushed rose petals wafted from the lace, so hauntingly seductive that I could not resist inhaling it wistfully.

That, I suppose, was the beginning of my undoing.

The fragrance came like a faint siren's call to stir my sleeping senses.

I fastened the red silk rosette buttons that secured the gown across my breasts and down to my waist. The lace clung to me from shoulder to hip; below, on the left side, the skirt fell in soft folds to the floor, while on the right side, the hem was hiked and anchored just at the top of my leg by another, larger rosette.

"Turn around slowly," directed my husband when I had secured the last button.

"That fits you nicely," he commented. "Madame Rullier was right. It does seem that I learned your body well—even with so few opportunities, and all of them in the dark. No, don't say a word. Come closer."

How can I describe my confusion as I obeyed? I moved toward him in a faint mist of invisible roses that filled my head with wisps of ancient dreams and slumberous longings. He took my hands and laid them on his shoulders. I felt his muscles move beneath my palms, under his white waistcoat, as he began to unfasten the first few little rosettes. The lace fell away. His fingers grazed my breasts but did not linger there. I closed my eyes for a moment; my contrived numbness began to have a tormenting pins-and-needles quality as my husband's hands glided slowly down my lace-covered back to my waist. His left hand slipped below the rosette at my right hip and came to rest upon my skin.

"Oh, you're lovelier than any painting," he said softly, leaning back to give me an appraising stare. "I've rarely seen such color in your face."

It was true. I knew my cheeks were brighter now than they could possibly have been made by the faint touch of carmine I had applied to them earlier, at my husband's wish, before we had gone out.

"Well, I'm very pleased with that," remarked my husband after a while. "You may take it off."

I roused myself and slipped out of the nightdress.

Next he directed me to put on a low-cut chemise of claret-colored silk, likewise redolent of a summer garden, thickly edged with creamy lace and matched with a pair of very short, loose drawers. Then he beckoned me to him again with that wordless, imperative tilt of his chin. Already disarmed by the languorous spell under which my senses threatened to pull me ever deeper, I approached him.

"One must be rather particular about garments like this," he told me, fingering the silken drawers like a connoisseur. "Unless they are generously cut, they can sometimes be obstructive."

These could not be faulted in that respect. His hand met no obstructing fabric as it plied its way slowly up the inside of my thigh and came at last to the tender flesh it sought. He cupped me in his palm then and curled his fingers slightly. At that small movement, I shuddered involuntarily. He pressed the heel of his hand against me for one singeing instant, giving me another, stronger jolt. I caught my breath in a sharp gasp.

"That will do," he said pleasantly, withdrawing his hand. But my fickle nerves had already begun to play me false; they clamored softly for me to pull his bold hand back and hold it there. Still they were, as yet, very weak, and I was quick to suppress them.

"I think I might even enjoy seeing you in your demure little patched gowns again," remarked my husband, "if they were merely camouflage for this."

I remained motionless, still struggling to collect myself in the aftermath of that brief and gentle assault. How had he succeeded in provoking my flesh to betray me so blatantly?

It occurred to me that, since my will alone might prove woefully inadequate to the challenges confronting it, perhaps a little wine would take the edge from my nerves and dull my ears to their perfidious whispers. I moved toward the little table and reached out to take the neglected glass my husband had filled earlier. He took me gently by the wrist.

"No wine," he said softly. "I want all your senses at their sharpest."

I might have resisted him easily. That numbing draught was within my reach, and his fingers lay upon me so lightly that the smallest exertion would have broken his grip. My pulse beat against his fingertips.

"I want you to feel everything," he said.

I took a step backward, and my wrist was my own again. The last thing I wanted was to feel any more than I already did, but under his steady, unsettling gaze, which held both a challenge and an appeal, that traitorous heat rose within me once again.

I pulled my gaze away. The moment passed. When I looked at him once again, I saw only a frosty glint of amusement on his face.

"I won't ask you to try on all those that are cut to the same pattern," he said, referring to the chemise and drawers I wore, which were replicated in a multitude of colors upon his bed. "But I *would* like you to remove the chemise and let me see you in those green stays, if you don't mind."

From among the silken pools of sapphire, topaz, amethyst, garnet, coral, and lapis lazuli, I drew out the emerald stays and examined them with a barely repressed quiver of dislike. They were thoroughly immodest, having been made to cup only the underside of the breasts. But convinced that to balk at my husband's wishes would simply turn the whole business into an interminable and degrading exercise, I slipped out of the claret-colored chemise with a sigh.

The stays, however, with which I had been instructed to replace it, laced up the back and gave me considerable trouble. To add to the difficulty, some of my hair, having fallen from its diamond pins, was already becoming entangled in the strings.

"What are you doing—it's useless to struggle with it," said my husband with a little laugh. "Just come here, for heaven's sake. . . . Now turn round and pin up your hair as soon as I have gotten it free."

I obeyed. While I restored my hair to its pins, he began to lace me.

As he did so, my renegade memory wandered back to our early rides together. My thoughts lingered in pleasant reminiscence on the graceful ease with which my husband had saddled and bridled his horses—he always began by whispering soft words to those high-strung creatures and by stroking them gently. He had taught me to do the same with Andromeda and had shown me all his ways of making certain that no piece of metal or leather tackle was so carelessly fitted as to pinch or chafe her.

Now he was securing the laces at my back, testing them to make sure he had left sufficient slack to permit me to breathe easily. Then his hands came around the swell of my ribs to stroke me lightly. He was behind me: That deft, almost soothing touch might have been anyone's. I felt my strength ebb further, like a gentle, outgoing tide.

At first he confined his explorations to the territory encompassed by the green satin. He ran his fingers up the whalebone ridges and downward over the smooth fabric of the interstices; he circled my waist with his hands and drew me into the embrasure of his thighs. His breath warmed my bare skin but his hands never touched it. They were content with satin.

As I grew weaker, he closed his knees around me, supporting me. His fingertips began to sketch little crescent moons upon the smooth fabric that only half shielded my breasts. My eyes fell shut.

At last he let his hands glide downward to the bottom edge of the stays. At last he crossed that dangerous border. He slid the tip of his index finger under the satin and ran it slowly along my skin. I felt my long-standing protection, that arid tightness within me, begin to loosen again alarmingly. I pressed my knees together, as if I imagined I could hold back the waves.

The hands drifted downward, the fingertips slipped beneath the band of the claret-silk drawers I still wore. I held my breath, fearing and willing those fingers to venture onward, into deeper regions, but they did not.

Instead my husband released me from his thighs, flattened his palms against my skin, and pushed the drawers slowly down my hips. They slithered to the floor. My body clenched in anticipation—was it a welcome or the last shred of resistance? I could not tell.

But it did not matter. The hands merely glided back to the place where his fingers had earlier tattooed those slender crescents. Idly he retraced their outline. His thighs closed round me again.

My unruly longings seemed about to choke me, but either my husband did not notice or else he did not care. He returned his attention to the lines of whalebone. His touch was even lighter now, almost absentminded, almost as if he were preparing at any moment to dismiss me with a yawn.

The fear that he might do so gave me an intense and shattering thrill.

He withdrew his hands. The thrill gripped me even more violently. I half dreaded that he had suddenly tired of these diversions. But he had not. He dropped his palms to my waist once again and again let them glide upward. This time they did not stop when they reached the top of the green satin. He spread his hands over my outthrust breasts, capturing my nipples between his fingers and pinching them lightly. They had grown firm long before, and now they tightened and swelled so violently that I knew myself to be on the verge of losing every shred of self-control.

A tiny sob broke against my closed lips and shook me. I could no longer hold my back straight. I fell forward like a broken doll, bracing my hands against my husband's knees.

His right hand deserted its post at my breast, drifted down my spine like a falling leaf, and then softly began to nuzzle into the moist heat between my legs.

This time my lips opened as I cried out.

He took his hands away.

I struggled in vain to part my thighs, to invite another tender invasion, but his knees held me like a vise, and I could not.

I continued to writhe in that iron grip for a moment, laboring for breath, and then gave up.

"There," he said, releasing his hold. "I know this has been difficult for you. I won't ask too much of you all at once. You may go now."

I stumbled forward. I was facing the doorway through which I had come earlier, but I was now so weak with hunger for all that I had barely tasted, as well as with the shock of disappointment, that I could have reached it only by crawling on my hands and knees.

I turned around unsteadily. My husband, reclining comfortably in the depths of his chair, wore a challenging look that conveyed a clear message.

He was daring me to disobey him.

"Good night," he said.

I glanced at the door behind me and then back at him.

"Take the dressing gown, if you like," he said indifferently, pointing toward a scarlet peignoir that lay at the end of the rainbow on the bed.

Modesty ought to have made me cover myself with it, but those casual and insinuating hands had driven away all my pretensions to modesty. I lifted my own hands to pull the pins from my hair and let them drop. I let my gaze drift back slowly toward my enthroned husband. His face showed nothing. I felt my skin grow brighter. I shifted my eyes and glimpsed my own image in the looking glass on the wall behind him. I was too drunk with desire now even to feel much amazement at who was caught there—that other woman, the one whose flesh had once burned so wildly that, long ago, unable to hold her pose for the man she loved, she had been driven to assume an even bolder one.

And now it was worse. Like that abandoned creature of the paintings, I was offering myself, not to my beloved Frederick, but to a man I did not love, for whom I had ceased to care in even the smallest way, and who now seemed bent upon teaching me how to hate.

The painted lady was real.

My husband watched me steadily. His expression did not change.

Not knowing what to do, how to curb my reckless impulses, and half swooning with desire, I dropped to the floor. My knees sank into that soft Chinese carpet, that thick expanse of blue as dark as the nighttime sea. My eyes came back to his rock-hard gray ones, and a tumultuous yearning, utterly unfamiliar, utterly debilitating, swept through me.

I closed my eyes. My hands began to move, as if of their own will, over my body, touching every spot where his hands had lingered earlier and where his adventuring fingers had probed. Thus, in the language that has no words, I recounted to him every fleeting delight he had inflicted upon me and avowed my hunger for more.

I no longer knew myself.

I had never imagined what it would be to fall so completely under the spell of another's sheer sexual power. My old self, even that long-ago self beloved of Frederick, the one he had called his *fleur du mal,* was a pallid and conventional creature compared to the woman I had now become, kneeling on the carpet before my enemy and proclaiming in this mute and urgent fashion my desperate longing to give myself up to him.

All that came back to me was stillness and silence.

At last I heard the sigh of a necktie being pulled free, the whisper of starched, boiled linen and soft wool falling to the floor, the click of a diamond stud striking a button. . . .

"Come here," said my husband huskily. He sounded shaken, no longer cool.

I opened my eyes and lifted my damp face. My husband was standing before the chair; his clothes lay at his feet.

I had never seen him naked.

As he had pointedly reminded me only a short time earlier, I had always insisted upon having the lights put out on the few occasions when we had made love.

Now I saw what I had always suspected: that my husband's lean and lightly muscled frame was as beautifully sculpted as any of those marble pagan gods and mythic heroes I had once admired in the Louvre.

He took only a half-step toward me, then halted. I came to my feet and moved forward slowly. Although he had not laced me tightly, my lungs felt starved and my breathing had a terrible, jagged urgency.

Only a few inches of carpet separated us when I reached the point where I could not go on without some sign of encouragement, some assurance that he would not simply fold his arms against me and rebuff my advances like a stony wall. I knew he had the strength to do that, in spite of the evidence of his own desire, if all he really intended was to teach me the cruel lesson he had hinted at, only days ago, in his study.

We faced each other, silent and immobile.

He took the final step and closed that tiny gulf. He brought his hands to my shoulders and bent his head to mine. His hair fell across my cheek like a curtain. My mouth melted under his demanding lips. Hours—or seconds—later his hands moved to my breasts.

I nearly stumbled with the shock of my response.

He drew backward and sank into the chair again, pulling me with him. Holding me by the waist, he lifted me slightly, as he forced my legs apart with his knees; in a moment I was straddling his thighs. His hands dropped to my hips and pulled me closer still. I brought my knees up, opening myself to him as he entered me. He used none of the restraint that I had come to expect from him. I didn't mind. He lifted his hips beneath me and then let them drop. The pleasure was nearly intolerable; I could no longer hold myself still. I thought he would object to this. Instead, I felt a whisper of soft laughter stir my hair, as he altered his rhythm slightly to mine, spurring me on.

My breasts strained toward his lips, his tongue, and, as they received his benedictions, my spine curved like a rainbow. Only his arms around my waist prevented me from falling away under those scorching, suckling kisses.

His skin was damp and tropical; his breath was a warm southern wind. There was no part of him that did not pulse and surge with fire. There was no inch of flesh on me that his insistent and intrepid hands did not claim for his own.

He showed me no delicacy now. His lips burned my ears with words I never dreamed any man would dare to breathe in my presence; he called me everything except my name and made my blood race madly. My body rose and fell, mastered at first by what had seemed to be his will and not my own; yet my every nerve responded so unhesitatingly and urged him on so strongly that I could not have said for the life of me which one of us truly set the measure for that headlong race.

Our bodies rocked together. His breath grew as ragged as my own; the sound of it incited me further. I heard myself yield to the cries welling up within me. I felt his excitement mount higher with each whimper of passion I could no longer contain.

"And how do you like me now?" he whispered. Again I heard that almost soundless laughter.

Sobbing, I bucked against the pressure of his arms, secure that they would never let me go.

But in the end, of course, they did.

Almost as soon as he had released me, I retreated in disarray.

He had thrown his head back, his eyes were closed, and he was breathing hard.

I staggered to the bed and pulled the scarlet dressing gown over my damp, smoldering skin.

He lifted his head. His face was still flushed but now otherwise icily impassive. I arranged my features likewise. I thought of the final taunt he had flung at me, when I was so far gone that, instead of bringing me to my senses as it ought to have, it had pushed me over the brink.

"Well," I said, "that's one out of the way. I trust that it was everything you hoped for."

"Not quite," he replied. I bridled slightly, for I could not imagine in what way I had disappointed him. "However," he continued, his breath still uneven, "I will admit that you surpassed my expectations." He pulled himself to his feet. "Good night. Again," he said.

His eyes were as impenetrable as granite.

I half turned to leave.

"Take your things with you," he tossed over his shoulder as he strolled off toward his dressing room.

I gathered up into the arms that only moments earlier had been entwined around his neck all the banners of colored silk still strewn across his bed. Then I retreated to my own room and began the lonely struggle to unbind myself from the green stays.

I did not see him on the following day, but a terse little note in his handwriting arrived with my breakfast tray. It told me that the coachman had been instructed to deliver me that afternoon to Victoria Station, to the train that would take me back to Charingworth.

XX

Alone at last.

At Charingworth, I did not dwell upon my recent misadventures in London. To have allowed—no, to have *encouraged!*—my detestable husband to evoke that blazing response from me—I could not bear to think of it. I preferred to occupy myself with visions of the future life which those weak-willed antics would help to buy me.

In a month or two I could return to Paris. Surely the gardens and boulevards which Frederick's death had so darkened and blighted would become, merely by virtue of my freedom to walk in them alone, almost bright again and lively. And with money enough to keep her, I could take Andromeda with me, leaving nothing behind to regret.

But as the days grew longer and the empty nights milder, my mind began to revert to what my husband had described to me as the culmination of his revenge: *Then your punishment will have just begun.*

Not a word came from him. I wondered how long the embargo would continue, whether he was already planning his next sally, and what form it might take.

The waiting became a subtle form of torture. I felt as used as a maidservant tumbled one evening and forgotten the next by her heartless, neglectful master.

Twelve days passed. Then, late one rainy afternoon, the sound of carriage wheels in the avenue announced my husband's return.

I had adopted the habit, when my husband was absent, of taking dinner in my sitting room. It was too depressing to preside alone over the huge table in the dining hall, like a solitary mariner cast ashore on a desert isle.

On the day of my husband's return, I had already arranged to have dinner brought up to me. I will admit that I *was* somewhat curious to see my husband, but at the same time I was extremely reluctant to come face to face again with the man who knew so much about me now, and all of it to my discredit. Most certainly I did not wish to dine with him.

I was not pleased, therefore, when Marie delivered to me, less than a half hour before dinner was to be served, another note in my husband's hand. This one commanded me to present myself at the table.

I made an effort to conceal my impatience with Marie's painstaking thoroughness as she helped me to dress. I feared if I was tardy it would bring my husband to my room before I was ready to confront him. However, I was unwilling to join him until I was in full panoply.

I chewed my lip with vexation as Marie carefully arranged my hair; the clock had already struck the hour. I wanted to snatch the comb from her hands and finish the job myself, but she had far more skill, and I could no more afford imperfection than could a knight being girded for bloody battle.

It was my aim to look austerely beautiful, concealing every haggard hint of anxiety. Only when I was satisfied that, in a sleeveless gold damask gown with a heart-shaped neckline, I appeared as splendid and impregnable as the flagship of an armada did I sail down the stairway. I entered the dining room with a deliberate, leisurely gait. It was twenty minutes past the hour. I expected my husband's expression to betray some surprise—perhaps even approval—at the sight I presented to him, but all his face revealed was irritation.

"You're very late," was his welcome. "I was about to come and fetch you."

"Good evening, Anthony," said I very graciously, making neither excuse nor apology.

We ate in silence. I watched him guardedly, but with new respect. He had dressed for dinner with his customary understated black-and-white elegance and appeared as remote and unprepossessing as always. Why, then, as the meal progressed, did my composure ebb, to be replaced by that tremulous anticipation which had come increasingly to plague me in recent days?

I could not resist an occasional, circumspect glance at the opponent whom I knew I must never again underestimate.

He caught me once. I dropped my gaze—but the damage had been done. His gaze fell over me like January sleet; I felt my face take on the telltale color that my accursed pale skin could not conceal.

We were alone. My husband disliked to have servants hovering at his shoulder after our plates had been filled. Now he laid down his knife and fork and leaned forward with his elbows on the table and his palms pressed together.

"I really have no objection, when you are alone, to your taking supper on a tray in your room, like a governess," he said. "But on the rare occasions when we are under the same roof, I will expect you to join me at the dinner table. And I will expect you to be punctual. I cannot think of any excuse for putting the kitchen staff to the trouble of keeping the dishes warm until you have managed to drag yourself to the table. Surely you—who have so little else to do—can at least exert yourself enough to show a modicum of respect for the work of others."

I burned at the rebuke. My husband's well-ordered household ran with a smoothness which concealed the enormous amount of labor thereby consumed. He behaved toward his staff with a courtesy that manifested itself not only in the politeness with which he addressed them but also in his scrupulous habit of advising them as early as possible of any anticipated disruption to the usual routine. For my part, I had tended to accept these tranquil and orderly functionings—to which, as my husband had indicated, I contributed virtually nothing—as evidence of his annoying lack of spontaneity.

Now, although I resented his tone, I could not dispute the justice of his observation. Nor did I dare; I had agreed to the bargain which made obedience, out of bed as well as in it, the price of my eventual freedom.

"I regret having been so inconsiderate," I heard myself say in a low voice. "It will not happen again."

As I indicated my acquiescence, I felt a sensuous languor slide over me. My nerves tightened for an instant, and then loosened softly, as if preparing to deliver me over to my adversary.

His eyes met mine again, and I had a sharp and vivid recollection of that moment of ecstatic release he had given me. I dropped my gaze and lifted my fork, but now my appetite, never hearty since the loss of my child, had completely deserted me, and I merely toyed with the turbot that adorned my plate until my husband directed me to ring for a footman to come and clear the table.

I went immediately to my bedroom when the meal had ended. My husband had disappeared in the direction of his study, where, I supposed, coffee or brandy would await him, along with a stack of papers demanding the instant attention of the absentee master. I ensconced myself among my pillows with the latest literary production of Mrs. Humphrey Ward. The reviews proclaimed that it lived up to the promise of her fabulously popular *Robert Elsmere*. I hoped it would. Neither *Robert Elsmere* nor anything else from that woman's pen had I ever been able to finish, but the spiritual torments of her vaguely repellent characters seldom failed to induce sleep.

Savoring one of the hard mint candies I kept in a covered

crystal dish on the table beside my bed—they had the pungency which Mrs. Ward's prose lacked and were the only sweets I ever craved—I opened the book. And, indeed, I soon began to nod. Yet when I gave in to the drowsiness and put out the light, my eyelids refused to remain shut.

The room had a brightness, half warm, half cool, that came only in part from the dying fire upon the hearth. The afternoon rain had cleared the sky, and now moonlight poured through the sheer, pale blue silk curtains, between the old-fashioned window hangings of heavy flowered chintz with which my husband had had my bedroom outfitted shortly before I took possession of it. These gave the room a quaint, cheerful informality which never could have been achieved with more fashionable velvet. I always opened them before I went to sleep to admit the moonlight.

At last I abandoned my bed to stand at one of the long windows, which offered a view of the silvery lawn's gentle descent toward the riverbank. As subtle variations in the dim landscape slowly began to reveal themselves, I thought I glimpsed a figure among the venerable oak trees. These cast such deep shadows that it was impossible to distinguish substance from illusion; the effect might have been only a trick played by the night wind, the tossing branches, the ragged little clouds sailing across the moon's face, and the dappled light she shed.

Then I saw a flicker of matchlight as my husband—for it was he below me on the lawn, the moon had laid her fingers on his hair and told me so—lit a cigarette. The bent head lifted. Was he looking upward at my window? I stepped back, out of the pool of moonlight, alarmed. The gauzy curtains fell shut.

He gave only the most perfunctory warning knock before opening the door to my bedroom a quarter of an hour or so later. I pretended to be asleep. Without a word, the invader lit a spirit lamp, banishing the moonlight. I sat up in bed, feigning as much confusion and dullness as if I had been dead to the world for hours.

He pulled the chintz window hangings closed and laid some wood upon the fire. When the flames were dancing to his satisfaction, he sat down in an armchair a little distance from the hearth. He was still dressed in the black tailless evening coat and narrow trousers he had worn at dinner.

"You seem to have had trouble sleeping," he remarked, by way of letting me know that he had seen me at the window.

"I had no trouble at all until you awakened me," I replied, to maintain the fiction that I had been rudely jolted from my dreams.

He met this with a long, slow, and knowing smile which told me I had chosen my words unwisely.

"Indeed," was all he said.

I felt myself turn crimson.

"Have you the necklace which I gave to you last month?" he then asked.

"Yes."

"May I have a look at it?"

"If you like. It is in my jewelry case." I made a small gesture toward my dressing room.

"Bring it to me," he said.

I left my bed unwillingly. In the dressing room, I opened the dark red morocco case, stamped in gold with my new initials, which contained the necklace and a few other pieces that he had given to me. My grandmother's jewelry was in a strongbox in a London bank.

I lifted out the necklace and delivered it to my husband.

"Have you any idea why I gave you this?" he inquired, holding it up to the glow of the lamp on the table at his left.

"You seem to enjoy decking me out in gewgaws and baubles," I replied.

"True." He was looking at the necklace and not at me. His eyes were narrowed critically.

"This has an imperfection in the clasp," he observed after careful inspection. "I am surprised that I failed to notice it earlier." He draped the diamonds over the fingers of his right hand and looked up at me. "If you use it roughly—as I fear you will, since you do not value it—the clasp may not hold."

"I do not intend to use it at all," I told him.

"Nevertheless, when I return to London, I will take it with me and have it repaired."

"As you wish."

"But for now, I would like to see it on you."

I thought the diamonds would provide a curious embellishment to my uninviting nightdress. However, I reached out obligingly to take them from his hand.

"I'll put it on you," he said. "Kneel down."

As I obeyed, that strange and dangerous feeling stole through me again, that soft, dizzying lethargy. I kept my head bent and my eyes lowered so that if my face revealed this, it would not be visible to him.

My husband lifted the hair that hung like curtains over my cheeks and let it fall behind my shoulders. His touch was as slow and delicate as a lover's. He laid the diamonds on my throat and secured them there.

"Lift your chin," he said.

Reluctantly I did so and brought my eyes to his. But already I felt as if my composed everyday face were being slowly chipped away from beneath by that other, purely sensual being, who was racing to take possession of me once again.

"That is not one of the nightdresses I bought for you," said my husband.

"No, it is not."

"Then it does not belong on you tonight."

"Shall I put on one of the others?" I asked, perhaps a shade too hopefully.

"No," he said. "Since I do not like this one, and you seem to dislike those I have chosen, we will compromise."

I did not like the compromise this remark foreboded.

"Shall I assist you?" he asked.

I began nervously to unfasten the buttons which secured my

nightgown from my collarbone to my waist. At last the white flannel slid over my shoulders and settled into a little snowdrift around my kneeling self.

"Don't look away," said my husband.

So I met his gaze, and although I was hardly a blushing innocent, my skin began to grow as rosy as if I were a maiden in imminent danger of debauchment.

My debaucher was lounging with his right leg thrown over the side of the chair. His right arm lay across the back, his hand propping his head. His other arm hung idly over the left side; it needed only an empty wineglass dangling between the fingertips to complete the dissolute effect of his posture, which made so great a contrast to his flawlessly pressed coat, starched shirt, and creased trousers.

His gaze drifted over me slowly and came to rest, with frosty approval, upon my traitorous nipples. At last he leaned forward and reached out languidly.

"These seem a little more eager to please than they once did," he remarked.

Or to be pleased. It was true—his presumptuous touch had me quivering with rebellion and delight. I pressed my lips together.

"Put your arms around my neck," he said as his hands continued their leisurely exploration of my breasts.

He leaned closer toward me and I toward him. I laid my arms upon his shoulders like a garland.

His breath warmed my cheek. I began to tremble and sigh under his touch.

"Here is what you'll wear for me tonight," he whispered. His hands left me. He slipped a tiny crystal vial from one of his pockets and twisted the cap. The light, fresh, springtime scent of lilacs spun around me as his fingertips touched the fragrance to my temples, my throat, my shoulders, to the insides of my elbows and the back of my neck, to my breasts—and then no more. He slipped free of the loose enclosure of my arms. I felt as incomplete as a half-finished painting, and drunk with lilac.

He held the vial toward me with a hard little smile that conveyed his wishes clearly. I opened my hand.

Slowly I clothed myself in those invisible flowers. They curled around my wrists and ankles and over my infertile belly, they wafted along my calves and wove themselves around my thighs.

When I considered myself fully arrayed in this remarkable fashion, I reached out to take the cap from his hand.

He shook his head.

"A little more," he said. "Between your lips."

I feared the potion would have a very bitter taste: With a slight frown, I lifted a hesitant hand toward my mouth.

"Not those lips," he whispered.

I let out a little sigh of protest and assent.

He was still draped lazily over the chair. With an inward shiver, I poured a droplet from the vial onto my fingertip and brushed it over the tender hidden flesh. I wished, suddenly and violently, that the brief touch were not my own.

"Be generous," said my husband softly. "Why deny yourself?"

Our eyes met and held. Instead of taking the obvious meaning, I chose another one.

I handed him the vial.

But he seemed not to understand me, for he merely took it from my fingers, replaced the cap, and laid it upon the table beside the lamp.

He unhooked his leg from the arm of the chair and stretched out both feet.

"Would you mind?" he said, with just a trace of his old diffidence.

I unlaced his shoes and slipped them off. He curled his toes and smiled at me, perhaps somewhat more warmly than before.

I did not smile.

The silent night held its breath.

With a somewhat moody and restless air, he then stood and wandered about the room. He lifted one of the panels of lavishly flowered chintz from the window where I had stood earlier, gazed outward for a moment or two, and at last let the hanging fall back. Next he strolled over to the bed, raised up Mrs. Ward from among the pillows, shook his head slightly as he examined her for a moment, and then lifted his eyebrows at me and his hand to his mouth in a pantomime of a yawn.

Against my will, a smile forced itself to my mouth. Well, how not? There *was* something wickedly amusing in his expression.

He let the virtuous matron fall and filled his arms instead with the pillows where she had lain. These he brought close to where I still knelt, now with my arms folded about me. He laid the pillows before the hearth.

"Lie down," he said.

With mingled reluctance and eagerness, I unwrapped my arms and attempted to arrange myself as modestly as possible among the lush hummocks of pale blue satin. I expected my husband to reclaim his seigneurial position in the chair, but instead, rather to my surprise, he removed his coat, laid *it* upon the chair, and lowered himself to the thick carpet at my side.

Regrettably, my unprincipled flesh still felt poised to welcome his touch; however, it was not to be. Slowly he removed his tie and loosened the high collar of his white shirt. The fear, or perhaps the wish, that he might bind me interestingly with the tie shot across my incorrigible mind. But he did not. He merely watched me quietly and thoughtfully, until I longed to snatch his coat from the chair and cover my persistent blushes.

"What is the trouble?" he said at last.

I shifted my posture slightly in a futile effort to better conceal myself amid the pillows.

"Ah," he said. "You feel yourself to be insufficiently clothed. I have something for that. If you'll go to my bedroom, you will find a small carved wooden box upon the mantelshelf. I'd like you to bring it to me."

I didn't move.

After a short while, my husband sighed, pulled out his watch, glanced at it with a frown, and threw an inquiring eye at me.

Thus rebuked, I stood up uneasily and took a step toward my dressing room, hoping to gain it, and a dressing gown, without interference.

My husband, alert as a serpent, shot out his hand and caught my ankle firmly.

"That's not the way," he said.

"But it will be cold out there," I protested, not wishing to voice my real objection.

"Yes," he agreed thoughtfully. "I think it may invigorate you."

There was nothing for it but to reveal my true concern.

"But . . . what if . . . if someone should . . . ?"

"No one will see you," said he rather impatiently.

Still I could not move.

"No one will see you," he repeated, now with a real edge to his voice. "No one is even remotely close by. It is one of the great pleasures of being the master of this house. I can depend on everyone to do exactly what I tell them. Even you."

This was a curious remark: My husband's behavior toward his servants had never given the smallest indication that he actually savored the power of ordering them about. In fact, despite the veneer of calm assurance, I had always thought his air suggested quite the opposite.

But my husband was proving that still waters may indeed run very deep, and I knew it would be unwise to provoke his anger.

I stepped into the dim passage that led from my rooms to the gallery and made my way, under the haughty painted stares of countless generations of Camwells, along the gallery's polished oak floorboards to my husband's rooms, in which I had never set foot.

If I had harbored any curiosity about his unknown bedchamber, there was hardly enough light now to satisfy it. The gas was low and the fire unlit. The chilly air from the open windows nipped at my skin.

I made my way to the mantelshelf and found the ornate little box. It was no more than four inches square and fastened with a little brass lock. Trying to envision a garment made of gossamer so fine that it could be folded into that tiny chest, I shook the box gently and heard a muffled jingle. I could have speculated all night on what lay inside, but I decided to return to him quickly and put an end to my curiosity and the charade.

My husband lay comfortably in the fire glow, resting on his elbows with his legs crossed. He lifted a lazy hand to take the box.

"The key is in the pocket of my coat," he said.

I found the tiny object and gave it to him.

Then, once again ensconced among the warm satin pillows, I watched him unlock the box. He drew out a piece of cotton wool and unrolled it to reveal a glittering tangle of delicate chains hung with miniature bells.

"Hold out your hand," he said.

I extended my arm. Slowly he glided his fingertips along the inside of my arm from elbow to wrist two or three times; then he brought them to my shoulder and traced the whole length of my bare arm. Slowly, slowly, he repeated those light, hypnotic strokes as I eased back among the pillows. My eyelids drifted downward. Just as I let them fall shut, persuaded that nothing in all the world could ever really destroy my peace again so long as that gentle, rhythmic touch continued, he clasped a tinkling bracelet around my wrist.

"Now the other hand," he said, and fastened the second flimsy manacle.

He got to his knees and moved along my body.

"Lift your foot."

The third little shackle claimed my ankle.

"This one."

But now, instead of merely engaging the clasp of the last of my fetters, he began to stroke my leg, as he had my arm, first only from knee to ankle, then extending his tender explorations along my inner thigh. I sighed and stretched involuntarily and jingled.

His hand glided back to my foot. I felt the anklet snap shut around me.

"Now," he said, looking down at me with a smile, "every time you quiver, all your bells will tell me of your hungers. Even if *you* won't."

I lifted my right wrist slowly and examined it.

By this time, I felt so captive to my longings that he might as well have hobbled me in irons. But my new adornments were not iron—they were not even silver. They had been fashioned of the most tawdry material imaginable—white brass. I do not say this with scorn: Amid all the ancient splendors of Charingworth, they seemed like a lovely little breath of life. They sang and chattered among themselves, cheerfully indifferent to the haughty disapproval of the frigid, aristocratic diamonds at my throat.

"What has made you smile?" whispered my husband.

I recomposed my face and did not answer.

With a little sigh, he got up, and began to wander about the room again with his hands in his pockets. At the table beside my bed he paused and eyed the crystal dish thoughtfully. He looked at me and back at the dish. Then he uncovered it and popped one of the hard mints into his mouth.

I almost laughed. Perhaps the poor fellow was not quite so confident as he seemed! Perhaps he imagined it was his *breath* which had once made his kisses unwelcome! He needn't have worried; his mouth was as warm and sweet as a summer pasture.

He strolled back with a sly, wolfish grin to where I lay. Then he knelt upon the pillows at my feet. He pushed my thighs apart gently and, with his mouth, deposited the mint between my legs, pressing it firmly with his tongue into the little crevice of flesh. I gasped and jingled.

"Ah," whispered my husband, lifting his head. "I think you are beginning to make your wishes known."

My knees tightened further; my hips rose.

He bent his head back to me and began slowly to lick the mint. Lost in strange and delicious sensations, I pressed my knuckles to my lips. But no matter how well I muffled my cries, those gossiping bells would not be silenced.

How sweetly did my husband's warm mouth console the tender skin where the menthol burned with a cool, distant flame, like melting ice. Slowly, slowly his tongue eroded the little mint; his languid concentration proclaimed that he was entirely absorbed in his own pleasures. Mine, although almost uncontainable, seemed purely incidental.

Yet I forgot everything except the promise of rapture. I could not have told you his name, or my own.

And then he took his mouth away and, with it, the last trace of mint.

I watched him stand up and bend to pick his tie from the carpet and his coat from the chair.

"What are you doing?" I whispered.

"I'm off to bed," he said with a little yawn. "You seemed disgruntled earlier at having been . . . awakened. I won't rob you any further of your sleep."

I rose to my knees. I could feel my face growing dark. I wanted to wrap my arms and legs around him. I imagined the faint scratch against my skin of the fine wool that covered his legs.

I watched him hang his tie around his neck without knotting it, fold his coat over his arm, and move toward the door.

Words of protest trembled on my lips—I couldn't have said whether I was struggling to push them back or to force them out.

And then, although I believed myself to be entirely petrified with confusion and dismay, the little bells spoke for me.

My husband, whose hand had just fallen to the door handle, turned.

"Did you say something?" he asked.

Everything that had made him seem almost warm and approachable earlier was gone. There was not even the hint of a smile. His face might have been carved from ice.

"Oh, don't go yet," I said helplessly.

"No? Why not?"

The four syllables I had spoken had exhausted my supply. He watched me for a short while with barely concealed irritation and then, with a shrug, turned and reached again for the door.

"Wait," I said.

He didn't even pause. He pulled the door open and stepped into the gallery.

"Please," I whispered desperately.

He began to draw the door slowly shut.

I was bereft of words, but desire pulled me to my feet and across the room. The bells made a soft clamor. I caught the door before it clicked shut.

With a sigh of exasperation, my husband stepped back into the room and closed the door behind him. He looked at me for a long while with an expression of severe disapproval.

Finally, he said, "I asked very little of you tonight. Would you agree?"

"Yes," I said, falling back from him.

"Did I force myself upon you unpleasantly in any way?" he asked.

"No," I whispered.

"Did I require anything that was objectionable to you?"

"Not really," I said, although I had not especially appreciated being asked to fetch things.

"And even so," he continued, "in one or two instances, you did not show quite as much alacrity as I have every right to expect from you. You know what I am referring to, don't you?"

"Yes," I said, reviewing my little failures.

He took a step toward me. I took a step back.

"You have disappointed me more than once tonight," he said. "When I express a wish, I like to see it fulfilled instantly, even with enthusiasm. I know, of course, that you are half dead and can feel no enthusiasm for anything, but I would have preferred an imitation of it, at least. Do you understand that?"

"Yes." I closed my eyes, too overwhelmed by confusion even to look at him.

"If I stay longer with you tonight," he said, his words seeming to reach me through a thick mist, "it will be on one condition. You will not balk at *anything* I ask of you. I leave it to you. I will go now and count tonight to your account, since, although you were occasionally dilatory, you acquitted yourself well enough, for the most part. Or I will stay, on *my* conditions—but at *your* wish. It rests with you. Do I stay or go?"

"Stay," I whispered.

I swayed and jingled as he led me back to the hearthside and laid me down upon the pillows.

"Undress me," he commanded when we were stretched out before the fire. "Slowly. As slowly as you can."

I moved closer to him and began to unfasten the buttons of his waistcoast.

He sighed.

"Don't rush," he whispered. "I can feel how eager you are, but try to control yourself. Take your time."

It was maddening to force myself to that unhurried pace, but in the end it only sharpened my hunger. As I contemplated the climactic pleasures in store—who could have said how long it would take to achieve them?—I could not help savoring the small but no less sweet ones immediately at hand. The slight drag against my skin of the fine wool that clothed him, more teasing even than I had imagined it; the almost imperceptible fragrance of lavender that wafted from his shirt, the hands which lay so lightly upon my waist as I absorbed the knowledge that the task he had set for me was not an obstacle to fulfillment but a means of enhancing it.

Yet I had unbuttoned only his waistcoat and his shirt when he told me to stop. He drew back from me a little. The very aura of controlled desire he radiated made me long to submerge myself in the impersonal heat and forgetfulness that his still presence next to me both promised and withheld.

I moved perhaps a centimeter closer to him.

"No," he said.

He began, in his calm, unhasty way, to remove his remaining clothing himself. I steadied my breath a little and watched the firelight move like a sculptor's fingers over his cool, hard body.

At last he leaned over me, but without touching me.

"You're so compliant tonight," he said almost tenderly. "You must be very hungry for your freedom, *mon fleur du miel.*"

I felt a twist of sadness. For an instant, I thought he had used Frederick's nickname for me. But he had called me something quite different—a flower, not of evil, but of sweetness . . . honey.

He brought his hand to my cheek and stroked it softly. I closed my eyes. Only the sudden sharp intake of my breath could have told him of the effect of that light touch.

He bent his head. I caught the scents of mint and smoke and my own secrets as his mouth moved close to mine.

I tipped my head back and opened my lips.

How long I had resisted those kisses! Now I craved his mouth, wanting to savor and prolong every sensation that could melt away my frozen, imprisoning armor of misery and isolation.

He barely grazed my lips with his.

Then he pulled himself to his knees and gently coaxed me into the same position, facing him.

Keeping his lips lightly on mine, he reached out and took my shoulders gently to bring me closer. My breasts brushed his chest with every long, shivering breath I took.

"You are free now," whispered my husband at last, releasing me, "to do as you like. . . . How will you use your liberty?"

For an answer, I put my arms around his neck, sank back upon the pillows, pulling him down to me, and brought my wild mouth to his.

I knew I was lost; his revenge was already complete. But then he betrayed himself; his kisses grew as hot and urgent as my own; his arms tightened around me, he gave a small, gasping moan, and in that instant I saw how I might turn his own unsparing weapons against him.

With a reckless exhilaration I had never known before, I seized upon the catechism of secret lore with which my grandmother had inculcated me, the practice of which I had begun and refined with Frederick.

As my husband's lips and tongue melded gloriously with mine, I moved one hand downward. My husband gripped my straying wrist. I caught his lower lip between my teeth and nipped it tenderly as a warning. He drew in his breath sharply and released my hand.

I found and tested his desire for me. And then I let my hand move further, to enclose, with the utmost gentleness, the soft rounds of delicate, pendulous flesh I had never ventured to handle. I pressed my fingers there with the assurance born of the harlot's knowledge and felt the violence of his response. I moved my fingers further.

My husband's arms fell away from me. His head dropped among the pillows we shared. He lay back, his eyes closed, his fine, long sinews tensed.

An even deeper thrill began to take possession of me as I observed his efforts to master himself.

At first the thought of going beyond this had seemed repugnant, but now the lust for power proved too much for me. I let my hand fall away and watched him press his lips together hard as if to curb a plea.

I waited a few seconds, and then I moved downward, between his hard thighs, and bent over him. Touching him lightly with my tongue, I lifted his hips gently and laid another pillow beneath them. My lips and tongue began to perform every act my hands had rehearsed before. I listened with maddening satisfaction to his sobbing breath as I laid my hands inside his thighs and pressed them further apart.

Nothing deterred me: His scent and his skin were fresh and inviting; to hear him groan softly and to feel him shudder as my fearless tongue explored him only spurred me on.

And then he broke free and sat up, panting. I knelt facing him. Frozen, we stared at each other like sleepwalkers jolted from their trance.

I watched the dazed expression ebb slowly from his face to be replaced by something like anger.

I closed my eyes.

When I opened them again, he was watching me with the cruel and wary eyes of a lion tamer.

"Come here," he said.

I inched closer.

He took my wrists and brought them together above my head, holding them in one hand. The other hand slid downward and began to play with me. He had regained his self-control, but within seconds he brought me to the limits of mine. He took his hand away. I shut my eyes again, knowing his were still open and upon me. Tears began to burn against my lashes as I strained toward him.

"Please," I whispered.

"Please what?" he demanded softly.

"Please, I want you," I said, but I knew I had failed him in some way.

He brought his lips to my ear as he began fingering me delicately once again.

"Use my name," he said.

I resisted for only a second or two. He moved his hand away.

"Please, Anthony," I gasped. It was the ultimate defeat.

He pushed me down upon the pillows, jammed my thighs further apart with his knees, and drove himself into me. I started to cry out against the force of his thrusts, but my cry was transformed before it left my lips as my pleasure shot toward its apex. He laughed softly and withdrew from me so abruptly that I had to choke back a whimper of loss. My body lifted itself to him.

I called his name, pleading.

When he took me again, it was even more roughly than before. The earlier taste he had given me only sharpened my hunger for this. All my pretenses had fled.

"Look at me," he said, and when I did, he was smiling down at me, but it was as much a smile of triumph as of anything else. I knew my own face was transparent. My eyes closed again, as he dragged me downward: I was falling like Lucifer, but falling into heaven, not out of it.

At last his body dropped against mine. For a moment I was intensely aware of every sensation: his silky hair falling on my cheek; the aroma and warm, dewy texture of his skin; the exhausted cadence of his breath. Then nothing.

I awoke to the sound of that slow, steady breathing. The fire still burned upon the hearth. I could not have slept, I supposed, for more than five or ten minutes.

I stared up at the ceiling, and I thought of my husband, to whom all that had just passed had been merely an exercise in power and revenge, and I thought of Frederick, whom, even at my most abandoned, I had never embraced quite so passionately. Frederick, to whom I had never given all that this unloved, unloving stranger had won from me.

It was too painful to contemplate—it led to the familiar thoughts of all those other things I ought to have done long ago and had not. They began, and ended, as always, with my failure to rouse myself from my own sorrows in time to have saved Frederick, to whom I'd sworn my love, from that dreadful, sordid death.

My husband stirred. I glanced at him cautiously, longing to lose myself in him again and wishing simultaneously that this night had never been. I would have given anything, then, to find myself back in that first shabby Parisian garret with my laughing artist, who had loved me, even if he had perhaps never roused me to quite that same pitch.

I had often thought that if I could imagine the circumstances vividly enough, if I could make every detail perfectly concrete, if I could somehow concentrate my mind sufficiently, I might, by the sheer force of will, be able to transport myself back into that old life . . . and mend it.

I closed my eyes and tried to let the studio take shape—the stacks of canvasses leaning against the wall, the cold northern light pouring through the windows, along with a little bite of chilly air. The fire was burning and the room was heavy with warmth. The familiar odor of garlic drifted upward from Madame Lemestre's kitchen below to mingle with the heady aroma of oil of cloves, which Frederick used to to keep his paint moist and plastic.

I was almost there. . . .

And then Frederick stood before me—wasted, mournful, and accusatory, the river mud clinging to his grave clothes and to his tarnished hair. I tried to move toward him; he lifted a skeletal hand to arrest me in my steps.

"Oh, what have you been doing, *mon fleur du mal?*" he cried in a strangled voice. And then, with a look of unspeakable reproach and sorrow, he drifted away, through the high, draughty window of my past, to dissolve among the snow-covered rooftops beyond, a lonely, restless, disappointed shadow.

That old, sweet love could not save me now.

"Oh, Frederick!" His name broke from my lips in a low, raw whisper, a whisper of resignation and farewell.

My husband pulled away from me and sat up.

I pressed my hand to my mouth. To think what he had uncovered in me that night! I was well on the way to proving the truth of his cruel predictions. *And then what will become of the cast-off Lady Camwell?*

"Perhaps you need to be alone," he said.

I did not refute him.

He got up calmly from the bed and began to dress. I longed for him either to hurry and go or to change his mind and stay, but he did neither. He was infuriatingly methodical, but he appeared abstracted and thoughtful as he secured each button.

Finally he stood over me with his shoes in one hand and his tie in the other.

He must have seen the anguish in my face.

"I want you to remember one thing," he said in a very quiet, steady voice. "It was not *my* faithlessness which brought you to this."

It was insupportable—to be accused of faithlessness by one husband from beyond the grave, and by the other, of the faithless spirit in which I had taken my marriage vows.

"Get out," I said in a harsh whisper. And then, as a final fillip, I added, "Anthony."

Of course, it had no effect on him. He merely turned and left silently, still enveloped in that inviolable air of dignity.

When he was gone, I ripped off the bells and flung the flimsy broken chains in the direction of the door through which he had vanished. I tried to yank off the diamond choker as well, but the clasp did not yield, in spite of its alleged weakness, and in the end I removed it in the usual way and restored it neatly to its little red leather tomb.

XXI

By the time I descended the stairway the following morning, after taking my breakfast in bed, my husband had departed for London. The ensuing fortnight dragged itself by in leaden shoes.

He did not communicate with me. I knew not when I might expect the pleasure of his company again. I was bored to distraction.

None of the scholarly tomes in my husband's vast library could hold my attention. I wandered about the grounds with my sketchbook, making little drawings in a desultory fashion, abandoning them before they were complete, and reviewing all too frequently that last night with my husband.

I had been unnecessarily cruel.

I tried to dull the sting of conscience by reminding myself of the unkind accusation of faithlessness he had flung at me. But I could not pretend that it was unjustified or that *he* had spoken cruelly. I still could hear the echo of his voice, laden with something like regret. I felt a twinge of regret myself, and shame as well, as I recalled my viperish response.

.   .   .

One morning, toward the end of April, a parcel arrived from Grosvenor Square—the first event of any possible interest to occur since my husband's departure. I could not imagine what it might contain.

I had it taken to my bedroom, where I opened it at my leisure a little while later. But first, in order to relieve my ennui, I teased myself by speculating upon its contents for nearly twenty minutes.

My patience was not pleasantly rewarded.

Within the parcel, wrapped in tissue paper, was a flamboyant dancer's costume of scarlet tulle. It would not even reach my knees and was alarmingly low-cut. There were black stockings, a pair of black net fingerless gloves, and a throat band of black velvet as well.

With a kind of fascinated dismay, I picked up the little envelope which had been nestled amidst the tulle and opened it.

"I will expect to see you in this when I dine with you in your sitting room on Thursday night. A."

These presumptuous words were the extent of my husband's communiqué.

So he would be home on the following night—and imagined that I would dress up like a little ballet girl to welcome him!

Which is, of course, exactly what I did.

I have said that I was suffering profusely from boredom.

Fortunately, I possessed a long, heavily embroidered, Japanese silk robe—a relic of my brief years of luxury in Paris. I was wrapped in this when dinner was brought to me and the dishes arranged upon a small table which had been set up before the fire.

Outside the heavens were pouring rain, but my sitting room had a bright and festive air. The table had been laid with a strip of gilt-trimmed, amethyst Indian silk over the white damask cloth; its centerpiece was a brass bowl of nasturtium flowers.

I was in a deplorably immature state of high-keyed spirits. But no one could have guessed this from my face or manner; I had every juvenile impulse firmly under control as, arrayed in Japonic splendor and sphinxlike dignity, I waited for my husband to join me.

Only after the servants had left did he enter my room and break my pose, for—impulsively—I rose to greet him. But although we had not seen each other for fourteen days, his "Good evening" was as casual as if we had not been apart for ten minutes.

He took his place at the table. I had started to take my own seat in the chair opposite his, when he stopped me by lifting his hand.

"Stay as you are," he said, so I stood beside the table and subjected myself to his cursory inspection.

"You may as well remove your robe," he told me. "It's surely warm enough in here."

I slipped out of the robe and laid it over the back of my chair. My husband examined me long and thoughtfully. I reddened under his gaze, but apparently not enough to please him, for at last he said,

"You're very pale. I like my women to have more color. Why don't you do something about your face."

This made me burn even more. I had already applied the barest touch of carmine to my cheeks—knowing that he liked it—but much more than that would have been indecent.

"Ladies don't paint their faces," I demurred, and then flushed even more deeply as I considered the flagrantly unladylike image I already made.

"No, ladies don't," agreed my husband, with placid good humor. "But you shall."

And with that, the wretch actually snapped his fingers. This sent me to my bath chamber to employ the rouge pot more industriously, while my husband waited before the covered dishes at the table.

I painted my lips and my cheeks carefully and was about to join him again—I almost fancied that I could hear his impatient fingertips beating a faint tattoo upon the cloth—when I paused to study my reflection one last time and to assure myself that the results of my efforts did not border on garishness.

And in that instant, I could not avoid noticing how vividly the picture I presented contrasted with the bloodless, ashen creature I had been until so very recently. Paint or no paint, I now looked brilliantly alive.

I remembered, with a surge of confidence, how I made my husband shiver and moan, and it occurred to me that perhaps I had not yet fully tested my powers. I had a sudden, intense urge to jolt him once again out of that attitude of cool restraint.

I went back to my rouge pot and applied more carmine, in a brazen, but what I knew to be an undeniably alluring, manner. Then I excavated, from my dressing case, a little jar of kohl which Frederick had given me years ago, that I might better represent his vision of the harem slave. With this I lined my eyes. After a final self-inspection, I returned to the table.

I had the profound satisfaction of hearing my husband's sharp inhalation, but he collected himself swiftly.

"That's a little better," said he in a tone of tepid approval.

I observed that in my absence he had rearranged the chairs at the table, so that my place was on the side perpendicular to his rather than opposite.

"Now you may serve me," he announced.

At this I mutinied.

"If you feel you must be waited on, why not ring for a foot-man?" I suggested.

"Is it beneath you? Very well," he responded pleasantly, as he got up from his chair and reached for the bell-handle.

I made a move for the robe which I had left lying over my chair, but it had vanished. I shot my husband a look of real terror. He withdrew his hand with a victorious smile.

Well, he had won that round.

I lifted the covers from the dishes and began to fill his plate. Although I had served Frederick his dinner countless times when we'd been poor, tonight my performance was far from adept. My hands shook with a combination of self-consciousness and mortified pride. Under my inexpert fingers, the steamy interiors of the silver dish covers rained little droplets upon the napery; I dribbled the gravy; I clanged the serving spoons against the china.

When I had finished, my husband pointed wordlessly to his empty glass. I filled it with wine, but not without spilling a little tear or two of Château-Lafitte upon the cloth.

Never had I felt so awkward and clumsy.

"Now you may take your seat," said my husband.

And then, to my astonishment, he rose and began, with infinite grace, to serve me.

At the end of that almost silent meal, my husband took a small leatherbound book from his pocket.

"Do you read Latin?" he asked.

"Of course I don't," was my quick and scornful reply. "My grandmother did not raise me to be a bluestocking," I added.

"No?" he said. He moved his chair closer to mine, leaned back in it, and, reaching under the table, began to stroke my black-swathed leg. His fingers drifted just above the stocking top and lingered there. I closed my eyes and commanded myself to be as still as a pillar of salt.

"And just what *did* she raise you to be?" he inquired eventually, withdrawing his hand.

"A lady," I told him.

He laughed.

"Indeed?" he said with a look that made me wonder whether he had somehow inferred the full truth about my upbringing. I flushed guiltily. His gaze dropped to my breasts, where the rouged aureoles of my nipples rose over the neckline of my costume. "And what would she think of you now?"

"She would be very sorry for me," I invented self-righteously.

"Then I'll make her sorrier still," he said with a smile, and I knew he meant not her but me.

He opened the little book and handed it to me.

"You have a most enchanting voice," he said, "although you rarely use it to say the things I want to hear. Tonight we will change that." He pointed to the top of the right-hand page. "You may start there."

In my ignorance, I stumbled a little over the meaningless words, written in a dull and lifeless tongue which surely deserved its fate of entombment between the faded covers of dusty little books.

My husband did not subject me to the pointless exercise for long.

"Shall I tell you what it means?" he asked before I had even reached the bottom of the page.

"If you like," I replied indifferently, handing over the book.

"If *I* like!" said he with a laugh. "Don't *you* want to know what you've just said to me?"

"Well, all right then," was the best that I, half curious, half reluctant, could manage.

"Those are the words of Ovid," he informed me. "From *The Loves*. And this is the meaning of what you have just spoken:

"Each thing has its place; yours is my bed,
And once you have come to it
Fill it with rapture;
I'll have no modesty there."

I felt my skin grow warmer. He went on:

"But once you have left it,
Your wildness must go, love.
In my bed alone will you ever be free
To fearlessly savor your secret delights."

His voice was like a caress. His eyes were on me, not on the book. I flushed more deeply.

My husband pushed back his chair and came round to my side of the table. Laying down the book, he continued, softly:

*"In my bed alone you must never feel shame
To throw both my clothes and your own to the
    floor . . ."*

His left hand slid down my throat and lifted my right breast free of my scanty bodice.

"To lie with your eager thighs open beneath me . . ."

He drew me to my feet.

"There it is right for our tongues to kiss . . ."

He twined his fingers in my hair and pressed his mouth to mine. Our tongues kissed. He held me tighter and moved his mouth away to whisper in my ear:

*"There may your splendid and boundless desire
Put every invention of love to the test. . . ."*

He let me go. I sank back into my chair.

"A disgraceful translation," he said. "I've improvised liberally, I'm afraid. But what did you think?"

My answer was a soft exhalation, half a laugh, half a sigh.

"We'll read more, if you like," he offered. "But not tonight. Too much instruction all at once dulls the appetite for it. Good night."

With one last smile, he walked toward the door.

I clung to the arms of my chair and swore that this time I would not call him back. And if I did not? Could he resist me? Would he really go?

"Sleep well," he tossed over his shoulder.

The door closed behind him.

I walked up and down the carpet until my blood had stopped pounding. Then I stripped off the despicable tulle, put on my plainest nightdress, and got into bed.

Sleep well, indeed!

I could not sleep at all. I wanted my enemy's hands on me. I wanted to feel his breath on my cheek, or that wolfish mouth at my throat. I wanted to hear him sigh. I ached to extort from him, once again, a helpless moan of passion and desire.

After a rather long time, I got up and, after still more hesitation, washed and repainted myself and changed back into my earlier attire. Then I put on my Japanese robe; the edge of a sleeve, peeking out from beneath the sofa pillows, had betrayed its hiding place.

I was not pleased to discover, upon being admitted to his quarters, that while I had been tossing in my bed, my husband had been happily occupied with his beloved photographic equipment.

There it was, all set up and gleaming: the big studio camera, with its leather bellows body, set firmly upon a sturdy, three-legged stand of polished oak. My husband, still fully dressed, was cleaning lenses. How I hate the way the male mind can skip from a woman to a piece of mechanical equipment as easily as a squirrel leaps from one tree to the next!

"And what brings you here at this hour?" he inquired with cool civility. I slipped out of the robe. His lips curved as he surveyed me, once again decked out like a scandal in red and black.

"Must you ask?" I whispered.

"I am afraid I must. I have learned that it is never safe to assume anything where you are concerned."

I bit my lip and began to saunter restlessly up and down before the fire with one hand on my hip and the other arm crossed over my waist.

At last I tossed my head and said, "Well, tonight you may assume anything you like."

He turned this over in his mind for a minute or two. Finally he said, "Very well. In that case, I will assume you are anxious to be free of me and eager to speed along the payment of your debt. Is that it?"

This being the least humiliating explanation for my presence in his bedroom, I did not repudiate it.

"You've read my heart," I told him.

"Amazing! And here I did not even credit you with having one."

I let that go.

"How I wish I could oblige you," he continued, with the specious regret of a lord dismissing a mendicant. "But I am afraid that now, as bad King Richard would have said, I am not in the vein."

My eyes fell to his trousers. I would have liked to reach out and test my suspicion that he was lying, but of course I could never have done anything quite so indecent.

He caught my glance and smiled.

"However, I can think of a way you *might* be able to *put* me in the vein," he offered suddenly.

"I am at your command," I replied, very cool and stiff.

That made him laugh. He reached out and pulled me to him and began to run his hands boldly up and down my body.

"At my command," he repeated, sounding very pleased. "So if I were to command you to go at once and leave me to my . . . less troublesome pleasures"—he tilted his chin in the direction of the camera stand—"you would depart as meekly as a mouse?"

He had me there. I knew I could not assent truthfully to *that* proposition.

"I don't see what pleasure they can give you tonight," I said. My voice trembled slightly. His fingers were lazily at work now, fanning the flames they had kindled earlier. "There's nothing here to photograph."

"That's just the dilemma that was worrying me when you arrived to present such an interesting solution."

I froze.

"No," I said.

"So much for being at my command," he responded with a shrug and let me go.

And so, like a fool, I put my head inside the noose for the second time.

We proceeded at a very leisurely pace, but eventually I had been propped against nearly every object in his bedroom and had decorated nearly every inch of sofa and bed, carpet and hearth, tables and chairs.

At intervals, he encouraged me to refresh myself with generous libations from a claret jug.

My pulse was soon racing madly, but the cool-eyed would-be recorder of these antics was exceedingly difficult to please. None of the ways in which I disported myself, at first somewhat grudgingly but soon with far too much zest, did he deem worthy to immortalize with his silver compounds.

Nevertheless, it was not long at all before his eyes began to dance. Worse still, I was disgracing myself with barely muffled laughter.

At last he said, with a devilish gleam, "You know, I'm not so pleased with that red thing after all. Take it off. I think I shall make this a true nocturne in black and white."

And so, with scarcely any hesitation, I shed the bright tulle and stood before him, laughing still, in nothing but the black stockings and gloves and the black band at my throat. He pulled back the coverlet from his bed to expose the glistening white pillows and sheets beneath and bade me lie down upon them.

I did.

With a perfectionist's thoroughness, he arranged me fetchingly, examined me carefully, adjusted my limbs a bit this way and that, at last pronounced himself completely satisfied, and commanded me not to move.

Then he disappeared behind the camera and aimed the lens at me. I sparkled recklessly back at him as I anticipated the joyous conclusion to this night of folly and delight.

I heard the shutter close.

"You're so piquant," he whispered, emerging from beneath the hood with tousled hair and an oddly tender expression upon his face.

But that earlier playfulness seemed to have fled. As he began to remove his clothes, I saw the familiar aura of restraint and self-control fall over him again like a veil. It only heightened my desire.

"Turn over," he said when he was done.

Silently I obeyed.

"Lift your hips."

I did; there was no posture I could pretend to be too proud to assume for him now.

From behind me, on his knees, he entered me quickly, sharply, without even the most perfunctory of preliminary caresses. I didn't need them. I wanted to draw him into me so completely that we would be no longer two bodies, but one. I wanted to absorb his cool, masterful dignity and make it my own. I felt myself tighten with the longing to bring him yet closer.

He groaned softly and shuddered. The sound and the sensation made me rock and writhe.

"Don't move," he whispered raggedly, and laid a cool hand on my cheek.

It was all I could do to obey, but obey I did. The clock on the mantelshelf ticked the minutes off as I bent against him, drowning in the exquisite agonies of wild longing and impossible self-control.

He stroked my hair and told me what a lovely little trull I was. I cried out then; my core exploded in one brief, violent spasm before I could bring myself in check again.

I felt my husband's lips nuzzle the back of my neck.

He brought his fingertips close to where our bodies merged and began gently to test delicate variations of pressure and rhythm. He found the right one quickly. It tore me loose altogether from the self-willed restraint into a frenzied dance of passion. But he was with me all the way.

When I awoke, the fire had died and the room was cold. Beneath the covers, I moved closer to my husband's warm body. He stirred. I felt him harden against me. I braced myself, with luxurious anticipation, to receive him again.

Instead he moved away.

"Are you still here?" he said with something like annoyance and surprise. "You should be off."

"Be off?" I mumbled in sleepy confusion. "Do you want me to go?"

"Please. You ought to have been in your own bed hours ago. Now run along. And wash your face so that you won't shock Marie when she brings your coffee."

Too stunned and wounded to protest, I slipped from the bed and departed—yes, as meekly as a mouse.

When I had gained my bath chamber, I stared with disgust at the sordid apparition in the glass. The rouge had streaked and faded; the kohl had run from my eyes and smudged my cheeks.

Dear God, was *this* the image that my heartless husband had captured only a few hours earlier?

A wave of horror and revulsion swept over me as I recalled, in every hideous detail, what I had done and what I had permitted him to do.

I thought of the way he had dismissed me and I nearly banged my head against the wall in a paroxysm of self-directed anger. How could I have been such an idiot? How could I have let my body rule me so completely?

The thought of the appalling photographic testimony to my immodesty that was now in my husband's possession made me ill. What would he do with it? Lock it away in an album to remind himself from time to time of my unworthiness once I was gone?

Stuff it carelessly into some drawer where God only knew who might stumble across it one day? Use it against me in some unimaginable way? Why, oh why, had I lacked the wit to destroy it while he slept! But I was so ignorant of even the barest fundamentals of photography, I would not have known what to smash or to steal—or even where to look for it.

On the chance that my husband had not yet returned to London, and not wishing to leave him with the impression that I was hiding out in shame, I forced myself to appear at the breakfast table the following morning. My face was scoured, my hair pulled up with ruthless severity, and, should that alone not make a sufficiently strong statement, I wore a gown nearly indistinguishable from the one I had preserved from Madame Rullier's dustbin.

My husband greeted this unappetizing vision with a slight, startled grimace, but rather than chastising me as coldly as I might have expected, he merely remarked, "I see you've dragged out the hair shirt again. Is it your penance for last night?"

He had a very self-satisfied glow. His little joke appeared to have amused him hugely.

"I'm sorry if it displeases you," I said without a milligram of regret. "I had supposed you would be on your way to London by now and that I might dress as I please."

My husband raised an eyebrow.

"And what made you think I was going to London?" he asked.

"You generally do," I pointed out, not adding the obvious conclusion to my sentence: *Once you have had your way with me.*

"I am beginning to find Charingworth more hospitable than it once was," he remarked as he returned his attention to the orange he was peeling with a small pearl-handled knife.

"By the way, if you can take any pleasure in an enemy's sorrows, I have a piece of news for you," he suddenly announced in an almost friendly tone. "Have you heard what has happened to that scoundrel Poncet? Apparently his daughter, who was the light of his life, has had a falling out with him. And she had an admirer, a musician, who is as poor as a church mouse and whom her father thought entirely unsuitable. He had higher aspirations for the girl. But she has gone to her musical lover and will have nothing more to do with her father, who is beside himself, for she was all he cared for: His sole ambition in life was to build her a fabulous dowry and buy her a gilded match."

I could not help taking a pinch of satisfaction from this news; I bore the girl no ill will and was pleased to think that in her own pursuit of happiness she had deprived her father of his. But I did not appreciate being reminded of Poncet, or of the paintings—not after the performance I had given for my husband only a few hours ago, not after the casual way he had dismissed me, as if I were nothing more than a girl he had bought for the night. And because of this, I said, "So you have become such good friends with that pander that he confides his troubles to you? Well, it doesn't surprise me. Like attracts like."

My husband froze and flushed darkly.

After a very long time he lifted his head and fixed me with a cold stare.

"You are mistaken," he said. "I merely chanced to hear the story from an acquaintance of mine. But now that you have pointed it out, perhaps I really ought to find more opportunities to do business with . . . your marriage broker." He paused thoughtfully and then went on, looking at the orange he was flaying and not at me. "After all, you made an extraordinarily provocative picture last night. What a pity that it is only in black and white and fails to depict the brilliance of your blushes. I wonder what it would cost me to have it copied in oils. Perhaps if I show it to our friend, he will recommend an artist. No doubt he'd welcome such a diversion from his private troubles."

I blanched.

He lifted his head again and caught my anguished eyes with his own remorseless ones.

"You must come with me when I go to Paris to see about it," he said.

I closed my eyes and shuddered.

"Oh, surely it won't be as trying as all that," he said. "Besides, think of the pleasure it will give me. *And* my kindred spirit," he added scathingly.

I could not respond. I already felt completely corrupted by the hungers, unhallowed by any glimmer of affection, which he had managed to awaken in me. Now the shock of such deliberate malice, coming on the heels of those recent intimacies which I had dropped my guard to partake in so enthusiastically, only sharpened my sense of vulnerability and betrayal.

The rain poured down in sheets. The wind blasted it against the leaded windowpanes and shook the branches of the ancient oak trees on the lawn outside. The air within the huge, high-ceilinged rooms of Charingworth felt dank and chill; the fires which had been lit provided only small comfort against the drafts.

"You wouldn't do that," I said at last. "I don't believe you are capable of such a thing."

He laughed.

"Oh, you have no idea what I'm capable of," he said. "Haven't you learned that yet? So don't provoke me by pretending to be coy, or you may discover there are worse things than having your picture painted."

I wished more than ever that I had resisted the call to that blinding, bewildering, and dangerous erotic sublimation. Now I understood—too late—how completely he had disengaged his affections; not even my helpless ardor had satisfied his lust for revenge. It had only whetted his curiosity to discover how far he could make me stoop on a whim.

I saw that I had never even guessed the true depths of his animosity.

·   ·   ·

On the following day, the rain stopped and the gray clouds parted to permit a few hours of watery sunshine. My husband left very early for London, and when the house was at last free of his oppressive, disturbing presence and I was able to think more clearly, I ventured boldly into his room. But the photographic equipment had vanished.

So there was no way to prevent him from carrying out his evil design. Still I knew I could not endure another moment in his company. How to escape? I owed him two more nights of fealty before he would be honorbound to set me free. It made me queasy, now, even to think of them. Was there no way out?

And then it came to me.

The diamond collar.

If he was truly determined to display that dreadful photograph to Poncet and, worse still, to have it reproduced in paint, there was little I could do to stop him. I could only pray that no one besides those two devils and the artist—oh God, what if it were someone I knew?—would ever see it.

But I would not suffer any further degradation at his hands, not for anything. It was even possible that if I fled, depriving him of the opportunity to savor the rigors of my intended humiliation, his wretched plan might lose its allure.

That fabulously expensive diamond collar would keep me indefinitely from destitution: I could leave at any time—I might have done so long ago.

But even as I considered this, I felt an uneasy premonition. I raced up the stairway, along the gallery to my chambers and into my dressing room. There lay the jewelry case in its usual place on top of a chest of drawers. I approached it slowly, my heart pounding. There was a key to it somewhere, but the staff at Charingworth had an air of such incorruptibility that I had never felt the need to use it. I lifted the cover.

The diamonds were indeed gone; in their place lay the broken chains of cheap little white-brass bells.

I withdrew into my bedroom and sank onto the bed. I hardly knew whether to laugh or to weep at my stupidity. He had told me he intended to have the clasp replaced, and *still* I had been as passive as a sleepwalker.

My grandmother would be turning in her grave. None of the self-protective instincts that she had labored so hard and so thanklessly to instill in me had been able to take root in the stony soil of my youthful foolishness. Now it was too late.

I thought of the way she had left her Italian count, fleeing his dilapidated palazzo in the middle of the night to go to her new lover, carrying with her all the jewelry the poor count had lavished upon her.

The image of my grandmother's ignominious departure from the one man who had truly cherished her, needed her—the man whom she was far too proud to go back to on her knees, pregnant, desperate, and remorseful—had always been repugnant to me. Was that why I had ignored, until too late, the glittering avenue to freedom which my farsighted husband had just sealed?

There were, of course, many other small objects of inestimable value at Charingworth, but something in me resisted even the idea of taking them. Perhaps it was the unpleasant thought of branding myself as a thief on top of everything else. Perhaps it was merely the fatalistic inertia that for so much of my life since the death of my child had held me in so cruel a grip.

XXII

The days that followed were not pleasant ones. The fear that at any moment my husband might attempt to carry out his threat poisoned my waking hours and skulked through my dreams.

He remained in Grosvenor Square for nearly two weeks, and during his absence I wrote a brief letter to Marguerite. I told her only that the business with my husband had gone badly, that he had adopted a cruel and vengeful attitude of injured self-righteousness and was making me horribly unhappy.

My husband returned to Charingworth very late on a Friday in May—long after I had retired for the night. But I heard his arrival and did not sleep.

At breakfast the next morning, he announced that he wanted me to come to London the following week. This made me distraught, for during my sleepless night, my dread had increased. From London, no doubt, we would go on to Paris. . . .

I excused myself from the table. I felt very ill and hoped that I might reach the stairway in the great hall before he could destroy my composure any further. But as I began to climb the stairs, a wave of nausea gripped me. The walls grew shadowy and began to spin. I clutched the newel post and swayed, shivering.

The next thing I knew, I was in my husband's arms.

"Are you ill, Fleur?" he asked, and I could have sworn that for an instant there was a note of stark concern in his voice.

"It's nothing, nothing," I said, clinging to him as if he had been my savior rather than my tormentor.

He lifted me easily and carried me up the broad stairs and along the gallery to my bedroom.

"You *are* ill," he announced after he had laid me upon the bed, removed my shoes, and drawn the counterpane over me. "I'll send for Doctor Blount."

"No!" I insisted miserably. "I don't need a doctor. I tell you, it is nothing."

I could not bear the thought of Dr. Blount's solemn examination, which would surely culminate in a portentous announcement to my husband that I must be suffering from an attack of nerves, a diagnosis which I was certain would provide my husband with no end of amused satisfaction.

Now he studied me in silence, his face growing ever paler and more perturbed.

Finally he said, "Are you with child?" His voice fairly shook: He sounded thoroughly alarmed.

"No!" I said.

"Are you *quite* certain?"

"Of course." There was no doubt of it.

"That would be unfortunate," he said at last.

"It would, indeed," I agreed bitterly. It was not a turn of events to which I had given much thought, since there seemed so little likelihood of my bearing a child, but at his chilly dismissal of the possibility as "unfortunate," I felt an unexpected surge of fierce protectiveness. Any child unlucky enough to come into the world as the result of the death throes of this marriage would need all the love I could lavish upon it. It could hardly hope to claim any affection from its father. But it didn't matter. There would be no child.

"Well, if you are not ill and you are not expecting, how do you account for your condition?" he asked, now with a hint of impatience.

I sank back among the pillows and closed my eyes.

"Just go away," I whispered. "Please. Just leave me."

"If you are not improved by this evening, I *will* send for the doctor," said my husband. He hesitated a few seconds longer, but at last, to my relief, I heard the door close behind him.

He had beef tea and blancmange delivered to me at intervals during the day, and by evening I had gathered enough strength to force myself to join him for dinner, thereby putting to rest the possibility that he might seek medical advice for what I knew too well was only a disease of the spirit.

We dined before the library fire.

At the end of the meal, when we were alone, he said to me, "As I mentioned this morning, you will be joining me in London for a few days at the end of the week."

I was now certain this was what I had feared. But I had given the matter some thought during the day.

"Perhaps *you* will be in London," I said. "But *I* will not."

"I think you will," he said. "That is, if you still wish to be free of this marriage."

"There's no need for me to dance to your tunes in order to get free of you," I replied. "I can as easily seek a divorce."

"Now *that* is an interesting possibility," he said. "What grounds do you intend to use?"

"Adultery and cruelty will be sufficient," I said. I knew my case was a weak one, but I wanted to test him.

He leaned toward me across the table.

"I think not," he said gently. "I haven't taken a second wife. I haven't slept with my mother or with any of the farm animals. I haven't sodomized you." He paused, eyeing me thoughtfully. "Although, if I should," he continued slowly, "I hardly think you will find it cruel."

I felt a small, unsettling stab of desire, mingled with distaste and curiosity. How could the suggestion of something which I

knew from my grandmother to be extremely unpleasant and which
I was fortunate enough never to have experienced, how could such
a suggestion from the man I hated have quickened my blood, if
ever so slightly?

"And if I decide to give you that pleasure," he continued, his
expression making it apparent that it would be a pleasure for him,
as well as for me, "are you naïve enough to believe that the scru-
tiny to which you'll be subjected, should you attempt to use that
to divorce me, will be easier to bear than the little courtesies I
require of you?"

"Courtesies!" I repeated with a laugh. "Is *that* what you call
them?"

"I did not guess you found them so unpleasant," he replied.
"From the eagerness with which you have begun to extend them, I
had supposed the opposite. I'm curious—what is it, precisely, that
you find so disagreeable?"

I ought to have ignored the question rather than rising to the
bait. It was here that I made my great mistake, believing that I was
dealing him a crushing blow rather than opening myself up to an
even more devastating one.

"There is no feeling in them," I said.

"True," he said placidly. "But *that* is what makes them so amusing. You are proving to be rather gifted at your true vocation. I
have no doubt you will improve remarkably with a little more
practice."

I rose from the table. I felt as if he had knifed me in the heart.

"And such an accomplished actress, as well," he continued. "I
have never seen a more convincing portrait of a refined and delicate woman than the performance you put on for me at the outset
of our marriage. Really, I have the greatest respect for *all* your
talents."

I put my hands on the edge of the table to steady myself. I
don't know why I felt so deeply wounded. What he had said was
no worse than I might have expected from him. But each word cut
to the bone, and rather than reveal this, I chose to retaliate.

"You bloody hypocrite," I said. "Since we're critiquing performances, shall we talk about the one *you* gave during those same interminably dull months? The perfect English gentleman, all chivalry and politesse. Who would have guessed that such a vengeful, sadistic nature lay behind that mask of civility?"

But my shaft missed its mark.

"I don't know why you complain of that," he replied. "It's obvious which you prefer—at least between the sheets. Things are not quite so dull for you now, are they?"

I ought to have let that be the coup de grâce, but I was unable to retreat from the battlefield. I knew I had lost, but now, far from a desire to strike back, I felt only sadness. I reached back into my memories for some recollection of love with which to console myself, but the now betrayed and accusatory shade of my darling Frederick sulkily refused to come to my aid, and instead I found myself thinking, very strangely, of the man who had led me into the magical forest of Fontainebleau.

"You were not always so unfeeling," I said at last. "Is your hunger for revenge so great that it has completely destroyed your better nature?"

Unfortunately, these words sounded melodramatic even to my ears, and the laugh with which he greeted them suggested that he found them so too.

"What you call my 'unfeelingness' is no part of my revenge," he told me candidly. "*That* is merely the result of disappointment and of my wish not to be deceived again. I will *never* believe anything you say, Fleur. However, that is not to detract from your recent performances, which have been perfectly delightful. If in a somewhat uninspired and mechanical way."

My cheeks flamed. If he had been vain enough to suppose that he had ever wrested a genuinely inspired and unstudied response from me, I could have summoned battalions of stinging words with which to undeceive him. But nevertheless, for him to dismiss my admittedly unloving, yet ultimately passionate, response as uninspired and mechanical was peculiarly irksome.

"I see," I said, and turned to leave the room.

"Wait, Fleur," said my husband.

But I did not want to hear any more. No matter what the justice of his case might be, the supercilious air with which he made it had routed my last, brief impulse to try to bridge the chasm between us. The short-lived concern I had heard in his voice on the stairway earlier in the day had touched me powerfully for an instant—until it was proven to have sprung only from his dread of fathering a child on me. I did not want to risk being undone once again.

"If you have anything left to say to me," I told him, turning back and only half masking a contrived yawn with my hand, "I hope you will make it brief and worth listening to, for once. All this ranting so quickly becomes tiresome."

"Very well then." His voice, which a moment earlier had been full of half-suppressed laughter, now became matter-of-fact. "There *is* one thing you ought to bear in mind—tiresome though it may be. If you should ever consider seeking a divorce, or even a separation, before my hand is played out, remember that I still have the paintings: And I won't hesitate to use them if that's what it takes to hold you to our bargain. I'm sure our friend Marcel can auction them as easily tomorrow as he might have in March. And I wouldn't mind recouping what they've cost me. So I advise you not to entertain the notion of leaving me before I am through with you. It won't be long—*that* I can promise you."

Although I could not imagine what worse threats he might make, I thought it would be reckless to incite him further. I left him, then, without another word.

When the coachman drove me to the railway station on the following Friday, I no longer felt that sick dread, but only the same terrible lassitude of my last years with Frederick.

Except for his luxuriously appointed bedroom, with its trappings of velvet, silk, and marble, and that ultramarine carpet so thick that one could drown in it, my husband's London home was furnished with a beauty that was almost stark in its simplicity.

Charingworth was the repository of priceless ancestral treasures, but in Grosvenor Square my husband had indulged his personal taste. He had restored the house to its original spare and classic lines, having stripped away the ostentatious embellishments favored by previous generations of Camwells. The clear, sunny colors he had selected for the interior offset what might have otherwise been an austere effect.

He was not at home when I arrived. I dined alone and went directly to my bedroom afterward. It was very late when I heard him return. He did not come to my room and left the house before breakfast the following morning.

Shortly after my solitary luncheon, I had an unexpected caller. I was in my sitting room, where I felt safe from any possibility of an accidental encounter with my husband should he return from whatever business or diversions had called him away, when a housemaid announced that Lord Marsden was downstairs.

I received him in one of the smaller drawing rooms, reminding myself that I must now call him Neville, which I found difficult. To me, he would always be Lord Marsden, Frederick's dazzling patron. Despite his air of genial, relaxed urbanity, today I thought he seemed faintly discomfited.

"I ran into Tony at my tailor's this morning," he told me. "He seems vastly improved, I am happy to say. When I last saw him, he looked so wretched that if he had been a dog, I'd have been tempted to put him out of his misery."

"When was that?" I asked uneasily. My husband was never ill.

"Oh, it was a chance encounter in Victoria Station. In March, I believe. Shortly after you returned from your visit to the charming Madame Sorrel. By the by, I hope that *she* has recovered completely."

"She is quite well now."

"I am glad of that. I was surprised when Tony mentioned to me that she had been ill, for I had attended a performance of hers the very night before you left for France, and she appeared to be in excellent health."

I did not reply.

"Well, that's a great actress for you," said Lord Marsden, extricating us from the awkwardness of silence. "But, as I was saying, Tony's spirits seem to have improved dramatically. He was alarmingly cheerful this morning. I haven't seen him glitter quite so dangerously since he embarked upon his campaign to throw his mother out of her own home."

"He *threw* her out?" I echoed faintly.

"Well, perhaps not in so many words. But it amounted to the same thing, really. It was when she still lived at Charingworth, you see, and he didn't want her there any longer. He began to assume such domineering airs that she couldn't continue to live under his roof. He made her life thoroughly disagreeable. It surprised her, I think, to discover that he can outdo her at her own pitiless games—when he chooses."

"I have no doubt of it," I murmured.

"Yes," continued Lord Marsden, leaning back in his chair. "It wasn't long after he'd come down from Cambridge. She'd lamed her hunter, so she took his favorite horse—without even asking him, I regret to say—and shattered its leg. He had to shoot it—he insisted on doing it himself, though any one of the grooms would have spared him that agony, and he did it cleanly, I must say, although it nearly killed him. I still remember the tears running down his face. Up until then, he'd always tolerated her highhandedness with astonishing good humor. I shouldn't have put up with it for a week. Still, you know Tony—he's slow to anger. But when he's pushed to it, he's completely unforgiving."

I couldn't help noticing how keenly Lord Marsden eyed me as he related this unhappy tale, although his tone was casual. I was reminded of the look on Watkins's face when he had told me, long ago, not to be deceived by the fact that my husband used a light rein. Too late had I learned the significance of *that* veiled warning.

As I handed Lord Marsden his tea, the spoon tinkled on the saucer.

There was a long silence while he sipped his tea. I did not fill my own cup. I could see, looking down, that my hands were still unsteady. I had become, I knew, the heir apparent to all the scorn my husband and his cousin shared for the infamous Lady Whitstone.

"I notice that you are not looking at all well yourself, my dear," Lord Marsden observed.

"I am perfectly well," I said tightly.

"I'm glad to hear that. I was concerned that perhaps whatever ailment seems to have afflicted your near and dear had communicated itself to you."

I was silent.

"Well, perhaps I'm imagining things. I tend to worry about you. That lovely painting of Hermione always reminds me of how you once looked. The contrast distresses me."

"Really, Neville," I said in a weak attempt at archness. "That is *not* very flattering. Everyone must grow older, and I am afraid that some of us age less attractively than others."

"In your case, that is nonsense," he retorted. "*You* are no more than a girl."

Oh, but I felt old. How long it had been since I had tasted the easy delights of youth! I shuddered inwardly as I remembered that recent night when I *had* momentarily forgotten my cares and my guilt and resentments, when I had drunk and laughed and kissed—and damned myself anew.

Lord Marsden set down his cup and leaned forward in his chair.

"Forgive me for speaking plainly," he said. "I have told myself repeatedly that I must not interfere, but to see two people for whom I care so much looking so miserable, each in their own fashion, compels me to greater candor than is my habit. I am sorry if this is difficult for you. I'm rather uncomfortable myself."

I was supremely uncomfortable and wished that I had had the foresight to have sent the housemaid back downstairs with the message that I was "not at home."

"I strongly advised Tony against marrying you," he said. "I thought it was a grave mistake."

I was glad, then, that I had not been holding a teacup, for it would surely have fallen to the floor at the astonishing revelation that he had campaigned against my marriage. I would have thought him my staunchest advocate.

"I did not believe you were in love with him," stated Lord Marsden bluntly. "I had known you as Brooks's wife. The difference in your manner toward Tony was painfully obvious to me. Of course, since he had not been acquainted with you then, and was so infatuated anyway, he could not see that—or much else."

"And you told him that!" I exclaimed.

"Oh, good heavens, no. As I have indicated, I find it difficult to speak as frankly as perhaps I sometimes ought. No, I merely remarked that it was much too soon after Brooks's unfortunate death for you to be able to give your heart to anyone. And that such a terrible loss can leave one so desolate and lonely that one is eager to clutch at any straw. I know."

His eyes, astoundingly, were full of sympathy. I remembered that my husband had once told me something about his cousin's devotion to his wife, who had died nearly a decade earlier.

"And in your case," he continued, "the emotional loss must have been aggravated by your other difficulties. I imagine you were feeling extremely vulnerable."

I flushed guiltily.

"That was my mistake," said Lord Marsden. "Up until then, Tony had discussed his intentions with me, but never with you. You see, he did respect your loss. But when I reminded him of your rather desperate circumstances and of how they might cloud your judgment, he seemed to fix upon that as a justification for advancing his untimely proposal rather than delaying it. He is rarely so incautious.

"Everyone knew that Brooks had been hounded by his creditors to the very hour of his death and that he had left you without a farthing. And when Tony fell so desperately in love with you, the temptation to play the hero and to rescue you from hardship proved irresistible. It made him wild to think of your having to pinch pennies while he lived in ease and comfort. Besides, he has always had such absolute faith in his abilities to master—through the sheer force of his will—any problem he sets himself to solve that he never doubted he could win your love. He admired you tremendously. I did, too."

I had always valued Lord Marsden's good opinion of me. The realization that I had forfeited this distressed me far more than had his earlier intimation of my husband's suffering—against *him* my heart was hardened. But I knew how well Lord Marsden loved his young cousin and where his strongest loyalties must lie, despite the compassion he had shown for me.

"Of course, when I realized that you were as determined as he to go ahead with the marriage after all, I made up my mind to voice no further reservations. It wasn't my affair. And it still is not. But I ought to have spoken out, even so. I see that only too clearly now. To fail to offer you whatever help I can at this juncture would only be to compound my error."

"You want to help *me?*" I whispered.

"But of course. It is easy to see who is most at fault in this unhappy contretemps and who has suffered the most. Tony has a knack, no matter how deeply he has been wounded, for shaking the dust off his heels and distancing himself completely from painful memories. I do not think that you have that happy faculty, my dear. Not only do you feel every cut—and I imagine that you have tasted a good many of those lately—but you assume that you deserve them, that all the guilt and all the responsibility are yours."

I could not speak. I could not believe my ears. I knew I was scarcely entitled to such kindness, but even so—to think that there existed another human being who comprehended my weaknesses and temptations and could yet have such faith in me made me feel faint.

"The fault was not Anthony's. It was entirely mine," I said at last in a low voice, although I still could not imagine any honorable means by which I might have extricated myself from Poncet's pincers.

"Nonsense. *I* don't condemn you for marrying Tony no matter what your reasons were. He can be very . . . persuasive. And the pressures upon you must have been overwhelming. Besides, he worshipped you, he wanted to lay the world at your feet, and seemed to demand so little in return. I expect you felt you would be doing him a favor and imagined that he could be satisfied with something less than love."

I could only blink my astonishment.

"But he, on the other hand, has everything to answer for. He had choices which you had not—that is the meaning of great wealth, it gives one infinite choices. And power over others. He understood the dangers—he was born to the knowledge that the best of women may be compelled to marry for the most sordid reasons having nothing to do with love. He had trained himself to some degree to use his wealth in a slightly more responsible way than merely to indulge his whims and his appetites. And then all that self-discipline collapsed. He wanted you, he had the power to buy you—ergo, he did."

This was more than I could absorb.

"You are correct," I said at last, "in surmising that your cousin has discovered there was far more truth in your warnings to him than in the vows I made when I married him."

"Well, it is as I suspected," Lord Marsden said with a sigh. "I was certain that nothing else could have reduced Tony to the state he was in when I ran into him in Victoria Station. However, he seems to have recovered his amour propre rather quickly. I must warn you, Fleur," he continued, "blameless as *I* may hold you, *he* will never forgive you. It is not in his nature. But one day he will come to his senses enough to acknowledge the not-so-shining part that he played. And that will be a very bleak day for Sir Anthony Camwell, for if he cannot forgive you, how can he forgive himself?"

Perhaps my husband *was* vulnerable on this score. I remembered the night he had come to my room and confessed his sense of guilt at having pressed his suit too soon.

"And that sad day *will* come, I guarantee it," continued the viscount. "But it seems, at present, to be rather a long way off. And in the meantime, I'm certain that my young cousin is cheerfully occupied in finding ways to make your life a misery to you and to remind you of how unworthy you are to bear his name."

"Something like that," I admitted. "You are very kind," I added. His kindness had finally vanquished the tremors in my hands. I took a deep breath and poured myself some tea. "I fear I have not behaved well, either," I confessed, "I think perhaps I have been far more unkind than . . ."

Than what? Than my husband deserved? He had shown me no mercy. Surely he did not deserve any.

". . . than I need have been," I concluded limply.

"Unlike your strong-willed husband," resumed Lord Marsden, "I have no illusions about my abilities to solve every dilemma. Yours I find particularly poignant because it was so predictable and yet I did nothing to avert it." He brooded for a moment or two. "It's a very painful thing to witness—two people, both so dear to me, who have succeeded in bringing only the keenest unhappiness to each other. What is to be done?"

"Yes, what is to be done," I mused, making it a comment upon the hopelessness of the situation rather than a question.

"Of course, there is only *one* truly civilized solution," declared the man of the world. It seemed that he had given the matter a great deal of thought. "A divorce would, of course, be unthinkable, and a legal separation would cause nearly as great a scandal; but I know that if Tony is brought to reason, you will be able to work out some polite arrangement that will keep you apart as much as possible, while preserving the social niceties."

I shuddered, almost imperceptibly.

"You don't approve," observed the viscount.

"It seems so . . . cold," I confessed, staring at the carpet.

"It does, doesn't it. But surely it can't be any worse than what I suspect you are enduring at present." He hesitated. "You *need* not go on like this, Fleur," he said at last. "I can put an end to it."

I lifted my eyes. My cheeks were hot.

"You can?" I whispered. "How?"

"I have told you that Tony's day of reckoning will come. He knows only too well that nothing good ever comes from squirming away from unpleasant truths. In the end, he will be compelled to face up to his own responsibility. When he has done so, his mood may not be charitable, but it will no longer be retaliatory. If he is left to himself, that may take weeks or even months. But if I were to intercede, if I were to put it to him bluntly, he would be forced to examine his conscience—sooner perhaps than he would like, but he is far too honest to turn away from what he must know is the truth."

I considered this carefully. If it were true, it would lay all my worst fears to rest, it would disarm my husband's threats, and free me from his dominion.

I heard my husband's voice. *How will you use your liberty?* and crimsoned, remembering the answer I had given him.

I pushed the thought away and considered, instead, Lord Marsden's great influence with my husband. I had never inquired as to its roots, but now I saw the reason for it. With such a heartless mother and, presumably, a weakling for a father—my husband had never spoken of the man, no doubt he was ashamed —how hungrily any child would have turned toward the aura of thoughtful, calm, worldly wisdom that Lord Marsden radiated.

"Well," I said carefully, "if I may reserve the right to accept your offer of help in the future, I should like to do so. But that is all. For the moment, I must ask you *not* to intercede on my behalf. I am very grateful to you, of course—immensely grateful. But for the present, I would prefer that you say nothing of this to Anthony."

"Certainly not, my dear, if that is your wish," said Lord Marsden, looking rather surprised. "But I can't imagine why you would refuse. I assure you, Fleur, Tony is not so unjust that he would blame you for confiding in me."

"It's not that," I said. "It's just that . . . well, Anthony is not close to many people. I know that you love him, and I believe you are one of the very few who are truly dear to him—the dearest of all, I think. How could I jeopardize that by putting you in a position where you might even *appear* to be taking my side, now that we are so divided? You say he would not blame me for confiding in you, and perhaps that is true. But he might well feel subtly injured by *you*, in spite of himself, and that would be a pity. I really believe, Neville, that the wisest and kindest thing you can do for *both* of us is simply to continue to be the loving, trusted, and unquestionably loyal friend to him that you have always been. No one who knows you can avoid being influenced by your goodness —Anthony least of all. You have no reason to worry about me. Your compassion and your generosity have done more to raise my spirits than I can say." *And I will try to be more deserving of them,* I vowed silently.

Lord Marsden gave me a long, searching look as he rose to his feet to leave.

"I think perhaps you have a warmer heart than you give yourself credit for," he said at last.

I held out my hand. He took it, bowed slightly, and left me feeling both comforted and troubled by his visit. In the end, I went outside to walk off my turmoil in Hyde Park.

By the time I had taken myself back to Grosvenor Square, I was resolved to curb my tongue and to extend toward my husband some of the same generosity with which Lord Marsden had showered me.

But how speedily do the best of intentions crumble under the smallest provocations!

When my husband returned late in the afternoon, he quickly undermined his cousin's salutary effect on my temper. He found me in my sitting room, where I had once again taken sanctuary, and wordlessly handed me an envelope. My first observation was that it had been opened; my second, that it bore Marguerite's return address. Nothing could have made me feel more violated; for a moment I bit back speech, out of fear of the rage that might otherwise spew from my lips.

At last I remarked calmly, "I never dreamed that you would stoop to open my letters. That's a new low—even for you."

"Perhaps you ought to turn the envelope," was my husband's equally calm rejoinder.

I did.

It was addressed to Sir Anthony Camwell, Bt., and Lady Camwell, at Charingworth, and had been dispatched thence to Grosvenor Square.

My husband, still standing over me, said nothing more. Perhaps he was expecting an apology, but an apology would have been absurd. Had not he himself boasted that I had no idea what he was capable of—how could I possibly be faulted for having assumed the worst?

I drew out the letter and read it. It was very brief—merely an invitation to the first night of Marguerite's new play, which was to open in Paris at the end of the week. The tone was cheerfully impersonal.

I was nearly overcome with emotion at my faithful friend's instantaneous response to the veiled appeal of my recent letter to her. I laid down the invitation carefully, without looking up. I did not want to let my husband catch my expression.

"Would you care to go?" he asked.

I composed my face and lifted my head.

"Do my wishes matter to you?"

"No, I suppose not," he conceded with a smile, and added, "I have decided to accept the invitation."

"For both of us?" I asked, trying not to reveal my eagerness.

"Oh yes," he said. "Aside from the fact that I have always enjoyed Madame Sorrel's performances, I am curious to discover what has inspired this unusual invitation, and there is not much likelihood of that, I think, if I don't bring you along."

It was true—the invitation was very much out of the ordinary. Marguerite, although she thought very highly of herself, was completely lacking in the kind of vanity that assumes one's friends must be eager to witness one's every triumph.

"Perhaps it is a particularly fine play," I suggested.

My husband's lips curved. He picked up the invitation and pointed to the play's title. *L'Embuscade.* The Ambush. It could only be yet another of those broad farces in which Marguerite invariably shone.

"That must be it," he agreed, with an expression which clearly told me that he found my explanation wanting.

He strolled off toward the doorway.

"Anthony," I called softly just as he reached it.

He turned.

"I am sorry," I told him with difficulty, "that I accused you of opening my letters."

His response was not encouraging.

"So am I," he said impassively, and left me to ponder his meaning.

XXIII

We dined out a good deal that week and entertained a little as well. Although we did not go so far as to wave white flags at each other and negotiate an armistice, there was a notable cessation of hostilities.

Perhaps I resisted the temptation to provoke my husband merely because I did not want to give him any excuse to deprive me of the tête à tête with Marguerite for which I so desperately longed.

Or perhaps I had been softened by the knowledge that, no matter how deeply I might have affronted their own high notions of honorable and decent behavior, I still had friends. I knew now that neither Neville nor Marguerite would abandon me to my husband's untender mercies. This was a great comfort, for his apparent interest in the trip to Paris still gave me moments of alarm. What seemed inconceivable in the light of day, or when he was smiling at me in company across a gleaming, candlelit table, seemed perfectly and horribly possible in the dark.

He treated me now, in public, with an air of remote, amused indulgence. He was never unkind; he was never affectionate. He appeared to enjoy the attention and admiration that I—or, at any rate, my striking new wardrobe—attracted wherever we went. But enjoyment, I came to realize, is not quite the same thing as happiness. When we were alone, he maintained a much chillier distance.

In Paris we stayed once again at the regally appointed Hôtel Continental on the Rue de Castiglione. But my husband had booked a larger suite than the one we had shared at the start of our honeymoon; this time, we lay in separate bedrooms.

Marguerite and Théo called upon us the morning following our arrival. Marguerite was so charming to my husband that I almost feared she had taken his side. Théo, who was looking very well, was even worse. He behaved with so much bonhomie that I was sure my husband must suspect it of being false. Yet my husband repaid him in kind, and soon—as if they had known each other all their lives—they were having a spirited argument about Puvis de Chavannes, whose paintings my husband admired considerably more than Théo did. They moved on to discuss their mutual enthusiasm for the works of Henri Rousseau.

The delightful visit was so brief that I barely had time to recover from my dumbstruck surprise before our guests departed. My fears that my friend had gone over to my enemy's camp were routed when, as she stepped forward to give me a final hug, Marguerite pressed a tightly folded bit of paper into my palm. I slipped it into my sleeve and returned her embrace with far more emotion than the occasion seemed to call for.

Perhaps my husband had recognized that indeed something was afoot, for after Marguerite and Théo's departure, he appeared suddenly reluctant to leave me alone. But as soon as we returned to our suite after luncheon, I declared myself to be very tired and in need of a nap.

"How I wish I were less fatigued. I was so looking forward to wandering about Paris. You won't go out and leave me here alone, will you, Anthony?" I added plaintively, for I wished to make certain that he would not slip out and meet with Poncet while I was feigning sleep.

"Certainly not," he assured me to my relief. "I would not dream of leaving you alone."

Unfortunately, this uxorious concern would soon prove to be my undoing.

Once I was safely sequestered behind the door of my bedroom, I drew Marguerite's note from its hiding place.

"Darling Fleur," she had written, "Do *not* come to the theater tonight. Your upstanding husband must come alone—for I would be *highly* insulted if *both* of you were to absent yourselves! *You*, however, are to plead a severe headache or any convincing ailment that is temporarily debilitating but unlikely to kill you!

"I have the impression from your letter that your husband has decided to occupy the moral high ground with respect to you, but I have discovered a few things that should speedily dislodge him from a position he has *no right to adopt!* Do not be distressed, I beg you, to learn that I have heard these things from Madame Germaine Mansard, *née* Poncet. She turned up as the scene painter on a production for which Théo did the playbill. We have become very good friends! Believe me, Fleur, she is a young woman of *fine* character and has the *greatest* sympathy for you. She will come to your room tonight at a quarter to nine to deliver what I hope may be a useful weapon against your husband.

"Forgive me, darling. I know how all this must pain you, but warfare is never pleasant, is it? And you will discover that your husband has no business accusing *you* of violating *his* trust!"

She was correct about one thing: I did not like the idea of once again looking into the limpid eyes of Germaine Mansard— *née* Poncet—eyes which had already seen too much, no matter how stoutly they might refuse to pass judgment. But I was in no position to refuse any weapon that might fall into my hands, and, to be honest, I was also ravaged by a perverse curiosity about what Madame Mansard might reveal.

When, after several hours, I still had not emerged from my bedroom, my husband finally came to rouse me. I sat up in bed and passed my hand over my forehead.

"I can't imagine what is wrong with me," I murmured faintly.

"You don't feel well?" he inquired.

"Not at all. The Channel crossing was so trying. And then that endless train ride. But I had hoped to feel better once we were settled here. It's unthinkable that I should miss Marguerite's first night after having traveled so far to see it!"

"Unthinkable, yes," he agreed, looking at me with an odd smile.

I sank back into the pillows. It was not difficult to look convincingly piteous: All I had to do was to contemplate the possibility that he might absolutely insist upon my going with him to the theater.

Fortunately, he was not yet so hardened a cynic that my performance failed to move him. As he surveyed me, his face grew increasingly troubled, and finally he repeated, with evident anxiety, the question which now seemed to prey most heavily upon his mind.

"Are you *quite* certain that you are not with child?"

His drawn look and his low tone told me, beyond any doubt, of the abhorrence with which he regarded this possibility.

At this realization, all my good resolutions failed me.

"Don't flatter yourself," I said sharply, momentarily forsaking the kidskin gloves.

He lifted an eyebrow.

"Well," I pointed out, "it *would* be practically a miracle, wouldn't it?"

His face darkened. And then he began to laugh.

"What a way you have of expressing yourself," he remarked. "You really have no heart at all, have you?"

"I don't know what you mean. Have I offended your sense of propriety?"

He sighed. "Oh no, Fleur," he said, looking down at the floor and shaking his head with amusement. "That is not what I was thinking at all." He lifted his gaze. "Perhaps you ought to rest a while longer. You may feel stronger by evening."

Some time during the evening, however, I began to feel a good deal worse, for—after agreeing that I appeared far too frail to get up from my bed; after arranging to have a tureen of soup sent up to me from the kitchens; and after descending to the hotel dining room to take his own meal—my husband returned, commented that I looked more peaked then ever, berated himself for having left my side, and declared that he could not even think of doing so for a second time.

I protested. There was no need for him to stay with me: Both my maid, Marie, and Stanford, his valet, had accompanied us to Paris; the hotel had a large and attentive staff. For neither of us to appear at the opening we had come so far to celebrate, when only one of us was disabled, would be such a disappointment to Marguerite.

My husband dismissed all my objections. He had given Marie and Stanford the evening off; nothing could be more impersonal than the services of a hotel staff; he would be a heartless churl to abandon me when I was so ill—even Marguerite must agree.

"But why deprive *yourself?*" I asked. "It serves no purpose. All I want is rest."

"And I intend to see that your rest is not disturbed," he said. "However, you will be comforted to know that I shall stay *very* close at hand, should you require *any*thing at all."

He closed the door and left me.

Thus thwarted, I tried to anticipate the events that lay ahead and decided that I did not want to face them in only the night-clothes I was wearing or, at best, a dressing gown. As noiselessly as possible—and trusting that my husband would keep his word not to disturb me—I put on the dress I had removed earlier. From the sitting room, I could hear the occasional faint but crisp rustle of my husband's newspaper.

At precisely a quarter to nine, I heard a rap at the outer door, followed by more rustling—as he presumably folded his newspaper and laid it down. I opened my door a crack. I hoped that as soon as she saw my husband, Madame Mansard might have the presence of mind to pretend that she had come to the wrong room.

And she did.

"Oh, I beg your pardon, monsieur," I heard her say breathlessly. "What floor *is* this? I seem to have knocked at the wrong door."

"Oh, I don't think you are mistaken, mademoiselle," was my husband's cordial response. "You are the nurse Lady Camwell sent for, are you not?"

I held my breath.

"Do come in and sit down," he continued disingenuously. "Her ladyship is sleeping now."

Oh, the gall of the man! I bit my lip.

Madame Mansard seemed to hesitate.

"I am on my way out," concluded my husband. "You are very late, you know. I have already missed the curtain, and I'll be lucky to catch much of the second act." He sounded piqued, as if she were to blame.

Madame Mansard stepped into the trap, and without making his exit, my husband closed the door.

That was when I left the wings and walked onto the stage of this private drama. Madame Mansard shot me an uncertain look.

"I am afraid that my husband has no intention of going anywhere," I told her. "And therefore you and I can have no business with each other, after all. I am very sorry to have—"

"On the contrary," interjected my husband firmly, "I suspect that we three have a great deal to talk about." He turned to me.

"Perhaps we should begin by discussing why you have gone to such lengths to arrange this rendezvous behind my back. I think it is high time to sit down and lay our cards on the table."

But it was Madame Mansard who took control of the situation.

"But, of course," she said with perfect aplomb. Then she turned to me. "May I put my coat in your bedchamber, Lady Camwell?" she asked.

I led her quickly to my bedroom, before my husband could stop us, and closed the door.

"Well, what shall we do?" she asked, removing her hat. "We had better be quick, I don't think he will let us remain alone together for very long."

"Does he know you?" I asked.

"He has never seen me before in his life."

"Then you must leave," I said. "There is no reason for you to become any further entangled in this sorry business. It was very kind of you to come here, but there is really nothing to be done, under the circumstances."

"But what about you? I understand, from Madame Sorrel, that Sir Anthony has not treated you well at all in recent weeks. His suspicions are already very high—if I should leave now, without satisfying his curiosity, might it not provoke him against you further?"

"I hardly think so. Anyway, it doesn't matter."

"I find I am rather tempted to take him up on his offer," continued Madame Mansard thoughtfully. She began stripping off her gloves. "I would love to confront him with his sins. He seems awfully sure of himself. I wouldn't mind knocking him down a bit. And I really don't believe it could make things more unpleasant for you. Quite the contrary. But it is up to you, of course. The risk is yours."

I considered this. There *was* something peculiarly intriguing about the notion of making my husband turn on the spit for at least a little while. I had occupied that unhappy position far too long.

My husband opened the door.

He looked excruciatingly uncomfortable.

"I beg your pardon," he announced to Madame Mansard, "but I am afraid I cannot permit you to say anything further to Lady Camwell that you do not say to me as well."

Madame Mansard and I exchanged glances.

"Well, if you really don't mind," I told her, "this may be rather interesting."

"Oh, I don't mind at all," she assured me. "I expect it will give me great pleasure."

She removed her coat, displaying a worn and paint-splattered dress. I liked it. I liked her.

With my husband at our heels like a sheepdog, we returned to the sitting room.

"Who the devil are *you?*" asked my husband ungraciously, as soon as Madame Mansard had taken her seat.

"I beg your pardon," retorted our visitor coldly. "I have not come here to be interrogated by you. I am here to give Lady Camwell some information, which she has very generously agreed to let me share with you, as well. Although none of it will be a revelation to you."

My husband frowned faintly as if he were trying to assess a most puzzling situation.

Madame Mansard turned to me. "May I speak frankly, Lady Camwell?"

"Oh, please do," I said. "Be as frank as you like."

"Lady Camwell," she then proceeded, "I understand that, as a result of having discovered a secret in your past, your husband has adopted an attitude of . . . extreme disapproval. Would that be correct?"

"Yes, I think so," I said. "Would you agree, Anthony?"

"Oh, I'm just here to listen," he demurred lazily.

He had erased the frown from his face and now reclined in his armchair, with his fingertips pressed piously together.

"Do go on, please, madame," I said.

"Yes, well, I wished only to bring to your attention, Lady Camwell, the sad fact that your husband's morals and behavior—his utter disregard for you and for the vows he made to you, long, *long* before he learned your unhappy secret—are far more condemning than anything *you* may have done."

This was what I was here for, and yet, as she spoke, I felt the unpleasant fiery shiver that comes when one begins to realize that one has been deceived. My husband, too, now looked very altered. He had straightened in his chair and was staring at his accuser keenly. His ordinarily pale face was suffused with color.

"I am afraid that I have learned a great deal about the baronet's lamentable habits from my father," continued Madame Mansard. "My father, with whom I am no longer on any terms at all, loves nothing more than to unearth—"

My husband leaned forward abruptly.

"I know who you are," he said softly. "You are Germaine Poncet."

"I was born Germaine Poncet," was her calm reply. "But that is no longer my name. As I was saying, Lady Camwell, my father likes nothing better than to collect any scandalous information he can about the weaknesses and appetites of the very people who have made him rich. Often he is able to profit from these—as he did in your case—but I believe he truly enjoys them for their own sake. What he gleaned about your husband, for example, did not lend itself to blackmail, but it gave my father endless hours of amusement to think how much money he was able to extort from you, Lady Camwell, so that you might retain your husband's regard, while your husband was betraying you with every courtesan in London—or at any rate, all those who were blessed with black hair and small waists."

My husband got up from his chair suddenly and went to the window. I would have liked to leave the room altogether, but I could not move. Yes, in the heat of his anger, he had said something about having mistresses, and yes, he had certainly implied that it had started long before he learned my bitter secret, but later . . . had he not assured me—that night when he had accused me of faithlessness while proclaiming his own fidelity—that none of it was so? I took a labored breath.

Now I realized that, in spite of all the evidence to suggest it, I had never truly believed that he had been with other women since he had married me. I had discounted his claims as something he had invented to taunt me; I had attributed even his erotic sophistication and his curious acquaintance with Madame Rullier to the experiences of bachelorhood.

"Lady Camwell," I dimly heard Madame Mansard saying with real concern, "I hope I am not distressing you."

I strove to bleach all expression from my face.

"Not at all."

My husband turned from the long window. His own face wore its customary look of imperturbability. His gaze did not waver from mine; it was mine that glided on, back to Madame Mansard, while he lounged against the window hangings with an air of arrogant disregard.

"I don't know, Lady Camwell, how much you wish to know. Your husband has had a series of mistresses—he never keeps any of them for long. He is said to be very good to them; no one has ever spoken ill of him in that respect. But he really did conduct himself disgracefully—"

"Disgracefully? Are those the morals your father taught you?" interrupted my husband with faint scorn.

"It is what my conscience tells me," retorted Madame Mansard. "Perhaps you would do well to listen to your own more often. Cast your mind back to that villa in St. John's Wood? Was not *that* a disgrace?"

"I'm afraid I am not certain of which one you are speaking. There have been several."

"The one where the three sisters lived."

A fond expression stole over my husband's face.

"Oh, that one! What delightful young ladies they were. I used to call them the Three Graces. But I cannot think of anything, with respect to them, that *I* would term '*dis*graceful.' Certainly not."

"And those notorious billiard games at Mrs. Hawkes's house? The players were very agile, to say the least, and the rules altered beyond belief!"

"Ah yes. The billiard games," murmured my husband. His lips seemed to be fighting a smile, and he had a faraway look in his eyes.

"Is that the worst of it?" I asked quickly, when I had managed to steady my breath.

"Oh, it's merely typical. No worse or better than the rest. Of course, there *is* the matter of the money he squandered on these women. There was one who had her nipples pierced to signify her devotion to him—"

"That was her idea, not mine," said my husband. "I forbade it, in fact, but she had a mind of her own—it was one of her greatest charms. And I will admit that, once the deed was done, I found the results utterly bewitching."

"And gave her those gold rings set with diamonds to wear in them—"

"That's right, I did," reflected my husband cheerfully. "I had forgotten about the diamonds. The rubies, although not as costly, were so much more becoming. They were my favorites."

"—while you left your *wife* to languish alone in the country, dressed in rags," pressed his relentless prosecutor.

My husband whitened as if he had been struck.

"I think I have learned as much as I wish to know," I interposed hastily. "There is only one other thing, a small thing, really. When did it start? Or have these always been his habits?"

"They were once—before he began courting you," said Madame Mansard. "After that—and even after the honeymoon, for a week or two—he led an exemplary life. But it appears to have been one of those sad cases of the leopard who cannot change his spots."

The leopard, having recovered himself, still leaned against the window, now looking as if he had been richly entertained.

"Thank you, madame," I whispered through stiff lips.

"Well then, if there is nothing more to be said on the subject, I will leave you," announced Poncet's daughter, getting to her feet.

I pulled myself to mine.

"Thank you so much," I said, forcing myself to show greater warmth as I followed her into my bedroom, where she collected her things. "It was kind and generous of you to offer me your help. If there is anything I can ever do for you—"

"I hate what my father did to you," she said bluntly. "And he's no better—" She jerked her chin in the direction of the room we had left. "But what a cool one! How can these men be such hypocrites!"

Unfortunately, as soon as she had gone, my facade began to crumble. My throat felt knotted, my eyes burned.

"Well, I can't imagine what the point of that was," declared my husband airily, once I had closed the door on the astonishing visitor. "A very admirable young woman. Who would have dreamed that that worm-eaten old tree could have produced such wholesome fruit? But it's not as if she told you anything I had not already told you myself."

"Yes, what a pity. I was rather hoping there might be something about your mother or a sheep."

"No such luck, I'm afraid. Even *my* tastes aren't *that* wide-ranging."

"And you never *did* tell me everything!" I cried stupidly. "Billiards, for God's sake! *I've* never seen you go *near* a billiard table!"

He started to laugh.

"Once I would have dearly loved to teach *you* my way of playing billiards," he said. "But, sad to say, you have never displayed the smallest enthusiasm for such pastimes." I opened my mouth to protest that he had never broached the subject with me, but I closed it again when he added, in withering tones, "Until recently, of course." He threw me a meaningful smile, but it faded quickly as he demanded, "Whatever are you doing now?"

"I'm going out. This room is an inferno."

"Let me open the windows. You can't possibly think of going outside. The air is very damp, and I believe it has begun to rain."

"Oh, what do I care!" I cried, throwing my coat over my shoulders.

"Then I will go with you," said my husband.

"What is the point of that?"

"You do not look well," he replied, "and I don't think much of your walking about alone at this hour—not in the state you appear to be in."

"Oh, do what you will," I said. "But if you must follow me about like a gaoler, at least be good enough not to talk."

He took his umbrella, and we made our exit.

XXIV

I walked blindly along the Jardin des Tuileries to the Place de la Concorde, where I turned toward the river. A fine rain was falling, like a balm to my blazing cheeks. I did not take shelter under my husband's umbrella, nor did he press himself upon me; at length he closed the umbrella. The soft, vaporous rain now fell upon his uncovered head—for in his haste to follow me, he'd left his hat behind—as he continued to walk silently beside me.

I could not unravel my tangled emotions. The help I had been secretly hoping for from Poncet's daughter—some scandal so far beyond mere adultery that I *could* petition for a divorce—had not been forthcoming; surely that was the reason for my misery. But would my turmoil have been less if she *had* told of some truly depraved act, such as I had spoken of to my husband after she had left us. No. In truth, I was relieved that at least she'd had nothing of quite *that* turpitude to relate.

But that meant, of course, that I was still bound to him. My husband had taken the slight little weapon Madame Mansard had handed me, and he had snapped it across his knee. Far from being embarrassed or chagrined enough by her account of his misdeeds to recognize the hypocrisy of punishing me for mine, he had relished each charming memory as it was rekindled.

And I, too vain and self-absorbed to have dreamed that he had flung himself into such pursuits, was unhappier than ever.

I thought again of his threat to have me painted. Now I acknowledged at last what I had always known—that he possessed far too much pride to do any such thing. Perhaps he had developed that hauteur in defense against his mother's representation that to marry a Camwell, a mere baronet, had been for her, the daughter of a marquess, an act of enormous condescension. Certainly I knew of no qualities that particularly distinguished the Camwell family, other than its old name and its great wealth. I had concluded long ago that my husband's deceased father must have been a virtual half-wit to have married so cold and unloving a woman as the present Lady Whitstone.

Perhaps my husband had come to the same conclusion about his parents' marriage. Perhaps this was why he had managed to blind himself to his own wife's lovelessness and why he had reacted so violently when the truth could no longer be denied.

But if he had been as blind as he had appeared, then he had been idling away the hours in those mysterious villas and enjoying those infamous games of billiards with his ruby-breasted mistresses even while he yet believed that I had married him for love.

And he—whose fundamental honesty I had never doubted— had lied to me.

These bitter thoughts carried me down the Quai des Tuileries, along the lovely, silent river where Frederick had drowned. A few tears scalded my cheeks, but they were cooled by the sweet, small rain that still blew softly down. I walked farther—along the Quai du Louvre, past that immense and dazzling palace where my husband's courtship had begun, past the Pont des Arts and on to the Pont-Neuf.

There I stopped and ensconced myself upon the stony bench within one of the bridge's graceful, curving bays, where lovers linger to whisper and kiss when the nights are warm and the weather fair. Turning to rest my arms upon the parapet, I stared up the river toward the Île de la Cité, where the forbidding walls of the Conciergerie, that severe medieval castle, press so heavily upon the island's edge.

I gazed for a long, long time at its stark towers, part fairy tale, part nightmare. And then, oblivious to the glow falling from the lanterns above me, oblivious to the people and carriages still passing over the bridge, I buried my face in my arms.

"I think you had better tell me what is troubling you," said my husband firmly after some time had passed.

I turned toward him.

"You!" I said. "You and your threats! I had hoped Poncet's daughter might have some bit of information for me that I could use to escape this miserable marriage, but it's no use—oh God!"

I looked down, down into the slow-moving water and thought of Frederick, who had been so warm and bright, and whose bones lay forever still in the cool, damp earth of a pauper's grave, on which this same soft rain must now be falling. I thought, too, of my tiny, nameless daughter's fate, and dropped my face back into the nest of my arms, all but sobbing aloud with an impossible grief that yet seemed strangely disconnected from those old, familiar sorrows. . . .

"Threats?" said my husband. "What threats?"

I lifted my head.

"Oh, you wretch, you devil!" I cried, to discharge some of that excess of emotion. "How can you act so innocent? What threats, indeed? Why, to have a painting made from that ghastly photograph, of course. And then to sell those other paintings back to that monster, who would drink my very blood, if he could!"

My husband sank down upon the hard, rain-slick seat beside me. He shook his head slowly.

"The photograph!" he exclaimed, staring at me with an expression of utter astonishment. "Lord love you, Fleur, are you a complete goose? Surely you know there was no plate in the camera, and even if there *had* been, there wasn't enough light in the room to capture the faintest image! I was playing with you that night—I thought you knew that! I even imagined you were enjoying it. That is, until you turned so nasty the following morning."

Now it was my turn to go slackjawed.

"No photograph!" I whispered.

"No photograph," he articulated, one syllable at a time.

I tried to clear my spinning head.

"But you took me at my word," he went on in a low, choked voice. "My God, even if you *are* a complete ignoramus about cameras, I thought you knew *me* at least *somewhat*. Did you really imagine that I was capable of anything so vile?" He shook his head once more in that baffled way. "Well, I suppose you did," he said at last. "But believe me, Fleur, I still have far too much"—he paused and then concluded rather stiffly—"regard for myself to do anything quite so ignoble as what *you* have credited me with."

"Well, *you* made the threats!" I said. "*I* didn't invent them."

"I *said* those things because it was the only thing I could think of to do that might stop me from smacking you. Can you possibly understand that?"

"Oh," I said. I still felt giddy, as if some horrible weight had been lifted, but it was not a pleasant sort of vertigo—my relief was tinged with bitterness that I had spent so many nights with fear coiled in my heart like a serpent, sometimes raising its head, sometimes baring its fangs, and only occasionally slumbering.

My husband, who had drawn himself up to explain himself to me, was now leaning forward with his forehead in his hand. Raindrops clung to his hair. Finally he raised his head and turned toward me. He wore a look of genuine remorse.

"Truly," he said, "I never meant to cause you so *much* distress."

"I think you did," I whispered.

A yet more shaken expression came over his face as he considered this, but he looked straight at me.

"Well," he said, still in that very low voice. "Perhaps I did. In any case, it was inexcusable. I most desperately regret it."

He paused. I said nothing.

"I don't know how to express how sorry I am," he concluded. "I never dreamed that I might have caused you any real suffering. Can you forgive me?"

"Forgive you!" I exclaimed. I thought of all I had endured, I remembered that painful interview with Neville Marsden, my frantic clutch at the lifeline of Marguerite's friendship, and, most particularly, the appalling revelations of the past few hours. My throat closed up entirely.

That was my answer.

After a very long time, my husband said coolly, "There is one other thing for which I owe you the deepest apology. About this evening . . ."

My heart seemed to lift, but it sank back to its usual depths as he continued, "I would never have been so unmannerly as to intrude myself into a private conversation, were it not for my fear that you had somehow fallen back into Poncet's power. I could not imagine why you were making such secretive arrangements. Then I recalled your last visit to Paris, and it occurred to me that perhaps he had somehow managed to gain yet another hold over you. I knew very well that, if that *were* the case, you would never confide your troubles to me, so I thought it would be best to uncover any intrigue that might already be underway."

"And once you realized that that was not the case," I replied, "you might have allowed me to speak with Madame Mansard privately."

He laughed.

"Oh? You think I ought to have slunk away, leaving the two of you to gossip about me, as if I were ashamed?"

"*Aren't* you ashamed?"

"No," he said. "Not in the least. Why would I be ashamed?"

"But you think *I* should be ashamed of *my* misdeeds."

"Oh yes. Absolutely."

I understood his own violent longings then. I yearned to push him from the bridge so forcefully that his proud neck would snap as his head struck the river bottom.

Instead, I said, "You lied to me."

He stared at me in apparent confusion.

Finally, he said, "Aside from those empty threats, I have never lied to you, Fleur."

I gasped with incredulous laughter.

"You told me you were faithful to me."

"I never did. In fact, I believe I indicated quite the opposite."

"I thought it was an idle boast. And you confirmed that when you told me you had *not* been unfaithful."

His eyes widened with undisguised bewilderment.

"I never told you any such thing, I swear it. I don't know what you can be thinking of."

"Have you forgotten so quickly? 'Remember,' you said, 'it was not *I* who was unfaithful to *you*.' But you were."

The puzzlement faded from my husband's face.

"Oh, that," he said.

"Yes, that. There you stood, chiding me for *my* bad faith, while avowing your own fidelity!"

"You are mistaken," said my husband. "You have distorted both my words and their meaning. Let me refresh your memory. What I said to you was, 'It was not *my* faithlessness which brought you to this.' I never said that I had been faithful. I merely said that *my* faithlessness was not the source of your troubles. How could it be? But you misunderstood me, of course, and took it as a slight against you."

"Wasn't it?"

He did not answer.

I leaned into the parapet. Finally, I said slowly, "If it wasn't to slight me, then what *did* you mean?"

Instead of answering, he said with a laugh, "I value my life too much to answer that. You already look as if you would dearly love to cut my heart out. Why is that? Why have you never asked yourself where all your anger rightfully belongs?"

"I suppose *you* think I ought to have gone to Poncet and stabbed him in his bath, like Charlotte Corday!"

"Not at all. If I believed he lay at the root of your suffering, or that his death would end it, I would have done the deed myself. With pleasure."

Instead of being flattered by the heroic assertion that he would have braved the guillotine for me, I said, "I think you are the most corrupt hypocrite on the face of the earth."

He laughed again. "Perhaps. But at least I cannot claim to have corrupted my high-minded wife. I am *not* the one who deserves the credit for *that.*"

Then I began to understand him. He was wise to fear for his life.

"I was completely faithful to Frederick," I said. "As he was to me. I loved him. I could never love anyone else. Yes, I modeled for those paintings you despise, it's true, but everything else about them is pure invention. *He* was an artist, thank God, not a prig and a whoremonger. He had an artist's imagination. I loved it. He was everything I ever wanted."

"I have no doubt of that," returned my husband placidly, to my surprise. "But your irreproachable behavior in your perfectly idyllic marriage to St. Frederick of Montmartre has very little bearing upon this one. *I* did not make you what you chose to become by marrying me, and my conscience certainly doesn't trouble me on *that* score."

"Ha!" I said, focusing with bitter satisfaction on his belittling reference to Frederick. "There it is! I knew it! You've always envied Frederick. He was everything you could never be."

"You're quite mistaken," said my husband. "I have never in my life wished that I might trade places with Frederick Brooks. Except once, perhaps," he added after a pause.

"He had everything," I persisted unkindly, "that all your wealth, all your noble connections could never give you. *He* had talent. He created masterpieces. *You* could only buy them. He had vitality, zest. He lived life to the hilt. And I loved him. Everyone did."

"You are utterly mistaken," repeated my husband calmly, after a long, alarming silence that almost made me regret my cruel words. "He was very talented, and fortunate in many ways. But I can tell you this: I would not change places with him for the world."

"That's easy to say—now that he's dead."

"And just *why* is he dead?" retorted my husband swiftly.

That brought my tongue to a halt. I knew the answer too well. He was dead because of me. It would have been kinder had I put a gun to his head, rather than sapping his vitality, his talent, by wallowing in my useless, vain despair.

"He is dead because he sold the woman he claimed to love and then drowned himself in absinthe to avoid having to think about what he had done," stated my husband brutally. "How could I envy a man like that?"

I floundered with shock.

"He loved me," I whispered.

"No doubt," said my husband dryly. "And it's plain to see how great a love this man of genius had for you, isn't it?"

I gasped. I felt as if he had kicked me in the stomach. I wanted to rip his eyes out. But I couldn't allow him to think such things of Frederick, so I pulled myself together and said in a cold and steady voice, "What do you know? You have no idea what it is to be poor. You don't know what it is to have creditors banging at your door, to fear being seen in the streets, having to duck down alleyways to avoid running into someone to whom you owe money."

Oh, how sordid it sounded! No wonder my husband's haughty and privileged patrician features gleamed with contempt!

"You are right, of course," he said disdainfully. "I have no idea what *that* might be like. But I know myself. And I know what I would have done, had I been your husband and had I believed that selling those paintings was the only way out of my difficulties."

"What *would* you have done?" I challenged. "*Do* tell me, what would you, one of the richest men in England, do if you woke up tomorrow to find you had nothing left—no money, no friends to whom you were not up to your ears in debt, nothing? Can you even *imagine* being so desperate! I think not."

He was silent.

I shivered and waited.

My husband seemed to be fighting with himself. After a very long time, he said quietly, almost gently, "It is clear to me that Brooks's views on love and marriage were somewhat different from my own. His apparently satisfied *your* tastes, mine do not. It really makes no difference, now, what I might have done had I found myself in his shoes. If you knew me better, you would be able to answer the question yourself."

"Oh, that's really low," I said. "To judge him so glibly—you, who have never tasted poverty! And you can't even say what *you'd* have done differently!"

"Call it whatever you like," said my husband equably. "If ours were the kind of marriage I dreamed of when I proposed to you, and if you had loved me at all"—for an instant his voice seemed to resonate with passion—"you would know instantly what I would have done differently. As it is, it hardly matters. You seem to approve of the way he handled the situation."

"He had no choice."

"Oh?" said my husband, and went on as if the words were breaking out in spite of his efforts to hold them back. "This man of so much vision and *imagination* had no choice?"

"Poverty gives people very few choices."

"I hope I have never condemned anyone for being poor nor for doing whatever they must to keep body and soul together," said my husband with frosty pride. "How could I presume to do that? It would be the very height of arrogance."

"Then you must exonerate Frederick. I know you despise him for being a wastrel and for leaving me penniless. But his only crime was that he liked fine things, as you do, and that he bought absinthe instead of women when he wished to forget his disappointments, and—oh yes, his worst crime—he had no hellish collieries and starving tenants to support his tastes, and therefore had to sell his paintings."

"It never crossed my mind to think of him as a wastrel," protested my husband, laughing. "Until I learned precisely what he had done to you. When did *you* learn of it, by the way? Poncet led me to believe it came as something of a surprise to you. I merely thought he was a brilliant artist who had succumbed to a tragic weakness. As for me, I am afraid I haven't got any hellish collieries —my soft-hearted father divested himself of that sort of thing, much to my mother's dismay—and if you see even so much as a starving dog on the lands over which I am fortunate enough to have stewardship, I hope you will tell me so."

I was still nearly choking on my fury. I could not have answered him to save my life.

"If you'd like to know where the money comes from that protected your reputation and now keeps you clothed and housed and fed," continued my husband calmly, "I am more than willing to review my investments with you. My father put his money where it wouldn't prick his tender conscience too painfully, and I have tried to honor his wishes in that respect, but—wouldn't you know —the returns have been embarrassingly great. However, if you find I have some particularly odious source of income that offends your sensibilities, I'll shed myself of it posthaste. Since my ill-gotten gains will be supporting you for the rest of your life, I would hate to have you feel they were too tainted for you to fully enjoy whatever you may spend them on."

To be honest, it was some of the places where his money had gone—far more than whence it had come—that troubled me the most, but I was still in a retaliatory vein.

"You surprise me," I said. "I was beginning to think you took real pleasure in holding the whip."

"Oh, I do," he agreed readily. "I like it better than anything. I don't think you can imagine how much pleasure it gives me to make others bend to my will. But it *is* a disagreeable trait, I fear, and one that I have struggled rather hard to overcome." He paused and threw me a sidewise glance; he now wore the cheerful countenance of a man whose conscience had never given him an uneasy night. "It's a thankless task to try to alter one's tastes, however; I suppose I ought to be grateful that your bad behavior has provided me with such a pleasant excuse to indulge them."

I knew this was a cut, but I did not rise to it; I was rather intrigued, in spite of myself, by the notion of my lofty husband wrestling with anything that he could deem a weakness. Even at his most superficially diffident, he generally conducted himself with an air of such underlying aplomb that I could never have suspected him of finding himself seriously wanting in any respect. And that, given his position in society, he would regard a lust for domination as a weakness to be resisted rather than as an appetite to be indiscriminately sated touched me in a curious way.

"Perhaps it is not so much a deficiency of character as it is a double-edged sword," I remarked pensively.

"I don't know why you would think so," said my husband in a tone of perfect indifference. He paused, then added, "The wind is rising, and it is becoming uncomfortably cold here. Shall we turn back?"

As we left the bridge and began to retrace our steps along the river, my husband appeared to be lost in his own thoughts. But suddenly he broke his silence. "You seem to feel that I have condemned you for what I believed took place in your previous marriage. Do you actually regard me as such a sanctimonious hypocrite?"

I laughed. "Of course, I do! Especially after tonight. What else can I think?"

"Your first marriage is really no business of mine. If I have impugned it, I had no right to do so. As for the paintings you went to such lengths to keep secret from me for so long, my opinion—which I know is worth very little to you—is that they are extraordinarily lovely and certainly no cause for shame."

His words, with their ring of sincerity, stripped me of yet another of my assumptions. My conviction of his hypocrisy and the sense of superiority it had once given me to believe that he had condemned not only me, but Frederick as well, had already begun to crumble under the fusillade of the evening's revelations. My skin burned.

But it was his next remark that completely demolished me.

"If you had simply told me the truth," he said, "I would have spared you everything."

"What?" I said with a short, disbelieving laugh. "*Before* we were married? Without judging me? Without demanding anything in return? You don't—"

He turned toward me on the dim, rain-soaked quai. The light from the lantern above our heads glistened on his hair and in the little puddles at our feet.

"I *loved* you," he said with an intensity that seared me. "Yes, I would have protected you. With or without marriage. With or without your love in return. What else could I have done? How could I *not* have admired a woman who would pose like that to please the man she loved. And herself. But what did you do? You sold yourself—no, not *that* self, but an empty husk of a woman— in a purely mercenary transaction, and based our marriage on a lie. And *that* is something I swear I will *never* forgive."

There being no possible rejoinder, we continued on our way in silence.

I was exhausted when we arrived back at the hotel. I felt as bruised and sore as if the sky had pelted me with stones instead of having merely misted my cheeks and hair with that fine, gentle rain. As for my husband, my emotions bounced between implacable rage at his presumptuous remarks about Frederick one moment, and a curious and humbling sense of astonishment and regret the next.

As we entered our suite, I stole a glance in his direction. His expression was set and remote as he helped me out of my coat with perfunctory politeness. I slipped quickly away to my bed- room, closed the door, and leaned against it, feeling dazed and bone-weary. I could hardly move, much less think. After a long time, I began to unfasten my dress and let it fall to the floor. My petticoat followed. Then, clad only in the silly, frivolous orchid-colored satin-and-lace underclothes I had selected that evening from the collection I was now obligated to wear in tribute to my owner, I sank down upon the edge of my bed. I felt too faint to go on. I wanted something—I needed something—but I couldn't think what it was.

A moment later I realized that I was only hungry.

I remembered having seen a large basket of fruit on a table in the sitting room. I supposed it was safe to go back there; surely my husband would have retired to his bed long ago.

But there he was, stretched out in a chair, his eyes closed. He had shed his wet topcoat but still wore the evening clothes in which he had dressed for the theater; his rain-soaked hair clung to his cheeks and forehead. I noticed, with a curious little pang, that his shoes were muddy.

I started to slip past him, toward the side table. I had my eye on the largest and rosiest apple.

My husband stirred slightly but did not open his eyes. I glanced downward. He looked so drained and pale that, had he been soaked with blood instead of merely rain, I might have supposed that he had been carried in from a battlefield, mortally wounded.

I reached down and laid my palm upon his damp forehead. He must have been half dreaming, because, without opening his eyes, he lifted his hand, took mine gently, and brought it to his lips.

"You don't look well, Anthony," I whispered. "Is there anything I can do for you?"

He stirred again, opened his eyes, and dropped my hand.

"What are *you* doing here?" he said. "I thought you'd gone to bed."

I wondered whose hand he had pressed to his mouth in his dreams.

"You look so wet and tired. Can I get you anything?"

"No. I'm all right. Thank you."

His tone was distant and dismissive.

I glanced across the room at the polished, gleaming apple and then back at the mud-caked patent leather of my husband's shoes.

"I don't think you are all right," I heard myself say. "You look half drowned."

I knelt down and took his left foot in my hands.

"You'll get dirty," he murmured in faint protest.

"It doesn't matter."

I slid off his left shoe and then lifted his right foot as he resigned himself, with an air of reluctant gratitude, to these ministrations.

After I'd removed his shoes, I went to my bath chamber to wash my hands and returned with a thick towel. He did not open his eyes as I came round behind him and gently began to dry his hair.

"What are you doing now?" he whispered.

"I'm drying you. Why aren't you in bed?"

"I'll go in a minute. . . . You're no better off yourself." He stood up wearily, took the towel from my hands, and hung it over my bare shoulders. Then, one by one, he pulled the pins from my own rain-wet hair. As it tumbled down, he toweled the dampness from it.

"Where is your comb?" he asked.

I brought it to him. He began to ease out my tangles.

At last he laid down the comb and the towel.

"That's better, isn't it?" he said softly. He stood so close to me that his breath moved my hair.

A wave of weakness swept over me. Only an hour earlier I had longed to throw him off the Pont-Neuf and watch him sink beneath the waters forever; now I felt softened, and tired, and so bereft of any comfort beyond the small ones he had just given me that it was all I could do not to move into his arms.

In spite of the warmth of the room, I shivered.

"You're chilled," said my husband. "Come with me."

He slipped off his evening jacket and laid it over my shoulders. Then he took me by the hand and led me to his bedroom.

"Sit down," he said. I did, but not on the chair he had indicated. I sat upon the edge of his bed, near the headboard. He took a decanter of Cognac from the little cabinet at one side of the bed, poured hardly more than a thimbleful or two into a snifter, and handed the glass to me. Then, as if once again overcome by exhaustion, he stretched out on the opposite side of the bed and closed his eyes.

I swirled the amber liquid slowly, inhaled the fumes, and idly surveyed my surroundings. Well within reach of my fingertips, on top of the little cabinet at the bedside, lay a small volume, open and facedown. I looked at it curiously. Except for his newspapers, and that incendiary Roman poet, all I had ever observed him reading were such things as treatises on progressive methods of crop rotation and soil reclamation, and tomes on the medicinal uses of native plants by the inhabitants of the Amazon rain forest.

But this was a collection of Shakespeare's sonnets. I turned it over to see what it might tell me.

> *Let me not to the marriage of true minds*
> *Admit impediments; love is not love*
> *Which alters when it alteration finds*
> *Or bends with the remover to remove.*

I laid the book down, but the familiar, once-loved words sang on in my mind. That sonnet to steadfast, immutable devotion was practically a taxonomy in its description of love as I had known it once, in my lost other life:

> *O, no, it is an ever-fixèd mark*
> *That looks on tempests, and is never shaken, . . .*

Oh, why did the words offer me no comfort now? Why did I feel so shaken, so desolate, so robbed of every consolation. I thought of the things my husband had said. Perhaps he had imagined that he had loved me thus, before the revelation of my deception had altered the emotion into something that would never again be miscalled "love."

It is the star to every wandering bark
Whose worth's unknown, although his height be taken.

I took a fiery sip of the brandy.

Love's not Time's fool, though rosy lips and cheeks
Within his bending sickle's compass come. . . .

I glanced down at my husband. His long dark lashes lay across his cheeks. Otherwise he was as pale and elegant as a sarcophagus.

Love alters not with his brief hours and weeks
But bears it out even to the edge of doom.

I emptied the snifter, put out the lamps, and lay down beside him. Only a little light from the wall sconce in the passage came through the open door to fall upon the carpet.

I moved closer to my unconscious spouse. I couldn't have said why. All I knew was that I did not want to be alone that night and that, since in any case he was now dead to the world, he could scarcely object.

He turned sleepily and put his arms around me. I laid my head against his shoulder and began to drift toward oblivion. His hand glided under the jacket that still covered me and came to rest against my breast. I sighed, lifted my arms to wrap them around his neck, and moved closer.

He pulled away, suddenly fully awake.

"Fleur? Why are you still here?"

"The brandy must have put me to sleep," I started to lie. Then I thought better of it. "I don't want to be alone."

What a pathetic admission!

"But you can't stay here." The abruptness of my husband's words did more to chill me than any rain had ever done. I sat up and drew his jacket more closely around me.

"Why not?" I whispered finally. Oh, shameless me!

"You know why," he said. "Or, if you don't, you ought to."

"I am afraid that mind reading is not one of my accomplishments," I said after a while. "If there is something I 'ought' to know, but don't, I think you 'ought' to tell me plainly."

"If you insist," he said. He leaned up on his elbow and looked me straight in the eyes. "Nothing," he said, each word as hard and well formed as a little hailstone, "would distress me more than to find that, in a moment of sheer folly, I had gotten you with child. I thought you understood that."

I felt a little pang—it was an unsettling possibility. But I reflected for a moment upon my inhospitable womb and decided there was not much danger of *that*. Besides, it was a very specious declaration on his part.

"That has scarcely inhibited you in the past," I pointed out.

"Regrettably, no. It ought to have. I have been unbelievably thoughtless."

I stood up. It was too much to absorb in one night—the mistresses, the horrible insinuations about Frederick, and now the unmistakable implication that my husband intended never to take me into his arms again. I couldn't even pretend indifference.

"Well," I said in a low voice, "obviously you have no qualms about scattering your seed in every brothel in London. But you won't defile yourself with your unworthy wife, is that it?"

My husband got up from the bed, switched on the incandescent lamp, and faced me across the rumpled counterpane.

"You had better go," he said. He sounded wearier than ever and dangerously taxed. "I really have nothing more to say to you. Nor have I the patience to listen to any more of your accusations and complaints. I might be tempted to say something very cruel, which you would undoubtedly take too deeply to heart and nurture in your bosom like an asp."

Thus dismissed, I congealed into myself and started toward the doorway. But when I reached it, a vision of my lonely room stopped me, as did the vague but unpleasant foreboding that I would very likely spend the night in sleepless and unhappy ruminations on all that had occurred in the last few hours.

I swallowed my pride, pulled the double doors together, and turned back to my husband, who had already drawn off his tie and was now halted in the midst of unbuttoning his waistcoat. I felt a deep, if sadly mistimed, surge of pure sensual hunger for him.

"Please, Anthony," I said stumblingly. His face had gone frigid with annoyance, making it nearly impossible to continue. "You needn't worry that your worst fears will be realized." I felt my voice start to break, so I turned and leaned my forehead against the door frame. "Really, I should be so lucky," I said with a shuddery little laugh. "It can never happen."

I closed my eyes and sagged against the lintel, feeling utterly drained.

Behind me there was nothing but silence.

Then I heard my husband move swiftly across the room.

From behind he wrapped his arms around me, bracing me.

"Oh, Fleur," he said.

Tears began to stream down my face. I was glad the room was dim.

Finally he said, "Are you sure? Has a doctor told you that?"

I took a deep breath and tried to wipe my cheeks surreptitiously.

"I don't need an *expert* to tell me," I said.

"But you can't be certain," said my husband gently. "Nor can I. It's not a chance I dare to take again."

Still with my back to him, I closed my eyes and let the weight of his words settle on me. I felt as if I were being pushed into a coffin and my husband was preparing to close the lid.

I wiped my cheeks again with my hand.

Finally I turned around.

"Please, Anthony," I said again. "I don't want to be alone." It was so hard to keep my voice calm and level. "I understand your feelings, and I respect them. But there are other ways." I paused with embarrassment, then pressed onward. "Ways of avoiding the risk."

I couldn't read his face in the dim light.

"What do you want from me, Fleur?" he said at last. He sounded as drained and hopeless as I felt.

"Can't we agree for one night to forget the injuries we have done to each other?" I pleaded softly. "Can't we set aside all this hatred and bitterness for at least an hour or two?"

I stopped to steady my voice, and then went on. "Can't we embrace, just once, without each of us thinking only of how to extract our pound of flesh?"

He shook his head. I could see his faint ironic smile.

"No pound of flesh? But in that case, tonight would not count toward your ransom." He paused. "No matter how trying it may be for you," he added.

"I understand that—I accept it."

His expression softened yet further. "It *would* make . . . an interesting change," he said at last. "But do you really think that you are capable of it?"

"Yes," I said. "I know I am. Are you?"

In lieu of a reply, he took my face in his hands and, bending his head to mine, kissed my mouth very softly. I opened my lips to him, and the kiss, still very slow and fragile, became a delicate adventure. When he had claimed my mouth serenely, his halcyon lips began to move down my throat, his hands over my breasts. I clung to his shoulders as the last of my strength flowed out of me like a spent wave sliding back to merge with the sea. His right hand slid under the satin at my hips; it caressed my buttocks, my belly, and finally stole between my legs. He fingered me gently, opened me.

My breath quickened. A moan of yearning escaped me. I

pressed my lips to his cheek to muffle it, but the scent and texture of his skin, so warm, with just the slightest, tantalizing trace of roughness, sharpened my longing, as he continued to cajole my body into those sweet tremors.

Only his left arm supported me. He guided me back to the bed, slipped the last of my clothing to the floor, and freed himself from his own.

When he was done, he lay down on his back and drew me to him. I found his lips with mine. His mouth was hungry, but gentle. There was nothing vengeful or cruel in his kisses; even now they still had the lingering tenderness that reminded me of how much he had once believed he loved me. So indolently sweet they were, so peacefully unhurried that, to my despair, tears rose to my eyes again.

Fearing that they might spill onto his own dry cheeks, I lifted my head, then began moving my lips downward along his smooth, warm chest, letting them press against his flat belly before I moved lower still. He sighed. I took him in my mouth; his body arched.

This was the act I had hinted at earlier; now, even as he gave himself over to it, I wondered whether, once his own desires had been quenched, mine would still be left to smolder.

But after only a moment or two, my husband slid out from beneath me. I tried to turn toward him, but he was above me, preventing me.

I could not help thinking, even as I succumbed, that he must wish to keep my face toward the pillows so as not to see it, to render me anonymous, to forget that it was I, his unloving and unforgivable wife, whom he might, by some slim, unfortunate twist of fate, be about to miraculously impregnate. At any other time, I would have welcomed this obliteration of my identity. Yet now, in the moment of my most complete surrender, it gave me no pleasure to think that I might have been any one in that succession of black-haired mistresses.

He pulled me up so that I was on my hands and knees.

Never had anyone done to me what he then proceeded to do.

At first I thought it was a mistake and moved my hips slightly to correct him. But calmly, almost tenderly, he persisted, and when I realized his intent, I felt a clutch of alarm and started to resist.

He made no effort to force me. While he waited for me to become still, he leaned toward the bedside cabinet, reaching past me to open it. From within he took a small, silver-mounted crystal flacon.

He uncapped it; the scent of laurel wafted through the air. He began to massage me slowly. The light aroma of the oil, as fragrant as the breezes blowing over a Mediterranean isle, gave me a pagan thrill. But when he had eased me completely, again he began that slow violation. Only the slight, sharp intimation of the pleasure I struggled against, which mingled inextricably with my anguish, prevented me from rising up and tearing myself away from him. But as the tantalizing, sweetly excruciating invasion continued, I could not restrain a moan.

"Ah, have I hurt you?" he whispered. He started to pull back. "Shall I stop?"

"Yes. No! I don't know!" I sobbed softly, trembling, half longing to break free of him, half yearning to take him even more deeply.

He became very still then, and began to pet my tossing head, my drenched cheeks, until a jarring ripple of pleasure melted me enough to allow him to proceed.

And so it continued, his hands calming and quieting me, his body scalding me as I relaxed enough to admit him further and further. Then his hands came around my waist, one rising to my breasts, the other falling between my thighs, stroking and caressing, until there was no pain at all, only heat washing through me in large, luxuriant waves. I sank onto the bed as he possessed me completely; my flesh was now utterly beyond my control. I was mortified by the violence of my response. It seemed to go on forever. Then I felt him go rigid with a final thrust, as he whispered my name, *my* name, stealing the last of my restraint.

He slipped free of me and collapsed upon the coverlet. I kept my face averted; I could hardly imagine what he must think of me now. But then he reached over and drew his finger along my jaw, coaxing my face toward his until I had to meet his gaze. I could not remember ever having seen in his eyes an expression of such undisguised sadness. He rolled to his side and held me close, cradling me in his arms. I surrendered to this, as well, and slept in his loose, easy embrace.

I awoke around dawn. The room was cool, but I was still warm in the curve of my husband's body. I remembered dimly how, after rising once to open the windows as was his habit, he had drawn the bedclothes over us, only barely breaking my slumber.

I gazed at his sleeping face, now heartbreakingly youthful and defenseless.

But how would those features arrange themselves when he awoke with the night gone, and, with it, that brief and glorious truce I had sued for and won?

I did not stay to find out. I was already in my own bed when the pale early sunlight slid down the river, from one graceful bridge to the next, gleamed on the lofty towers of Notre-Dame and on the lowly wet cobbles, and lovingly caressed the leaves of the great horse-chestnut trees that are everywhere in Paris.

We did not speak of that night again.

Never had my husband seemed more stern and unapproachable than he did a few hours later, when he took me to the Gare du Nord and put me on a train bound for Calais.

I was on my way back to England. Alone.

XXV

Although the truce had expired, my husband's next offensive was a subtle one. In mid-June, after leaving me to wonder how he might be enjoying himself apart from me, he summoned me again to London. His request for my company had been occasioned by a desire to take me to the theater.

As we were about to enter his box at the Haymarket, he was greeted by a fellow who cast a look at me and said with a laugh, "So you're back again, Tony?"

My husband introduced us. The other immediately straightened his back, took his hands from his pockets, and bowed to me with grave respect.

"What a pleasure it is finally to meet Lady Camwell," he said. "I could not resist coming to see the adorable Miss Neilson once again," he added to my husband. "But I see that cannot be *your* motive."

"Julia Neilson is pretty enough," agreed my husband, in a way that would have made me feel rather slighted had I been the adorable Julia. "But I thought that Fleur might enjoy the play."

"Well, perhaps you won't *enjoy* it," he murmured a little later as we took our seats. "But I think you may profit from it."

"You have seen it before?"

"In April, when it opened."

I wondered who had sat at his side then, and since he seemed to do little that was not calculated to remind me of my sins, what humbling lessons lay in wait for me.

I recognized the playwright's name. I had seen him once, not long before my second marriage, when he had been the toast of Paris. Marguerite had pointed him out to me in a café.

I was severely disappointed, however, once the curtain had risen on *A Woman of No Importance.* It seemed to me that the play sorely lacked the emotional depth my recollection of the play-wright's admittedly vain but kindly face had led me to hope for. It was wonderfully amusing—breathtaking in its cleverness—but so frothy and insignificant, so deliberately brittle, that I felt vaguely irritated every time it wrenched a smile from my lips.

Still, to my surprise, at the beginning of the Second Act, I was struck with a pang, rather than a giggle, when Lady Stutfield spoke of how women are always trying to escape from men: "Men are so very, very heartless. They know their power and use it." And although I actually laughed when Mrs. Allonby declared, "Nothing is so aggravating as calmness. There is something posi-tively brutal about the good temper of most modern men," it was at the astuteness, and not the apparent absurdity, of her percep-tion.

It was not until the Fourth Act, however, that I began to feel very uneasy. I had no reason now to wonder why my husband had selected this play. For, although I was irreligious and detested the melodramatic Mrs. Arbuthnot to boot, I felt thoroughly admon-ished when she explained why she would rather endure disgrace and social ostracism than marry the father of her son. "How could I swear to love the man I loathe. . . . No: Marriage is a sacra-ment for those who love each other."

My discomfort took yet a sharper edge when even the puritan-ical moralist Hester—played by the ravishing Julia Neilson—called Mrs. Arbuthnot's choice not to legitimize her son an honorable one and reminded us all that real dishonor lies in marrying without love.

Although by this time I was moved and shaken by the tone the play had assumed, I was not sorry when the final curtain fell.

My husband then decreed that we would have supper at Romano's, in the Strand. Perhaps that noisy exuberance of sportsmen, Gaiety girls, army officers, and theatrical managers all jammed together in the famous dining room—so long and narrow that it had been nicknamed the Rifle Range—was not quite the correct milieu for a well-bred gentleman's wife, but I didn't object. I was thrilled at the chance to glimpse this livelier side of English life. But after we made our way into the restaurant, and after my husband had acknowledged a few greetings from the Rifle Range, we were led upstairs to a private room, there to enjoy our supper in quiet and intimate splendor.

"Now tell me, did you enjoy the play?" my husband asked.

"As much as anyone can enjoy being tried and condemned, however amusingly," I replied. "That *was* what you intended, was it not?"

My husband shrugged. "Perhaps I merely wanted to see you laugh. But if the shoe fits, of course . . ."

"Even so," I said, "I could not help but admire the play. I take its deeper message to be a more generous one. Perhaps it can remind us *both* of the dangers of any hardness of heart."

"Indeed?" said he indifferently. But I saw his color rise.

"For example," I continued with a magnanimity which was, alas, not unmingled with spite, "it suggests to me that perhaps I ought to judge you less harshly for the vices which you concealed from me so well and for so long."

Again he laughed. "To which of my vices do you refer?"

"To your famous succession of mistresses. And the other pleasures of the demimonde which you apparently enjoy to the hilt with God-knows-whom."

I had not missed the knowing, admiring glances my husband had garnered from some of the bolder-looking girls downstairs, nor the whispers, which I could not make out, nor the appraising eyes directed at me.

My husband laid down his fork, and resting his left forearm and his right elbow on the edge of the table, pointed his knife at my breast.

"Oh yes," he said. "Those mistresses whom I have at least had the decency not to flaunt in your face, although you have never given me any reason to suppose that you cared anything about where, as you once put it, I went crawling. I'll have you know, the only time in my life that I have *ever* crawled was in trying to make you happy. And what a thankless task that was."

My gaze fell, but finally I lifted my eyes back to his.

"Yes," I said very slowly. "You *were* discreet. And considerate. And I *have* been thankless."

My husband's expression did not soften.

"And if you were sincere about taking the play as a caution against judging other people harshly," he continued severely, "there would be no need for me to point out that I had every intention of being faithful to you until you proved to be such an unsatisfactory wife."

"That's entirely false," I said, my temper flaring again. "You know as well as I do that you took up with your mistresses long before you became disenchanted with me."

"But only after you made it painfully clear not only that you took no pleasure in our marriage bed but that you were perfectly satisfied with that state of affairs and did not wish to change it," he retorted. "That account you received of me from Madame Mansard, although accurate in every other respect, exaggerated the haste with which I broke my vows. It took me somewhat longer than a *week* or two to swallow my pride and admit to myself that I could never thaw *your* frozen heart."

"How *much* longer?" I whispered.

"How *much* longer? Well, if you must know . . . perhaps you recall the night you told me outright that I could never give you any pleasure?"

I shadowed my face with my hand and did not reply.

"I did not break my vows to you until the following evening."

"The *very* next evening?" I whispered.

"The very next evening," he repeated without even a hint of remorse.

I turned my head away and pressed my fingers against my lips. But still he continued.

"Before you upbraid me further, ask yourself this. Why do you suppose all my mistresses had black hair? And why do you think I turned to those other diversions you are so eager to condemn? One must do something to whet one's appetite for a woman when she is not the woman one wants . . . one wanted."

I reached for my champagne glass, but it was already empty and my husband, who valued privacy above service, had dismissed the waiter. I twirled the stem slowly between my fingers as I considered his admission.

My husband took the glass from my hand. He filled it, set it down, and after he had returned the bottle to the ice pail, he covered my hand with his for a moment.

"Drink," he said.

So I did. I took one sip, and then another; slowly the sparkling anodyne dulled the edge of my distress.

"I hoped the play would make you laugh," continued my husband more gently. "And once or twice I think it did. Now tell me truthfully, heathen that you are, did you not like Lord Illingworth in spite of yourself?"

That *did* make me smile.

"Very much so," I admitted. "And didn't you, in spite of yourself, find Mrs. Arbuthnot's mother love somewhat excessive?"

"Cloying," he agreed. "But I think I have every right to call the grapes sour. What about you? Were you no luckier in your upbringing? Didn't your grandmother love you like a mother?"

"I really know nothing of how mothers love, but I suppose she loved me in her way," I said. "Unfortunately, it was a way that made me desperate to escape her plans for me."

"What plans were those?" he asked.

I had told him so little about her—he knew what she had been, but nothing of what she had intended for me. I recalled his scathing remark, made only a few weeks earlier, about my "unfortunate antecedents." But it was all water under the bridge now. The champagne, and the sense that I had nothing left to lose, unfettered my tongue. I began to speak with astonishing candor about my girlhood, about my grandmother. But now a cascade of soft, unfamiliar feeling for her washed over me. I recalled the play's gentle admonitions against moral inflexibility. I wanted to defend my grandmother from my husband's contempt.

"You can have no idea what it was like for her, to be so poor— how hard she had to work and how much she had to sacrifice. She took in washing. She took in sewing. She helped out when there were dinner parties at the vicarage—not at the dinners themselves, of course, for her past was no secret and her presence would have outraged everyone, but before and afterward. Sometimes she would be there most of the night, washing up and cleaning. For her betters. They thought they were being charitable."

And I had been ashamed of her.

"She was so bravely determined that I should never want," I continued, despite the lump that had risen to my throat as I thought of how ready I had been to judge her, and of how much I owed her. "She made everything possible for me, everything."

Without doubting the sincerity of Frederick's love for me, I felt pierced by the sudden, painful realization that, had it not been for the sophistication, the education, and the grace with which my grandmother had endowed me, I could never have commanded the attention of such a pampered aesthete.

My husband was silent as I sat lost in thought, vainly regretting my thanklessness.

Finally I lifted my head from my reverie to notice that my glass was empty once again and my husband was refilling it.

I took another swallow and said to him, rather shakily, in what must have seemed to him a complete non sequitur, "Perhaps you would have judged me less harshly, as well, had your cocoon of wealth not given you such glib notions of integrity."

The bright color flooded his cheeks again. He said nothing to defend himself.

I lifted the glass to my mouth yet again: It seemed that I was tearing through the bottle at a phenomenal rate.

"Well, *she'd* have been pleased with me, at any rate," I continued tactlessly, as my thoughts turned back to my grandmother. "She would have felt I had surpassed even her hopes for me—in the very moment that I was going down for the third time."

My husband's color rose even higher.

"So that is how you felt about marrying me," he said after a long silence, as if to himself. "Well, perhaps the fish will have to be content with his four nights and cast Jonah back upon the shore."

At this I was overwhelmed by confusion. Very likely it was due to the vast quantity I had imbibed. I looked away and found myself wondering whether Jonah had sometimes missed his fearsome intimacy with that great creature, had ever awakened in the dark of night longing for the belly of his devouring protector once he had been flung free of it.

But of course I did not say this.

My husband may have had a little too much champagne himself, for, although we did not say much more across the table, later, when we had climbed into his carriage for the journey back to Grosvenor Square, he said, "You know, for a moment or two tonight you reminded me of the way you looked the first time I ever saw you."

"When you called on me with Neville?" What could have reminded him of that fateful day?

"Oh no. It was long before that."

At first I was puzzled. Then I understood. "Oh, you mean Neville's painting from *The Winter's Tale.*"

"No. Not the painting. You. It was in Paris. I was dining with a friend—it was Phil Harborough, as a matter of fact. You may remember meeting him at the reception for Caylat."

"Oh yes, Philip. The talker."

My husband laughed.

"No, Fleur," he corrected me gravely. "Philip, the raconteur. In any case, we were at the Coq d'Or. It was the autumn of eighty-eight. You were across the room with your husband and Marguerite and Théo and another couple. You were in an emerald green dress and you had a red rose in your hair."

My mind shot back across the years to that ancient tavern in the Rue Montmartre. If my husband had gone down on his knees to me, then and there, and declared his undying love, he could hardly have astounded me more. How could I not remember that joyous night at the Coq d'Or? Even now I can see the candlelight dancing over Frederick's laughing face, I can reel off the names of everyone who stopped by our table. I recall everything—everything except the pale Englishman who must have been gazing at me from across the room.

"You were positively incandescent. I thought your husband must be the happiest man on the face of the earth. I remember making some idiotic remark—well, I was still very young—about understanding for the first time in my life why a moth would fly into a flame. Phil told me who you were. Of course, I ought to have recognized you from Neville's painting, but I hadn't—there was no comparison between the painting and . . . the real thing.

"Neville knew how much I admired that particular masterpiece, not to mention the others he owned. I had been urging him to introduce me to your husband—I had hoped to commission something equally magnificent for myself. But once I had seen you, it was out of the question. I was forced to recognize the wisdom of the Tenth Commandment."

The carriage rattled us softly through the dark London streets. I thought of my husband's cold mother, of the civilized cruelty in which he had been raised, and of how stingingly that, and his purchased pleasures, must have contrasted with the mellow, tender joie de vivre of the love feast he had witnessed in Paris.

"Your face was glowing. I attributed that to the warmth of your nature." Now his voice had taken on its familiar, ironic edge. "But I suppose you were just full of champagne, which seems to do as much for you as paint."

I shook my head, still lost in that bittersweet remembrance.

"I'd had nothing to drink. Frederick had just gotten a commission for a group of paintings that would pay more than anything he'd ever done before. We were celebrating. It seemed like the happiest night of my life—I didn't know it was the end of everything."

"The end?" said my husband, puzzled.

"Yes, that was the night I lost my daughter."

I stopped, my voice catching. I had said far too much.

My husband turned toward me. I could not read his expression.

"Your daughter!" he exclaimed.

I could answer only with a sharp little nod.

"So you *did* have a child," he said softly.

Again I felt that vague surprise at how little he knew about me. But of course I had never mentioned her to him.

"What happened?" said my husband.

"She was born three months too early," I said, now in the toneless voice I had found safest to adopt at the time of her death. "She died."

"How devastating for you."

"I am afraid I took it a little too hard," I said, still in the same flat voice.

"*Too* hard? What do you mean?"

"Well, it isn't as if she were ever truly a person," I lied as crisply as I was able to. "But I grieved excessively. Why, I can't say. I hadn't actually *known* her so, of course, there was really no reason to feel quite so—"

"My God, Fleur, how can you say that! You carried her in your body for months! How much closer could you have been to her?"

I glanced at him, amazed. But already tears, idle tears, useless tears, had begun to spill from my eyes. I turned my head and brushed them away angrily.

"You must think I do nothing but weep. I don't know what is wrong with me these days. I used to have *some* self-control. I never cried."

"Surely you wept for your child?"

I thought about that rainy night on the Pont-Neuf. Even then, I had not yielded fully.

"Hardly," I said with a certain pride. Everyone I had ever loved hated tears. My grandmother regarded them as a sign of weakness, unless they were used deliberately and with the greatest caution and self-control as a weapon. Frederick had regarded them as one of the grotesque and depressing excesses of the previous generation. "I mean, one would hate to be like the Queen, making a fetish out of mourning, parading one's sorrows endlessly—it's so morbid and undignified," I explained, thinking of my husband's air of dignity, which I had come to admire greatly, and which I longed to emulate.

"Perhaps," said my husband. "But you talk as if there is no difference between making a cult of grief and simply allowing oneself to weep. What could possibly be more natural and healing than tears?"

"What have tears ever healed?" I asked bitterly.

"I'm sure I don't know," said my husband, who did not seem disposed to argue the point any further. "Is your face dry now? Let me see."

I lifted my damp eyes reluctantly to his. It was too dim in the carriage to see very much at all.

"Why don't you tell me something about your daughter," he whispered. "Just a little. Only as much as you feel you can."

For a moment I was at a loss for words. No one had ever acknowledged her reality, that there might have been something —some*one*—to talk about. Everyone, even my darling Frederick, had behaved as if the only tragedy was that she had never existed. I had never demurred. But she *had* existed; *that* was my tragedy—or my weakness—to have entertained, as I had whispered foolish, loving bagatelles to my distended belly, the absurd fancy that I could feel the force of her tiny personality's response to me. To have watched her fight for her life, and die, and then to have had to seal my lips and pretend that she had never been, because *that* eased the disappointment for—

I cut off the thought.

"What did you call her?" asked my husband gently.

How could he have suspected my folly—the silly nicknames I had given her when I didn't even know her sex?

I almost smiled. I opened my mouth to answer him, but before I could say more than a few halting words, I started to sob. Once I had started, I couldn't stop. I no longer even cared about stopping. I buried my face in my hands and wept as heedlessly as Niobe.

My husband, beside me, put a tentative hand upon my shoulders. Rather than recoiling from the comfort he offered, I turned to him. He drew me into his arms and wholly absorbed that flood of tears. Between my sobs, I told him things I had never told anyone.

I pulled myself upright in a daze and tried hastily to arrange my tumbled hair and rumpled clothing when the carriage came to a halt in Grosvenor Square. But then my husband called out to the coachman and asked him to go on, to drive us around Hyde Park.

"If you don't mind, it will give you a little more time to compose yourself," he said to me.

Mind! He must have understood completely how I would have detested having to exhibit my reddened eyes to the butler and Marie.

I leaned back into the soft upholstery with a sigh. I was still feeling my sadness more profoundly than I had ever permitted myself to feel it, but now it seemed to expand, like a shimmering, trembling bubble, to encompass not only my lost little daughter, but my poor, weak Frederick and my fierce, devoted grandmother. And, not least of all, the man sitting silently beside me, whose love I had betrayed and forfeited.

Yet now, rather than being overwhelmed by sorrow and remorse, I had a curiously buoyant sense of relief. It did not mitigate my regrets but blended with them, both softening them and deepening them.

"I thought *you* had the stiffest upper lip in England," I remarked after a while. "Where did you learn about tears?"

"Oh, I'm not half so unflappable as I like to appear," he replied. "My father died when I was still a boy—it was the summer I turned fourteen. He'd been planning to take me on the Grand Tour of Europe that summer, but by then he was too ill. I adored him."

This was something I had never known and had never even suspected.

"I was completely devastated when he died. I had really not thought it was possible, and I had no idea what to do. When I was among other people, I was so afraid I might break out in tears that I simply refused to speak to anyone at all. That lasted for days. It drove my mother wild. But I knew exactly what she would have said otherwise. 'Show your breeding, Anthony. Have some backbone, for heaven's sake! You don't see *me* sniveling like a girl.'" He mimicked her to perfection. "Of course, whenever I was safely alone, I cried like a baby."

The thought of such private, extravagant emotionality lying under his cool self-possession gave me a dusky thrill. That he would admit to it so freely surprised me. Of course, I reminded myself, he had been much younger then, only a boy.

"What was your father like?" I asked.

"Oh, rather retiring and scholarly. Hardly dashing or heroic. And certainly not as . . . demonstrative as one might have liked. But he was kind, very kind, and very gentle. Too much so, I think, for his own good. But I loved him for it."

XXVI

Outside my bedroom door, we hesitated for an awkward, silent moment. I longed to reach up and take his face between my hands, to bring my lips to his. But I was too overwhelmed by a peculiar shyness and a deep, incomprehensible and debilitating tenderness. It was so disarming that I wanted to hide. Scarcely knowing what I was doing, I dropped my fingers to the door handle.

"Well, good night," he said, and moved down the passage.

On the following day, I was despatched to Charingworth, where my husband joined me several days later, but only to attend to some business there.

I saw very little of him, and when we did encounter each other, we behaved with extreme politeness. By unspoken, mutual consent, we had once again laid down our weapons. But the few meals we took together during this state of fragile peace were almost silent; it seemed that, having ended our sparring, we were left with nothing to say.

My husband retreated behind his customary air of remoteness, and I reminded myself of his remark about being unable, ever, to forgive me. It was better, really, that he was not tempted to sweeten his revenge by exploiting the dangerous softness he had discovered in me.

But the tender weather of late June did not assuage my vague longings. It was easier to keep them at bay during the blue, sweet days; but the evenings, all muted violet shot with glowing red and gold, and cruel with seductive and unfulfilled promises, undid me.

Everything about my life had become ambivalent. My husband lingered at Charingworth longer than one would have thought necessary, but barely spoke to me. What his intentions might be I could not guess. He had hinted at releasing me without extracting his full due—yet now he made no move either to set me free or to collect the final payments.

Meanwhile the moon fattened. On the night it came to fullness, my husband had dined elsewhere. I had not seen him since breakfast, yet I had rather deftly managed to ascertain from Mrs. Phillips that he had not returned to London. Now, as I lay in bed, I heard my husband's light tread upon the stairway. Soon it faded down the gallery toward the wing where he slept. I tried to imagine how he had occupied himself that day and with whom he might have dined. But I could not. I knew virtually nothing about him; for nearly the entire duration of our brief marriage, I had absented myself as much as possible from his company. I had shared neither his troubles and worries, if he had any, nor his pleasures. I had shunned his pastimes and allowed anything he might have revealed about himself to pass over me like smoke.

The moonlight spilling through my window illuminated everything except the small mysteries which occupied my restless mind. It coaxed me from my bed. The night was mild; rather than merely standing at the window, I put on my dressing gown and stepped out into the empty gallery. The great house was dim and still; there was no danger, at this hour, of running into my husband or anyone else.

Barefoot, I stole down the angled wooden staircase, with its

quaint turned banisters and elaborate newel posts, each one sur-
mounted by a fabulous mythical beast. I crossed the chilly tiles of
the great hall, passed through a dark passage, and entered the
music room, which lay on the same side of the house as my own
bedroom.

The polished piano gleamed in the moonlight. I thought of
the expensive lessons my grandmother had insisted upon, and of
how rarely I had ever opened the piano at Charingworth. I ran my
hand over the cover longingly, and then passed to the French
windows. I unlatched them and stepped outside.

The grass was cool and moist underfoot as I wandered over the
long terraced lawns and then down to the edge of the river, where
the light shimmered like silver foil on the water. A few birds,
deluded by the brilliance of the sky into believing it was daylight,
chirped and twittered in the treetops.

I turned my face to the moon. For how many hundreds of
thousands of years had she stared down upon her sleepless subjects with that same cool, archaic smile? Now, for all but a few of
those whose paths had brought them under her detached, benefi-
cent gaze, whatever sorrows, labors, or joys kept sleep at bay had
long ago waxed and waned and vanished forever, beyond even the
reach of memory. The Greeks had made a minor deity of her. To
me she remained a goddess, silent, remote, and constant. A goddess for everyone who walked in the shadows while quieter souls
lay cushioned in the slumber of the righteous and the just. I
thought of my husband dreaming quietly in his own dark bedroom.

But this only exacerbated my loneliness, and the beauty of the
night, which seemed made for magic, impressed upon me only
more heavily the weight of my own empty existence. I sent a brief
prayer skyward. I asked my goddess only to lighten my heart for a
few hours. But now her blank, closed smile no longer appeared
benign, and feeling melancholy indeed, I turned back toward the
house.

As I approached the last turn of the stairway, I heard a door close and the sound of boots striding along the gallery. I looked up. There was my husband, dressed in riding clothes, and as startled at seeing me, it seemed, as I was to see him.

"Where have *you* been?" he demanded.

"I went out to look at the moonlight on the river," I stammered. "Were you looking for me?"

"Why would I do that? It never occurred to me that you were not asleep in your bed until I saw you drifting up the stairway like a ghost."

"I could not sleep."

"How unfortunate. Neither can I," he said coldly, and started to pass me on the stairway.

"Where are you going?" I asked.

The words were scarcely out of my mouth before I realized my faux pas. Of course he would be going to a woman.

It made me ache. He had made love to me so seldom and, I was pretty certain now, intended never to again. I was certain, too, that he must still be conducting his careless infidelities in London. He had a real taste for such pleasures, and no reason to give them up. I tried not to think of this too much. But I had not divined, until this very minute, that he could also betray me so close to home.

He had already reached the second landing; now he paused and looked back at me.

"I beg your pardon," I said, trying to muster some dignity. "I did not mean to pry."

But he was gazing at me thoughtfully and appeared more conflicted than annoyed.

"Well, if you can't sleep, put on your riding clothes and come out with me," he said, somewhat ungraciously, and then added, "if you like."

My heart leapt.

"I'll just be a minute," I said. "Shall I meet you in the stable?"

"As you wish," he replied indifferently, as if he already regretted the invitation. He hurried on down the stairway.

At Charingworth I never rode sidesaddle. It was scandalous, of course, to ride like a man, but my husband did not object at all and had cheerfully paid for my outré riding habits. Now I dressed quickly, not bothering with stays, not taking even the time to pin up my hair—I pulled it back and tied it with a red velvet ribbon.

But once I was dressed, I lingered, despite my promise to be quick, to inspect my mirrored image carefully and to make the countless tiny adjustments by which I hoped to render my appearance more fetching.

When I reached the stable, I found Andromeda already saddled for me.

We trotted out of the stableyard together and down the long avenue. The strange cool light and the stark black shadows had altered the pleasant landscape from its daytime aspect and made it as newly glamorous as the first snowfall. Every cluster of trees was touched with wonder and mystery. I felt altered as well, dazzled and expectant. To have found druids gathering beneath the oak trees could not have amazed me more than had my husband's invitation to ride with him.

"Can you keep up with me?" he asked when we reached the high road.

"I'll try," I said.

He brought Perseus to a gallop; Andromeda needed no urging to follow. The sound of the hooves, the rush of the night air over my cheeks, the blur of hedgerows and meadows on either side were as intoxicating as the moonlight. I drank the fragrant breeze. At the crossroads, we turned onto the road that ran along the river. We raced for miles over the still, silent countryside. Andromeda never faltered; she might have been flying. Each hoofbeat seemed to strike a burden from my heart; useless regrets, petty concerns, and grudges fell away. I wondered how long I might outrun them; would it be days or hours or only minutes before they found me again?

At last we turned and retraced our way back, slowly, as if unwilling to end the adventure. When we were close to an old apple orchard, my husband brought Perseus to a halt. I pulled up next to him. My spirits were still high. In fact, I felt as giddy as a schoolgirl on the verge of her first taste of longed for and forbidden pleasures. But underneath the excitement lay the strange sense of peace that had stolen like a drug through my veins during the long ride.

We let the horses drink a little from the river.

"We must go back," said my husband at last.

"Oh, not yet," I said. "Let's walk in the orchard."

"It's late. You ought to be in bed."

"But it's so mild, and the moon so bright," I pleaded. "Please, Anthony. Let's just climb to the top of the rise and see what the view is from there tonight."

My husband sighed, as if he did not altogether approve of my whim, but he followed me across the road and into the orchard. There he dismounted and reached toward me to help me from the saddle. I slid into his arms and knew, instantly, that he wanted me. In the same instant he released me and stepped back. We tethered our horses to a tree and began to climb the gentle slope.

It was not until I caught the toe of my boot under a fallen branch that my husband took my arm. At his touch, my strumpet soul rudely pushed the fainthearted Lady Camwell aside, brought my feet to a halt, and turned my face eagerly toward his as if to steal a kiss. It was all she had time for: Before my husband could do more than draw away slightly, I had the troublesome wench in irons once again. He moved decisively apart from me. To cover my embarrassment, I wandered off in the opposite direction and let myself surrender to an equally unseemly but more innocent form of playfulness. I found an open patch of grass and began to turn cartwheels; it was a trick I had learned from a schoolmate in Montreux. I hadn't practiced it for years.

My husband started to laugh.

"What has come over you?" he asked.

I cartwheeled back to the tree under which he stood and

pulled myself up onto a low-hanging branch, from which I then hung by my knees.

"Sheer lunacy, I suppose. Brought on by the moon, no doubt, to whom I will now pay homage." I smiled blithely up at her through the mesh of branches. Then I reached behind me to tug at my husband's sleeve. "Would you care to join me, Sir Anthony, in showing your devotion?"

By now I was laughing a little, too, because I knew very well that my husband would never dream of dangling from a tree by his knees. My jacket was pulling at me; I slipped it off and let it fall to the ground.

"You *are* a pagan," said my husband.

"I suppose so," I admitted, pulling myself upright. "Well, one must have faith in something. And my heathen goddess is in a generous mood tonight. She has already answered one prayer."

"What did you ask for?"

"No more than this," I said, smiling down at him in the moonlight. "Catch me."

I dropped into his arms, so suddenly that he was obliged to catch me whether he would or no, and then, still moonstruck and reckless, I put my arms around him and kissed him.

For a moment he froze.

"Why are you doing this?" he whispered, sounding agonized.

But then he was returning my kisses, more fiercely and cruelly than I had ever known him to, and I could not have answered his question even if my lips *had* been free.

What self-control he still displayed lasted only long enough for him to remove his jacket and to lay it next to my own, spreading them both out over the rough earth like a blanket. Then he pulled me to the ground with him. He ripped off my shirt, scattering two or three buttons, and cursed my clinging boots and breeches roundly before he got me out of them.

Gone was all that elegant self-possession; gone was the cool and ironic restraint with which he had so confidently directed the pace of our other conflagrations; gone, the air of amused detachment and the cache of sophisticated erotic refinements. He was still half dressed when he fell upon me like an avenging demon.

Never before had I suspected how much unbridled anger he might be capable of turning on me. When I lifted my hands involuntarily to ward off that flood of rage, he yanked the red ribbon rudely from my hair and knotted it around my wrists.

"Oh no, you witch," he said dangerously, "you can't have it both ways."

But I didn't want it both ways any longer. I was no longer afraid of him: I hadn't failed to notice that even in the midst of his fury he had slipped his fingers under that strip of velvet to make sure he had not bound me too tightly. I felt gloriously pacified. As he tore into me, all my own very weakly curbed desires sprang forward to envelop him.

What I thought was the height of my passion came swiftly. I heard myself cry his name. But nothing would appease him.

"Damn you," he sobbed as he hammered into me mercilessly. "Damn you, Fleur."

And still I felt safe.

Somehow he got up and pulled me upright. My arms were around his neck. He lifted me slightly, leaned me against the tree, and pulled my legs around his waist. I had thought that I could not climb any further, but already I was soaring again.

"Say it," I heard dimly through my ectasy. "Why can't you say it, you bitch!"

He must have been slamming me against the tree, but I was as supremely indifferent to discomfort as if I were being plundered in a goosedown bed.

I shuddered, went limp, and beamed up at him like a happy idiot.

"Goddamn you, Fleur, I hate you," he said with a gasp, as he came.

He broke away from me instantly and lay down prostrate in

the grass, panting. His face was turned away from me, his cheek to the ground.

I slumped and sank slowly to my knees. Under the moon's cruel glare, I saw the marks which bark and twigs had left on his shirtsleeves, and on his wrists, and on the backs of his hands; in some places they were all but raw. He had wrapped those arms around me, and that was why I had felt no pain as this man, who hated me, had ravished me against the tree.

I felt a tear slide down my cheek and a sharp biting cramp deep inside, as all that would never be a child mingled and began to seep out of my exhausted body into the cold, dark earth.

After a while, my husband stood up.

"It's cold, why aren't you dressed?" he said sharply, when he had arranged his own clothing. His glance fell upon my hands, "Oh."

Rather than struggling with the knot, he merely drew his pocketknife and cut the ribbon with a quick, savage gesture. I supposed he must be wishing that all the ties that bind might be so easily severed.

XXVII

The cramping torments of my complaint did not ease until late the following morning. By the time I arose, my husband was already gone from Charingworth.

I would have been really inconsolable had I not received a letter from Marguerite. She would soon be at loose ends, for *L'Embuscade* would close at the end of the month. For the remainder of the summer, all the theaters of Paris, except for the opera and the Comédie-Française, would be dark.

Marguerite, who loved her work, could barely tolerate the enforced idleness that was to be her lot until she began rehearsals for a September opening.

But, from my point of view, it could scarcely have been more fortuitous.

I immediately invited her to Charingworth.

Marguerite created something of a sensation at our village station. She arrived with fourteen trunks and a dozen hatboxes, although she intended to stop with me for only a week. And she knew how to make an entrance. She paused, so charmingly, before stepping down from the carriage that all eyes were drawn to her. She smiled at everyone as if from behind the footlights. Her frank enjoyment of the admiration she had drawn resulted in a general hoisting of feminine eyebrows. While seasoned gentlemen surveyed her from the platform with broad smiles, dazzled youths abandoned their tottering, bombazined grandmothers to assist the fairy princess in her descent to earth. But there was nothing helpless about Marguerite, and with mingled sweetness, gratitude, and faint reproach she speedily dispatched each of them back to where their less bewitching duties lay.

Upon her arrival at Charingworth, my effervescent friend showed no signs of having just completed a long and arduous journey. She admired all that met her eyes profusely—at Charingworth every keyhole was a work of art—and rebuked me for my past indifference to my surroundings. She could not be persuaded to sit down to tea in the drawing room but insisted upon being given a tour of the house at once.

She must inspect the library, and exclaim over the venerable manuscripts and some previous baronet's priceless collection of ancient coins; she must glide slowly through the music room and put her lovely hands to every instrument; she must glory in the view offered by each window; she must inspect every painting in the picture gallery—the Rubens, the Canaletto, the Vermeer, ad infinitum. She must rapturously examine each of the gilt mermaids who supported the arms of the Linnell sofas and be ravished by the picture gallery's pièce de résistance: a huge Pietà, which had originally graced the altar of a Florentine church but now occupied a thoroughly secular position above the chimney piece.

"The English, such pirates!" declared my friend, studying it lovingly. At last she spun around to demand, "What! Are there no Gainsboroughs? No Sir Joshuas?"

"They are upstairs in the portrait gallery," I murmured rather faintly.

"Oh, the portrait gallery! Is it next? I am very eager to see that!"

"Then you might move a little faster," said I, ungraciously.

Eventually, after innumerable delays, we reached the portrait gallery. Marguerite lingered annoyingly before the first Sir Anthony, a mere knight, but unswervingly loyal to his doomed sovereign, with whom he had died at Bosworth Field, leaving a young widow and an infant son to fare as well as they might under the buccaneering Tudors.

"I see *your* Anthony has something of his namesake in him," Marguerite remarked thoughtfully.

"I think not," I said. "He is pure Cercy, I am afraid."

But I recognized my error instantly. The resemblance *was* there, in the calm set of the beautifully formed mouth, and in the unwavering eyes, softened only by those long, dark lashes. I wondered, shockingly, how this other Anthony had behaved in the bedroom, and how those lips had tasted.

I felt a pang of longing. *He hates me,* I reminded myself. *My husband does not lie.* My eyes stung. I moved back from the painting to brace myself against the balustrade.

Marguerite proceeded cheerfully along the gallery.

"Well, you'll look very lovely up here," she declared at last, having sated herself.

"No doubt," I said bitterly. "All five of me."

She whirled upon me then.

"Oh, Fleur, will the two of you never put that behind you and make your peace!"

"What are you saying? Why, it was *you* who—"

"Arranged to expose *his* sins to *you.* Yes, I know. Let me see your bedroom."

Greatly relieved that she had changed the subject, I led her to my private quarters and endured her effusions in praise of the chintz hangings, the carved oak overmantel, the vista from every aperture, ad nauseam.

"And where," she inquired archly, when she had exhausted her store of both French and English accolades, "does the baronet sleep?"

"His bedroom is in the other wing," I said, and added rather defiantly, "naturally."

"Naturally," said Marguerite satirically.

"Naturally," I repeated. "I believe Théo has his own bedroom, has he not?"

"He has," conceded Marguerite. "I insisted upon it—separate bedrooms are essential to a happy marriage. One must always have the freedom to sleep alone. However, if Théo actually *used* his freedom more than two or three times a month, I think I would be exceedingly disgruntled. Well," pressed Marguerite, "is that next?"

"Is *what* next?"

"The baronet's bedroom."

"Certainly not! I would not dream of going in there!"

"Oh, what is it? A Bluebeard's closet?" demanded my naughty guest.

"Indeed it is not!" I retorted. Poor Marguerite could not say anything on the subject of my husband that did not needle me. If she seemed to favor him, I felt betrayed; if she mocked him, ever so lightly, I was outraged.

"I would not think of setting foot in there without his knowledge," I continued rather stiffly, and immediately felt foolish, remembering how I had stolen into his bedroom in the hope of destroying that nonexistent photographic plate.

"Oh, you English," said Marguerite with ill-concealed disappointment. "Always standing upon ceremony, even in your own homes! Well, what about tea? I declare, I am absolutely famished!"

How Marguerite rhapsodized over the Niderviller porcelain and the silver Paul Storr tea service! But it seemed to be my fate to have disconcerting news dropped upon me while I was juggling cups and saucers.

"So, your Valorys are not for show," remarked my friend. "Théo would be wounded. Where do you keep them—in London?

Or the attic?" She glanced up at the ornate plastered ceiling. "Attics, I suppose," she added wryly.

"I don't know *what* you are talking about. I have nothing of Théo's. I dearly wish I had. He would never sell to Frederick, you know."

"I mean the ones Tony bought, of course," replied Marguerite.

The priceless fifteenth-century apostle spoon with which I had been about to stir my tea—fittingly, it was the Judas spoon—went flying to the carpet, and it was all I could do to prevent the cup and saucer from following.

However, I managed to set them down carefully, pick up the fallen spoon, and finally confront my friend's innocent gaze.

"*Tony?*" I said, unable to prevent sarcasm from oozing into my voice. "And when did *you* become such good friends?"

Marguerite turned crimson.

"Oh, Fleur! Do you really mean to say that you don't know!"

"I know nothing," I said. "How the baronet occupies himself is a complete mystery to me—except for such sketchy but intriguing reports as I may occasionally receive from Neville and the Mansard woman. And now, it now seems, from you."

"Impossible! Why it was all your doing!"

"*My* doing! My dear Marguerite, you are thoroughly mistaken."

"But it was you who kept insisting that Neville must visit Théo's studio! Surely you remember how he finally managed to corner Théo on your wedding day!"

I continued to gape at her in angry confusion, for I did not see what this could possibly have to do with my husband.

"Well, Neville found Théo's work . . . challenging at first, but it so fascinated him that he kept coming round and soon he decided he absolutely had to own one or two of Théo's more accessible canvases. He was dying to show them to Tony, but, as you know, your husband never had any time for Neville during the first few months of your marriage. However, Neville brought it off at last, and after that nothing could have kept Tony out of the studio. He has such a passion for color. . . . Are you angry, Fleur?"

"Not in the least," I lied. "Please, tell me all."

"Well, Tony would have bought the lot, I think, but he did not wish to seem greedy, so he brought round some of his radical friends, and Théo has now become quite a sensation with the most daring collectors."

"Really? And when did all this occur?"

"Oh, let me think . . . his first visit was a few weeks before you came to Paris for that dreadful meeting with Germaine's father. I assumed that you knew then—in fact, I rather feared you might suppose that was my reason for seeming to take Tony's part —he having become a sort of patron of Théo's, you know. And then, when I heard from you again, when you were so very unhappy, I was indescribably relieved to think that you still knew you could turn to me!"

"And so ready then to betray your husband's patron by arranging that meeting between me and Madame Mansard! Really, Marguerite, how do you contrive to serve such opposing interests?"

"Is that what you think!" Marguerite fairly flung down her cup as she leaped from her chair. She then threw herself on her knees at the foot of my own chair and looked at me piteously. "Forgive me, Fleur. Perhaps I *was* wrong to meddle. But how can Théo and I take sides when we are so fond of you both? I wanted only to bring the two of you together. I thought that besides impressing Tony with how little right he had to sit in judgment upon you and extract some horrid kind of penance—what was it, exactly? You've never told me, you know!—Germaine might also show *you* the danger your marriage was in before it was too late. I never intended it as a betrayal. One can scarcely fault Tony for taking mistresses after all *you* have told me! But neither could I overlook his cruelty to you! Do you call *that* double-dealing?"

Cruelty. I thought of the silks and perfumes, the diamonds and the white-brass bells. Which of us was indeed the crueler one? I burned with discomfort as I recalled how I had seduced my husband among the apple trees, exploiting what must have been for him no more than a demanding biological urge, without the smallest regard for the concerns he had expressed about children. No wonder he hated me.

How could I melt that hatred? Why did I yearn to?

"Did you ask him why he never brought me to Paris with him when he came to visit Théo?" I asked irrelevantly, after a long silence.

"Of course I did, but you know how he can be. He simply drew the blinds in that way he has and said something about your being disinclined to travel. I hoped *that* meant we might be receiving happy news from you shortly; however, it was not to be. It is no wonder—separate bedrooms, separate lives! Where is Tony now?"

"I'm sure I don't know. I might as well ask you," I admitted sadly. I reached out and took her hand. "Never mind, Marguerite. I know you meant well. To tell the truth, I rather wish you had succeeded in your object."

Marguerite got off her knees and returned to her chair. There was a little flush upon her cheeks.

"Ah, does that mean you are more favorably inclined toward your 'Sir Galahad' these days?" she asked hopefully.

"And if I were? He *hates* me, Marguerite."

"Surely not! I have never had that impression from him!"

"And why would you? You *are* my dearest friend, and he is very adept at concealing his emotions. I myself did not suspect the full degree of his antipathy until lately."

"I am sure he does not hate you. His manner with you may be calculated to make you feel rather small. I saw how it was when Théo and I called upon you in Paris, but even with all that, I can tell you this: He was a good deal happier then than I have ever seen him when he is apart from you. Oh yes, it would break your heart if you knew—he mopes like a lovesick dog."

The woman could not help herself, of course. She was an actress and had the characteristic disease of her profession: a compulsion to dramatize, embellish, and romanticize even the most arid incidents and situations.

"Perhaps he is yearning for his Three Graces and Mrs. Hawkes," I said bitterly, unwilling to allow myself to entertain any notion that he might still care for me. "I doubt they travel with him when he calls on you. No, Marguerite, I will not deceive myself. He hates me. He has told me so point-blank, and he never lies."

"So you choose to believe him."

"I have no reason to believe otherwise."

"It suits you to believe him, since *you* hate him."

"I do not," I said. "That is so far from what I feel!"

I thought of the reckless, unrestrained passion he had revealed to me, and of my joyous response to it—until its source had proven to be hatred.

"Ah? At last you begin to see what you have thrown away."

"I have learned that perhaps I do not know him quite as well as I imagined I did," I conceded.

"I do not think that is quite all," said Marguerite softly. She had been watching me carefully. "You really *must* give serious thought to how you feel, Fleur."

"I have learned *not* to think about how I feel," I countered, not wishing to reveal all the confusion that had been plaguing me lately and to which I had, in fact, begun to give a great deal of thought. "Thinking too much about how I felt was what brought my life with Frederick to ruin," I continued, but with more uncertainty than conviction. "Introspection is very morbid. I will not indulge in it again. These days I try to confine myself to thinking about what needs to be done. And then to grit my teeth and do it."

"Ugh, how disagreeable," said Marguerite with a little shudder. "I would not adopt *your* philosophy for all the world! Was that how you spent your honeymoon? No wonder he has mistresses and you sleep alone!"

· · ·

In spite of its unpromising beginning, in the end Marguerite's visit was a great success. How painfully I would have otherwise felt my loneliness during those long summer days without even the briefest communication from my husband! Besides, I had absolute faith in Marguerite's goodwill, and once I had accustomed myself to her and Théo's improbable friendship with Anthony, I felt oddly bolstered by it, although I am afraid I continued to resent the easy familiarity with which she bandied his nickname about.

But I put off charging her with the commission I had decided to entrust to her, and several days—very pleasant ones—passed before I dared to broach the subject.

"I have decided to leave Anthony," I told her rather grandly one afternoon, and was immediately punctured by her crushing reply.

"*Mon Dieu*, Fleur, don't be absurd! How can you leave a man who has left you?"

"I mean," I amended quickly, "I have decided to leave Charingworth."

"I think you must be crazy," she pronounced. "First you snub your husband. Now you want to turn your back on all this splendor!"

"Anthony will be very glad to see the last of me. His only reason for avoiding Charingworth is that I am here. He loves this house."

"Do you mean that he wants a *real* separation! I can hardly believe he would court such a scandal!"

"Why not?" I said with a sigh, yet rather proudly. "He cares nothing for what society thinks. He would not live a lie to please even the Queen herself!"

"Oh, you don't speak of him at all in the way you once did," observed Marguerite. "What admiration there is in your voice! What feeling!"

"You must help me, Marguerite! I have told you that Anthony hates me and wishes to be rid of me. I accept that. He cannot—or will not—forgive me for the way I deceived him. I accept that. I have done other things to set him against me still more, if such a thing is possible. I cannot go on living here."

"If only you could show him your love," said Marguerite, "I think he would forgive you anything."

"Love!" I cried, shaken. "Surely you don't believe that I have fallen in love with my husband!"

Marguerite regarded me with a dubious smile and said at last, "Look at yourself, Fleur! You are as lovesick as he is!"

But I continued to protest her unsettling diagnosis until at last she said, *"Eh bien,* my friend. And how does this latest folly of yours require my assistance?"

"Well, you see," I said, "Anthony has promised that he will support me once I am gone. But I am beginning to think that I cannot take his money."

"By all the blessed saints, Fleur, you *are* an utter fool! First, you scorn the man! Then this house! And now the money! What can you be thinking of?"

"I *must* leave before things get any worse!"

Lately I had been haunted by a vision of the welcome I might have been tempted to give my husband were he to visit Charingworth and find me there alone. I saw myself in tears at his feet begging for his forgiveness and for his love. I saw him, having steeled his resolve and sated his physical appetites with other women, turning away from me with a chilly and ironic smile, savoring his ultimate victory: my wanting him when he no longer wanted me. *Then your punishment will have only just begun.*

"I cannot take his money, Marguerite. That would put me on the same level as the coldest fortune hunter! Yes, I married Anthony to save my reputation. My reputation has been saved. *Voilà.* To take anything more from him would be to compound the wrong I did him."

"So you wish to restore his good opinion of you?"

"In whatever small way I can," I acknowledged humbly. "And not to sink any farther in my own eyes."

"I see," said Marguerite. "And, of course, you cannot retrieve your self-respect except by plunging yourself into abject poverty. Really, Fleur, living in England seems to have made you very dim. I do not know why you cannot simply say to him that you are very sorry for what has happened in the past and would like to start anew."

"It is impossible," I said.

"I don't see why. All you need do is say, 'I'm sorry, Tony. If you can forgive me, I would like to—' "

"You don't understand," I cried. "We *cannot* stay together under *any* circumstances."

"Why is that?"

"He absolutely does not want children," I said, surrendering up nearly the last of my secrets.

"Really? I declare, the man has no vanity at all! And you?"

"I do! More than anything."

"You don't mean to say you would marry someone else!" cried Marguerite.

"Oh never!" I cried rather too ardently, and then added in a stiff and far more rational tone, "I merely wish to escape from a situation where I am daily reminded of the difference between how things are and how they might have been."

"Well," said my friend with a sigh, "I will do whatever I can to help you, Fleur. How sad it is. . . . I wish there were another way. But never mind. Tell me what I must do."

"I am afraid I will need to borrow a little money," I said. It nearly killed me. How Frederick had had the stomach to make such a request, not once, but repeatedly, of the people he had called his friends was incomprehensible. I would do almost anything, I thought, to ensure that I would never find myself in so mortifying a position again.

"But of course," said Marguerite. "How much?"

"Only enough for me to get to London and for a night or two at a hotel."

"Why, that is nothing," said Marguerite. But she was looking at me rather strangely. I recognized the look; I had often seen it in my grandmother's eyes. She was appraising what my dress must have cost, and my shoes.

"Yes, I know," I said, fingering the satin rosettes at the wrists of my gown. "Anthony pays for my clothes." I was becoming nearly tongue-tied with embarrassment. "I . . . I haven't a penny to call my own."

"Oh, my dear!" cried Marguerite, turning white. All her heart was in her voice. "How dreadful! He has really pinned you to wall, hasn't he! But has it never occurred to you to nick the silver? And I recall seeing some very fine gold plate in the dining room!"

"Yes, but that would make the nobility of my intentions rather suspect, wouldn't it!" I said with a choked little laugh. "No, my grandmother left me a little jewelry, which I keep in a bank in London. If I can get there, I can sell it. It should raise more than enough money to keep me until I can find work."

"What sort of work?"

"Whatever I can."

"You shall come to Paris," ordained Marguerite. "You may as well come back with me. You can stay with us for as long as you like. Théo will be delighted."

"Oh no," I protested weakly. "That would be a terrible imposition! And if Anthony is Théo's patron—"

"What of that!" cried Marguerite. "*He* may be Théo's friend, but *you* are mine! Besides, if you are so foolishly in love with your husband that you are willing to endure poverty to prove your honor, I hardly think Tony will blame us for wanting to be sure you do not starve! My house is large—it will be delightful to have your company until you both have sorted things out."

I knew *that* day would never come, but her warm-hearted assurances and intermittent scoldings finally persuaded me to accept her offer. However, I did not return to Paris with her. I told her I would follow in a fortnight. I wanted time to make my farewells to Charingworth. I was pretty certain, now, that my husband would not intrude upon them.

XXVIII

I spent hours out of doors, riding through the countryside or sitting with my sketchbook in a hedgerow or a woodland glade, struggling, now that my time there was running out, to capture the beauties of Charingworth, so that I might carry a record of them with me into the future.

A morning came when I reached the last page of my sketchbook.

I closed the book and gazed at the bright ripples of the little stream I had come to draw. It was time to leave. I knew it. Already I had lingered too long; I felt weaker, not stronger, at the prospect of departure.

If only I could have been as clear, as transparent with my husband as that unpolluted stream. But I was not transparent—not even to myself.

I recalled Marguerite's advice: *All you have to do is say* . . . What could I lose by speaking to my husband? Were our differences—even those regarding the propagation of little Camwells—beyond even the realm of discussion? The mere idea of initiating so open and fearless a conversation made me shrink; but the prospect of swallowing my unarticulated desires and burying my vague hopes was more painful still.

I stood up at last and climbed into the saddle, still musing on these matters.

I was far from the house but close to a copse that lay on the border of my husband's lands and the neighboring estate. As Andromeda carried me across the stream where I had loitered for most of the morning, a shot rang out. Andromeda whinnied and fell to her knees. I lost my seat and landed in the water, striking my right shoulder on the sharp edge of a large rock.

"Hold your fire, you idiot!" I cried as I clambered toward Andromeda. But no one answered. At first I feared that my horse had been hit, but she was quickly back on her feet and showed no signs of harm. Her hoof must have slipped on one of the slick stones in the streambed when the shot had startled her.

I led her back to the house, sick with guilt. If only I had not been so preoccupied with my own thoughts, I would have found a less treacherous place to cross the stream. As for the shots, I had often heard gunfire on Lord Sparling's property, but never so close.

We reached the stables. I told Watkins what had happened.

"It's that Sparling brat again," he muttered, shaking his head. He inspected Andromeda carefully and assured me that she had suffered no injury. Then he asked me whether I'd been hurt.

"Oh, not at all!" I lied. My shoulder was throbbing violently, but I was too proud to complain. Even when I went to my room to change from my sodden habit, I didn't ring for Marie to help me. I was embarrassed that I'd been thrown; I didn't want to explain the livid bruise.

No sooner had I changed into one of my old dresses than Mrs. Phillips asked if she might speak with me; she wanted my approval for the arrangements she had made for dinner that night, in honor of my husband's return.

"Sir Anthony is here?" I gasped, forgetting to conceal my surprise.

"No, my lady. He arrives on the three o'clock train from London," said Mrs. Phillips.

"Ah yes," I said, pretending that I had forgotten, although my heart was pounding with a mixture of anxiety and joy. I examined the menu carefully, and for the first time in the entire history of my life at Charingworth, I hesitantly suggested some small alterations, which I hoped might please my husband's tastes, and then proceeded with the same diffidence to offer some other suggestions as to the flowers which would grace the dinner table. Mrs. Phillips, although she could be faulted in no other respect, was somewhat conservative about mixing colors, and I thought a bolder floral display than we usually enjoyed might delight my husband's eye.

"*Very* good, my lady," she said with a happier expression than she had been accustomed to wear of late.

When she had gone, I surveyed my collection of dresses thoughtfully.

During my last visit to London, my wardrobe had been further replenished by Madame Rullier, although my husband had not remained with us to monitor the fittings. Now I selected what I believed was one of the prettiest of all her creations, an afternoon dress of vibrant amber silk, with a few vertical green satin ribbons extending from shoulder to hem and along the sleeves, which were puffed at the shoulder and tightly fitted down the lower arm to the wrist.

After luncheon, I visited Andromeda to assure myself yet again that she was unharmed. Then I stopped by the kitchens to review the dinner menu once again, this time with Monsieur Borchet, my husband's chef.

After that, I changed into the amber silk and wandered through the gardens. When the hands on the face of the old clock which surveyed the gabled roof stood at a half past two, I was seized by yet another whim. I thought of all the times I had returned to Charingworth alone, to be met only by the coachman, and of how disheartening I always found it not to receive a warmer welcome at the end of a journey.

I returned to the stables and learned that my husband had arranged for one of the undergrooms to meet him at the railway station with the dogcart.

"No," I announced to the undergroom. "I shall meet him myself."

My nerves were as tightly strung as piano wire when I drove the dogcart down the avenue to reach the station five minutes before the train did.

And then, shrieking and hissing, it arrived.

I stood upon the platform, waiting with an unfamiliar flutter in my heart for my husband to appear. When a young gentleman leaped flamboyantly from the train, I scarcely noticed; never in a million years would my husband have broken into a run.

But the impetuous figure was rushing toward me, and a once familiar voice was crying, "Fleur Brooks!"

It was my long lost friend, Guy.

Now I was flying toward him. We both stopped awkwardly, just short of an embrace.

Out of the corner of my eye, I saw my husband step down from the train. He was looking straight at me. For an instant, it seemed to me, his face wore a stricken expression. But if it had been there at all, it was gone in a moment.

"Come," I said, seizing Guy by the hand. "Let me introduce you to my husband."

We walked slowly across the platform toward my husband, who was approaching us with his usual calm dignity.

"Good afternoon, Fleur," said my husband.

"Welcome home, Anthony," I stammered. He must have thought it a very odd welcome to find his wife all but in the arms of another man. "Let me introduce a very old and dear friend of mine, Guy Hazelton. Guy, my husband, Anthony Camwell."

They greeted each other amicably.

"But what brings you here?" I asked Guy. "I could scarcely believe my eyes when I saw you."

Even as I spoke I half feared my husband would regard this as a spur-of-the-moment invention.

"Nor I mine," said Guy. "I'm on my way—well, I *was* on my way, and my luggage still is—to spend the weekend at Lincroft with the Kendalls when I saw you from the train. What could I do but jump off? It is so lovely to see you, Fleur, after all these years. You're looking marvelous—radiant!"

I thought this must be a gallant exaggeration. As Guy spoke, I felt my husband's curious, piercing glance upon me once again.

"You've captured a real prize," declared Guy to my husband with the unstudied charm I had always found so endearing in him, although at this juncture it embarrassed me sorely. "I would not have believed that any man on earth could have beguiled Fleur away from Paris."

My husband smiled.

"Why don't you come back to Charingworth and have tea with Fleur?" he said. By not saying "tea with us," he had rather delicately indicated he would give Guy and me the opportunity to talk alone. "You must have a great deal to tell each other after so long. My carriage can take you to Lincroft later on, if you like. It is not far at all."

"Oh, I wouldn't dream of putting you to the trouble," said Guy. "There'll be another train along in an hour or so. I'll just telegraph the Kendalls to let them know that my luggage and I will be arriving separately."

"Really, it would be no trouble," said my husband.

But Guy was firm in his refusal.

"Perhaps you'd like to wait here, then, and give yourselves a little time to talk," said my husband to me. And then, as Guy dashed off to send his telegram, my husband added, "I'll leave the dogcart for you. It's such a fine day—I shan't mind the walk at all."

"Oh, I'll walk!" I said quickly. "You must be tired after your journey. Take the dogcart—I brought it for you. It is such a lovely day that I'm afraid I rescinded your orders and came to meet you myself."

"That was thoughtful of you," he said. I realized with a pang that I had rarely given him much opportunity to speak of me thus. "But I insist upon walking."

"Have you no luggage?"

"None," he said. Then, with another long look, he added, "Everything I could ever want is here."

I felt my cheeks color as I looked at him until he turned away and left.

"He's very gracious," said Guy, returning, "and so good-looking. But he seemed, oh, slightly upset. . . . Is he the jealous sort?"

"I don't know," I said, feeling dazed. I watched my husband's straight back disappear round the corner of the livery stable.

"You don't know!" exclaimed Guy. "You don't *know* whether your own husband is subject to fits of jealousy! Believe me, Fleur, if anyone married to *you* had a jealous bone in his body, you'd have found it out long ago."

I thought again of the terrible things my husband had implied about Frederick, but I thought too of how long he had held his peace before breaking out with them.

"But I *don't* know," I repeated. "We have never been close. I'm afraid ours has not been a happy marriage, Guy. In fact, we are about to separate."

"I am so sorry," said Guy politely. He looked thoroughly perplexed. "But why?" he finally demanded. "It's obvious that he adores you."

"I don't think so," I said in the brittlest voice I could manage. "We must be rather good at putting up a false front. I'm surprised it fooled *you*, however. You were once so perceptive."

"And you care for him," persisted my friend. "It was written all over your face."

I lifted my hands to my cheeks.

"I do," I whispered at last.

Then I lapsed into silence again, until Guy took my hand and led me to the bench against the station wall.

We sat down.

"But enough of this," I said with forced briskness. "Tell me, how is Harry?"

"Very well. He is at Lincroft."

"I am glad you are happy," I remarked, with a touch of envy.

"Oh, Fleur," said Guy as if he'd caught my thoughts, "do you think that I have achieved happiness without a struggle?"

"What struggle? You love Harry, he loves you. It seems to me your happiness was inevitable."

"You know better than that, Fleur!" exclaimed Guy. "Nothing is inevitable. Look at my life in England. It was an absolute hell of duplicity and deception. I ended *that* only by resolving to return to Paris—with Harry or without him. When I left for France, I left alone."

"But . . . why are you here?" I stammered.

"Because Harry has made his choice. He is at Lincroft because, before leaving for France, he chose to tell his favorite sister—she is Mrs. Kendall—the truth about why he is going away. He half feared she would never speak to him again. But in point of fact she responded by inviting both of us to Lincroft before Harry returns to France with me."

"What an excellent woman she must be."

"And as for you, your troubles are not so different from anyone else's," continued Guy rather brutally. "Just because love was so effortless with Frederick . . ." I barely heard the rest of what he said.

Had love really been so effortless with Frederick? Yes, there was something endearingly feckless about him—it invited love. He was so cheerfully unashamed of his need to be shielded from all the inartistic, tedious business of daily life! He was so openly, charmingly helpless about everything he regarded as unpleasant, unaesthetic, and therefore beneath him. He was never imperious —he didn't have to be. He exerted his will with sunny gaiety and cajoling compliments, making resistance seem surly, making resentments seem mean-spirited and carping. I could never have voiced them!

Yes, I loved him! Yes, I would have raised him from the dead! But the Frederick of my cherished memories—the Frederick I yearned to have restored to me—had been altered greatly from the flesh-and-blood Frederick of our last years together. I did not yearn for drunken kisses, for scattered piles of dirty clothing, for empty bottles and overturned glasses, for the litter of crumbling sticks of charcoal lying about everywhere, for the filthy paintbrushes it was *my* thankless job to clean, or for the mountain of debts *I* had not incurred. . . .

". . . and you can't let the rough patches get the better of you," Guy was saying.

"Rough *patches!*" I said with a laugh, still thinking of the hardest stretch of that old life.

Then I realized with a jolt that Guy was still, of course, speaking of my present marriage.

"Why do you sound so bitter?" he asked.

I took a deep breath, decided to tailor my answer to his question rather than to my private thoughts, and confessed what seemed now well on the way to becoming common knowledge rather than a dark secret.

"I did not marry Anthony for love."

"You!" cried Guy. "Madame All-for-Love married for a baser reason!"

"I felt I had no choice," I murmured, crimson with embarrassment.

"And he found you out!" pursued Guy. "And now you find that you are developing a certain tenderness for him!"

"Well, perhaps it is something like that," I admitted cautiously.

"Well, then tell him so, for heaven's sake, you silly creature. Very likely, he'll be overjoyed. I'm sure you won't have to humble yourself half as much as you think. Harry always had the upper hand with me, you know, until I refused to take it any longer. The happiest day of my life was the day he swallowed his pride and told me that he would follow me anywhere."

"I am so very glad for you, Guy. No one deserves happiness more than you."

"I would be even happier," said Guy, "if I believed you would take my advice and go to work to mend your bridges instead of burning them beyond any hope of repair."

"I will confess, I have been considering it," I admitted nervously.

"Well, that's better, then," said Guy cheerfully. "Let me know what comes of it. Here is my address in Paris."

I took the precious bit of pasteboard and tucked it into my purse.

"You know, Guy," I said, "I am so sorry I failed to answer all those letters of yours so long ago. Someday I'll tell you the reason. But not today. Today I will take a leaf from Frederick's book: We have so little time that we ought to dwell on only happy subjects."

"Yes, that was Frederick to the hilt," murmured Guy with a smile.

Much too soon his train arrived.

"Let me know how it goes with Camwell," were his last words to me.

My husband was nowhere to be seen when I returned home from my tête à tête with Guy.

"Will you take tea upstairs or in the drawing room, my lady?" inquired Mrs. Phillips.

"Oh, in the drawing room," I said absently. "Where is Sir Anthony?"

"He has gone out. It seems that young Percy Sparling has been shooting at our doves while the master was away, so he has gone off to have a word with Lord Sparling about it."

"Oh dear," I said. How unfortunate to meet with nothing but trouble as soon as one crosses one's own threshhold! But I was very glad the poor doves had so ready a champion. "Then I will have my tea upstairs, after all."

I drifted up the stairway to my sitting room. The brief encounter with Guy had left me hungering for more of the intimacy that only the truest of friendships can offer. I decided to write to Marguerite.

I sat down at my writing table and had committed a few sentences to paper when there was a knock at the door. I supposed it would be Ellen with my afternoon tea. But it was not. It was my husband.

"Is it all settled then, about the doves?" I asked. How I wished my voice did not betray my nerves!

"Oh, it never is," said my husband with a sigh. "I am afraid eternal vigilance is the price of having Sparlings for neighbors."

"What a trial that must be."

"It is, indeed. Lord Sparling is inclined to forgive his son's trespasses. 'Boys will be boys,' is his litany—so long as it is *his* boy and not someone else's!"

This was true; in his role as local magistrate, Lord Sparling seldom forgave the trespasses of less exalted youths.

"I swear, Fleur," my husband was saying, "I would set mantraps throughout that copse if only there were no danger of catching something more innocent than that Sparling brat."

I considered the problem presented by Percy Sparling—how I wished I might have been able to present my husband with some neat solution to it. But nothing glimmered in my brain. All I could think of was what a sorry homecoming my husband had received. Well, at least the dogs must have slobbered over him enthusiastically.

At this point Mrs. Phillips herself arrived with the tea tray.

"Would you please send up a second cup, Mrs. Phillips?" I said quickly. And when she had left, "You will stay and have tea with me, Anthony, won't you?"

"If you wish," said my husband after a pause, as if he were both bestowing a favor and accepting one.

I thought he, too, seemed somewhat ill at ease. What had brought him to my room? Now that he had fallen silent on the subject of the doves, he seemed to have been struck dumb altogether. Perhaps he was waiting for the second teacup to be delivered, that he might then speak without fear of interruption. What was taking Mrs. Phillips so long?

I began to babble rather inanely about my pleasure at seeing Guy once again. Perhaps it would have relieved any jealousy my husband might have felt had I told him about Harry and the history of my friendship with Guy, but to have done so, without having received Guy's express permission, would have been to betray a confidence. And, in any case, why would my husband be jealous? He hated me; he wanted nothing more to do with me.

Still, the more I chattered on, the more I began to feel that even if the friendship between Guy and me had not unsettled my husband at the outset, it must seem as suspect by now as it would have been had I assiduously avoided the subject. There was nothing for it now but to take the bull by the horns and confess to my husband that what had brought me to the station was my feeble hope of salvaging our marriage. Yet I must wait for that second, laggard teacup!

At last Ellen arrived with the overdue bit of porcelain. I fairly snatched it from her hands, told her that we wanted nothing more, and, as the door closed behind her, filled the cup for my husband and handed it to him.

"I would like to assure you, Anthony," I said in words stilted by embarrassment and emotion, "in the event that you may have suspected otherwise, there is nothing more than friendship between Mr. Hazelton and me, nor could there ever be."

"Why have you felt it necessary to tell me that?" asked my husband. There was no warmth in his voice, but neither did he sound particularly hostile.

"I was concerned that you may have been unpleasantly surprised by the sight of us."

"Not at all. To see such a smile on your face is always a surprise, but never an unpleasant one." This he said in a most chillingly ironic tone. "Do you think I would be so small and mean as to resent the man who put it there?"

Oh, that stung! How could I persuade him that yes, indeed, I had been overjoyed at the sight of Guy, but that the tremulous eagerness which had possessed me all day and had at last impelled me to set out for the station had been for *him*, and him alone.

"Anthony," I said, blushing, "there is so much I must say to you. Do you think—"

But it was so difficult to find the words. I set down my cup, rose from my chair, and turned my back on him to look out across the lawns to the river, as if I might see the proper phrases floating past me downstream and reach out to pluck them from the water. How could I ask for what he had told me he could never give? Even the thought of begging for that impossible forgiveness brought tears to my eyes.

"Do I think what?" said my husband softly. He had risen, too, and was standing behind me.

"Oh," I said with a little sob.

His hands, the hands I longed for, dropped lightly to my shoulders. I gasped, wincing involuntarily with pain from that still fresh bruise I had momentarily forgotten. I jerked away and turned toward him. He saw the tears on my face.

"I beg your pardon," he said coolly.

He was moving toward the door.

"Wait!" I said.

At the doorway he turned.

"No," he said gently. "I've waited *too* long, Fleur."

And with that he was gone.

The courage and hope with which Marguerite and Guy had infused me did not fare well under this latest blow. But what would my good angels have thought of me if I were to give up so easily, even in the face of that latest rejection?

I contemplated the curious fluctuations in my husband's manner.

Could I discount the slim possibility that he was, in fact, as open to a reconciliation as I was? He had reached out to me, as I had to him, and it was no fault in either of us that the attempt had failed. Only an unlucky accident had deflected me from my purpose.

The dinner table yet awaited us, with its bright flowers and its carefully orchestrated menu.

But when I arrived in the dining room, the table, to my dismay, was set for only one. I swallowed my pride and asked the footman to send Mrs. Phillips to me.

In the glare of the chandelier, it seemed to me that both Mrs. Phillips and the flowers had a crestfallen look.

"Why does Sir Anthony not dine here?" I asked her.

Her face became inscrutable.

"He is in his study, my lady. He has a great deal of work to do tonight and asked to have his dinner sent to him there. He does not wish to be disturbed."

Did I imagine that little flicker of compassion in her face?

"Work!" I said, forgetting myself. "What 'work' is it that cannot wait even an hour or two!"

"I'm sure I do not know, my lady," she replied in such an opaque way that I rather imagined she *did* know but that not even the threat of the rack could have persuaded her to reveal it.

I pushed back my chair and started to rise. I had lost my appetite completely, and I could not bear the thought of sitting in that huge hall alone, staring down one delicacy after another until the interminable torture ended.

Mrs. Phillips gazed with bleak eyes at the beautifully laid table.

I sank back into the chair.

"Well," I said, "you may as well tell them to bring on the soup."

"Yes, my lady."

Although I could eat very little, I scrupulously sampled each painstakingly prepared dish: the *saumon, sauce verte;* the *Châteaubriand aux pommes.* . . . If anything could have tempted a sluggish appetite, it was these.

I barely tasted them.

My head was splitting when I left the table. However, I did not go to my bedroom. I went to the library, where I picked up one dismal book after another and stared at meaningless pages of type. I heard the clock strike ten . . . quarter past . . . half past . . . and then my eyes fell shut.

"There you are," said my husband. He sounded surprised.

I pulled myself upright, too befogged and uncertain of myself to speak.

"I've been wanting to have a word with you," he said, "but it is already past eleven, and I thought you would be in bed by now. Is it too late?"

"Not at all," I said.

I thought he seemed as ill at ease as he had been earlier in my sitting room. Again he appeared to be at a loss for words.

"You will be pleased to know that I have lost the taste for my exercise in revenge," he said finally. His voice was flat and dismissive; his eyes were hard and distant. As I stared at him, bewildered, he turned and disappeared into his study, whence he shortly returned with a check folded inside a sheet of notepaper which bore the address of Smalley & Brown, his London solicitors. The check was for a princely amount.

"You may leave anytime," he said. "I have instructed my solicitors to send you checks for this amount every quarter. You need only keep them informed of your whereabouts."

Even if words had come to me, I could not have spoken them. I was mute with shock.

"I return to London tomorrow and shall stay there until you are gone from Charingworth." He reached into his pocket and pulled out a crisp little stack of bank notes. "Here is something to help you on your way. How much time do you want to make arrangements to leave? Will two or three weeks suffice?"

"Two weeks will be more than enough," I managed faintly.

"If the money I have arranged for you to receive proves to be inadequate to your needs, or if you wish to communicate with me for any other reason, I must ask you to do so through Smalley & Brown."

"Was it to tell me this that you came to my room today?" I said after another long silence.

"Yes," he said.

He seemed reluctant to meet my eyes.

I waited, longing for him to hold out one glimmer of hope. He said nothing more.

"Then why did you put your hands on me?" I whispered at last.

He turned back to me. The hard, distant gaze was gone; now I saw that gentler look which I'd glimpsed in his eyes when he'd left me at the station. I hadn't known how to interpret it then; I soon learned that all it expressed was pity.

"It was a . . . a reflex, if you will," he said. "I felt sorry for you. You were trying so hard to be pleasant this afternoon—I could see what an effort it was for you. It made me realize what a scoundrel I've been to hold on to you for the sake of exacting my revenge. That's over, Fleur," he concluded. He sounded exhausted. "I want you to go."

After a while I said, with a coolness that rivaled his own, "I suppose you will want a divorce then."

He shrugged.

"I have given you the justification you need," he said. "Whether or not to use it is entirely up to you. For my part, I have no wish to marry again. My experience of marriage has done nothing to recommend the institution to me. Good night."

He turned quickly and left the room.

XXIX

I took what little clothing I thought I would need, but I could not bring myself to take the diamond collar, which had been mysteriously restored to the case in my dressing room, nor any of my husband's other gifts of jewelry, except for the broken chains of white brass.

There was very little that I carried away from Charingworth— a few old dresses, some books and sketches, and my father's last letter to me. I left a note for Mrs. Phillips with instructions to have my remaining possessions shipped to Marguerite's house in Paris.

Shortly before my departure, I took Andromeda out for a long ride. To her patient ears, I confided all my confusions and regrets. I knew it was foolish, but I didn't care. She was steadfastly unjudgmental and offered me no useless advice. Finally my eyes blurred, so I slipped from her back and stood against her with my arms wrapped around her neck and tears sliding down my face, until she whinnied softly and bent her lovely head to nuzzle me.

Watkins gave me a curious look when I returned. I supposed my eyes were still red. He knew I would be leaving that afternoon, for I had asked him to arrange for someone to drive me to the

railway station. But he could not know—could he?—that I had
been told never to return.

I spent a little time in the stables, making my sad farewells to
the other horses. I had become fond of all of them. Magnificent
Perseus, my husband's favorite, who held his head so proudly and
moved with such flair and grace. Patient old Canute. Older even
than Canute was Hadrian, who had long ago outlived his useful-
ness. He had been stiff and half blind for years, but was still
cherished and indulged. My husband could have never sold him
off or sent him to the knacker's yard.

And the others, so well trained and so lovingly cared for. In a
burst of unjust and irrational self-pity, I wondered how much better I might have fared had I been one of my husband's horses.

After leaving the stables, I went to my room to change into my
traveling clothes. That done, I took a sheet of notepaper from my
desk and the check my husband had given me. His instructions
had been to communicate with him only through Smalley &
Brown, but I ignored this command.

"Dear Anthony," I wrote. "I hope you will understand why I
cannot accept this check from you. I shall be gone from Charingworth by the time you receive this, so I hope you will feel free
to return as early as you like.

"I am not able to take Marie with me, and, under the circumstances, I am sure that any reference I might give her would do
more harm than good. But you will agree that it would be unjust to
let her suffer because of a situation that is in no way her fault. She
was an excellent maid to me in every respect. I know I can depend
upon you to look out for her interests.

"If you can give Andromeda a little special attention, that she
may not feel suddenly abandoned, I would be very grateful. I truly
regret whatever unhappiness I have caused you, and I wish you
only the best. Believe me. Fleur."

I folded the note around the check and put them into an
envelope, which I addressed to him at Grosvenor Square.

There was a certain irony in the comfort I gleaned from knowing, beyond any doubt, that he would have concerned himself about Marie whether or not I had asked it of him. His earnest sense of responsibility, which I had once scorned as a lack of spontaneity, guaranteed that she would never suffer for my sins. I knew he would do everything in his power to find her a new situation as a lady's maid, and that if he could not, he would keep her on at Charingworth.

Shortly before I left the house, I had a very odd impulse. I went into my husband's bedroom, where I had scarcely ever set foot. It was very different from his bedroom in London; I liked it better. It reminded me of him powerfully.

It was chastely furnished, almost Spartan in its simplicity, but filled with a haunting, verdant sweetness, for the windows were open to the mild summer air, open to the birdsong soaring from the treetops, open to the flowers in the gardens below.

I lay down upon his bed and thought about all the things I would never have the opportunity to say to him. I had barely ever had a warm word for him, and certainly never an affectionate one. I wondered why this had continued to be so, even after my feelings for him had softened.

Perhaps it was because I could not bring myself to trade in the coinage I had debased. Long ago, when he'd asked me whether I loved him, I had answered yes; I had corrupted the language of the heart. How can it hope to reveal its secrets, when words have lost their meaning?

I contemplated this now with regret but without despair. I felt open to every sad truth, yet strangely peaceful. The realizations came, I accepted and acknowledged them, and let them pass on. The unrestrained tears I had shed earlier had left me with an exhausted sense of calm. I did not resist the currents of my thoughts.

My mind drifted back to Andromeda. I wondered whether my husband would take her out occasionally and let her run. He had never ridden her; I had had a proprietary attitude where she was concerned. Now I hoped he would. I knew he admired her passion for speed.

As I contemplated this, I felt a curious twinge of envy for my little horse. I let myself imagine what it would feel like to be his mount, controlled by the warm pressure of his knees and calves and by the delicate, assured touch of his hands on the reins. My blood sang softly at the vision of having the passionate impulse liberated and at the same time skillfully directed.

Now, as the scent of new-cut grass drifted up from the lawn and the curtains rustled softly in the breeze, unsettling images sprang into my consciousness like water rising from a subterranean stream to replenish a woodland pool.

Perhaps if I had been able to transmute myself into a beautiful, four-legged creature, built for speed and schooled to respond to the most subtle, expert hands, my husband would have kept me— might, in fact, have taken some delight in me.

The idle fancy was seductive, compelling. To be prized and petted, curried and groomed, to be coolly, masterfully used, to have nothing more demanded of me than silent, sensitive responsiveness. . . . Oh yes, this was the adventure I craved, the experience to which I ached to surrender. As I acknowledged the secret hunger so long disowned, I understood at last why my husband had been able to unleash such an astounding torrent of sensuality on that distant night in London, why he had awakened in me a response of such profound obeisance.

He had stopped talking of love. He had offered me the only thing my frozen heart could accept. He had catered to my deepest, most inadmissible wish—to surrender myself, not to love, but to a power worthy of respect and admiration, a power that weighed and measured its demands instead of insisting that it must have everything.

Could he have perceived that dormant yearning when he married me? And if he had, why had he waited so long to assert his own appetites, which so perfectly complemented my own? My mind wandered back to the beginnings of his courtship. I knew, from what he had told me when we had stood together on the Pont-Neuf in that gentle rain, that he had always been aware of his own darker desires—the lust for power, the joy in exercising it —and that, although he had guarded against these, he had never disguised his hungers to himself as I had mine.

Perhaps, at the very beginning, his recognition of me had been only barely conscious, and untrustworthy in the face of the smooth, unassailable facade I had presented to him once we were wed.

But I did not blame myself now for the huge gulf between the woman I had seemed and the woman he had revealed me to be. How could I have known that other aspect of myself?

I thought of my beloved Frederick, easy, laughing, and indulgent. Frederick, who had not shrunk from passion, but who, on the other hand, had never insisted upon it. Never could he have steeled himself to such sublime and necessary ruthlessness. Never could he have exercised such glorious, implacable severity. Even the paintings that brought me down had been done in a playful spirit; they had never affected Frederick's perception of me.

But my husband, seeing them through the lens of his own self-knowledge, would have recognized exactly how much I had withheld both from him and from myself, would have discerned in them instantly that capacity for passionate submission that the artist had unwittingly captured.

I stood up. I supposed this greater awareness, so painfully acquired, could help to clarify the past, with all its confusions and ambiguities, but it would serve me little in the future. The opportunity for that was gone.

I straightened the coverlet and the pillows, to erase any evidence of my visit to my husband's room, and left.

PART THREE

1893

XXX

I t was Théo who found me the position in Geneva.

He had a cousin who ran a girls' school there. The English mistress had been called away suddenly by a family crisis, and Théo's cousin needed a temporary replacement until Christmas.

"If I recommend you," Théo told me, "Elisabeth—Madame Vignon—will take you on in a second. She'll work you like a dog, of course, but she's very decent."

The luster of success was becoming to Théo; he was more amiable and less volatile than I remembered. He and Marguerite would have extended their hospitality indefinitely. But I was eager to supplement the tiny nest egg I had gained by selling the last of my grandmother's jewelry. I kept only one poor little emerald necklace with which I could not bear to part.

"The only thing is," Théo went on, "my cousin is anxious to protect the school's reputation and to avoid anything that might bring it notoriety. So it would be best if you were to use an assumed name."

That was how I became, once again, Caroline Flora Hastings. Only Théo, Marguerite, and Guy knew where I had gone and the name I had taken. I did not attempt to communicate with my husband, who had said he wanted nothing more to do with me.

During the few months I would be at the Vignon School, I was sure my secret would be safe. No one could mistake a plainly dressed, respectably widowed schoolmistress for the infamous Lady Camwell, that parvenue who'd scandalized English society by bolting her marriage, throwing over both her handsome husband and his immense fortune—and for what? Or, as some people whispered, for whom? The behavior of the abandoned husband provided no answers: He had neither opened his lips to illuminate the mystery nor taken action against his errant wife.

The sensible thing would have been to forget him. It was impossible. Although Madame Vignon, the endless demands of her pupils, and the almost unquenchable flow of idle conversation from the sewing mistress, Mademoiselle Hubert, with whom I shared a tiny attic room, commandeered most of my attention during my waking hours, my estranged husband was my first thought when I awoke in the morning, my last as I fell asleep at night. It was useless to think of forgetting.

I tried to harden my heart against him: What could be said for a man who, motivated by vengefulness and hatred, had deliberately awakened a woman's sleeping passions and slaked his own merely so that he might then enjoy the crueler satisfaction of casting her aside?

I swore he would never learn from any action of mine how well he had succeeded in exacting the revenge he'd forecast with such coldness and held to with such determination.

Or had he?

When I felt my implacability faltering, I would sternly remind myself of his infidelities. Or I'd think of the joyless, virtually silent meals we had shared, when it seemed that we could find nothing to say to each other, even as the sham of our marriage was collapsing about our heads.

But my thoughts kicked over the traces; they persisted in wandering back to the moment he had turned to me in the darkened carriage and gently invited me to talk about my daughter.

There was little point, however, in dwelling upon the past when my future was so uncertain.

Madame Vignon expressed great satisfaction with my work, but it went without saying that I would be redundant once the regular English mistress returned after the New Year.

Marguerite, although she scorned my lowly ambitions, acknowledged that with Madame Vignon's recommendation, she might be able to help me find employment as a governess in theatrical and artistic homes where my identity, which could probably not be concealed for long, might not be as severe a handicap as it would be elsewhere. She agreed to try to arrange several interviews for me in Paris during the Christmas holidays.

In early October, she wrote, "I saw Guy and Harry at the Opéra last week. Guy seemed dismayed to hear of your plans for the future. Nevertheless, he knows *so* many people, I asked him please to keep you in mind should he learn of any position which might suit you, and he has promised to apply himself to that.

"I must tell you that I have seen Anthony," she added to my chagrin. "I don't think he can be sleeping well—he was as haggard as a *ghost* and begged for news of you. I kept your secret, however —though I had to bite my tongue, I felt so sorry for him!—and did nothing more than assure him that you were safe and well. That seemed to ease his mind somewhat, but I think he is far from happy. His *apparent* composure is beginning to wear *very* thin."

I puzzled over this last bit for a long time. I knew he would never come to Geneva and expose my identity, even if Marguerite had been foolish enough to tell him where I had gone. But why had my husband, who'd made it clear that he wanted no further communication, sought news of me? I couldn't stop my thoughts from wandering back to this question on many an occasion.

. . .

Of all the girls at Vignon, I was particularly fond of Nina Lewingdon, the moody, precocious, and often wildly dramatic daughter of a London solicitor. Unfortunately for Nina, the dirt and congestion of the sooty metropolis where her family made its home had proven too much for Nina's fragile respiratory system, and, upon the advice of the family doctor, she had been sent away to the wholesome shores of Lac Leman. She was desperately homesick, and she was lonely: Having just turned thirteen, she was the youngest girl in the school.

There was nothing meek, however, about the poor little misfit. She had an impudent tongue and clashed endlessly with Mademoiselle Hubert, who disapproved of Nina's undisciplined stitches. But she quickly developed a strong attachment to me. This concerned me a little; my tenure at Vignon would end at Christmas, and I sometimes worried that Nina might then be lonelier than ever. I raised the subject with her once.

"Oh, I shall miss you fearfully," replied Nina offhandedly. "But I shall never surrender to despair! You see, you *have* taught me something!"

"I can't think what you are talking about," I said with a laugh.

"You set such an example," declared Nina. "Here you are, all alone in the world, your adored husband dead—"

The adoration was a pure flight of fantasy on her part; I had never discussed my "adored husband" with Nina Lewingdon or with anyone else at Vignon!

"—no relatives to take you to their bosom and to give you a home where you are cherished and beloved. Forced to work for a living, and worse, to share a room with that gargoyle Hubert, which I would consider a fate worse than being thrown down the oubliettes at Chillon!" declared the extravagant Miss Lewingdon. "But you are always cheerful and kind, and no one has ever heard you grouse or get in a wax about anything."

"No one is always cheerful, Nina! But I do consider myself very lucky to be here."

"I wish I did! But I like it better than I did at first. If only La

Hubert were leaving, instead of you, I might be entirely happy. You ought to hear how she talks about you! I don't know how you bear it! She finds you unduly mysterious and speculates about you constantly. She thinks you are hiding something! It's your own fault though, for being so tight-lipped."

Perhaps it was true. At Vignon, I had revealed as little as was humanly possible of the details of my life.

"For example," pursued Miss Lewingdon, "where were you born?"

I hesitated.

"Oh, you needn't worry, I won't betray your confidences to Hubert. But we *are* friends, aren't we?" she concluded plaintively.

Oh, what harm could it do?

"In Brighton," I said.

"Brighton!" she repeated happily. "I was there one summer. It is so very sad, the condition of the Royal Pavilion. It must have been beautiful once, but the Queen doesn't keep it up at all! If *I* am ever rich, I shall restore it and live there. Is Brighton where you grew up?"

"No, I grew up in a little village in Kent."

"What was it called?"

"Holwich," I said. I was not enjoying the innocent interrogation at all, but neither did I wish to fabricate a history or to seem "unduly mysterious."

"And your parents, do they still live there?"

"My mother died when I was born, and my father went to America."

"Oh, my goodness! Were you sent to an orphanage, like Oliver Twist? No wonder you think yourself lucky to be at Vignon!"

"My grandmother raised me," I said. "You will be relieved to know that she was not at all like Mr. Bumble. And *that* is the last such question I intend to answer today."

. . .

How strange that Nina should regard me as an example of courage in the face of misfortune just as I was coming to the humbling conclusion that I had never shown any courage at all! It was true that at Vignon I had managed to rise above self-pity. But as the weeks passed and my bitterness toward my husband relaxed, I began to look back upon both my marriages with new eyes.

I thought of how my idyllic romance with Frederick had cracked under the first real strain. It had seemed so easy to love, but what could be said of "love" that was nothing more than a feeling? Was it possible that I had never loved Frederick until the day I had dragged myself—too late—out of my self-imposed, despairing isolation, had committed myself to try to reverse the disastrous course our lives had taken, and had asked him for his help?

I burned inwardly as I dared even to consider that the great romance of my life had been little more than a case of passion without love, a passion that had survived, thanks to a happy compatibility of temperaments and inclinations, until circumstances demanded more of it. And even if I had managed to rise to the challenge, had Frederick?

As I entertained the searing possibility that perhaps Frederick had *not* been able to fully return my love, and that my isolation had *not* been entirely self-imposed, I was consumed with a mixture of anguish and pity.

Later I went on to contemplate not only the sad events that had led to Frederick's death but those that had followed it as well. Had they perhaps been, not simply the result of fate and unhappy circumstances, but the inevitable consequences of choices made— not only Frederick's but my own.

I had chosen fear over love.

I had chosen not to put my faith in the love I had glimpsed in my suitor's eyes at Fontainebleau.

I had chosen to turn away from my husband every time he had come to me and begged me to open my heart to him.

He'd sworn he would make me feel passion without love—

what mortal being has such power to engineer another's feelings! And if he *had* possessed such remarkable abilities, *was* it passion without love that he'd have chosen to make me feel? If that was all that I felt, perhaps it was because that was all I had wanted or dared to feel.

And when my heart had begun to move past fear, past indifference and resentment and hatred and blind desire, to feel that strange blend of admiration and compassion—love?—for my husband, I had barely expressed my softer impulses. I had bowed without resistance to the separation my husband imposed.

Which one of us had chosen that final estrangement? Was it my husband's choice, simply because he had initiated it? Or was it more truly my own? Had I yielded too readily to his decree? Had I wilted under the lash of a few petty rejections merely because I lacked courage—or the motivation to challenge them? I could not avoid comparing my behavior to that of my husband, who had exposed himself to rejection over and over again during the first months of our marriage, as he'd sought the way to reach my heart.

I had chosen to believe him when he said he would never forgive me, because it was easier than asking for forgiveness that might come slowly and painfully, or not at all. It was easier than trying to express feelings for which I had no words.

Each night, as I slipped between the cool sheets of my narrow bed, I thought of these things. I yearned to bridge the gulf between my husband and myself. But I could not imagine where or how to begin, nor could I even have said what outcome I desired.

I did not wish to leave matters as they were. But still less did I want to return to the strained silences that had been so much a part of my empty, idle life as Lady Camwell.

By mid-November, thanks to the efforts of my friends, I had four prospects for a new position. Madame Vignon took an active interest in them.

"How many children are there?" she demanded, when I received a letter from the secretary to a Mr. Henry Blake, an Englishman dwelling in France who wanted a governess for his children and who had obtained my name from Guy Hazelton. Mr. Blake would be in Geneva in December and wished to meet with me then. "And what are their ages?"

I scanned the letter again.

"He doesn't say."

"Throw it away!" cried Madame Vignon with a shudder. "I know that trick! To omit such pertinent information means only one thing: There are so many children and they are all so small that the truth would prejudice any sane woman against him!"

"Oh, it can do no harm to meet with him," I said. My prospective employers were not so numerous that I could afford to reject any of them out of hand. I wrote to accept the date Mr. Blake had suggested for our meeting. Madame even offered me the use of her study for the interview.

In late November, Nina's father came to Vignon to pay his daughter a visit. While he was at the school, he requested an interview with me. In contrast to his scrawny, high-strung daughter, the solicitor was a rotund, placid-looking gentleman.

"Ah, Mrs. Hastings," he greeted me warmly. "Such a pleasure to meet you at last. My daughter writes of you so glowingly! My wife and I want you to know how much we appreciate the time you have taken to help her feel less lonely here. We are sorry to think that you will be leaving Vignon next month."

"Nina is a delightful young lady," I replied.

"I have come to Geneva on business as well as pleasure," continued Mr. Lewingdon after we had spoken of Nina for a few minutes longer. "And, as a matter of fact, my business is with you."

His somber tone gave me a shiver of alarm. He was, after all, a London solicitor. Perhaps he was even employed by the firm of Smalley & Brown. But what could they want with me? Had my husband decided to divorce me after all? *Could* he? Was that why he'd tried to get news of me from Marguerite?

And had I unwittingly given myself away? How desperately I

wished that I had been less open with Nina on the subject of my origins!

"One of my firm's branches in the United States has requested our assistance in trying to locate a *Miss* Caroline Hastings, born in Brighton and raised in Holwich, Kent," he continued. "It's proven to be a most difficult assignment."

I could only stare with growing anxiety.

"I hope you can forgive me for allowing my daughter to play the detective," he continued. "She knows nothing of my reasons for wanting to learn a little more about you." His expression was distressingly grave. "If you are who I believe you are," he concluded gently, "I am afraid I have some very sad news for you."

My mind shot backward to the first time I had heard words like that, spoken in just that tone, one chilly morning in Paris not so very long ago—the words that had summoned me to Frederick's lifeless body.

"Oh no!" I whispered, forgetting everything except my dread. "Not Tony!"

"What was your father's full name?" the lawyer asked me once I had recovered enough self-possession to assure him that he need not call for smelling salts or burn a goose quill under my nose.

"Harold Barclay Hastings," I replied wonderingly.

"I am very sorry to tell you this," said Mr. Lewingdon, "but a gentleman of that name passed away last June in San Francisco, California."

"Please forgive my first reaction," I managed to say after a long while. "I feared you brought other news."

Silent tears—but now of a much milder sorrow—were still sliding down my cheeks.

"I never knew my father," I explained. "I have not known for years whether he was dead or alive."

Dimly I heard Mr. Lewingdon telling me that once I had established my identity satisfactorily, I would inherit my father's estate. It was not insignificant. My father had founded a chain of dry goods stores in the American West; in his later years, before he'd sold them, they had become very profitable. There were no other heirs. My father's second wife had died, childless, only a few months before his own death. In short, Mr. Lewingdon concluded bluntly, my father had left me the means to live in comfort for the rest of my life.

However, at the time of preparing his will, his health and memory already failing, he had been unable to recall my married name or any other details of my marriage. To the best of his recollection, I had eloped with a penniless musician or actor and gone to France. The difficulty of tracing me had been compounded by the fact that my very name had been a point of contention between him and my grandmother: To the end of his life, my father had always insisted upon referring to me by the name he had given me at birth.

I had enormous difficulty focusing on Mr. Lewingdon's words. I could think of nothing but the emotions which had flashed through me in the instant when I had imagined my husband dead. How could I have been so blind to my own feelings? How could I have repressed them by pretending that the world I had left behind would remain conveniently static until some distant moment when I could resolve my conflicts without sacrificing my pride and risking further pain?

There would never be such a moment.

My father, whose rejection of any relationship with me I had accepted without complaint, yet who had never forgotten me, was gone now, forever beyond my reach. Dead and beyond the reach of my love were my grandmother, Frederick, and my daughter.

But my husband, who had loved me better than any of them and who might have been—*would* have been—equally dear to me had I only found the courage to open my heart to him, still lived.

I knew then that I cared far more for him than I had ever dared to acknowledge.

Now Mr. Lewingdon was assuring me that he did not expect the question of my identity to present insurmountable difficulties. That was when I mentioned that I still possessed one souvenir of my father—the letter he had written to me upon hearing of my first marriage.

When I produced it, Nina's father started visibly at the sight of the envelope, which was addressed to Mrs. Frederick Brooks. After a long silence, he remarked, still in that dispassionate tone, "I trust you are aware, Lady Cam—"

I raised my hand quickly to silence him.

"Mrs. Hastings," he amended dryly.

Now another melodramatic vision filled my mind. He knew my secret. It would ruin the school. He would take Nina away immediately. Inevitably, other parents would hear of the scandal. When it came time for the school to reopen after the Christmas holidays, the pleasant classrooms and pretty little bedrooms would be empty. Poor Madame Vignon!

"Mr. Lewingdon," I began, my voice raw with anxiety, but before I could frame my plea he interrupted me.

"It is my business to keep confidences, Mrs. Hastings," he said. "I hope you will forgive my slip of the tongue. It will not happen again. And let me add that I see no evidence of your having been anything but a most salutary influence upon my daughter and, I can only assume, upon the other young ladies. So let us say no more upon the subject."

That night I wrote a letter to my husband.

I told him that I had been living in Switzerland but would be visiting Marguerite and Théo in Paris at Christmastime and that I hoped he would give me an opportunity to meet with him then. I added that I had given a great deal of thought to our marriage, since we had separated, and that I was ready to extend myself to him as unreservedly as he had long ago extended himself to me.

I told him that I loved him.

How I wished that I might have spoken those three words, which I had once rendered so untrustworthy, in person, instead of having to inscribe them on a piece of paper. But I could not withhold them until the perfect moment. I had already waited too long.

When I posted the letter, I again ignored my husband's instructions to communicate with him only through his solicitors. I sent the letter to Charingworth. Then I waited in a frenzy of anticipation for his response.

It never came.

The night before the Christmas holidays began, I dreamed I was on the train from Paris to Fontainebleau, but this time I was not sitting demurely across from my suitor cutting prim, measured little wedges from a pear with a silver knife. I was lying across the seat with my head in my husband's lap and lifting the ripe, intact fruit to his mouth, and he was laughing down at me as he bent his head to bite into it. . . .

If only there were a way to bring the dream to life.

The next morning I began to pack my trunks for my departure. It was still early in the day, but the mood of giddy anticipation that always marks the advent of school holidays had begun to dissipate as, one by one, the young ladies took their leave. Nina had just gone, with hugs and promises.

My husband's refusal to respond to my written appeal had crushed my spirits momentarily, but I was determined to persist. I vowed I would not lose heart with each disappointment. I had decided that when I left Vignon I would go, not to Paris, but to England—and to him.

Now, as in preparation for my journey, I folded the well-worn and mended gowns I suddenly realized I need never wear again, my thoughts were interrupted by the sound of Madame's brisk footsteps on the attic stairway.

They came to a stop outside the open door to the little room I had shared with Mademoiselle Hubert.

"Mrs. Hastings, did you forget, in all the excitement, to write to Mr. Blake to cancel your interview?" she inquired with a very odd look.

"No, of course not, madame," I replied. "I wrote weeks ago to cancel *all* my interviews. Why do you ask? He is not *here*, is he?"

"Yes, and he claims that he never received any such letter. He insists upon speaking with you personally. I have tried to make him understand that it can be to no avail, but, although he is extremely polite, he is quite intractable. You are fortunate to have escaped the necessity of working for your bread, for if his innumerable children are anything like him, you'd have had your hands full with them! I am at my wit's end, Mrs. Hastings. I cannot persuade him to leave!"

"I *did* send the letter," I repeated. "I don't know how he could have failed to receive it! But let me go and set him straight!"

He must be an alarmingly stubborn man, I thought, for Madame, at her most forbidding, could have easily routed the whole Swiss Army. I followed her down the stairway, happier than ever that I was no longer in need of a position.

We entered her study.

He was seated on the sofa at the far end of the long room, and rose to greet me languidly, with a faint smile.

"Mrs. Hastings, I presume—" he began calmly.

"Anthony!" I whispered. I lifted my hem and broke into a run in his direction.

For one splendid instant I thought I saw my husband's self-possession shatter. He was staring at me with a shaken look.

It was Madame who brought me up short.

"*Mrs.* Hastings!" she exclaimed in a low but arresting voice. "Please be good enough to remember where you are!"

XXXI

I sank into one of two armchairs that stood opposite the sofa. To my horror, Madame, her posture issuing a clear challenge, had taken the other chair.

No one spoke.

My husband continued to stare at me with a look of confusion, but slowly some color began to return to his face.

I gazed back at him in a hopeless effort to communicate with my eyes what Madame's chastening presence had prevented me from expressing more indecorously.

Madame looked from one of us to the other with the severe expression she was accustomed to assume while waiting for an explanation from two students who had been found quarreling.

Why did my husband look so taken aback? Had he expected to find someone else? A *real* Mrs. Hastings?

I began to feel ever more uncertain and mystified. Perhaps he had not come here for me at all! And why was *he* using a false name?

The silence continued.

Madame Vignon did nothing to reduce my discomfort.

Then, after a long time, my husband's expression relaxed and the corners of his mouth began to twitch.

"I have asked Madame Vignon whether I might have a word or two with you privately," he began with perfect sangfroid, addressing himself to me, "but she has adamantly refused. On grounds of propriety. Naturally I respect her wishes, so I suppose we will have to conduct our interview accordingly."

His voice was light; his face, inscrutable.

I turned to Madame.

"Madame," I said hardly above a whisper, "this gentleman's name is not Henry Blake. This is Sir Anthony Camwell."

"Oh?" she said. "And what business has this Sir Anthony Camwell with you?"

Uneasily I eyed the open door; beyond it lay the entrance hall —still a thoroughfare for departing young ladies. Even now someone's trunks were being bumped down the carpeted stairway. My husband must have heard them, too. He went to the door, shut it softly, and returned to face Madame's unsmiling face, which accused him as a masquerader.

But I was an impostor as well.

"Forgive me, madame," I said. "Sir Anthony Camwell is my husband."

I waited for the explosion—a very controlled explosion, for Madame's shot always went deep, but never wide.

"Risen from the grave, with a new name *and* a title," said she. "What an astonishing metamorphosis!"

She gave us a moment to savor her witticism.

"But it does not come entirely as a surprise to me," she went on. "I suppose you both ought to know that Monsieur Valory and I have very few secrets from each other. *We* both have too much respect for the truth."

I flushed under the implied rebuke. My husband had dropped his gaze; his cheeks too had darkened with what I could only suppose was chagrin. I ached for him; to think that he should find himself in this wretched situation because of *me*.

He brought his gaze back to my employer.

"I apologize, madame, for the deception," he said quietly.

"I too," I whispered, but my words were meant for him.

"Apologies accepted," said Madame brusquely. "I cannot pretend that I did not know what I was getting into, although I never dreamed"—here she stopped and subjected my husband to a long, appraising look—"that you would actually storm the gates."

"I came more as a Trojan horse, I fear," said my husband.

"So you did," said Madame with a little smile. "And *you*," she went on, turning to me. "To my pupils and to the other teachers here, you are still Mrs. Hastings, whose husband is deceased. I cannot permit anything which might call the decorum of our otherwise irreproachable English mistress into question. If you wish to have a *brief* private conversation, I will allow you to have it here, but that door *must* remain open. Certainly *I* have no intention of eavesdropping, but I shall be outside to make sure that no one else yields to the temptation. If you keep your voices low, I think you will have as much privacy as you require. However, there are still a few young ladies here, so if you two have some quarrel, be good enough to take it elsewhere. And if you have any peacemaking to do," she concluded, "you may arrange the preliminaries here. But do not go far in your negotiations until you are *well* away from these premises."

She stood up. My courteous husband sprang to his feet as well.

"Thank you, madame," he said.

"*Have* we a quarrel, Mrs. Hastings?" he asked softly as soon as she had left us.

I couldn't speak. I closed my eyes and shook my head.

"Then why did you make it so difficult for me to find you? I scoured Paris for weeks. Marguerite and Théo were no help at all. If I hadn't come across your friend Hazelton I don't know what I would have done. I am grateful that you *have* such a friend, for I was in so wretched a state that he finally took pity on me and scouted La Sorrel's orders to keep your whereabouts a secret. Thank God for his kindness!"

"But I *told* you where I was. Why have you never answered my letter?"

"What letter?" he inquired with a blank, rather startled look. "You sent me a letter? Where did you send it? When?"

"To Charingworth! Weeks ago!"

The look of bewilderment fled from my husband's face.

"Of course it never reached me! Do you suppose that Charingworth is any kind of home to me now! Why do you think I told you to send everything to Smalley & Brown! No doubt your message has been playing hare and hounds with me all across Europe! Well, never mind that—what did it say?"

Beyond the open door a tiny cluster of young ladies were making noisy farewells.

I looked at the door and back at my husband in agony. If I breathed even a word of what I had written, I was sure I would lose the last shreds of my self-control.

"Please, Anthony," I appealed to him at last. "Not here."

My husband, too, had glanced toward the doorway, but his expression was one of pure irritation. Yet, within seconds his look reverted to that earlier one of bemused wonderment.

"Well, I suppose I shall have to wait then," was all he said. "I seem to have become better at that than I once thought."

"You don't have to wait—for anything," I told him, praying that he would understand me.

But instead of giving any sign of comprehension, he got up and walked away from me. He stationed himself at one of the long windows and stood there silently looking out. I could see only his back and, beyond it, the fine little snowflakes making their eddying descent to earth. Some of them struck the window, melted slowly, and slid down the glass like tears.

After a long time, he turned around and with a little smile, said, "Well, I think I will at least have to wait until you are released from your obligations here. When will that be, Mrs. Hastings?"

"Oh!" I replied, coming back to reality as I recalled that I had committed myself to assisting Madame Vignon with a number of last-minute tasks. "Not until this evening! This is my last day here," I added.

"In that case, I suppose I ought to leave you to your work," he remarked without much enthusiasm.

"Oh, not quite yet!" I protested. "We have a *little* time. And there is one thing I *must* know. Why have you come here, if it was not because of my letter?"

"Did you really imagine I could accept your obstinate insistence upon living in poverty! I came here to find out for myself *why* you have so stubbornly and foolishly refused everything that was due you from me!"

"You owe me nothing."

"I am your husband. Didn't I vow to endow you with all my worldly goods?"

"Yes, but we have both made—and broken—a number of vows," I pointed out.

"Ah. But *mine* were in earnest, even if I have strayed from them occasionally."

At this, I bit my lip; it was still a sore point with me.

"But not lately," remarked my husband casually, as if he had read my thoughts. "Not, in fact, since the first night you slept at Grosvenor Square. If it matters to you."

He was watching me closely. My heart beat faster, but I could not open my mouth to tell him how much it mattered.

"One reason I came to Geneva was to restore this to you," he went on.

He picked up a small, plainly wrapped parcel from the table beside the sofa and handed it to me. I took it dumbly.

"You really can't refuse it," he was saying. "If you do, I shall be forced to keep it for you and to send you exorbitant bills demanding compensation for the inconvenience of having to safeguard it. That would be a pity. From the look of you, I do not think you can manage many unnecessary expenses."

I peeled off the paper to reveal a jeweler's case. I raised the cover. Inside lay the diamond collar.

"Really, Mr. Blake," I said, striving for a lightness that would match his as I attempted to hand it back to him, "this is a most inappropriate gift for a governess."

"It is not mine to give." He left the open box in my outstretched hand. "It belongs to you, Mrs. Hastings. It ought to make your life somewhat easier. Has it never occurred to you *why* I gave it to you?"

"I've always assumed that it was part of your campaign to turn me into a lady of fashion."

"A doomed campaign, I see, in spite of some temporary victories," remarked my husband, casting a disapproving eye at my gray dress. "But that was not why I gave you the diamonds."

"Why *did* you, then?"

"We had been married for six months, and you were desperately unhappy. You would not, or could not, tell me why, nor could I discover where all your money was going. Nevertheless, it was clear that you had some pressing need which required every penny. There would have been nothing to prevent you, you know, from having the necklace copied in paste and exchanging the real thing for cash. I hoped it might present you with a discreet solution to your difficulties."

I stared at him in disbelief. "You imagined that I would stoop to that!" I exclaimed, before I realized what a ludicrous protest it was.

But my husband did not laugh.

"Where's the dishonesty in that?" he asked.

"To accept such a precious gift and then palm off a copy on you! That would be stealing!"

"I don't see why. Once I've given you something, do you suppose that I still consider it mine? The necklace was yours to do with as you wished. There would have been nothing underhanded about selling it." He hesitated before adding, "And if the lack of money was all that prevented you from bolting your marriage, it would have given you the means to do so."

Now I was truly shocked.

"You *wanted* me to leave you! And like *that!*" I exclaimed in a very low voice.

"It was the last thing I wanted! But what could I do? You were miserable, you would barely talk to me. . . . I was racked with memories of how much happier you had seemed when I knew you in Paris. The diamonds, I thought, might give you the means to return to that other life, which seemed to suit you so much better than your life with me. Of course, I hoped you wouldn't leave me! Of course I still struggled to delude myself that you loved me! But, more than anything, I wanted you to choose me freely. . . . I had no way of knowing, then, that you were caught in a snare from which not even these diamonds could have sprung you."

"Well," I said when I had absorbed his words, "I *have* been sprung from the snare of poverty, at any rate." I told him briefly of my legacy.

"Oh," he said. "So *that* is why Mr. Blake's offer no longer interests you and why you wrote to turn him away! And *I* feared that it was because you had pierced my alias!"

"Then you did receive *that* letter, at least!"

"Shh!" he exclaimed with an expression of alarm. "Don't let Madame Vignon hear you! She has terrorized me quite enough today. I would not like to let her discover that I am an even more incorrigible liar than she already believes me to be. My untruthfulness, in fact, is my second reason for having come to see you."

"*Your* untruthfulness?"

"I told you once that I never lied to you. And then I lied to you not once but twice. I told you I hated you. That was a lie, or at any rate, it was not the whole truth. I want you to know that."

I found this tepid comfort.

"And the other lie?" I said.

"Yes, the other lie," he said somewhat haltingly. It seemed a more difficult one to confess to. "Well, you may as well know that when I came to your room that last time, it was *not* to ask you to leave. And when I put my hands on your shoulders, it was *not* because I felt sorry for you. I merely said that, after you pulled away, to cover my . . . Well, your manner seemed so altered when you met me at the station that . . . But then . . ."

He seemed to be having trouble completing his sentences.

"Oh, if only you knew what happened that day!" I burst out. "Andromeda threw me, and I bruised my shoulder horribly. It nearly killed me when you—"

"Good heavens, Fleur!" interrupted my husband. "You know better than to be thrown! How the devil could you have let something like that happen? Why, you might have—"

"I know," I said humbly. "It was inexcusable. I wasn't paying attention. I might have broken her leg."

"—been seriously injured!" concluded my husband.

He sank down upon the sofa, shaking his head.

"Thank God nothing happened to you before—" he began in a choked voice. Then he brought his eyes back to mine.

"I was wrong about everything, Fleur," he said more calmly. "Since you have been gone, I have begun to realize how little I troubled myself to understand you."

I began to wonder whether I was dreaming again. Perhaps this conversation was as unreal as last night's train ride.

"That's not true!" I protested. "You went to endless trouble, again and again, only to be rebuffed each time!"

But he pressed on. "I was so harsh, so inflexible. As you so often pointed out, I have never known poverty. How could I imagine the kind of desperation it can lead to? It was unreasonable and unjust of me to insist that you ought to have trusted me enough to confide so delicate a matter as the source of your difficulties. I never deserved your trust. I have a great deal to answer for."

"Oh no! It was I who wronged you! I did not value you at your worth."

"No," he persisted. "I think you *did* value me at my worth, which has proven to be very small. I have always prided myself not on *being* a gentleman—which is merely an accident of birth—but upon *behaving* as one, which is another thing altogether. And I was no gentleman to you, Fleur."

Again I started to speak. I wanted to say that I had liked him better once he had ceased to be the perfect gentleman, but he lifted his hand to silence me.

"A gentleman," he said, "would have simply bought the paintings, locked them safely away for a couple of centuries—only because they are far too lovely to be burned—and said nothing about them. He would have behaved as if he had never seen them, as indeed he should not have. They were never meant for my eyes. To use them as I did was to trample upon the most intimate act between man and wife. I knew you never wanted anyone but the man you loved to see that aspect of yourself.

"There is no excuse for what I did. I was beside myself with envy and jealousy. It made me so wild to think that you had given so much to another man, who betrayed you—I know you resent my saying that, but I must—that I managed to ignore my own worse crime. The use to which I put those paintings was just as heinous a betrayal."

"No it wasn't," I said after a while. "It wasn't a betrayal of trust. Or of love."

My husband looked at me thoughtfully for a long, long time. Finally he said, "It was an abuse of power. My wealth and our marriage had given me power over you, and I used that power against you. It is *not* a lesser crime."

"*I* betrayed *you*," I whispered at last. "Can you forgive me?"

"If I had any right to judge you, I would forgive you everything," was my husband's reply.

I tried to absorb this but, alas, I was painfully conscious that it was nearly time for luncheon and that I was expected to preside over one of the tables where the few remaining students were to take their last meal of the term.

I had to seize the moment.

"You will let me come back to you, then?" I said with a kind of graceless urgency.

"Do you think that would be wise?" asked my husband gently.

"I have missed you, Anthony," was the best I could manage in reply.

"Have you?" he said. "And so much so that you want to come back with me to England and live with me forever?"

"Yes. There—or anywhere."

"And all because you *miss* me."

"Yes," I faltered, and then added, "Really, I have missed you more than I can say."

There was a frown on my husband's face now, and his lips were pressed tightly together. He seemed lost in some vexing internal debate. I could almost see the subtle clash of conflicting impulses. He turned away from me and began to walk slowly up and down Madame's prized Aubusson, his hands in his pockets, his head bent in thought.

When he finally came to halt before me, his eyes were both guarded and searching.

"I don't know what is in your heart, Fleur," he said, "beyond what you have seen fit to say under these rather difficult circumstances. But I *have* to know. For one thing, there is the whole question of children."

How could I have forgotten?

He was right, of course. He had made it clear, time and again, that he did not want children. And I did—I yearned for them. No longer did I cherish the hopeless conviction that nature had condemned me to barrenness.

So there *was* a reason, after all, to hold back from making that final leap. Suppose I *did* return to him and gave him all the love that I had once reserved for Frederick and Frederick's memory. Would I torment him, then, to put aside his own wishes in order to gratify mine? Would I have insisted upon bearing children to a man who did not want them? No. I would have wordlessly resigned myself to childlessness, killed my own hopes out of devotion to my husband—and made only the first of those endless, unspoken sacrifices that love demands and which breed the resentments and silences that gnaw away at love like worms.

There had to be another, a better way to love.

My nails dug into my palms as I thought of the children I would never know. I could see them so clearly—a little girl with hair like moonlight and gray eyes; a tiny boy, dark-haired like me and luminous with infancy. They were as real to me as if they already existed somewhere in time, waiting for the moment when they could finally be embraced. Oh, how had I, once again, let something that could never live become so precious to me! I wanted to reach out and pull them to my breast.

Instead, I opened my hands to let them go.

Dimly, I felt my husband press something into one of my empty palms—a snowy, perfectly folded handkerchief.

"You must understand," he explained gently. "It's not that I dislike the thought of children. I long for them. And I do think that, under happier circumstances, you'd have made a wonderful mother. I'm certain of it. But I will not risk bringing children into the world whom you might find yourself unable to love, because you do not love their father."

"Oh, but I would!" I burst out without stopping to think. "My God, I would love them with all my heart. How could you suppose—"

But there I stopped. I thought of his mother and of the interpretation that he must have put upon her lovelessness. If that was the crux of the matter—and I was certain that it must be—could I *ever* make a case for myself? Could I ever overcome his doubts and convince him that I loved him and that my love was true? Could I place my weightless hopes and imagined possibilities in the scales against the heavy reality of his own experience, the unloved child of a woman who had surely claimed to love her husband but who had not?

How could I ask him to take that chance?

I thought of the children who would never live except in my dreams unless I fought for them, and I opened my lips to try.

The ten-minute bell for luncheon rang imperatively and jarred me from my thoughts.

My husband continued to stand before me, motionless and silent, as if he had been carved from stone.

I groped vainly for words. I knew I was on the verge of breaking down completely, and that if I were not careful, within seconds I would be violating every code that governed how a respectably widowed English mistress ought to conduct herself in an interview with a prospective employer.

"But I *can't* leave without saying good-bye to Mrs. Hastings, madame!" came a high voice from the hallway.

"This is hopeless," said my husband with an oath.

He reached into his pocket, drew out his silver card case, and penciled something swiftly in the corner of one of his cards.

"Here is the address of the hotel where I am staying in Geneva," he said as he handed the card to me. "You can find me there after eight o'clock this evening." He paused and then added with evident difficulty, "I have the impression that you feel more kindly disposed toward me, now that you are your own woman again. But unless you can say that you love me—and convince me that your words are true and that your love for me is as strong as mine is for you—I cannot take you back. I *won't* put myself through that again."

And with that he was gone.

I stared at the doorway through which he had vanished, paralyzed with a bizarre mixture of bleak despair and wild elation. He loved me still! But what protestation of love could I ever make that would not render me as suspect as the boy who cried wolf?

And yet he loved me. As long as that was so, I would never turn away in defeat no matter what challenges he flung at me. Somehow I would find a way to prove that my love was stronger than his doubts.

XXXII

When I announced myself to the discreet desk clerk as Lady Camwell, he barely blinked and told me that Sir Anthony was out.

I had arrived at the hotel too soon—it was only a quarter to eight—but nevertheless, as I proceeded to settle down to an anxious vigil on one of the palm-screened sofas, I felt bitterly disappointed. It seemed that my husband was not champing at the bit quite so eagerly as I.

Just then a gentleman raced in from the street, hair and tails flying, in a neck-or-nothing dash to the desk.

"Has a lady—?" he gasped.

The impassive clerk made a tiny gesture in my direction.

But I was already on my feet.

My husband paused for a moment before he turned, as if to assume, like a shield, the air of quiet dignity that I had once regarded as his very essence. When he faced me it was with a faint, unruffled smile; only the color in his cheeks betrayed him.

He advanced toward me calmly as he peeled off his right-hand glove.

"Forgive me, Fleur," he said, holding out his hand with the utmost self-possession. "I hope I have not kept you waiting long."

"Oh, not long at all," I assured him breathlessly. But my voice, my savoir faire, everything dissolved as my fingers locked around his. "Tony," I managed to choke out, "I—"

He moved closer, protectively.

"It's all right," he whispered. "There's no need to say anything."

He led me to his suite and closed the door behind us with that same familiar air of calm dignity. But that was the last I saw of my self-possessed, unflappable, eternally, infernally, exasperatingly imperturbable husband for some time.

In seconds we had tumbled, entwined, against the door and on down, down to the carpet.

Under the deluge of my kisses, his splendid facade was disintegrating like a sandcastle under a tidal wave; he pulled me across the ruined fortifications and into the depths of his soul.

So he had fallen to me at last.

All the tumultuous, unbridled passion I had once longed to wrest from him—by calculation, by bitter provocation, by skillful erotic techniques—were mine, in exchange for nothing more than my unencumbered heart.

"Don't you know how much I love you!" he whispered as he held me. "How could you dream that I would settle for less than this?"

I couldn't see his face—I was crushed against him too closely —but I knew that not all the hot tears upon our cheeks were from my eyes.

"How did you know?" I asked when I could speak.

"Your eyes," he said. "I hardly dared to believe what I thought I glimpsed in them when you walked into the study at Vignon. But now—downstairs—it was still there."

"They say the eyes are the windows to the soul," I remarked, stretching against him luxuriously. "Do you know, I dreamed last night that we went back to Fontainebleau, you and I. Do you ever think of that day?"

"For a long time I thought of it far too much," was my husband's wistful reply. "That was the day that I knew I had fallen hopelessly in love with you."

"Not until *then?*" I exclaimed. "And you led me to believe that you'd been carrying the torch for me ever since you saw me at the Coq d'Or!"

"That! That was pure enchantment! Oh yes, I'd lost my heart to you long before we went to Fontainebleau. But it was there, when you tried to shield me from the rain, that I *knew* I loved you. After that day, I lost all sense of caution. All I could think of was the way you looked, standing there in the downpour in that hideous, shapeless old dress of yours, with your face glowing, as you declared that we might as well give in to Nature!"

"I only meant the rain!" I reminded him.

"Yes, you made that clear. But it was already too late for me. I wanted to go down on my knees and kiss your hem!" declared my husband extravagantly. "*Me!* Wanting to press my lips to the disgusting, threadbare hem of that horrible gown! And utterly tongue-tied at the thought of all the perfections it must have hidden. *Now* you know why your limitless supply of ugly dresses always drove me to the wall! They were a perpetual, stinging reminder of the moment you enslaved my heart. What a relief it was to get you out of them! And here you've found yet another! Do you breed them like rabbits?"

"I left my other gowns with Marguerite when I came to Switzerland. I feared a schoolteacher dressed by Madame Rullier might raise a few eyebrows!" But as I glanced down at my old gray dress, I *did* feel a keen twinge of regret. "I wish I'd had something else to wear tonight," I concluded sadly.

"Oh please! Don't apologize. This will do perfectly!" exclaimed my husband. He lifted up the offending hem and, yes, he did, he kissed it.

"There," he said, looking up at me with a transparent, joyous smile. "At least *that's* out of my system."

Then he unbuttoned my shoes and began to kiss my ankles and the soles of my feet.

"Oh, I'm absurdly fond of your ugly gowns, Mrs. Hastings," he announced. "It's a good thing you've got money of your own now. Otherwise I'd make you wear nothing but these heartrending little rags for the rest of your life."

"I never guessed. . . ."

"And then you were my wife—and suddenly so spiritless. It terrified me."

"Terrified you!"

"Oh yes! I had dreamed of ravishing you in a thousand ways. But once we were married, you seemed so . . . broken, so fragile, so unable to assert yourself. Not the woman I had fallen in love with at all. The only signs of life you gave . . . Well, there *was* that day with my mother when you were so magnificent, but aside from that, you were so distant. You would never give any indication of what you were feeling. I hardly dared to touch you, out of a fear that I would drive you even farther away."

"Oh, why did *you* seem so cold?" I whispered as he brought his tender, consoling kisses back to my mouth. "Why were you so cruel to me?"

"Cruel!" he exclaimed. "I was never cruel to you! God knows, I longed to be!"

"Have you forgotten so quickly! You were *very* unkind! You stayed away from Charingworth for weeks on end, while I was awaiting your return—"

"Then why on earth didn't you tell me so!"

"What! And give you the satisfaction of knowing that you'd accomplished exactly what you'd set out to do! You don't know what I went through! I felt like a pariah! You always threw me out of your bed after making love to me or sent me away! How *could* you have done that if you still loved me? I was so ashamed of wanting you the way I did! Do you think I could have told you that?"

He rocked me against him.

"Oh, Fleur," he said. "I never dreamed you felt any of it. I thought you hated me. I didn't know what to do. I knew I had no right to hold you against your will, but I could hardly bear the thought of letting you go. When I conceived my revenge in anger, I thought it would be so simple, that I would tire of my icicle wife in no time. . . . But I never wanted it to end. No, it wasn't the pleasure of making you suffer—that satisfied nothing, not even my hunger for retribution. But every so often, in spite of yourself, when you condescended to smile or merely to blush, I fell in love with you all over again. If I hadn't stayed away from you, kept you at a distance, and thrown you out of my bed, believe me, you'd have won your freedom in less than a day." He paused to reflect upon his words. "Well, *two* days, perhaps," he amended with a laugh. "I would not like to exaggerate my powers and raise your expectations."

I found his mouth again, but he pulled back a little.

"Not so fast. What was that you said about waiting for me— did you really? I always had the distinct impression, whenever I came to you, that you'd been on your knees praying that I had been struck dead by an omnibus."

"I was angry that you could stay away so long."

"I see. *You* were *angry!* Well, Mrs. Hastings, I'd like to know how you intend to take *your* revenge?"

"Perhaps I'll use your methods," I whispered.

". . . But not here upon the carpet," protested my husband gently. "This *is* our wedding night."

He found the strength to break away. Then he lifted me in his arms and carried me to his bed.

From the softness of his breathing as he lay quietly beside me, I knew he slept. But I could not.

His lovemaking had told me all the things that no words were needed to say. I knew how well he comprehended every contra-diction of my body and my heart—the longing for a sublimation that was not a defeat; the yearning to be driven toward surrender by a man who would not assume total possession as the spoils of his victory, a man to whom I could yield everything and lose nothing.

And how much more he had revealed of himself to me. He had given me leave, tonight, to explore him with a freedom he had never before permitted me, and he had responded without reserve. We had drunk, from the same cup, the dazzling liquor of love and power.

And yet, he would be forever a mystery to me, separate and inviolate.

What was it he had once said? That if I had ever loved him, I'd have known what he would have done differently had he been in Frederick's desperate shoes.

And I *did* know.

It was so simple, after all. He would have talked to me. Before taking such a step, he would have insisted that together we discuss every avenue, every possibility, and every danger. Never would he have exposed me to such a terrible risk without my knowledge and without my consent. Never would he have robbed me of the freedom to choose. And never would he have drunk himself into a lethal stupor and left me to face the consequences alone.

"Never doubt my love for you," Frederick had told me, and tonight I made my peace with Frederick as well. He had loved me as well as he was able. But he had not had the courage to take love to its limits.

I turned to my sleeping champion, who had saved me from no dragons but had attempted a deed far more heroic: He had assured me of his love and had then challenged me to call out my dragons and face them down. He had failed at first, and love had failed, as well.

But here we were, after all.

I brushed his silky hair away from his cheek and brought my lips closer to his ear.

"I love you. I *do* love you, Tony," I whispered.

I thought he was too deep in dreams to hear me, but I was wrong.

His arms tightened round me and he drew me closer.

"I've always loved you, Fleur," he said.

And that is how I came to join the household of that intractable impostor, Mr. Henry Blake, and to raise with him those unnumbered children. In the end, it turned out, there were three.

AUTHOR'S NOTE

It would be almost impossible to cite all the sources on which I depended as I tried to recreate fin de siècle Paris, but I must credit one in particular. With its vivid, amusing, and lavishly detailed commentary on Parisian life and its engaging illustrations, *The Praise of Paris* (Harper & Bros., New York, 1892) by the American art critic, Theodore Child, was invaluable. Among its colorful accounts of duellists, ragpickers, and couturiers is a fascinating description of the Salomon family, from which I drew very heavily. Yes, they really existed; besides making toys, Abraham Salomon was the curator of skates, and professor of skating, for the Paris Opera. I am grateful to Mr. Child for having immortalized this family and so much else of turn-of-the-century Paris.

—LG